ACE

$7.99 U.S.
$8.99 CAN

P9-DCJ-308

ISBN 978-0-425-25613-8

9 780425 256138

5 0 7 9 9

S ⊳ EAN

ILONA
ANDREWS

New York Times Bestselling Author of *Magic Slays*

GUNMETAL
MAGIC

A NOVEL IN THE WORLD OF KATE DANIELS

"The world Kate inhabits is a blend of
gritty magic and dangerous mystery."
—*The Parkersburg News and Sentinel*

continued . . .

"I have read and reread this book, and it's perfect. The action, the romance, the plot and suspense . . . I cannot wait for the fifth in the series."   —*Smexy Books*

"Balancing petrifying danger with biting humor is an Andrews specialty, leaving readers both grinning and gasping. Put this on your auto-buy list immediately!"   —*RT Book Reviews*

"Delivers on the promise of 'One hell of a good read.' You will not be disappointed!"   —ParaNormal Romance.org

MAGIC STRIKES

"Andrews's crisp dialogue and layered characterization make the gut-wrenching action of this first-person thrill ride all the more intense . . . mesmerizing."   —*RT Book Reviews* (4½ stars, Top Pick)

"Andrews blends action-packed fantasy with myth and legend, keeping readers enthralled. *Magic Strikes* introduces fascinating characters, provides a plethora of paranormal skirmishes, and teases fans with romantic chemistry."   —*Darque Reviews*

"Ilona Andrews's best novel to date, cranking up the action, danger, and magic . . . Gritty sword-clashing action and flawless characterizations will bewitch fans, old and new alike."
                                            —*Sacramento Book Review*

"Doses of humor serve to lighten the suspense and taut action of this vividly drawn, kick-butt series."   —*Monsters and Critics*

"From the first page to the last, *Magic Strikes* was a riveting, heart-pounding ride. Story lines advance, truths are admitted, intriguing characters are introduced, and the romance between Kate and Curran develops a sweetness that is simply delightful."
                                            —*Dear Author*

"Write faster . . . I absolutely love the relationship between Curran and Kate—I laugh out loud with the witty sarcasm and one-liners, and the sexual tension building between the couples drives me to my knees, knowing I'll have to wait for another book."
                                            —*SFRevu*

MAGIC BURNS

"Fans of Carrie Vaughn and Patricia Briggs will appreciate this fast-paced, action-packed urban fantasy full of magic, vampires, werebeasties, and things that go bump in the night."
—*Monsters and Critics*

"With all her problems, secrets, and prowess both martial and magical, Kate is a great kick-ass heroine, a tough girl with a heart, and her adventures . . . are definitely worth checking out."
—*Locus*

"With a fascinating, compelling plot, a witty, intelligent heroine, a demonic villain, and clever, wry humor throughout, this story has it all."
—*Fresh Fiction*

"A new take on the urban fantasy genre, the world Kate inhabits is a blend of gritty magic and dangerous mystery."
—*The Parkersburg News and Sentinel*

"If you enjoy Laurell K. Hamilton's early Anita Blake or the works of Patricia Briggs and Kim Harrison, you need to add Ilona Andrews to your reading list."
—*LoveVampires*

"Andrews . . . demonstrates her mastery at balancing dark humor, clever mystery, and supernatural jeopardy. Andrews is the total package!"
—*RT Book Reviews* (4½ stars, Top Pick)

MAGIC BITES

"Treat yourself to a splendid new urban fantasy . . . I am looking forward to the next book in the series or anything else Ilona Andrews writes."
—Patricia Briggs, #1 *New York Times* bestselling author of *Fair Game*

"Andrews shows a great deal of promise. Readers fond of Laurell K. Hamilton and Patricia Briggs may find her work a new source of reading pleasure."
—*SFRevu*

"Andrews's edgy series stands apart from similar fantasies . . . owing to its complex world-building and skilled characterizations."
—*Library Journal*

GUNMETAL MAGIC

ILONA ANDREWS

ACE BOOKS, NEW YORK

THE BERKLEY PUBLISHING GROUP
Published by the Penguin Group
Penguin Group (USA) Inc.
375 Hudson Street, New York, New York 10014, USA

Penguin Group (Canada), 90 Eglinton Avenue East, Suite 700, Toronto, Ontario M4P 2Y3, Canada
(a division of Pearson Penguin Canada Inc.) • Penguin Books Ltd., 80 Strand, London WC2R 0RL,
England • Penguin Group Ireland, 25 St. Stephen's Green, Dublin 2, Ireland (a division of Penguin
Books Ltd.) • Penguin Group (Australia), 250 Camberwell Road, Camberwell, Victoria 3124, Australia
(a division of Pearson Australia Group Pty. Ltd.) • Penguin Books India Pvt. Ltd., 11 Community
Centre, Panchsheel Park, New Delhi—110 017, India • Penguin Group (NZ), 67 Apollo Drive,
Rosedale, Auckland 0632, New Zealand (a division of Pearson New Zealand Ltd.) • Penguin Books
(South Africa) (Pty.) Ltd., 24 Sturdee Avenue, Rosebank, Johannesburg 2196, South Africa

Penguin Books Ltd., Registered Offices: 80 Strand, London WC2R 0RL, England

"Magic Gifts" was previously published on www.ilona-andrews.com.

This is a work of fiction. Names, characters, places, and incidents either are the product of the authors'
imaginations or are used fictitiously, and any resemblance to actual persons, living or dead, business
establishments, events, or locales is entirely coincidental. The publisher does not have any control over
and does not assume any responsibility for author or third-party websites or their content.

GUNMETAL MAGIC

An Ace Book / published by arrangement with Ilona Andrews, Inc.

PUBLISHING HISTORY
Ace mass-market edition / August 2012

Gunmetal Magic copyright © 2012 by Andrew Gordon and Ilona Gordon.
"Magic Gifts" copyright © 2011 by Andrew Gordon and Ilona Gordon.
Fractal series illustration by Ilona Gordon.
Cover illustration by Tony Mauro.
Cover photograph of rusted metal © Péter Gudella/Shutterstock.
Cover design by Judith Lagerman.
Interior text design by Laura K. Corless.

ISBN: 978-0-425-25613-8

ACE
Ace Books are published by The Berkley Publishing Group,
a division of Penguin Group (USA) Inc.,
375 Hudson Street, New York, New York 10014.
ACE and the "A" design are trademarks of Penguin Group (USA) Inc.

PRINTED IN THE UNITED STATES OF AMERICA

10 9 8 7 6 5 4 3 2 1

ALWAYS LEARNING   **PEARSON**

To the fine people of Texas,
who have taken us in and treated us as their own

ACKNOWLEDGMENTS

At the core, *Gunmetal Magic* is a book about a deeply damaged person finding her place in life, and in the beginning stages, it was also a very damaged book in need of help. We would like to thank Anne Sowards, our editor, for once again making it better, and our agent, Nancy Yost, for invaluable advice and friendship.

We'd like to thank the following people for making the book a reality: Production editor Michelle Kasper and assistant production editor Andromeda Macri for overseeing the production and putting up with our craziness, and editorial assistant Kat Sherbo for her patience and attention to detail. Special thanks to the long-suffering art department, cover designer Judith Lagerman, and artist Tony Mauro. We deeply appreciate everything you've done on our behalf. We're grateful to the interior designer Laura K. Corless for making a manuscript into a beautiful book, and to publicists Rosanne Romanello and Brady McReynolds for tirelessly promoting the book.

In addition, we owe thanks to Marsheila Rockwell, Sue Staltare, Susann Max, and Shannon Martinez for their expertise with reclamations, construction, and fallen buildings. Thank you to Shiloh Walker for her knowledge of snakebites and explanation of medical terms, and to Cassandra Brulotte for her legal expertise. Any errors of law, medicine, or construction found in this book are due purely to us and not to them.

Thank you to our beta readers for suffering through the first draft.

Thank you to Jeaniene Frost for being there and to Jill Myles and Meljean Brook for the tea war.

Finally, we'd like to thank our readers—thank you for making it all possible.

CONTENTS

GUNMETAL MAGIC

The world has suffered a magic apocalypse. We pushed the technological progress too far, and now magic has returned with a vengeance. It came like an invisible tide, ripping planes out of the sky, dropping monsters onto crowded streets, sucking the power plants dry, and jamming firearms. Some people awoke and found themselves shapeshifters. Others died, cut down by a magic-fueled disease, and rose again as mindless undead, robbed of their ability to reason and driven only by their all-consuming hunger. Gods became real, curses gained power, and telekinesis and telepathy were no longer the products of illusion and special effects.

For three days the magic raged and then it vanished without warning, leaving the world reeling, its population decimated, its cities in tatters.

Since that day, the day of the Shift, the magic comes and goes as it pleases. It floods the planet like a wave crashing on the shoreline, hissing and boiling, leaving its dangerous gifts, and then recedes once again. Sometimes a wave lasts half an hour, sometimes three days. Nobody can predict it and nobody knows what our future holds.

But we are resilient. We will survive.

"40th Anniversary of the Shift"
The Atlanta Journal-Constitution

CHAPTER 1

✦

Thud!

My head hit the sidewalk. Candy jerked me up by my hair and slammed my face into the asphalt.

Thud!

"Hit her again!" Michelle squeaked, her teenage voice shrill.

I knew it was a dream, because it didn't hurt. The fear was still there, that sharp, hot terror, mixed with helpless rage, the kind of fear that turns you from a human being into an animal. Things become distilled to simple concepts: I was small, they were big; I was weak, they were strong. They hurt me, and I endured.

Thud.

My skull bounced off the pavement. Blood stained my blond hair. Out of the corner of my eye, I saw Sarah take a running start like a kicker before a field goal. The flesh on her body boiled. Bones grew, muscles wound around them like cotton candy over a stick, hair sprouted, sheathing the new body, half human, half animal, in a coat of pale sandy fur dappled with telltale hyena spots. The bouda grinned at me, her malformed mouth full of fangs. I clenched up, curling my ten-year-old self into a ball. The clawed foot crashed into my ribs. The three-inch claws scraped a bone and it crunched inside me like a snapped chopstick. She kept kicking me.

Thud, thud, thud!

This was a dream. A dream grown from my memories, but still just a dream. I knew this, because ten years after my mother took eleven-year-old me and fled halfway across the country, I came back and put two bullets through Sarah's eyes. I had emptied a clip into Candy's left ear. I still remembered the way her skull had blossomed with red when the bullets tore out the other side. I had killed the entire werehyena clan. I wiped those bouda bitches off the face of the planet, because the world was a better place with them gone. Michelle was the only one who had escaped.

I sat up and grinned at them. "I'm waking up, ladies. Go fuck yourselves."

My eyes snapped open. I lay in my closet, wrapped in a blanket and holding a butcher knife. The door of the closet stood slightly ajar, and the gray light of early morning slipped through the narrow gap.

Fantastic. Andrea Nash, decorated veteran of the Order, hiding in her closet with her knife and a blankie. I should've held on to the dream long enough to beat them into bloody pulp. At least then I wouldn't feel so completely pathetic.

I inhaled, sampling the air. The normal scents of my apartment floated to me, the hint of synthetic apple from the soap in the bathroom, the fragrance of vanilla from the candle by my bed, and strongest of all, the stench of dog fur, a leftover from when my friend Kate's poodle Grendel had kept me company. That freak of nature had slept at the foot of my bed, and his distinctive reek was permanently imprinted on my rug.

No intruders.

The scents were muted, which meant the magic was down.

Thud-thud-thud!

What in the world?

Thud!

Someone was pounding on my door.

I kicked off my blanket, rolled to my feet, and ran out of the closet. My bedroom greeted me: my big bed, intruder-free; the crumpled mess of the blanket on the rug; my jeans and bra, discarded last night by the bed, next to a Lorna Sterling paperback with a pirate in a poofy shirt on the cover; bookcase, stuffed to the brim; pale blue curtains on the barred window, undisturbed.

I dropped the butcher knife onto my side table, pulled on my pajamas pants, grabbed my Sig-Sauer P226 from under the pillow, and ran to the door. Waking up with a gun in my hand would've made a lot more sense, but no, I'd woken up clutching a knife. That meant I must've gotten up in the middle of the night, run into the kitchen, taken a knife from the butcher block, run back into the bedroom, grabbed a blanket, and hidden in the closet. All without realizing where I was or what I was doing. If that wasn't crazy, I didn't know what was.

I hadn't slept with a knife since I was a teenager. This blast from the past wasn't welcome and it needed to go away real fast.

Thud-thud!

I reached the door and stood on my toes to look through the peephole. A tall black woman in her fifties stood on the other side. Her gray hair stuck out from her head in a mess, she was wearing a nightgown, and her face was so twisted by worry, I barely recognized her. Mrs. Haffey. She and her husband lived in an apartment right below me.

Normally Mrs. Haffey viewed her appearance as serious business. In terms of battle readiness, she was my hero—I've never seen her without her makeup and hair perfectly done. Something was really wrong.

I unlocked the door.

"Andrea!" Mrs. Haffey gasped. Behind her, long white strands covered the landing and the stairwell. I was one hundred percent sure they hadn't been there when I'd dragged myself into my apartment last night.

"What's wrong?"

"Darin's missing!"

I pulled her into my apartment and shut the door. "I need you to tell me from the beginning, slowly and clearly: what happened?"

Mrs. Haffey took a deep breath. She had been a cop's wife for twenty-five years and her experience from dealing with a lifetime of emergencies kicked in. Her voice was almost steady. "I woke up and made coffee. Darin got up to take Chief outside. I took a shower. When I came out, Darin wasn't back. I went out on the balcony, but he wasn't in his usual spot."

I knew exactly where the usual spot was: two stories under my bedroom window, where the Haffeys' bulldog, Chief, preferred to mark his territory. I smelled it on my way to work every morning. Of course, Chief smelled my scent and it only made him more determined to pee his way to territorial supremacy.

"I called and called Darin, and nothing. I tried to go downstairs. There's blood all over the landing and a white substance on the stairs and it's blocking the way."

"Did Mr. Haffey take his gun with him?"

Mr. Haffey had retired from the Paranormal Activity Division of the Atlanta Police Department. PAD cops took their guns seriously. As far as I knew, Darin Haffey never left the house without his Smith & Wesson M&P340 snub-nosed revolver.

"He always takes his gun with him," Mrs. Haffey said.

And he hadn't fired it, because his revolver ate .357 Magnum cartridges. When he pulled the trigger, the shot sounded like a small cannon going off. I would've heard the gunshot and recognized it even through the dream. Whatever happened, happened fast.

The mysterious "white substance" must've appeared as a result of the magic wave last night. Kate, my best friend, had warded my apartment months ago. Invisible spells shielded my place in a protective barrier. She'd covered the perimeter walls, the ceiling, and the floor. Anything magic would have a hard time breaking in, which probably explained why I'd slept safe and secure through the night.

"You know Darin's blind as a bat." Mrs. Haffey twisted her hands. "He can't even see what he's shooting at. The other day he comes running out of the bathroom, screaming and foaming at the mouth. He'd brushed his teeth with Aspercreme instead of toothpaste . . ."

A note of hysteria slipped into her voice. At five ten, she had eight inches of height on me and she was leaning over. "I called down to the station, but they say it will be twenty minutes or longer. I thought since you were with the Order . . ."

I used to be with the Order. When I was a Knight of Merciful Aid, it was my job to help people when the cops wouldn't or couldn't assist them with the magic hazmat. I had decorations and a stellar service record, but none of it mattered when the Order found out that I was a shapeshifter. They branded me mentally disturbed and unfit for duty and "retired" me.

But they didn't take away my training or my skills.

I pressed a latch in my wall. A panel slid aside, revealing a small niche that used to be a hallway closet and which I had converted into my own personal armory. A row of gun barrels gleamed in the morning light.

Mrs. Haffey clicked her mouth shut.

Let's see. I'd be bringing my Sigs, but I needed something with more power. The AA-12, an Automatic Assault 12-gauge shotgun with a 32-round clip was always a good choice. It fired 300 rounds per minute with minimal recoil. I filled mine with steel slugs. Squeeze the trigger once, and get a single shot that would punch through a car door. Hold the trigger, and anything on the other end, no matter how much hard body armor it wore, would become a smoking pile of meat in six and a half seconds. I'd paid a fortune for it and it was worth every dollar.

I grabbed the AA-12 and put on a hip holster, into which I stuck my Sig and its twin. "Mrs. Haffey, I need you to stay here." I gave her a nice big smile. "Lock the door behind me and don't open it until I come back. Do you understand?"

Mrs. Haffey nodded.

"Thank you, ma'am."

I stepped onto the landing and heard the deadbolt slide shut behind me.

The "white substance" stretched in long pale strands over the walls. It resembled a spiderweb, if the spider was the size of a bowling ball and instead of working in a spiral had decided to weave only in a vertical direction. I crossed the landing and inhaled. Usually there was an up-draft here, the air rising from the front entrance to the top of the building. Today no movement troubled the stairway, but I smelled the sharp metallic odor of fresh blood all the same. Tiny hairs on the back of my neck stood up. The predator in me, the other me sleeping deep inside, opened her eyes.

I padded down the stairs, moving silently on the concrete steps, my shotgun ready. Even though magic made my existence possible, it didn't mean that magic and I played nice. Give me guns over spells any day.

The web grew thicker. At the Haffeys' landing, it swallowed the walls and the wooden stair rail. I turned, heading down. The stench of blood assaulted my nostrils and I tasted it on my tongue. All of my senses went into overdrive. My heart beat faster. My pupils dilated, improving my vision. My breathing sped up. My hearing sharpened and I caught a distant noise, muffled, but unmistakable: the deep, throaty bark of a bulldog.

I took a few more steps down. Blood stained the stairs. A large amount, at least a couple of pints, possibly more, all in big round drops. Either someone bled and walked, or someone bled and was carried. Please don't be Darin. I liked Darin and I liked his wife. Mrs. Haffey was always kind to me.

The first floor landing was a narrow tunnel within the web. The door to apartment 1A was intact, but buried in white strands. The same solid wall of white sealed the way downstairs, and none of it was torn. No sign of Darin going that way. The door to 1B lay in a splintered wreck. Bloody marks stretched across the threshold, pointing into the apartment. Someone had been dragged inside.

I stepped into the hallway. A new scent tugged at me, a slightly sour, prickly odor that set off instinctual alarms in my head. Not good.

The apartment had the exact same layout as mine: a narrow hallway, opening into the kitchen on the right, the living room on the left, then the first bedroom, and then a short perpendicular hallway leading to the utility room and guest bathroom, and finally to the master bedroom with a bathroom en suite.

I moved in, nice and easy, slicing the pie around the corner: starting at the wall and moving at a ninety degree angle away from it, leaning slightly away from the wall to see the threat around the corner before it saw me. Jumping around the corners was very dramatic but would get your head blown off.

Kitchen—clear.

I moved into the living room.

On the left, by a coffee table, sat a large wicker basket full of yarn. Two long wooden needles stuck out of it at an angle. Next to the basket lay a severed human arm. The blood had pooled from it, soaking the beige wall-to-wall carpet in a dark red stain.

Pale skin. Not Darin Haffey. No, this was likely Mrs. Truman who lived in this apartment with her two cats. She liked to play bridge with her knitting club and collected yarn for "special" projects, with which she never did anything. Now her torn-off arm lay next to the basket with her knitting stash. No time to absorb and deal with it. I still had Darin to find.

I moved on. The sour prickly scent grew stronger.

Bedroom—clear. Bathroom—clear.

A huge hole gaped in the floor of the utility room. Something had smashed through the floor and tile from below.

I circled the hole, shotgun pointing down.

No movement. The floor below me looked clear.

A muffled noise cut through the quiet.

My ears twitched.

Woof! Woof!

Chief was still alive somewhere in there. I jumped into the hole, landed on the concrete floor of the basement, and moved away from the light streaming through the hole. No need to present a clear target.

Gloom filled the basement, dripping from the web into dark corners. The walls no longer existed. There was only web, white and endless.

My eyes adjusted to the darkness. Shapeshifter vision guaranteed that as long as there was some light, I wouldn't bump into things.

Wet dark smears marred the concrete. Blood. I followed it.

Ahead the concrete split. A long fissure ran through the floor, at least three feet wide. The apartment building was already none too sturdy. The magic hated tall buildings and gnawed on them, pulverizing brick and mortar until the structure crashed down. The bigger the building, the faster it fell. Ours was too short and too small and so far we had escaped unscathed, but giant holes in the basement didn't exactly inspire confidence.

A snorting noise came from inside the gap. I leaned over it. A whiff of dog-fur stink washed over me. *Chief, you silly knucklehead.*

I crouched by the hole. The bulldog squirmed below, snorting up a storm. He must've fallen into the fissure, and the drop was too sheer for him to jump out.

I put my shotgun on the ground and leaned in, grabbing Chief by the scruff of his neck. The bulldog weighed eighty

pounds at least. What in the world were the Haffeys feeding
him, small elephants? I yanked him out and jumped to my
feet, shotgun in my hands. The whole thing took half a second.

Chief pressed against my leg. He was an Olde English
Bulldogge, a throwback to the times when the English Bulldog
was used for bull-baiting. A powerful, agile dog, Chief feared
neither garbage trucks, nor stray dogs or horses. Yet here he
was, rubbing against my calf, freaked out.

I took a second to bend down and pet his big head. *It will
be okay, boy. You're with me now.*

We started forward, moving slowly out of the first narrow
room into a wider chamber. The web spanned the walls, cre-
ating hiding spots in the corners. Creepy as hell.

I carefully rounded the corner. At the far wall to my right,
two furnaces sat side by side: the electric for the times when
technology had the upper hand and the old-fashioned coal-
burning monstrosity for use during the waves, when the magic
robbed us of electric current. To the right of the coal furnace
stood a large coal bin, a four-foot-high wooden enclosure
filled with coal. On the coal, half-buried, lay Mr. Haffey.

Two creatures crawled on the concrete in front of the bin.
About thirty inches tall and at least five feet long, they resembled huge wingless wasps, with a wide thorax-chest slimming
down before flaring into thick abdomen. Stiff brown bristles
covered their beige, nearly translucent bodies. Their heads,
bigger than Chief's massive skull, bore mandibles the size of
garden shears. Their claws scraped the concrete as they
moved—an eerie, nasty sound.

The left creature stopped and planted its six chitin-sheathed
legs. Its tail end tilted up and a stream of viscous liquid shot
out, adhering to the wall. The creature scrubbed its butt on the
floor, anchoring the stream, and moved away as the secretions
hardened into pale web.

Ew. Ew, ew, ew.

Mr. Haffey raised his head.

The creatures stopped, fixated on the movement.

I fired.

The shotgun barked, spitting thunder. The first steel slug
punched into the right creature, cutting through the chitin like
it was paper-thin plywood. The insect broke in half. Wet

innards spilled onto the floor, like a bunch of swim bladders strung together. Without a pause, I turned and put a second shot into its buddy. Chief barked next to me, snapping his jaws. The creatures jerked and flailed, dragging their body chunks. The sour, spike-studded odor filled the air.

Darin Haffey sat up in the bin. "I see Kayla dragged you into this."

I smiled at him. "No, sir, I just came to borrow a cup of sugar."

"Heh."

The web obscuring the rest of the room to my left tore.

"Incoming," Mr. Haffey snapped, raising his firearm.

The first insect burst into the open. I fired. *Boom!*

Two more. *Boom, boom!*

Boom!

Boom, boom, boom!

The broken chitin bodies crashed into each other, making a pile of jerking legs and vomit-inducing entrails.

Boom, boom, boom! Boom!

An insect leaped over the pile, aiming for me. I swung the shotgun up. The impact exploded the creature's gut, spraying foul liquid over me. Bug juice burned my lips. Ugh.

A smaller insect dashed toward me. Sharp mandibles sliced at my leg. You bastard! Chief rammed the creature, ripping into the thing before I could sink a slug into it.

Boom! Boom!

I kept firing. Finally the revolting flood stopped. I waited, listening, but no more skittering came. My calf burned. The pain didn't bother me too much, but I'd be leaving a blood trail, which would make me ridiculously easy to track. I had five shots left in the AA-12. No way to know if I had killed them all or if this was the calm before the second wave of insects. I had to get Mr. Haffey out of here.

He was sitting in the coal bin, staring at the pile of insect parts. "Damn. That's some shooting."

"We aim to please," I told him.

"You aim like you mean business."

Funny thing, praise. I knew I was a great shot, but hearing it from the PAD veteran made me all warm and fuzzy anyway. "Have you seen Mrs. Truman?"

"I saw her body. They ripped her to pieces, the assholes."

Poor Mrs. Truman. "Can you walk?"

"The fuckers got me in the leg. I'm bleeding like a stuck pig."

That's why he'd hidden in the coal. He'd buried his leg in the coal dust to smother the scent. Smart. "Time to go, then."

"You listen to me." Mr. Haffey put some cop hardness into his gruff voice. "There's no way for you to get me out. Even if I lean on you, I'm two hundred and twenty pounds and my weight will just take you down with me. Leave me a gun, and you get out of here. Kayla must've called over to the station. I'll hold them off until . . ."

I swung the shotgun over my shoulder and picked him up out of the coal. I wasn't as strong as a normal shapeshifter, although I was faster and more agile, but a two-hundred-pound man still wasn't a challenge.

I double-timed it to the hole, Chief at my heels. The bulldog had a death grip on a chitinous leg as long as he was. He had to lean his head back to carry it, but the look in his eyes said no army in the world could take it away.

"This is embarrassing," Mr. Haffey informed me.

I winked at him. "What, Mrs. Haffey never carried you over the threshold on your wedding night?"

His eyes bulged. "That's just ridiculous. What are you?"

I'd spent most of my life pretending to be human. But now the hyena was out of the bag, and sooner or later I had to start owning up to it. "A shapeshifter."

"Wolf?"

"A bouda." Well, not exactly. The truth was more complicated, but I wasn't ready for those explanations yet.

We reached the hole. If I were a regular bouda, I could've jumped out of the hole with Mr. Haffey in my arms. But I knew my limits and that wasn't happening. Throwing him out would injure his dignity beyond repair. "I'm going to lift you. Can you pull yourself up?"

"Is the Pope Catholic?"

I lowered him down, grabbed him by the hips, and heaved. Mr. Haffey pulled himself over the ledge and I got a real close look at that wound. It was a four-inch rip down his leg and touching his sweatpants left my palm bloody. He needed an ambulance yesterday.

I tossed Chief and his prize out of the hole, jumped, caught the edge, and hopped up.

"Will you at least carry me fireman-style?" Mr. Haffey huffed.

"No can do, sir. I'm trying to keep your blood from dripping out of your leg."

He growled deep under his breath.

I picked him up and started out. "It will all be over soon." He guffawed.

I caught the familiar scuttling sound behind me, coming from the master bedroom.

"I thought the Order didn't allow shapeshifters."

"They don't. When they figured me out, they fired me."

The scuttling chased us.

"That's bullshit right there." Mr. Haffey shook his head. "And discrimination. You talk to your union rep?"

"Yes, I did. I fought it as long as I could. Anyway, they retired me with full pension. I can't appeal."

Mr. Haffey gave me an appraising look. "You took it?"

"Nope. Told them to shove it."

I dropped him to the floor as gently as I could and spun, shotgun ready.

A huge pale insect lunged at us. I pumped two slugs into it and it thrashed on the floor. I gathered Mr. Haffey up and double-timed it to the door.

"Listen, most of my contacts have retired, but a few of us have kids in the department. If you need a job, I can probably fix up something. The PAD will be glad to have you. You're a hell of a shot. Shouldn't let that go to waste."

"Much appreciated." I smiled. "But I've got a job. I work for a business. My best friend owns it." I started up the stairs.

"What sort of business?"

"Magic hazmat removal. Protection. That type of thing."

Mr. Haffey opened his eyes. "Private cop? You went private?"

That's cop mentality for you. I tell him I'm a shapeshifter and he doesn't blink an eye. But private cop, oh no, that's not okay.

"So how's business?" Mr. Haffey squinted at me.

"Business is fine." If by fine, one meant lousy. Between Kate Daniels and me, we had a wealth of skills, a small sea of experience, and enough smears on our reputation to kill a dozen careers. All of our clients were desperate, because by the time they came to us, everybody else had turned them down.

"What does your man think about that?"

Raphael Medrano. The memory of him was so raw, I could conjure his scent by just thinking about him. The strong male healthy scent that drove me crazy . . .

"It didn't work out," I said.

Mr. Haffey shifted, uncomfortable. "You need to drop that silliness and get back in uniform. We're talking retirement, benefits, advance in rank and pay . . ."

I ran up to my door. "Mrs. Haffey!"

The door swung open. Mrs. Haffey's face went slack. "Oh my God, Darin. Oh God."

In the distance the familiar sirens blared.

The cavalry arrived with guns and in large numbers. They loaded Mr. Haffey into an ambulance, thanked me for my help, and told me that since I was a civilian, I needed to keep the hell out of their way. I didn't mind. I'd killed most of what was down there and they had gotten all dressed up and gone through the trouble of bringing flamethrowers. It was only fair to let them have some fun.

I tended the cut on my leg. There wasn't much to do about it. Lyc-V, the virus responsible for shapeshifters' existence, repaired injuries at an accelerated rate, and by the time I got to it, the gash had sealed itself. In a couple of days, the leg would be like new, without scars. Some Lyc-V gifts were useful. Some, like berserker rage, I could live without.

I was scrubbing the bug juice off my face with my makeup removal washcloth, when the phone rang. I wiped the soap off my face and sprinted into the kitchen to pick it up.

"Hello?"

"Nash?" a smooth voice said into the phone.

The smooth voice belonged to Jim, a werejaguar and the Pack's security chief. He usually went by Jim Black, if you didn't know him well. I'd dug through his background during my tenure with the Order. His real name was James Damael Shrapshire, a fact I kept to myself, since he didn't advertise it.

Atlanta's Shapeshifter Pack was the strongest in the nation, and my relationship with it was complicated. But the Pack backed Cutting Edge, the business Kate owned and for which I now worked. They had supplied the seed money and they were our first priority client.

"Hey, Jim. What can I do for you?" Jim wasn't a bad guy. Paranoid and secretive, but then cats were odd creatures.

"One of our businesses got hit last night," Jim said. "Four people are dead."

Someone obviously had a death wish and that someone wasn't very bright, because there were much easier ways of committing suicide. The Pack took care of their own and if you hurt their own, they made it a point to take care of you. "Anybody I know?"

"No. Two jackals, a bouda, and a fox from Clan Nimble. I need you to go down there and check it out."

I headed into the bedroom. "No problem. But why me?"

Jim sighed into the phone. "Andrea, how many years did you spend as a knight?"

"Eight." I began pulling my clothes onto the bed: socks, work boots, jeans . . .

"How many of those did you spend on active cases?"

"Seven." I added a box of ammo to the clothes pile on the bed.

"That's why. You're the most experienced investigator I've got who's not tied up in something, and I can't ask the Consort to look into it, because A) she and Curran are working on something else and B) when the Consort gets involved, half of the world blows up."

Kate the Consort. The title still made me grin. Every time someone used it, she got this martyred look on her face.

"This mess looks to be complicated and the cops are in up to their elbows. I need you to go down there and untangle it."

Finally. Something I could actually sink my teeth into.

I held the phone between my shoulder and my ear and took a pencil and a notepad off the nightstand. "You've got an address?"

"Fourteen-twelve Griffin."

Griffin Street ran through SoNo, one of the former financial districts, sandwiched between Midtown and Downtown. The name came from "South of North Avenue." It was a bad, unstable area, with old office buildings crashing down left and right.

"What were the shapeshifters doing there?"

"Working," Jim said. "It's a reclamation site."

Reclamations. Oh no. No. He wouldn't do that to me. I kept my voice even. "Who was in charge of the site?"

Please don't be Raphael, please don't be Raphael, please don't . . .

"Medrano Reclamations," Jim said.

Damn it.

"Raphael is being questioned by some cops, but I've sent some lawyers down to make sure they don't keep him. He'll join you as soon as they spring him out of there. Look, I know things aren't good between you and Raphael, but we all have to do things we don't want to do."

"Jim," I cut him off. "I've got it. A job is a job. I'm on it."

CHAPTER 2

It took me forty-five minutes to make my way through the twisted wreck of the city to SoNo. The magic had really done a number on Atlanta. Downtown had suffered the most, but both Midtown and Buckhead had taken a beating. Once-stately skyscrapers lay in ruins, like the gravestones of human hopes, toppled on their sides. Overpasses crumbled into dust and new wooden bridges spanned the asphalt canyons. Debris choked the streets. Atlanta was still alive and kicking and the city was rebuilding little by little, but the sheer weight and volume of the fallen concrete made it problematic. I had to make a wide circle north around the wreckage.

On the corner of Monroe and 10th Street, something fluorescent had exploded, drenching the walls of the new houses in electric orange that smelled like day-old vomit. The city Biohazard crew narrowed the traffic to a single lane guarded by two guys with stop signs, who let the vehicles and riders through a few at a time, while the rest of the Biohazard team washed the orange pus down with fire hoses.

Around me, the morning traffic neighed, brayed, and defecated on the street. Gasoline vehicles failed during magic. My Jeep had two engines, one gas and the other enchanted water, so even when technology was down, my car still got me where I needed to go, reliably but not very fast. Buying a reconditioned car like mine was expensive, so most people opted for horses, camels, and mules. They worked whenever. They just didn't smell very good. It was the middle of May, and a hot one at that, and the reek rising from the pavement would have sent anyone running for cover.

To my left a man atop a white horse leveled a crossbow at

the stop sign. The string twanged and a bolt punched through metal, right into the *O*. Bull's-eye.

The Biohazard guy thrust the injured sign against the Biohazard service truck, pulled a shotgun from the truck bed, and leveled it at the crossbowman.

"Make my day, bitch! Make my day!"

"Fuck you and your sign!"

"Hey," a woman yelled. "There are children here!"

"Piss off!" the rider told her and pointed the crossbow at the Biohazard dude. "Let me through."

"No. Wait your turn like everybody else."

I could tell by their faces that neither of them would shoot. They'd just talk shit and waste everyone's time and as long as the Biohazard guy bickered with the moron on the horse, he wasn't waving the traffic through. At this rate I would never make it to my crime scene.

"Hey, dickhead!" one of the other drivers yelled. "Get off the road!"

"This here is a Falcon Seven," the rider told him. "I can put a bolt through your windshield and pin you to your seat like a bug."

A direct threat, huh? Okay.

I pulled down my sunglasses a bit so the rider would see my eyes. "That's a nice crossbow."

He glanced in my direction. He saw a friendly blond girl with a big smile and a light Texas accent and didn't get alarmed.

"You've got what, a seventy-five-pound draw on it? Takes you about four seconds to reload?"

"Three," he said.

I gave him my Order smile: sweet grin, hard eyes, reached over to my passenger seat, and pulled out my submachine gun. About twenty-seven inches long, the HK was my favorite toy for close-quarters combat. The rider's eyes went wide.

"This is an HK UMP submachine gun. Renowned for its stopping power and reliability. Cyclic rate of fire: eight hundred rounds per minute. That means I can empty this thirty-round clip into you in less than three seconds. At this range, I'll cut you in half." It wasn't strictly true but it sounded good. "You see what it says on the barrel?"

On the barrel, pretty white letters spelled out PARTY STARTER.

"You open your mouth again, and I'll get the party started."

The rider clamped his jaws shut.

I looked at the Biohazard guy. "Appreciate the job you're doing for the city, sir. Please carry on."

Ten seconds later, I got through the roadblock, steered the Jeep down Monroe Street, and turned right onto North Avenue. I made it two blocks before the street ended in a mountain of crushed glass. This intrepid adventure would have to continue on foot. I parked, checked my guns, took my crime scene kit out of the trunk, and jogged down the street.

Maybe Raphael wouldn't be there.

Sooner or later I would have to interview him. My heart rate sped up at the thought. I took deeper breaths until it slowed. I had a job to do. The Order might not think I was worth much, but the Pack obviously did. I would be professional about it.

Professional. Just the facts, ma'am. Move along, there is nothing to see here. No need to panic.

This wasn't my first case and this wasn't my first murder. It was a chance at work that mattered and I would not blow it by making a spectacle of myself.

Fourteen-twelve Griffin resembled a small hill of twisted metal, decorated with chunks of concrete, mixed with dirty marble, piles of shattered bluish glass, and fine gray dust, the result of magic's fangs grinding at the substance of the building. A backhoe and some other heavy-duty construction vehicle the name of which I didn't know sat across the street, next to a tent.

A reinforced tunnel led inside the hill, with two shapeshifters standing guard. The one on the left, in dark jeans and a black T-shirt, was a male bouda in his late thirties, lean, dark, with an easy smile. I'd met him before—his name was Stefan and he and I had no problems. Like most boudas, he was good with a knife and occasionally, if his opponents really pissed him off, he would scalp them after he killed them.

The other shapeshifter, on the right, was larger, younger, and dark-eyed, with chestnut hair cropped short. I inhaled his scent. A werejackal.

I came to a halt before the tunnel. Stefan's eyes widened. "Hey, you."

"Hey, yourself."

The jackal gave me a long look. I wore a white long-sleeved shirt, brown pants, and a leather vest over it. The vest's main advantage was its million pockets. My two Sigs rested in twin shoulder holsters. The jackal's nose wrinkled. That's right, I don't smell like a normal bouda.

"Jim sent me," I told Stefan.

Stefan raised his eyebrows. "That Jim?"

"Yup. Did Raphael make it back from the cops?" My insides clenched up.

"Nope."

Thank God. I was a coward. A terrible, sad coward. "I need to examine the scene."

The jackal finally identified the scent. "You're . . ."

Stefan sidestepped, casually stomping on the jackal's foot with his steel-toed work boot. "She's point on this case. Come on, Andrea, I'll show you around."

He ducked into the tunnel. I took off my shades, tucked them into a vest pocket, and followed him. A dry stone odor greeted us, mixed with something else. The secondary scent coated my tongue and I recognized it: it was the faint, barely perceptible reek of early decomposition.

When magic attacked a tall building, it gnawed on the concrete first, attacking it in random places until it turned into dust. Eventually the building crashed like a rotten tree. Concrete and breakable valuables perished, but metal and other valuable scrap endured. Reclamation companies went into the fallen buildings and salvaged the metal and anything else that could be sold.

Fallen wrecks like this one were unstable. It took a special kind of insanity to burrow into a building that could collapse on your head at any moment. Shapeshifters turned out to be well-suited for it: we were all insane to start with, enhanced strength let us work fast, and Lyc-V-fueled regeneration knitted broken bones together in record time.

Whatever other faults Raphael had, he made sure to keep the broken bones to a bare minimum. The passageway was six feet wide. Thick steel beams and stone pillars supported the roof and metal mesh held back the walls. I was five foot two, but Stefan had six inches on me, and he didn't have to duck either. A string of electric lights ran along the ceiling, blinking dimly. Dimly was plenty. We paused, letting our eyes adjust to the gloom, and walked on.

The tunnel angled down.

"Tell me about the building," I asked.

"It fell about seven years after the Shift, right in line with the Georgia Power building behind the Civic Center. Before it crashed, it was a thirty-floor tower of blue glass shaped like a V. Built and owned by Jamar Groves. Jamar was a real estate developer and this baby was his pride and joy. He called it the Blue Heron Building. People told him to evacuate, but he got it into his head that the building wouldn't fall. He's still here somewhere." Stefan nodded at the ceiling. "Or at least his bones are."

"Went down with his ship?" The stench of decomposition was getting stronger, clinging to the walls of the tunnel like a foul patina.

"Yep. Jamar was a weird guy, apparently."

"Only poor people are weird. Rich people are eccentric."

Stefan cracked a grin. "Well, Jamar owned a huge art collection and he had some interesting ideas. For one, he had a Roman-style marble bathhouse on the second floor."

"So you're after the marble?" I asked.

"Screw the marble. We're after the copper plumbing. The whole structure had old-school copper pipes. Copper prices are through the roof right now. Even copper wiring is expensive. Of course, if you smelt the plastic off of it, it's worth twice as much, but we won't be doing that. The smoke is toxic as hell, even for us. There is steel, too, but the copper is the real prize. That's why Raphael bought the building."

"He bought the building?" A few months ago when Raphael and I were together, he mostly did work for hire: the owners of various buildings would employ him to reclaim the valuables for a percentage of anything he recovered.

Stefan grinned. "We can do that now. Playing with the big boys."

The tunnel kept going, lower and lower, burrowing down.

"Why dig so deep under the building? Why not come from the side?"

"The Heron is a toppler," Stefan said. "It went over right above the sixth floor. And it never caught fire."

Magic took buildings down in different ways. Sometimes the entire inner structure collapsed and the building imploded in a fountain of dust. More often, the magic weakened parts of the building, causing a partial collapse until the whole thing crashed, toppling on its side. Topplers were valuable, especially if they didn't catch fire, because anything underground had a decent chance of surviving.

"We were trying to get into the basement," Stefan confirmed. "There are fire-suppression and heating systems down there, generators, access to both freight and regular elevator shafts—that's a lot of metal right there. And you never know, sometimes you can get computer servers out. Stranger things have survived a fallen building. Here we are."

Ahead the passageway widened. Stefan flicked the switch and the twin lamps in the ceiling flared into life. We stood in a round chamber, about twenty-five feet wide. Four bodies lay on the dirt floor, two men and two women. At the far wall, a six-foot-tall disk of metal thrust out, revealing a round tunnel filled with darkness—a vault door left ajar.

"A vault?"

Stefan grimaced. "It wasn't on any of the blueprints and none of the building-related correspondence we had access to mentioned it. We were merrily digging our way up and ran into it last night. We screwed around with the door for about an hour, but we didn't have the right tools for it, so Raphael posted two guards here and two by the entrance, and we cleared out. A locksmith was supposed to come in this morning and open the sucker. Instead we found this."

Four people dead, sprawled in the dirt. Last night they had hugged their loved ones before going on their shift. They had made plans. This morning they were my responsibility. Life was a vicious bitch.

"Okay, let me see the log."

"The what?"

"The crime scene log? The record of who's been down here and at what time?"

Stefan gave me a blank look.

"Eh . . ."

God damn it. I took a small notebook and a pen out of my vest pocket and kept my voice friendly. "I tell you what, we'll start one. Here, I'll be the first."

I marked the date at the top of the page and wrote: "Andrea Nash. Time In: 8:12 a.m. Time out: _____. Purpose: Investigation." I signed it and passed the notebook and the pen to him.

"Now you write yourself in. When people come to pick up the bodies, you make them write themselves in, too. We need to keep a record of who comes and goes down here."

I set my crime scene bag on the side, opened it, took out gloves and put them on. Next came the Polaroid Instant Digital camera and a stack of paper envelopes for crime scene photos and evidence. Other cameras took better pictures, but magic played havoc with digital data. Sometimes you'd get crystal-clear high-definition images, and sometimes you'd end up with a blurred gray mess or nothing at all. Polaroid Instant Digital cameras produced photos faster than anything else on the market and stored the image digitally as a bonus. It was as close to an instant record of evidence as we could get.

"Have the bodies been moved at all?"

Stefan shrugged his shoulders. "Sylvia found them, she checked their pulses, examined the vault to see that nobody was there, and backed right out of the dig. We know the drill."

If they knew the drill, they would've kept a log. "Where is Sylvia now?"

"With Raphael, being hassled by the cops."

In legal terms, the Pack had similar rights to a Native American tribe, with the ability to govern itself and enforce its own laws. If a shapeshifter died in the Pack's territory, it was a Pack matter. These shapeshifters had died within city limits, and the PAD wanted in on the action. They weren't exactly shapeshifter fans, with a good reason.

We lived in the gray zone between beast and human. Those of us who wanted to remain human lived by the Code, a set of strict rules. The Code was all about discipline and moderation and obeying the chain of command. Sometimes the human brakes failed, and a shapeshifter threw the Code out the window and went loup. Loups were sadistic, murderous freaks. They reveled in killing, cannibalism, and every other violent perversity their insane brains could think up. The Pack put them down with extreme prejudice, but that didn't keep the PAD from viewing every shapeshifter as a potential spree killer. Whenever a shapeshifter murder occurred in the city, they tried to muscle in on it.

Not that they would accomplish anything. The Pack's lawyers were ravenous beasts.

I crouched by the nearest body and aimed the camera. The flash flared, searing the scene with white light for a fraction of a moment. The camera purred, printing out the image. I pulled it out and waved it a bit to dry, before sliding it into a paper envelope.

The dead man appeared to be in his late fifties. Shapeshifters aged well, so he could've been in his seventies, for all I knew. The skin on his forehead was olive, a warm shade particular to those from the Indian subcontinent. That was the only patch of exposed skin left undamaged. Large blisters swelled everywhere else on his cheeks, neck, and arms, the skin peeling up from muscle, stretched taut and completely black.

Another Polaroid.

"I've never seen anything like that before," Stefan said.

I had. "Has the ME been through here?"

"Yeah. But we chased them off."

That's right, even if Pack members died outside of the Pack's territory, the Pack still had the right to claim their bodies. And technically the building was Pack property, since Raphael had bought it. I should've remembered that. Getting rusty, Ms. Nash. Getting rusty.

I handed him the Polaroid camera. "Could you hold on to this for a second?"

He took the camera. I pulled a knife from my belt and sliced the man's shirt straight down his chest. The thin fabric parted easily. I made a cut through each sleeve and gently turned the body on its side. A large swelling marked the top of the left shoulder, just above the clavicle. I flicked the knife across the bottom edge of the blister. Body fluids gushed out, black and streaked with blood. The stench hit me instantly, the foul, putrid reek of rotten flesh.

Stefan cursed and spun away.

"If you're going to puke, kindly do it in the tunnel."

He bent double and shook his head. "No, I'm good. I'm good."

I stretched the deflated skin down. Two ragged punctures marked the man's back, close to the top of the shoulder near the neck. The swelling had hidden them before.

"What is that?"

"A snakebite."

"Aren't we immune to snake venom?"

I shook my head. "Nope."

"You're kidding me."

"No, I'm not. Shapeshifters don't exactly advertise this fact, for obvious reasons, but yeah, a copperhead bites you, you'll feel it."

Stefan blinked at me. "We regenerate broken bones, and we're immune to disease and poison."

"We're very resistant to poison but not immune. Remember Erra?"

Stefan's eyes darkened. "Yeah. I remember."

Erra was Kate's aunt and her secret. Kate's family was magic, the kind of magic that leveled cities and altered the course of ancient civilizations. Her aunt had slept for thousands of years, but the onset of magic had awakened her, and she came to Atlanta looking for trouble and nearly destroyed the city. One of her creations, which she named Venom, broke into one of Clan Wolf's houses in the city and poisoned everyone within. They died in agony. It was a wakeup call to the Pack. The shapeshifters could be poisoned, if the poison was strong enough.

"Most diseases are viral or bacterial in nature," I said. "Lyc-V is a jealous virus, so it terminates these other invaders. Ingested poison is localized to the stomach. The second it tries to enter the bloodstream, Lyc-V will shut it down. A snakebite is another story."

I rose, pulled a rag from my pocket, and wiped my hands. "The snake injects toxins directly into the body, and these toxins are biological: enzymes, coagulants, and so on. Some just attack the area of the bite, but some attack the nervous system, and Lyc-V doesn't recognize them as a threat until the damage starts to spread."

"So what's this one?"

"Hemotoxic. Probably from a viper. The moment the venom enters the victim, it begins to coagulate blood and clot the blood vessels. Lyc-V exists in all tissues, but most of it is in the bloodstream. Clog the arteries and the virus can't get to the venom fast enough to destroy it. I once knew a werebuffalo who fell into a nest of rattlesnakes. Looked just like that when we pulled his corpse out."

Stefan peered at the body. "How did a snake manage to bite him on his back? He wouldn't have been lying down in the dirt. Sitting, maybe."

Shapeshifters took personal hygiene seriously. "Filthy animal" was a common insult people hurled our way. The guards wouldn't have been lying down in loose soil unless they absolutely had to.

"I don't know." I took a ruler from my bag and held it up to the bite marks. Three and three-eighths of an inch. Two inches would mean a big snake. Two and a half inches meant a fifteen-foot rattler. Three and three-eighths was crazy.

"I can tell you that if I was an intelligent snake, this is the place I'd bite," I said. "If you cause coagulation in the arteries leading to the brain, death will follow like that." I would've snapped my fingers, but I was wearing latex gloves.

"So we have giant super-smart vipers who slithered in here, killed our people, opened the vault, stole something from it, and slithered out, undetected?"

"Appears so."

"Okay. Just wanted to make sure it wasn't something dangerous."

I flashed him a quick smile and set about processing the scene.

The scene was a nightmare. Raphael's workers had been in and out of it barely twelve hours ago and two dozen scent signatures clung to the ground, not to mention the stench of decay rising from the bodies. In the Georgia heat, even this deep underground, corpses decomposed fast.

A cursory examination of the bodies showed multiple snakebites. I noted four different fang spans and wrote them down. I divided the scene into rows and searched it, wall to wall, picking up every bottle cap and every hair.

A truck arrived from the Pack to take the bodies back to the Keep, the Pack's huge headquarters just outside Atlanta that everyone insisted was not a castle, despite it being a dead ringer for one. I jotted down some notes for Doolittle, the Pack's chief medmage, outlining my snake theory. He would be the one examining the bodies. I packaged the fingerprints I had collected into a large envelope and addressed it to Jim. The Pack had its own fingerprint database, and Jim was in a much better position to identify the prints than I was. I knew the theory behind fingerprint analysis and had been taught some rudimentary skills in the Order's Academy, but in practice I just saw a bunch of whorls I had no idea what to do with. I also wrote out a quick preliminary assessment for Jim, requested background files on Raphael's entire workforce, and sent the whole kaboodle to the Keep with the body crew.

I went into the vault and stood in it for a bit, visually examining the contents. It was filled with antiques. A pair of elegant, long-necked cats, pure black, with eyes of what were probably real emeralds sat against the wall. To the left of the cats, a stone tablet as tall as me rested on the floor, carved with figures in robes and weathered with age. To the right, a small wooden chair, gilded with gold and painted with brown, stood, its feet fashioned into the semblance of lion paws.

On the shelves were an ornate gold necklace resting in a glass box on top of a scarlet velvet pillow; a set of small bottles, crystal wrapped in bands of gold; a wooden cabinet, empty; a large chunk of sea-foam crystal on black velvet with a carving on it—three men on one side and a woman waving good-bye. Or maybe hello.

Nope, it was probably good-bye. Life was mean like that.

Age permeated the scene, emanating from the items like an aroma from a flower. How many people had died for these things? I knew of at least four and I had a feeling the body count would continue to climb.

I called Stefan down and catalogued the vault, item by item, and had him sign the whole thing as a witness. The list was so long my pen was in death throes by the end of it. Something must have been taken out of the vault, but what? I crawled over every inch of the damn place, looking for any indication of a missing item, but the vault was dust-free. No mysterious outline, no empty hooks, nothing that would give me any sort of clue about what had been taken. For all I knew, instead of taking something out, the attackers had put something in. Wouldn't that be the pits.

By the time I finally emerged from the tunnel, covered in dirt and bone tired, the sun had almost completed its escape below the horizon. Scene processing was a slow and tedious job. The next time, I'd find myself someone to slave with me.

Stefan rose from the steel drum on which he was sitting. "Done?"

"Yes. Any news from Raphael?"

"No."

Either the cops had held him up or he was going to great lengths to avoid me.

"Stefan, that stuff in the vault is very old. We have no way of knowing if any of it is magic or not. You guys need to keep away from it. Don't touch it, don't sniff it, don't try to transport it. I'll ask someone with magical knowledge to come down with the Keep. They will move it and quarantine it."

Stefan squinted at me. "I get what you're saying, but you'll have to talk to Raphael about it. He'll probably come by here after the cops let him go. You want to leave him a note?"

Good idea. "Got something to write with?" I shook my exhausted pen. "Mine is all out."

"Sure, in the tent."

I glanced at the work tent sitting a few yards away. "Thanks."

I walked to the tent, pushed the entrance flap aside, and stepped into it.

It smelled like Raphael.

His scent permeated every inch of the space, from the tent walls, to the foldout desk and chair, to the papers neatly stacked on the desk. Every object pulsed with it, calling to me, singing, "Raphael . . . Raphael . . . Mate . . ." The scent enveloped me, warm, welcoming, *mine*, and every inch of me screamed in frustration. I stumbled back out and nearly fell over a rock.

"Are you okay?" Stefan called.

"Yes." I had to get out of there.

I turned and marched away.

"What about the note?" Stefan asked.

"I'll leave a message on his phone."

I kept walking, trying to put distance between me and that cursed tent. If someone had barred my way, I might have shot him.

I stopped by Cutting Edge's office—it was locked, Kate absent—deposited my trace evidence into our office vault, and drove home. I climbed the stairs, which turned out to be web-free and singed with dark soot from the PAD flamethrowers, and stopped by the Haffeys' apartment. Nobody answered my knocking. Hopefully Mr. Haffey had made it through.

I walked to my apartment, got inside, and leaned against the door, afraid that the world outside would somehow bust in and get me.

My place was dark and empty. It served as my little haven, especially in the three weeks I had holed up here, trying to come to terms with being thrown out of the Order. It was my safe little prison cell, just me, myself, and I. Well, and Grendel, but the poodle, as good of a listener as he was, couldn't really hold up his end of the conversation.

My place didn't seem safe now. It felt stifling and barren.

No Raphael. I remembered what it felt like to wake up in the morning and find him holding me. If I closed my eyes, I could hear his laugh. He made me so happy, but more importantly, I made him happy. Whatever my shortcomings were, I knew that I could make his day. I never realized how much joy it brought me. I didn't have to even do anything. I just had to snuggle up next to him on the couch, while he peered at his business reports, and his face would light up.

And now he was gone.

This sucked. This sucked so, so much.

"This sucks," I said, my voice alarmingly loud in the silent

room. I knew exactly what I had to do. I had to pick up the
phone and call him and tell him how I felt. I should've done it
weeks ago, but lifting that phone felt like trying to pick up
Stone Mountain.

Our happily ever after ended in one fight and both of us
were to blame for it. Back when Erra was rampaging through
Atlanta, Kate and I had barely survived a huge fight with one
of her creations at the Order. The Order's office was half
burned, half flooded, every window shattered, the walls still
smoking. That's when an emergency call came in from Clan
Wolf. They were under attack by Erra too and they were
dying. Kate and I wanted to help. Ted, the resident knight-
defender, ordered us to stand down. He needed us at the Order.

Kate ripped off her Order ID and walked out. I didn't. I
was a knight. I had sworn an oath and I didn't get to pick
which orders I obeyed.

Raphael took it personally. In his mind I had rejected the
shapeshifters, the Pack, and therefore I had rejected him. He
was the prince of Atlanta's boudas, the favorite son, loved,
admired, and supported on every turn. To him being a shapeshifter was the most natural thing in the world.

To me being a shapeshifter meant being hurt, degraded,
and living in fear. Every bone in my body had been broken by
shapeshifters before I was ten years old. I've been stabbed,
punched, kicked, whipped, and set on fire. I've watched my
mother being beaten to a bloody pulp repeatedly and with
vicious glee. I had rejected that life and chosen the Order
instead. The knights were my pack and Ted was my alpha.

Raphael knew all this, or most of it. I had told him about
my childhood. But to him all that abuse had been inflicted on
me by "bad" shapeshifters. The Atlanta Pack consisted of
"good" shapeshifters, with laws, discipline, and safety. He
thought they deserved my loyalty above everyone else simply
because all of us turned furry. He had expected me to walk
away from everything I'd worked so hard for and be his bouda
princess. We had an ugly fight and went our separate ways.
Neither of us said we were through. We just stopped talking.

I meant to call him. I had planned to do it after we finally
took Erra down, but in that last fight I was injured. My shapeshifter status came out, and the Order cordially requested my

presence at its headquarters. It wasn't the kind of invitation one declined. So I went to stand trial. I thought it was my chance to change the Order for the better. There were other people in the ranks like me, closet shapeshifters, secret not-quite-humans. I wanted to prove that we were worthy of knighthood. I had a stellar record, years of exemplary service, and the decorations and awards to prove it. I thought I had a shot. I had tried, so desperately tried, and in the end it was all for nothing. The Order got rid of me and that was that.

I couldn't change the past, but I could work on the present. I was miserable without Raphael. I knew exactly why I hadn't picked up the phone. Sure, some of it was pride. Some of it was anger. I was tired of everyone judging me. The Order judged me for being a shapeshifter. The shapeshifters judged me for having the wrong kind of father. In a time when my life really sucked, I had needed Raphael to be that one person who didn't judge me, and I was angry because he did. But deep under it all was fear. As long as I didn't call him, Raphael couldn't tell me that we were over.

How is it that I could run into a gunfight against over-whelming odds and put myself between bullets and civilians, but I couldn't scrape together enough courage to speak to the one person who mattered the most to me?

I walked into the kitchen, picked up the phone, and dialed Raphael's number. We had something, damn it. We loved each other. I missed him. He had to miss me, too. We needed to stop being stupid and sort things out.

The phone rang.

He would understand. If he just gave me a chance, I would make him understand all of it.

Something wet touched my cheek and I realized it was a tear. Jesus Christ. I wiped it off. It was good that I was alone and nobody could see it.

The answering machine clicked on. Raphael's voice said, "Raphael Medrano. Leave a message."

Keep it together. Keep it professional.

"Hi, it's me. Jim asked me to look into the murders at your work site. I need to interview you, so I thought maybe we could meet at my office tomorrow morning." Neutral territory, no memories to get in the way. I hesitated. "I know we didn't part on the best terms, and I regret that. We both made some mistakes. I hope we can put this aside and try to work together on this investigation."

I miss you. I miss you terribly.

"I would like a chance to clear the air. I . . . I have some things to tell you that are long overdue. I'll see you tomorrow."

I hung up.

It hadn't sounded right. That wasn't exactly what I wanted to say. But then again, crying hysterically into the phone and sobbing about how his scent made me want to curl into a fetal position wouldn't do any good. Sorry and tears had to wait until we met and were alone.

I could do this right. I just needed to sleep on it.

CHAPTER 3

------◆------

The morning brought light and magic. I took a few extra minutes to decide what to wear. Not that it would make any difference, but I put on my pale blue shirt. It matched my eyes and looked nice. I put on my favorite jeans and looked at myself in the mirror.

Full-on makeup would be too much. I brushed some mascara on and styled my blond hair, which was doing its best to grow out of its shorter hairdo. Right after I got kicked out of the Order, I'd "frosted" the tips of my hair blue, but now the dye was all gone and I'd ended up with a head full of highlights instead.

Like a kid before the prom: gussying up and shaking with nerves. I crossed my arms and glared at myself in the mirror. Sniper, death, kill, tough, hooah. Okay, that was better.

Raphael always brought out a strange side of me. The wild side, the one that was knitted from pure emotions. That wild Andrea loved him completely and did irrational things, like sitting by the phone with her heart beating too fast, waiting for him to call, or running headfirst into danger against overwhelming odds to fight by his side. That wild Andrea once got arrested. We had gone away for a romantic retreat and while I left the hot tub in the courtyard of the hotel to use the bathroom, some floozy had attached herself to Raphael, not taking no for an answer. When I returned, instead of beating a swift retreat she suggested we should all have fun together. I had dunked her a couple of times. Unfortunately, I was pointing a gun at hotel security at the time, and the sheriff's deputies showed up. Raphael ate it up. I was finally acting like a mated shapeshifter: irrational, possessive, and head over heels in love.

I didn't know if that part of me was my hyena side or just that uncompromising fifteen-year-old girl that lives inside every woman, but now wasn't the time to let her out. I had to stay rational, so I could apologize and try to mend things between me and Raphael.

Cutting Edge occupied a sturdy building on the northern edge of Atlanta, about an hour from the Keep. The Beast Lord, also known as Kate's sugar woogums, had chosen the location, and he pretty much picked the closest place to the Keep that was still within city limits. Curran didn't like to be without Kate and Kate didn't like to be without Curran.

The door was unlocked. Great. I walked in. Ascanio looked up from his broom.

Despite having very few clients, Cutting Edge had an excess of employees, partially because Kate kept hiring them. According to her, Ascanio Ferara was an intern. In reality nobody with a drop of sense would hire him as an intern or anything else, except maybe as a traffic jam generator. If you stood him on a street corner, sooner or later some female driver would wreck.

Fifteen going on thirty, with glossy black hair and green eyes, Ascanio was beautiful. Not just pretty, not just attractive, beautiful. He had that whole fallen angel thing going—there was a devious, sly mind behind that innocent face and pretty eyes.

Like most male children of Clan Bouda, he was treasured and babied, more so because he was lost for most of his life and his mother had just found him a few months ago. In this short period he had gotten into every possible trouble imaginable, culminating with being arrested for having a threesome on the courthouse steps. The boy did not understand how the Pack worked, and finally Aunt B foisted him off on Kate. It was that or kill him. Kate's solution was to make this raging ball of problems and hormones into our intern. How her mind worked, I would never understand. It was a mystery.

Ascanio snapped to attention and saluted me, holding the broom like a rifle.

I pointed at the broom. "No."

"Why not?"

Because it would've made every ex-military instructor I

ever had foam at the mouth. "You salute with your weapon as a sign of respect."

He presented me with an expression of puzzled innocence. "I don't have a rifle or a sword. The broom *is* my weapon."

Smartass. "Kid, you make my head explode."

"Ave, Andrea! Ianitori te salutant!"

Hail, Andrea, those who janitor salute you. Kate was forcing Ascanio and Julie, her ward, to learn Latin, because a lot of historical magical texts were written in it and apparently it was an essential part of their education. Since the lessons were conducted in the office during our copious spare time, I was learning the language along with them.

I pointed at Ascanio. "Not another word. Latin is a dead language, but that doesn't mean you get to molest its corpse. Finish sweeping, *ianitor.*"

He spun the broom with the dexterity of a Marine on Silent Drill Platoon, planted the handle into the ground, jumped, spinning around it, his legs straight out, and landed on one knee, his head bowed, his right hand extended, holding the broom in his fist parallel to the floor.

"You had coffee this morning, didn't you?"

He looked up at me and nodded, a big grin plastered on his face.

Teenage boudas. Enough said.

I sat down and tried my best to concentrate on going through my case. The survey of the evidence only confirmed what I had already realized last night: I didn't find any smoking guns. Most of what I had picked up looked just like common trash, which didn't necessarily mean it was trash. It was evidence, the significance of which wasn't immediately apparent. I catalogued it anyway. Crimes were rarely cracked by the super-brilliant detectives in a blaze of intellectual glory. Most of them were solved by the patient and the meticulous grunts just like me.

The roar of a water engine–powered vehicle thundered outside of our door and died. Raphael. Had to be. Kate would have parked in the far corner of the parking lot on the side, because she had trouble backing out.

I pretended to be absorbed in my likely worthless evidence. I had spent the entire drive to the office trying to figure out what to say, how to say it. I wanted to explain why I had done things. I wanted to tell him I loved him. I had tried to prepare myself for the possibility that he would tell me off, but most of me hoped with a desperate naive hope that he would forgive me and we would go home together.

A knock sounded through our absurdly reinforced door.

"Periculo tuo ingredere!" Ascanio proclaimed.

What the hell did he just say? *Ingredere* . . . Enter . . . Enter at your own risk. "If it's a client, I'll shoot you," I told him.

The door swung open. A new scent swirled around me, a heavy fragrance—rose, patchouli, and coriander—an expensive perfume. A tall woman stepped inside. She was close to six feet and her shimmering golden heels added another four inches to her height. Her hair, the color of luminous white gold, fell down over her shoulders past her butt. She wore a really short black dress or a long T-shirt, I couldn't quite decide which. Whatever it was, it was cinched to her improbably narrow waist by a white belt with golden studs. Her face, pretty and painted with makeup to near perfection, had that slightly vapid expression sometimes seen on models: she was either sleepy, horny, or just badly needed to sneeze.

A dark figure stepped into the office behind her. Six foot three, lean, wearing a black leather jacket and faded jeans . . . He stepped into the light. Dark blue eyes looked at me and the world fell apart around us. His face, framed by soft black hair, wasn't perfect in the way Ascanio's was, but it was masculine and handsome, and his eyes communicated a kind of sexual intensity, a promise and a challenge, that made women lose all of their self-respect and try to proposition him in plain view of their dates. The familiar scent washed over me like a pain-filled perfume.

Raphael.

As if in a dream I saw him put his hand on the woman's butt, gently pushing her toward the two chairs by my desk.

Oh sweet Jesus.

He replaced me.

He replaced me with a better version of me.

And he brought her to the office. To rub it in.

The planet snapped back into place with an agonizing crunch. I stood up, saw myself extend a hand, and heard myself say, "Good morning."

"Rebecca." The woman shook my hand.

I concentrated so I wouldn't crush her finger bones into cartilage pancakes.

"I got your message," Raphael said.

And I've got yours, loud and clear. Inside me, the other me, the one that grew claws and fangs, howled in helpless fury. She didn't understand nuances. She understood only that the person who loved her and cared for her had betrayed her and now she hurt. *He was mine. Mine!* The other me screamed inside me, tearing at the walls to be let out.

I struggled to keep her in check, imposing logic over emotion. Moving on was one thing. Moving on I could understand. It would break my heart, but I would understand it. This was a giant "fuck you" spelled out in glowing letters.

I forced my mouth open. My voice sounded flat. "Please sit down."

They sat. Behind them Ascanio stared at us, his jaw hanging down.

"Ascanio, would you mind getting our guests some coffee."

"Black, please," Raphael said, his voice pounding a sharp spike into me. "Cream and sugar separate."

"I don't drink coffee," Rebecca informed us. "It stains your teeth."

"Did you have any trouble with the cops?" I asked, my control so tight that if I let myself go a hair, I would snap.

He looked directly at me. "Just minor formalities. Did you have any trouble at the dig site?"

"None at all. Stefan helped me."

"He's a good man, Stefan."

"Yes, he is. Who is your lovely associate?" I unleashed my best smile in Rebecca's direction. Raphael leaned forward, sliding his left arm along the back of Rebecca's chair, his body half turned to shield her. He recognized the smile—it was the kind that meant someone was about to get shot.

"I'm his fiancée," Rebecca said.

Fiancée? *Fiancée.*

Raphael's eyes widened a fraction. He hadn't wanted me to know, but it was too late. She had let the cat out of the bag.

"How lovely," I said, sweetness dripping from my voice. "I hadn't heard the announcement."

"We're engaged to be engaged," Rebecca said. "We're waiting until the end of the physical year to officially announce."

"You mean fiscal year?" Dear God, she was a moron.

"Yes, that's what I meant."

Raphael slid his hand over Rebecca's fingers tipped with hot pink acrylic nails.

I closed my eyes for a long second. "Congratulations to the happy couple."

"Thank you," Rebecca said.

Raphael toyed with a lock of her hair.

That did it.

"I see you've upgraded to the deluxe model," I said. "Must've set you back quite a bit."

"Worth every penny," he said.

"You always had expensive tastes."

"Oh, I don't know." He shrugged his muscular shoulders. "I've been known to slum on occasion."

I will kill you. I will hurt you, you wretched bastard. "Be careful with that. Sometimes slumming can be dangerous for you."

"I can take care of myself," he said and winked at me.

"What are you talking about?" Rebecca asked.

"My car, doll." Raphael picked up her hand.

No. No, he wouldn't.

He kissed her fingers.

Every nerve in my body burst on fire.

"You seem like such a well-matched couple." I smiled at them. "Physically and intellectually. Rebecca is so stunning."

"Don't forget loyal," Raphael said. "And loving."

So is a dog. "I'm sure your mother is simply delighted with you both."

A muscle in Raphael's face jerked. My goodness gracious, I'd hit a sore spot. Aunt B, his mother and the head of Clan Bouda, was a legend. Boudas were wild, and she ruled them with sweet smiles and razor-sharp claws. One look at Rebecca and Aunt B would have an instant apoplexy.

Raphael's eyebrows furrowed. "My mother's approval isn't necessary."

Aha. "Does she know that?"

Ascanio approached, carrying a coffee mug on a platter, with a small jar of sugar and a cup of cream.

"She is a terrible woman," Rebecca said.

Ascanio froze.

I stared at Raphael. *Are you going to let it slide? Honestly?* Aunt B was his mother, but she was also his alpha, and Ascanio was a member of the clan.

Raphael leaned toward Rebecca, his voice intimate but firm like steel wrapped in velvet. "Sweetheart, never insult my mother in public."

"She insults me. And you don't do anything about it."

Ascanio focused on Raphael, waiting for a cue. Aunt B ruled the clan, but Raphael was the male alpha.

Raphael leveled a warning stare at Rebecca, but it had no effect.

"She's rude and spiteful—"

Ascanio picked up the jar of sugar and emptied it over Rebecca's head. The white powder spilled over her hair and dress.

She gasped and jumped off the chair.

"Oh no!" I opened my eyes wide. "I'm so sorry. Teenage boys are such a clumsy lot."

"Raf!"

Raf? What was he, her poodle?

"Why don't you go outside and wait for me in the car," Raphael said.

"But—"

"Go outside, Rebecca."

She marched out of the office, pouting. Raphael's eyes sparked with a deep ruby glow. He looked at Ascanio, as if deciding what he should do about him. The boy ducked his head and said nothing, his gaze firmly affixed to the floor.

Ascanio was a talented young shapeshifter, but I had fought beside Raphael. He could go through a room full of Ascanios in seconds and leave none of them alive.

"Ascanio," I sunk so much quiet menace into the word, the boy froze, as if petrified. "Did your alpha look like he needed help?"

Ascanio's voice was clipped. "No, ma'am."

"Go outside and wait until I come to get you."

Ascanio opened his mouth.

"Outside. Stay in the back lot. Don't speak to Rebecca."

He clamped his jaw shut and took off. A moment later the back door closed.

Raphael had shattered my heart into tiny little shards and they were hurting me. Never in all of our time together had he so much as mentioned engagement. And now he had found a pretty, empty-headed idiot and he was going to marry her. Why her? What was she giving him that I hadn't?

The answer came to me in a painful burst. She was there for him. I hadn't been. I'd shut him out. I'd thought he would wait while I sorted myself out. My own damn fault.

I leaned forward, my voice steady. "Are you high?"

"What?"

"Did you smoke something before you decided it was a good idea to flaunt her in front of me? Maybe you ate some weird-looking mushrooms?"

He smiled at me. It was a brilliant Raphael grin, sharp like the edge of his knives.

"You know I could kill her before you could stop me."

"No danger of that," he said. "That would mean you'd act like a shapeshifter and we all know that's not going to happen."

Ouch. "My memory must be malfunctioning. I don't remember your being this cruel."

"People change," he said. "Did you expect everyone to pause their lives while you were having your little pity party? Was I supposed to sit there and wait like a good boy, until you were 'in a good place'?"

It hurt so much, I was beginning to go numb. "I didn't bar my door. My phone still worked. If you wanted to get in touch, you could have."

"Please! You think I have no pride? I loved you, I cared for you, I offered you a place in the Pack beside me, and you betrayed everything that was important to me. How did that turn out for you, Andrea? Was it worth it?"

I winced. "No. It wasn't."

"My door wasn't barred either."

He had saved it all up since the night we'd fought. Now everything was coming out.

"You betrayed me, you let the Order treat you like shit, and then you hid in your apartment. That wasn't the Andrea I knew. I thought I could count on you. I thought you had my back." His face was a furious mask. "I would've done anything for you."

I would have done anything for him, too. If it had been him in that Wolf House, I would've run there so fast, the entire Order wouldn't have been able to stop me. My other self was howling in my ears, loud, so, so loud . . .

"You spat on everything I am. You picked the knights over my people, which means you picked your precious Order over me."

I was shaking, straining to contain myself. My body struggled to counteract the stress, betraying me.

"Anything to say?"

"I'm sorry I hurt you."

"Too little, too late. I'm tired of waiting for you to stop running away from who you are. You want to know what the best thing about Rebecca is?"

His eyes were pure ruby and they burned. I was hanging on by a thread.

"She isn't you."

My humanity tore and the other me spilled out.

Raphael stared at me, suddenly silent.

The shreds of my clothes fluttered around me. I had this curious feeling that I was watching it all from some point above my head. My arms still rested on the table, but now soft sandy fur with a scattering of brown spots covered the hard muscle. I knew what my face looked like: a meld of human and hyena, with a dark muzzle and my blue, human eyes above it.

Most shapeshifters had two shapes, human and animal. The more talented of us could maintain a warrior form, halfway between animal and beast. I didn't have an animal form. There were only two choices: my human self and my other me, neither human nor hyena, but an odd creature in between. I was beastkin. My father had started his life as a hyena, caught the Lyc-V virus, and turned into a human. For that, other shapeshifters hated me and some tried to kill me on sight.

I examined myself sitting there. I'd held back for so long. I'd been good for so long. I always did as expected. I followed rules and regulations. Look where it got me. Being good hurt.

"I didn't mean that," Raphael said.

Why had I wasted all my time pretending to be someone I wasn't? I was tired, so very, very tired of standing on my own brakes. I felt . . . right. I felt free. I hadn't felt like this since I'd lost control and slapped Aunt B. She had backhanded me right down two flights of stairs, but it was worth it. It was so worth it.

What did I have to lose anyway?

I took a deep breath and let the old good Andrea go. Magic coursed through me, making me stronger, sharper. Scents filled my nose, stole through my mouth, and expanded my lungs.

"Andrea?"

I tilted my head and looked at him. He'd brought another woman into my office. Whatever made him think I would stand for that?

I opened my mouth and showed him my sharp teeth. Most shapeshifters couldn't speak in a half form, but then I wasn't most shapeshifters.

"You meant every word. I told you I was sorry. I took responsibility for my actions. It is over now."

My voice was deeper, permeated with the rough notes of a growl.

"This office is my territory. If you bring your woman here again, I'll consider it a challenge."

He leaned forward, inhaling my scent. His upper lip trembled, betraying a flash of his teeth. "Been studying the Pack's Law?"

I laughed and heard an eerie hyena cackle in my voice. "I don't have to study. I know *all* the laws."

"Then you know you can't attack a human."

"Who said anything about attacking a human? If you bring her here again, it will be your fault. I'll beat your ass and not even your mommy will be able to stop me."

Raphael leaned closer, his eyes glowing. "Promises, promises, honey."

I snapped my teeth at him. "I'm not your honey. Your honey is out in the parking lot."

The beginnings of a snarl reverberated in his throat, but his eyes were puzzled. He wasn't sure what to make of me.

I wanted to bite something. I wanted to rend and carve things with my claws and get rid of my hurt. I wanted him to leave. But if he left, we would have to do it again. I still had a job to do. This sonovabitch would not keep me from it. I would get the information I needed and I would not let him bother me any further.

I picked up the pen with my clawed hand. "I find your scent disturbing. Let's finish this up so I can air the place out and get you and your girl candy out of my life. The Blue Heron building. How did you buy it?"

He stared at me.

"We have four dead people. Your people. Do try to keep up."

Raphael leaned back, studying me. "It was a sealed bid auction."

"Were there any other buyers?"

"Yes. It was a very valuable building."

"Do you know who they were?" A sealed bid auction meant that each of the participants submitted a confidential bid for the building, but Raphael would've done his homework and researched other buyers to know how much to bid against them.

"I can give you the top three," he said.

"I'm all ears."

"Bell Recovery. Kyle Bell has been in the business for a long time. He does decent work, but he's expensive and slow. I can usually underbid him."

I wrote it down. "What's your relationship with him?"

Raphael shrugged. "We don't like each other."

"Was he bitter that you outbid him?"

"Kyle exists in a state of bitter."

"In your opinion, would he stoop to murder?"

Raphael shook his head. "No. Kyle makes a lot of noise and stomps around. He might get his people to rough someone up, but he wouldn't get into anything that required outside help, like magic snakes. He doesn't trust anyone."

So Stefan had already told him about my visit. "Got it. Next."

"Then there is Jack Anapa of Input Enterprises." Raphael leaned forward, resting his forearm on the table. His scent was scraping against me like fine-grain sandpaper. "Anapa is an ass. He has mountains of money and he plays with it."

I squinted at him. "Don't like him much?"

Raphael grimaced. "He dabbles. He dabbled in construction, he dabbled in shipping, now he's dabbling in reclamation. He'll get bored and move on; for him it's a game. For us it's business."

"Was he upset at losing the bid?"

"Initially he won it, but his permits weren't filed properly, so they went to me as the second-highest bidder. A skyscraper has a lot of mercury. It's in the thermostats. When a building crashes, mercury drips to the bottom. Before you can reclaim a building, you have to prove to the city—"

"That you're qualified to safely remove it," I finished. "I remember." I was with Raphael once when he filed for permits. "Would you say Anapa is capable of murder?"

"Yes. But I don't think he'd murder my people. He doesn't seem to have the motivation. I was there when he lost the bid. He was looking over some papers his assistant shoved under his nose. He waved his hand and said, 'Yes, yes. *C'est la vie.*' Oh, and he invited me to his birthday bash before he left."

Interesting. "The third bidder?"

"Garcia Construction. I've known the Garcias for a long time. They were in business for about ten years before I started. It's a family-operated business. They mostly took medium-sized reclamation jobs and didn't get very ambitious until about two years ago, when Ellis took over the company from his father. They went big real fast, too fast, and bought rights to a huge apartment complex." Raphael grimaced again. "It was a monster of a building. I wouldn't have taken it."

"Too expensive?"

"Not too expensive to buy, but too expensive to reclaim. The way it fell, you'd have to shift a ton of rubble before you got to anything decent. Too many man-hours. Ellis started it that May and last February the Garcias were still digging in it when a section of it collapsed. Killed seven workers. Apparently Ellis had sunk all his resources into the building and let the insurance lapse. The insurance companies hate us. The premiums are through the roof. The Garcias did the right thing and paid out the death benefits anyway, out of their own pocket. The company was finished after that."

"So how can they afford to bid on Blue Heron?" I asked.

"Word is, they got a substantial investment. This was their comeback attempt. They are decent, hardworking people, Andrea. They wouldn't kill my crew."

"Somebody did, Raphael. What about the seller?"

"The city of Atlanta."

That was a dead end for sure. "Did you know about the vault?"

"No." He scowled. "Rianna, one of the guards, just had her baby three months ago. It was her second day back on the job. Nick is her husband. You remember Nick Moreau?"

"Nick the carpenter? The one that redid our, no, I'm sorry, *your* kitchen?"

Raphael nodded. "Yes."

I remembered Nick. He'd cracked jokes while he had installed the cabinets and showed me a picture of his wife and told me she was the most wonderful woman on Earth. He'd said they were trying to have a baby and if it was a boy, they would name him Rory, and if it was a girl, they would name her Rory, too.

Raphael had teased him that they were setting the baby up to be made fun of, to which Nick had pointed his hammer at Raphael and told him that if he wanted to name babies, he would just have to make some of his own.

"Was it a girl?" I asked quietly. "Baby Rory?"

"It's a boy," Raphael said.

And now his mother was dead. I would get those bastards. I would find them and make them pay.

I got up. "Thank you for your cooperation. We're done. I'll inform you when I have a lead." *This interview is over. Get the hell out of my office and out of my life.*

"Do that."

Raphael rose and left.

Work was the only thing I had left. Everything else was gone now. I would find the murderers. I would find them if it was the last thing I did. I had to do it to prevent them from killing anyone else, to offer their victims vengeance and solace, and most of all I had to do it to prove to myself that I was still worth something.

I pulled out a phone book and tracked down the three addresses of the bidders.

His scent was still here. I snarled at it, but it refused to vanish.

Hurt and frustration bubbled in me. I was keyed up too high, my skin was on too tight, and I wanted to shoot something just to vent all the pain boiling up inside.

So Raphael had replaced me with a seven-foot-tall dimwit, so what? Good riddance. I was better off on my own.

The back door opened with a faint creak. Ascanio walked into the office and froze.

"What?" I asked.

He opened his mouth, his eyes wide.

"Speak!"

"Breasts," he said.

Female shapeshifters didn't have breasts in warrior form. There was no need for them. They were either flat-chested or sported rows of teats. I had breasts. They were covered with fur, but they were recognizable adult female boobs.

"It's not your first time seeing a pair, is it?"

"Um. No."

"Then do act like you've been around the block before."

Ascanio closed his mouth with a click.

"Don't test Raphael," I told him. "If you do, he'll cut you into itsy-bitsy pieces and leave them in a pretty pile on the floor." I decided I liked my beastkin voice. It was deeper, more powerful, and sounded better. In an attractive female monster kind of way.

"Oh, I don't know." He gave me a look suffused with teenage arrogance. "I think he might find it difficult."

"No, he won't. We once fought a dog the size of a two-story house. Raphael ripped one of its heads off."

Ascanio blinked. "One?"

"It had three." I got up and pulled a change of clothes from my bag. My other me was about twenty-five percent larger, but my long-sleeved T-shirt had a lot of stretch in it. I pulled it on and put on my pants. They were more like capris now and they were tight on my calves. "I'm going out."

"Like that?"

I pulled out my knife and sliced the hems of my pants. Much better. "Who's going to stop me?"

"But you're . . . not in human shape."

Yes, and I was sick of being ashamed of who I was. I looked at him for a long moment. "If I change back into a human, I'll need a nap. I don't have time for naps. If someone has a problem with the way I look, fuck them."

"Uhh . . ."

"And stop looking so scandalized. I covered my boobs, didn't I?"

"But I still know they're there. I saw them."

"Treasure the memory." I grabbed my bag off the table.

Ascanio jumped in front of the door. "Can I come with you?"

"No."

He fluttered his eyelashes at me. "I'll be very quiet."

"No."

"Andrea, I'm sick of being stuck here by myself. Please, please, please, can I come with you? I'll be good."

He'd been cooped up in the office for the last few weeks, at first because he was injured, then because he wasn't and we wanted to keep him that way.

"I'm going to look for a murderer. If you come with me, you'll get hurt when we run into trouble on the way. And then I will have to have a very unpleasant conversation with Aunt B, which will go like this: 'You won't join Clan Bouda, you broke up with my son, and you let that sweet precious boy get hurt.'"

Ascanio picked up my desk with one hand and held it four feet off the ground.

"It's not your muscle I'm concerned about. It's your brains. Or lack thereof."

He set the table down. "Please, Andrea."

He was going stir-crazy and doing broom drills. I could relate. I'd been there.

"Can you drive?" If I put my seat all the way back, I'd fit into the Jeep, but driving with my size-twelve feet and three-inch claws would be a challenge.

"Do the People navigate vampires? Of course I can drive."

"Alright."

He jumped three feet in the air.

"Now, while you're with me, you will be acting as a representative of our firm. That means you will be respectful and polite. If some jerk calls you an asshole, you'll call him sir. Even if you have to throw him on the ground and break his legs, you will still call him sir while doing it. You follow my lead and you follow my orders. That means not taking the initiative and starting fights without my express command. Do you get me?"

"Yes, ma'am."

"Excellent. Go get your knife."

He ran into the supply room and came out with a tactical bowie knife in a sheath on his belt. The bowie, a "Mercenary Guild" model, boasted a sixteen-inch black blade and weighed almost two pounds. You could chop small trees down with it. It would be sufficient.

"Let's go."

He hesitated. "Carrie and Deb are in our parking lot. I saw them from the window."

I went to the back and carefully glanced out of the window. Two boudas waited for us by my Jeep. The one on the left, Carrie, a tall Italian-looking woman in her mid-forties with dark shoulder-length hair, leaned against the vehicle, her hands in the pockets of her jeans. Olive-skinned, Carrie had a kind of raw-boned hardness about her that said you'd have to rip her arms off before she'd stop coming after you. Deb, her buddy, was about ten years younger, looked softer, rounder in the face, and stood two inches shorter. Her red hair, cut in a fluffy carefree bob, flared about her tan face. Her brown eyes brimmed with humor. She cracked up easily and usually went for the gut in a fight.

Aunt B used them for light enforcement jobs. That old bitch was at it again. Aunt B and I never saw eye to eye. She'd helped me once during the flare, when the magic made me lose control over my body, but that was the only moment of kindness I had ever seen from her.

"What are you two doing here?" I murmured to myself.

"Maybe they have some pamphlets that will save our souls and make sure we're right with the Lord," Ascanio said.

"Did those nice church ladies come by again?"

He nodded. "I asked them if a man died and then the woman remarried, and the three of them met in heaven, would it be a sin for them to have a threesome, since they were all married in God's eyes. And then they decided they were late to be somewhere else."

A little bit of knowledge was a very dangerous thing.

In the parking lot, Deb crossed her arms and kicked a tiny rock. It flew out of our view like it had been shot from a cannon. Deb watched it go, winced, and hid behind the Jeep. Carrie shook her head.

Any shapeshifter in the Pack's territory had three days to present themselves to the Pack, at which point they would either obtain a visitor's permit, allowing them to carry out their business; they would petition to join the Pack; or they would be asked to leave. While I was in the Order, Aunt B made no move to bring me into the fold. I thought she didn't want to cause a problem with the knights. I discovered I was wrong—she left me alone because Raphael had a thing for me and then we became an item. The moment we had a falling out, she came after me like a shark.

Aunt B wanted me to play ball, join Clan Bouda, and be one of her girls. I'd been in a bouda clan once. No thanks.

"We could go out the front door," Ascanio said.

They thought they could intimidate me. Well, they should have brought a lot more people, because I was done doing things by the book. "Hell, no. We're going out the back. Whatever happens, you stay out of it or I will never take you with me anywhere."

"Yes, ma'am."

I marched out through the back door.

The boudas took me in, fur and all. Their eyes widened.

"Where the hell do you think you're going like that?" Carrie asked.

Wrong thing to say. Wrong, wrong thing to say. "Wherever the hell I please."

"I don't get it." Carrie shook her head. "Are you trying to

provoke Aunt B? What, your life's too nice and you need some misery?"

I grinned at them. *See the teeth? Take note, you'll see them up close if you're not careful.* "Can I help you, ladies?"

"Sure," Carrie said. "You can tell us what the meeting between you and Raphael was about."

"And why would I do that?"

"Because Aunt B wants to know," Deb said.

They must've tried to listen in, but before Kate got this office, the same Jim who put me on this case had remodeled it. I didn't know what he put into the walls, but the place was shapeshifter soundproof.

"Aunt B's tailing her own son now?" I asked.

"That's none of your business," Carrie said. "Look, we can go with Plan A, where we all have a nice chat and go our separate ways, or we can do Plan B, where we have a more vigorous chat and tune you up a bit until you feel like sharing. Either way, Aunt B will get what she wants."

"How about Plan C?" I asked.

"What plan would that be?" Deb asked.

"The one where you go fuck yourselves." A snarl crept into my voice. "You come here to my territory and you think you can push me around? Well, come on. Push. See what it will get you."

Deb blinked.

"Fuck you, you stupid bitch," Carrie growled. "You want a lesson, I'll give you one."

Carrie's body flowed, snapping into a new shape: half-person, half-animal, wrapped in sparse, sandy fur. Thick ropes of muscle corded her massive neck, supporting her round head with giant jaws and a forest of sharp fangs soaked in drool. The muscle continued to knot between her shoulder blades, forming a hump. Colossal biceps powered her arms, the network of veins bulging through her hide. Her feet and hands bore three-inch claws that would shred flesh like a knife cut through a ripe fruit. She looked like the stuff nightmares were made of. If you didn't know any better.

I took a couple of steps forward, so I'd have plenty of room to maneuver. My furry me was proportionate: my limbs were properly formed, my jaws fit together into a neat muzzle, and although my hands and feet were oversized and armed with claws, my fingers weren't misshapen. Maintaining this form came effortlessly to me. But Carrie was a regular shapeshifter and her warrior form was on the shaky side. Her jumbo biceps bulged from her too-long arms, limiting her movement, while her short legs barely had enough meat to support her top-heavy frame. She hunched over, because her spine fit into her pelvis at an angle, and no effective kicks would be coming my way. She didn't specialize in combat, which meant she'd fight just like any other civilian shapeshifter: claws, teeth, nothing fancy. Good enough to tear most normal humans into pieces.

Next to her Deb raised her arms. No warrior form, but she was good at boxing.

Carrie's eyes stared at me, shining with ruby light. She outweighed me by a hundred pounds. She thought the fight was in the bag.

Inside my head, Michelle's squeaky voice mocked from the depth of my memories, *"Hit her again, Candy. Hit that beast-kin bitch. She deserves it."*

Never again.

Carrie charged me. She thundered across the pavement and lunged at me, swiping with her right arm diagonally and down, trying to gash my chest open. I leaned back. Her claws sliced through the air, an inch from my chest. I caught her wrist, yanked her massive arm straight and smashed the heel of my hand into the back of her elbow. The cartilage crunched, the joint popped, dislocated, and her arm bent the wrong way, its elbow inside out. Carrie howled and dropped to one knee, her right leg bent, her left almost flat on the ground. I stomped on that weak calf. I sank all the power of my hip and butt muscle into it. Like getting hit with a jackhammer. The leg didn't stand a chance. Carrie screamed as the bone broke.

Deb bladed her body, standing sideways, trying to present less of a target. Her hands were up, curled into fists.

I took a step, spun, and hammered a roundhouse to the back of her thigh. My shin smashed into her leg. Her knee bent, her thigh suddenly powerless. She gasped, dropping her guard, and I turned, swinging into the punch, and landed a haymaker to the side of her head.

The blow took her off her feet. She flew, rolling, and smashed into the stone wall bordering the parking lot.

That's right. No shapeshifter would ever beat on me again while I curled into a ball on the ground. Especially not a bouda.

Carrie sprawled facedown on the pavement, out cold. The pain must've been too much and Lyc-V had shut her down while it made repairs. Deb moaned weakly by the wall. Ascanio still stood by the door, his eyes opened wide, his face glazed over with shock and something suspiciously resembling admiration.

I walked over to Deb, grabbed her hair, and pulled her face up. She stared at me, her eyes terrified.

"Now you listen to me," I said. "You tell the clan that I'll come to see Aunt B when I'm damn good and ready. And if I catch any of you at my place of business or near my apartment, you will regret it."

I let go of her and straightened. "Ascanio! I need that motor running."

He ran to the Jeep and began to chant. Fifteen minutes later we drove out of the parking lot. As we turned, I saw Deb pick herself up and stagger over to Carrie. For better or worse, she would deliver my message. I was sure of it.

CHAPTER 4

Bell Recovery was headquartered in a sturdy brick building on the edge of a large industrial yard on the southwest side of Atlanta, all ugly ruins surrounded by bright green growth. Nature waged a relentless assault on the city. People burned it and cut it, and still it came back, fed by magic and growing faster than ever.

Ascanio parked and didn't bother shutting off the engine. It would take too much chanting to start it back up and considering the Pack's paw stenciled on its door and the fact that I exited it flashing my claws and teeth, there wouldn't be anyone dumb enough to try to steal it.

Ascanio and I marched through the front doors.

A harried receptionist raised her head from the papers on her desk and jumped a little in her seat. She was middle-aged and her hair had been dyed an unnaturally red color.

"Good morning," I said, smiling.

She pushed her chair as far back as it would go.

"We're here on behalf of the Pack to chat with Kyle Bell."

"He's on site," the receptionist said. Her eyes told me she would answer any question just to get us out of her office.

"Where would that be?"

She swallowed. "The east end of Inman Yard."

You don't say. "At the Glass Menagerie?"

The receptionist nodded. "Yes."

"Thank you for your cooperation, ma'am."

We headed back out to our Jeep.

"Kyle Bell is either really ballsy or really stupid. Probably both."

"Why?" Ascanio asked.

"Because doing any sort of reclamation at the Glass

Menagerie is suicidal. Especially with the magic up. It's also illegal. And now we have to drive through the Burnout to get there. I hate the Burnout. It's depressing."

We got back into our Jeep.

"Take the right, then another right. We need to get on Hollowell Parkway and make a left there."

"What's the Glass Menagerie?" Ascanio asked, steering the Jeep out of the parking lot.

As far as I knew the Glass Menagerie was off-limits to adventurous Pack persons below eighteen. For a good reason, too. "You'll see."

As the road climbed north, the landscape changed. The ruins of warehouses and the greenery remained behind. Around us old husks of burned-out houses crouched, accented by an occasional spot of green.

Being stuck holding the fort at the Order left me with a lot of free time, so I had read guidebooks and familiarized myself with the city maps. In my spare time I'd jogged through random Atlanta neighborhoods on the off chance I might have to visit them in my professional capacity. My guidebooks mentioned that years ago a devastating fire had swept through the western section of Atlanta, taking out the older residential neighborhoods north of 402. The fire had burned with an intense, unnatural orange and raged for almost a week despite heavy rains and many attempts to put it out. When it was finally over, the land had lost its ability to support plant life. In other parts of Atlanta, any spot of clear ground was immediately claimed by vegetation that grew like it was on steroids. The Burnout remained weed-free for a decade. The plants were finally coming back—kudzu draped a crumbling wall here and there and bright yellow dandelions and crimson bloody dandies, the dandelion's magic-altered cousins, poked out between the fallen bricks.

A few months ago, during Indian summer, Raphael and I had a picnic under a giant oak in a field outside the city. I had always wanted to have one of those movie picnics with a red-and-white checkered cloth and a wicker basket. We ate take-out fried chicken, washed it down with root beer and cream soda, and lay about on our tablecloth. I had picked a bunch of dandelions and bloody dandies and made two flower crowns.

It seemed so stupid now. What the hell did I do that for? Like some besotted silly ten-year-old.

"Why didn't you just fight Rebecca?" Ascanio asked. "You'd win."

"Of course I would win. Even if she spat frag grenades and sweated bullets, I'd win. She's a human. I'm a shapeshifter with ten years of combat experience and some of the best martial education you can get."

"In nature you have to fight off your competition."

In nature, huh? I'd heard that one before. "In nature, hyena cubs are born with open eyes and a full set of teeth. They start fighting from the moment they come out of their mother. They dig tunnels in the den, too small for adults to get through, and they fight there. About a quarter of them don't grow up. So if this was nature and you were a twin, you'd have to murder your newborn sister or brother. Should we dump all of the bouda babies into a playpen and let them starve until they start killing each other?"

Ascanio frowned. "Well, no . . ."

"Why not? It's natural selection. Just like nature." I wrinkled my nose. "Boudas love this argument, because it gives them an excuse to do all the wrong things. 'I'm sorry I screwed your sister and got my penis stuck in your German shepherd. It's in my nature. I just couldn't help myself.'"

Ascanio snorted.

"Don't be that guy," I told him. "It's bullshit reasoning. We are not animals. We are people. And a good thing too, because it wasn't hyenas who conquered the world. And yes, I know it's ironic as hell, given that I'm all fur and claws right this second, but the human part of me is still in the driver's seat. We all know what happens when the animal side starts running the show."

"We go loup," Ascanio said.

"Exactly."

Loupism was a constant threat. It claimed fifteen percent of shapeshifter children, some at birth, some in adolescence, forcing the Pack to humanely terminate them. For boudas, the number was even higher—almost a quarter. Both of Raphael's brothers had gone loup and Aunt B had had to kill them. That's why any surviving adolescent in the bouda clan was treated like a treasure.

If I ever had babies with Ra . . . The thought twisted in me like a knife in the wound. There would be no little bouda babies. No Raphael. That door slammed shut and I needed to put him out of my mind. In this life you're lucky if you get one shot at happiness, and I had missed mine. The fact that it was a joint screwup just hurt more.

Water under the bridge.

"But she is stupid," Ascanio said. "She insulted Aunt B!"

"And for that we should rip her throat out?" I glanced at him.

"Well, no."

"Suppose I did beat the snot out of her. What would it accomplish? In nature animals fight to demonstrate superiority. The more powerful you are, the better your genetic material is. Stronger animal, stronger babies, a better chance of survival for the species. Raphael already knows I'm a better fighter and he chose her over me anyway. That's a lesson for you—when you get a chance to be happy, you take it and you treat the other person the way they deserve to be treated. Don't take things for granted."

Giving advice was easy. Living by it was much harder.

We took a right at the fork, heading farther north. The charred houses continued. To the right, a large sign nailed to an old telephone post shouted DANGER in huge red letters. Underneath in crisp black letters was written:

IM-1: Infectious Magic Area
Do Not Enter
Authorized Personnel Only

A second smaller sign under the first one, written on a piece of plastic with permanent marker, read:

Keep out, stupid.

"We aren't going to keep out, are we?" Ascanio asked.

"No."

"Awesome."

We rolled by another blackened home. To the left a large blue-green shard protruded from the ground at an angle. To the right, by the metal carcass of a fire-stripped truck, another sliver, pale blue, waited to bloody someone's ankle. The first signs of the Menagerie.

Here and there more shards punctured the soil, and in the distance, far to the right, a jagged iceberg rose at a steep angle twenty feet high, glowing with translucent green and blue in the morning sun.

Ascanio squinted. "What is that?"

"Glass," I answered.

"Really?"

"Yes."

"Where did it come from?"

Ahead more icebergs crowded in, forming a glacier. "Some of it is from Hollowell Station. Before the Shift, Inman Yard used to be Norfolk Southern's train yard. It was huge. Over sixty-five tracks in the bowl alone. Not only that, but CSX's Tilford train yard was right next to it. Together they handled over a hundred trains per day. Then they built the Hollowell Station. It was supposed to be a new, super-modern terminal and most of it was glass. Guess what happened when the magic waves started hitting?"

Ascanio grinned. "It crashed."

"Yes, it did. There were hills of glass everywhere. The magic waves kept causing train crashes, but the railroad hung in there. Over the next few months some railroad employees started to get the idea that the glass hills were multiplying. Nobody else paid much attention to it. Then during the second flare, creatures popped out of the glass and killed half of the railroad workers."

"What kind of creatures?" Raphael asked.

"Nobody knows."

Flares—intense, terrible magic waves—came once every seven years. Things that were impossible during normal magic waves became reality during a flare. The flare's magic held for three days straight and then disappeared for a long while, but its consequences were often deadly.

"Eventually the military came back to reclaim the yard. There were roughly two hundred trains in there, and some of them were full of goods. The soldiers found that the glass had expanded and encased the trains. When they tried to chip it off, they were attacked by creatures. Nobody ever figured out what the creatures were, but they caused multiple casualties. Finally the MSDU gave up and cordoned off the Inman Yard with barbed wire. The glass never stopped growing. Helicopters were still flying once in a while back then, so one of the reporters looked at the place from above and dubbed it the Glass Menagerie."

Ahead two glass icebergs met above the road, fused into a massive arch. We passed under it and into the labyrinth of glass. Peaks of green, blue, and white towered above us, some connected, some standing apart, some curving, others perfectly sheer. The light turned turquoise, as if we were underwater. The glass cliffs crowded the crumbling road, painting the ground with colored shadows.

The back of my head itched, the nerves prickling, as if some invisible sniper had sighted me from the scope of his rifle. Someone was watching us from the icy depths. Ascanio fell silent, focused and tense. He'd sensed it, too.

The road in front of us glittered.

"Stop," I said.

The Jeep came to a stop.

A sheer ridge of glass crossed the road. A few yards before it reached the asphalt, it had shattered into a heap of shards. An identical heap marked the other side. Bell Recovery must've blasted through it. Kyle Bell was trying to reclaim the trains. The metal alone would be worth a fortune, not to mention the contents of the cars. Once reclaimed, he would have to transport the metal out and he needed a road in decent repair. Except now there was broken glass all over it.

I got out of the vehicle and padded forward, careful not to step on anything too sharp. My paw-feet were calloused, and Lyc-V would seal any cuts the moment they were made, but it would still hurt. Ascanio followed me.

The shards littered the asphalt, large slivers of glass at the edges, and smaller crushed glass dust in the center. I crouched for a better perspective. Crushed glass ran in two parallel rows.

"Track vehicle," I said. "They're using a tractor or a bull-

dozer." The glass would slice our tires into shreds. "Park the
Jeep. We're going on foot."

We hid the Jeep behind a glass mountain and shut off the
engine. The sudden silence made my ears ring. I took a crossbow and a longbow out of the vehicle.

"Why two bows, mistress?" Ascanio asked, sinking a sudden English accent into his words.

"The crossbow has more power but takes longer to reload."
I strung the longbow. "Sometimes you have to shoot fast. And
can you go ten minutes without being a smartass?" I grabbed
the quiver.

"I don't know, I've never tried, mistress." He shook his
head. "But arrows bounce from monsters."

"These don't." I pulled one out and showed him the incan-
tation written on the arrowhead. One of the Military Supernatural Defense Unit's mages wasn't averse to moonlighting.
He was expensive but worth it. "But if you have doubts, why
don't you go stand over there. I'll shoot you and we'll find out
if it hurts."

"No thanks."

I picked up the spare bow and the second quiver and
handed it to him. "Then shut up and carry this."

I started forward at an easy jog, skirting the road. Ascanio
followed a couple feet behind. The glass swallowed all footsteps and we glided like two shadows.

A flicker of movement appeared in the corner of my eye.
Something crouched atop the glass ridge to the left. Something with a long tail that hid in the shadows. I kept running,
pretending I didn't see it. It didn't follow.

A muted roar announced water engines being put to good
use. We passed under another glass overhang, running parallel
to the road. Ahead the ribbon of asphalt turned, rolling
through the opening between the glass peaks into the sunlight.
I slowed and padded on silent feet to the nearest iceberg ledge,
about fifteen feet off the ground. Too smooth to climb. I gathered myself into a tight clump and jumped. My hands caught
the glass edge, and I pulled myself up. Ascanio bounced up
next to me. We crawled along the ledge to the opening.

A clearing stretched in front of us, about half a football
field long. To the right the ground climbed up slightly, the

slope studded with pale green glass boulders. A large construction shelter perched on top of the raised ground, its durable fabric stretched over an aluminum frame. To the left a mess of glass bristling with shards curved away, deeper into the glass labyrinth. The tail end of an overturned railroad car stuck out of shards.

An enchanted water engine sat nearby, powering up a massive jackhammer that two construction workers with hardhats and full facial shields pointed at the glass encrusting the train car. Eight other workers, wrapped in similar protective gear, pounded away at the glass with hammers and mining picks.

Three guards milled about the perimeter, each armed with a machete. The nearest to us, a tall, broad-shouldered man in his mid-thirties, looked like he wouldn't hesitate to use his. With the magic up, guns wouldn't fire, but the security seemed too light for a reclamation in the Glass Menagerie. They must've had something else up their sleeves.

"You see what they're doing?" I murmured to Ascanio.

"They're trying to salvage that railcar," he said.

"Why is it illegal?"

He thought about it. "It doesn't belong to them?"

"Technically the railroad has gone out of business, so this is abandoned property. Try again."

"I don't know."

"What are we sitting on?"

He looked down at the turquoise surface under our feet. "Magic glass."

"What do we know about it?"

"Nothing," he said.

"Exactly. We don't know what makes it grow and we don't know what would make it stop."

"So anything they take out of that rail car could sprout glass," Ascanio said.

"Precisely. They're going to sell whatever they reclaim and they won't tell the buyer where they got it. And when another Glass Menagerie sprouts someplace, it will be too late."

"Shouldn't we do something about it?"

I held up my empty hand. "No badge. We can report it when we get out of here and see if PAD wants to do something about it." Besides, it wasn't our job to report it and I was pretty much done with acts of civic responsibility. It wasn't my problem.

"They have to know that what they're doing is illegal," I said. "And this area is dangerous, so they should have more than three bruisers walking about with oversized knives. They have some security we're not seeing. Be ready for a surprise."

Ascanio's eyes lit up with an eerie ruby glow. "Can I shift now?"

"Not yet." Shifting took a lot of energy. Change your shape twice in rapid succession, and you would have to have some downtime. I needed Ascanio fresh and full of energy, which meant once he shifted, he'd have to stay that way.

We jumped off the ledge and walked down the road straight into the guard. He saw my face and drew back.

"What in the bloody hell are you?"

"Andrea Nash," I said. "This is my associate, Robin of Loxley."

Ascanio saluted with the bow. Thankfully no Latin spilled out.

"I'm investigating a murder on behalf of the Pack. I need to talk to Kyle."

The man stared at me. This was clearly outside of his normal duties.

"You got some sort of ID on you?"

I handed him my ID—a miniature copy of my PI license endorsed by the Georgia Secretary of State with my picture on it.

"How do I know it's you?" he asked.

"Why would I lie?"

He mulled it over. "Okay, you've got something that says you're from the Pack?"

Ascanio coughed a bit.

I swept the hand from my forehead to my chin, indicating my face. "Do I look like I need to prove I'm from the Pack?"

The guard pondered me. "Okay, fine. Come with me."

We followed him to the tent. It looked bigger close up, almost forty feet tall. Inside, a middle-aged man pored over some charts next to a taller, thinner man with acne scars on his narrow face. Both wore hardhats.

The middle-aged man looked up. Stocky, well muscled, he might have been quick at some point in his youth, but probably not. He looked like one of those linemen that plant themselves in front of the quarterback, except in his case he'd let himself go a bit and most of his muscle now hid behind a layer of fat. His hair was gray and cropped short, but his dark eyes were sharp. He didn't look friendly. He looked like the kind of guy who could order a shapeshifter murder.

Kyle gave me a once-over and focused on the guard. "What the hell is this?"

"Some people from the Pack want to talk to you," the guard said. "About some murder."

Kyle leaned back, his face sour. "Tony, do you remember that time I told you to just let any asshole in here?"

The guard winced. "No."

"Yeah, I don't remember that either. Felipe, you remember that?"

"No," the taller man said.

"That's what I thought."

Tony paused, obviously confused. "So what do I do?"

"Throw them the fuck out. If I want to talk to any ugly bitches or punk kids, I'll tell you." Kyle looked back to his papers.

Tony put his hand on my forearm. "Come on."

"Take your hand off of me, sir."

The guard pulled me. "Don't make this hard."

"Last chance. Take your hand off of me."

Kyle looked up.

Tony tried to yank me back. I raised my arm up sharply and elbowed him in the face. The blow knocked him back. Tony dropped his machete. It bit into the dirt, handle sticking upright. Blood gushed from his nose, its scent piercing me like a shot of adrenaline.

"Sit on him," I said.

Ascanio tripped Tony, pulled him to the ground, facedown, and leaned one knee on his back. "Don't move, sir."

He remembered. I felt so proud.

Tony tried to push up. "Get off of me!"

"Do not struggle, or I'll be forced to break your arm."

Tony shut up.

Kyle looked at me. Behind him, Felipe carefully took a couple of steps back.

"We can talk about the murders now." I smiled.

"And if I don't feel like talking?"

"I'll make you," I said. "I've had an unpleasant day and four of our people are dead. I feel like having some fun."

"You shapeshifters are getting ballsy," Kyle said. "You think you can just come in anywhere and screw with regular decent people."

"As a matter of fact, I can." I looked at him.

"The boys down at PAD will just love that," Felipe, the taller man behind Kyle, said.

Ha! He was threatening me with cops. "The boys down at PAD won't give a shit. This area is designated as IM-1. You are here in violation of two city ordinances, one state and two federal statutes. Anything you reclaim is contaminated with magic of unknown origin. Taking it out of here is punishable by a fine of not more than two hundred thousand dollars or imprisonment for not more than ten years, or both. Selling it will get you another dime in a state penitentiary."

Kyle crossed his arms. "Is that so?"

"Greed is a terrible thing," I said. "When you extract your metal and sell it to a builder, and then the new school or hospital in the city starts sprouting glass, they will come looking for you. At the moment, it's not my problem. I'm here to ask questions. Answer them and I'll thank you and go away. Do keep in mind that if you piss me off, I can slaughter the lot of you and nobody will give a crap."

And I could. I could just twist his head off and nobody would be the wiser. This was the Glass Menagerie and if he died, the cops would just think he got what was coming to him. Now there was an interesting thought.

A creature walked into the tent, moving on all fours. It used to be human, but all fat had been leeched off it, replaced by hard, knotted muscle and skin stretched so tight, it looked painted on. Its head was bald, like the rest of its repulsive frame and the two eyes, red and feverish with thirst, bore into me like two burning coals. Its oversized jaws protruded, and as it opened its mouth, I glimpsed two curved fangs.

A vampire. The revolting stink of undeath swirled around

me, raising my hackles in instinctive disgust. Ew. Well, that explained the light security. They had an undead guarding them. And where there was a vampire, there was a navigator.

Infection by the Immortuus pathogen destroyed a human's mind. No cognizance remained. Vampires were ruled only by instinct and that instinct screamed, "Feed!" They did not reproduce. They did not think. They hunted flesh. Anything with a pulse was fair game. Their blank minds made perfect vehicles for necromancers. Called navigators, or Masters of the Dead, if they had talent and education, necromancers piloted vampires, driving them around telepathically like remote-controlled cars. They saw through the vampire's eyes, they heard through its ears, and when an undead opened its mouth, it was the navigator's words that came out.

Most of the navigators worked for the People. The People and the Pack existed in a state of uneasy truce, hovering on the verge of full-out war. If the People were running security for this site, my life would get a lot more complicated.

A man followed the vampire. He wore ripped jeans, a black T-shirt that said MAKE MY DAY in bloody red letters, and sported a dozen rings in various parts of his facial features. He could've been one of the People's journeymen, but it was highly unlikely. Strike one, he followed his vampire instead of sitting somewhere outside being inconspicuous, pulling the undead's strings with his mind. Strike two, the People's journeymen looked like they just emerged from arguing a case before the Supreme Court. They wore suits, had good shoes, and were impeccably groomed.

No, this knucklehead had to be a freelancer, which meant I could kill him without diplomatic consequences, if he didn't kill me first.

"Where the hell have you been, Envy?" Kyle said.

I looked at him. "Envy?"

Ascanio chortled.

"Around," Envy said.

"I want them gone," Kyle said. "Do your fucking job."

The vamp hissed. Envy smiled, showing bad teeth.

Ascanio gathered himself. "Can I shift now?"

"No." I turned, stepping closer to the machete Tony had

dropped on the ground and looked at the navigator. "You have a chance to walk away. Take it."

"Can I kill them?" Envy asked.

"You can do whatever you want," Kyle told him.

I had to do this fast. Getting into a hand-to-hand brawl with a vampire would end badly. I would've preferred to wrestle an enraged mama grizzly. "Walk away. Last chance."

Envy grinned. "Pray, bitch."

"Are you affiliated with the People?" I asked.

"Fuck, no."

"Wrong answer."

Outside, glass shattered. A scream tore through the quiet, the raw painful scream of a man experiencing sheer terror. Two more followed.

"What the hell now?" Kyle growled.

We piled out of the tent.

The rail car had split open at the top, like a can of bad beans, and creatures poured out, climbing onto its roof. Thick pale-gray hide covered their squat, barrel-chested bodies, supported by six muscled bearlike legs. Hand-paws tipped each limb, and their long dexterous fingers carried short but thick ivory claws. A narrow carapace ran along their backs and when one of the creatures reared, I saw an identical bony shield guarding its stomach and chest. The carapace terminated in a long, segmented tail with a scorpion stinger. They had large round heads with feline jaws and twin rows of tiny eyes, sitting deep in their sockets. The eyes stared to the front, not to the side. That usually meant a predator.

The beasts scuttled across the sleek surface, sticking to the glass as if they had glue on the pads of the paws. The largest of them was about six feet long and had to push three hundred pounds. The smallest was about the size of a large dog. That meant some of them were babies. Hungry, hungry babies.

The workers backed away, brandishing their tools. Only one exit led out of this glass bowl and it lay on the opposite side, almost directly behind the train car and the creatures.

The horde focused on the people, watching them with the intense attention of hungry predators who were trying to decide if something was food. The larger of the creatures raised its head. Its wide jaws parted, revealing a small forest of crooked fangs. Meat-eater. Of course.

The workers stopped moving.

The largest beast stared at the people below, turning left, right, left . . . Muscles bunched on his shoulders.

"Back away," Kyle called out. "Don't provoke it. Envy, get in there."

"In a minute," the navigator said.

The beast leaped, aiming for the center of the crowd. People scattered, splitting into two groups—the eight people closest to us ran toward the tent, while twice as many sprinted away in the opposite direction, toward the glass wall.

The beast chased after the farther, larger group. One of the guards, a large dark-skinned man, charged at it. The beast hooted, like a colossal owl, and snapped its teeth. The guard dodged, swung, and chopped at the beast's neck. The machete cut bone and gristle like a meat cleaver.

The beast's head drooped to the side, half severed. The scent of blood hit me, bitter and revolting. My predatory instincts backpedaled—whatever that thing was, it wasn't good to eat.

The creature staggered and crashed down. Dark blood, thick and rust-brown, spilled onto the glass.

The horde broke out in alarmed hoots.

"Not so tough," Felipe told Kyle, the relief plain in his voice.

The ground trembled. The walls of the railcar burst. A behemoth spilled out, huge, grotesquely muscled, its forelimbs like tree trunks. I'd once seen a dog as big as a house. This was larger. It was taller than the construction tent. How the hell did it even fit under there?

Kyle swore.

The beast sighted the dead offspring, opened its maw, and bellowed. She looked just like her babies, except for the bone carapace that sheathed most of her upper face as if someone had pulled her skull out and clamped it over her ugly mug. Her four eyes were barely the size of Ping-Pong balls. Trying to shoot them with an arrow would be a pain in the ass.

"Okay," Envy said. "I'm out."

Kyle's eyes bulged. "I paid you, you maggot!"

GUNMETAL MAGIC 69

"Not enough," Envy said.

The vamp grabbed him, swinging the navigator over its back, and dashed away, leaping over people and dodging beasts. A moment and it vanished into the glass forest.

Kyle's face turned purple in a fit of sudden rage. He struggled to say something.

Spurned by their parent's roar, the creatures slunk toward the larger group.

Felipe grabbed my arm. "Help us!"

"Why?" I was done with the civil servant bit. It was no longer my job to save every idiot from the consequences of their own stupidity. They walked into the Glass Menagerie on their own, knowing the risks. Why should I put my life in danger for the people who tried to sic a vamp on me? I owed them nothing. I just had to get the information I needed from Kyle and make sure that Ascanio and I got out of there in one piece.

The beasts circled the larger group. The workers hugged the glass wall. It wouldn't be long now before one of the creatures got brave enough.

"Please!" Felipe's eyes were desperate. "My son is down there."

So what? Everyone was somebody's husband, wife, somebody's son, somebody's Baby Rory . . .

Aw, shit.

I looked at Felipe's face and saw Nick there. Their features were nothing alike, but that's exactly what Nick must've looked like when told his wife was dead. Felipe stared at me with wide-open eyes, desperate and terrified, his face sharpened, as if he were about to wince in pain and cry out. Every wrinkle gouged his skin like a scar. All of the rules society imposed on men, all of the obligations to be the brave one, to never panic, to handle themselves with stony dignity, all of them were wiped away, because he was about to lose his son. He was helpless. He begged me for his child's life and I knew that he would trade places with his boy without a moment's hesitation.

I couldn't just stand there and watch him as his son was eaten alive. It was not in me. The person who would walk away from that man wasn't who I was or wanted to be.

I slipped the scabbard off my arm and handed it to Ascanio. "Arrow!"

He yanked an arrow out and put in my palm. I notched it. "I'll be shooting fast. Have the next arrow ready."

I drew the bow.

The bravest beast jumped, aiming for the nearest worker.

The bow string and the arrow sang together in a vicious happy duet. The arrowhead sliced into the creature's throat. The first beast fell, hissing, trying to swipe at the shaft with its paw. The arrow whined. A blue light sparked at the wound and the beast exploded.

I held my hand out and Ascanio put another arrow into it.

The second beast followed the first. A moment later, the second explosion hurled chunks of flesh and bone into the pack. I didn't have time to watch. I kept shooting, fast, precise, filling the air with arrows.

The beasts panicked. They dashed to and fro amidst their exploding siblings, biting and clawing at each other. The Mother Beast roared, snapping massive jaws at random, unable to figure out what was killing her babies.

"Run!" I screamed.

The workers dashed toward us, running along the wall. The beasts chased them. The air whistled in a nonstop deadly chorus, as my arrows found targets.

Felipe grabbed a pickaxe out of another man's hands and ran toward the group. A woman to my left charged in after him, and so did Tony—the guard—and two others.

One of the workers, a small woman, stumbled, fell, and slid down the glass slope. Two beasts fell on her, ripping into the woman with wet, gurgling growls. I sank two arrows into them, but it was too late. The woman screamed, a short guttural cry, cut off in mid-note. Blood drenched the glass. A moment later the arrow detonated and human and beast rained over the glass in a bloody deluge.

The first runner made it to the tent and collapsed behind me. The rest followed. Finally Felipe and the dark-skinned guard made it in, both splattered with gore.

The Mother Beast spun toward us. Finally found the enemy, did you?

"Form a perimeter!" I barked. "Time to fight for your lives! Use whatever you got."

The workers scrambled to form a line.

The monster ducked her head, and I saw a narrow slit in her carapace, located high between her eyes. Soft pink tissue expanded and contracted, filling the foot-wide slit and then retracting. *Hello, target.*

The beast swung her head again and bellowed in my direction. The wave of sound hit me like the roar of a tornado. I'd have to take the mother out or none of us would get out alive.

"Can I shift now?" Ascanio asked.

"Yes. Now."

Ascanio's skin ruptured. Powerful muscle wound about his skeleton, skin sheathed it, and pale brownish-gray fur sprouted through it. A dark mane grew on his head and dripped down the back of his neck, over his spine. Pale stripes sliced his forelimbs, ending in five-inch claws. His face, like his body, became a meld of human and striped hyena. His eyes flashed with red.

The Mother Beast lifted one colossal front paw and took a step forward. The ground shook.

The bouda opened his mouth and roared back, breaking into bloodcurdling hyena laughter. My hackles rose. *There's my pretty boy.*

"Keep her occupied!" I barked. "Make her face this way."

Ascanio leaped over the workers' heads and dashed down to the monster. He swatted a smallish beast out of the way. It yelped and the behemoth swung in his direction.

I drew my bow. *Not yet.*

Ascanio backhanded another creature.

Not yet. I had time.

The behemoth ducked down, snarling.

Not yet . . .

The huge teeth snapped at Ascanio. He ducked, escaping by a couple of inches.

I let the arrow go. It sliced through the air, propelled as much by the bowstring as by my will, and sliced straight into the unprotected area of her head. *Yes! Nailed it!*

The arrow whined and exploded. Blood shot out of the behemoth's nostrils. She shook her head . . . and charged Ascanio. He leaped up and left, bounced off the glass, and jumped behind her, slicing the behemoth's leg with his claws on the way.

Damn it. It didn't even faze her.

Ascanio and my arrows weren't doing enough damage. Neither would machetes. We could hack at her all day, and we'd do no good.

The behemoth chased Ascanio. The boy jumped back and forth, dashing like some mad rabbit. He couldn't keep this up forever.

If only we had something, some weapon, something . . .

The monster swung her tail, right over the heavy jackhammer laying abandoned on the glass. It was still attached to the tank by the hose that pumped enchanted water into it. The hose was way too short to reach the beast.

I spun to Felipe. "Will it work without the hose?"

It took him a second. "Yes!" He jerked his hand up, fingers spread. "Five minutes."

I threw down my bow and sprinted to the jackhammer. My paws slipped on the glass, slick with beast blood. I slid, jumped, landed by the jackhammer, and heaved it off the ground. A heavy bastard.

A tree-trunk-sized monster leg loomed in front of me. I leaped and clawed my way up the beast to the top, hauling the jackhammer with me. The freaking thing must've weighed three hundred pounds, and I had to drag it one-handed. My right arm felt like it would wrench out of the socket. I pulled myself up, digging into the monster's hide with my left hand and my hind claws.

The creature moved, chasing Ascanio. Her muscles bulged under me. I clung to her, like a flea, and scrambled up.

I made it over the shoulder and ran toward her head. She roared again and I planted the jackhammer right at the base of her neck, the only spot unprotected by the carapace.

I flipped the jackhammer's ON switch.

Nothing.

Below people were yelling something. I flicked my ears.

"Chant! Chant it to start!"

Aaaargh. I chanted, praying it would start faster than our cars did.

Ascanio dashed around the work site, buying me time. Below, the smaller monsters attacked the line of workers.

Work, I willed, chanting. *Work, you blasted stupid tool.*

Work.
Work.

The jackhammer shuddered in my hands. I dug my foot claws into the beast's back and plunged the jackhammer deep into the behemoth's flesh. The chisel pounded into the creature's muscle. Hot blood drenched my feet.

The beast howled in agony, deafening me with the sound of her torture. The jackhammer ate its way down, into her body, and I clung to it, sinking in.

The behemoth shook like a wet dog. I gripped the jackhammer and drove it deeper and deeper. It pulled me in. My arms sank into wet flesh. I took a deep breath and then my nose and my face connected with bloody mush. Pressure ground me. I heard a dull rhythmic sound and realized it was the beast's heart beating next to me.

Suddenly the full weight of the jackhammer hit my arms. I fell.

The jackhammer hit the ground, dead, and I landed on top of it, its handle conveniently impacting with my rib cage.

Ow. That's a cracked rib for sure.

Above me the beast stumbled, a red hole in her chest dripping blood and liquefied flesh.

I sprinted away, running for my life.

The creature teetered, blocking out the sun, and crashed down with a deafening thud. The glass floor of the clearing shattered from the impact. Fractures raced from her body up into the translucent glass icebergs. For a fraction of a second nothing moved, and then giant chunks of glass slid from the walls and plummeted down, exploding into razor-sharp shrapnel.

I threw myself behind the enchanted water tank.

All around me glass fell with thunderous blasts, as if I were crouched in the middle of an artillery salvo. Shards slashed at my hide, stinging me like a swarm of bees. I smelled my own blood. The ground shook.

Gradually the bursts slowed. Silence claimed the clearing. I straightened.

Where is the boy?

The tent lay in shambles, crushed beneath a chunk of amber glass the size of an SUV. A man was crying, his leg sliced open. People were slowly rising from hiding. I scanned the survivors. Felipe was hugging a young man. At least his son had survived.

No Ascanio.

Please be alive.

A loud hyena cackle rang through the clearing. I turned. He stood on top of the beast. Blood drenched his fur. His monster-mouth split in a happy, psychotic grin.

I exhaled.

Gradually it sank in. The Mother Beast was dead. I had killed her. The taste of her blood burned in my mouth. Behind her, a deep black hole bore into the ground beneath the remnants of the railroad car. It must've been her underground lair. She had raised her brood there, safe and far away from everyone, until Kyle's crew invaded her den.

Such an awful waste. None of this was necessary. At least one person died, many others were injured, and this great magnificent beast and her brood lost their lives all because Kyle Bell wanted to make a quick buck on the side. He stood by the remnants of the tent now, arms crossed, barking orders.

I marched over to Kyle. He saw me, opened his mouth, and I backhanded him. The blow knocked him to the ground. "This is your fault. You brought these people here. You knew this place was dangerous." I pulled him upright and spun him toward the dead beast. "Look! People died because of you. Do you understand that? If it wasn't for you, I wouldn't have had to murder her. She was just protecting her children."

"She tried to kill us!"

I backhanded him again. "She tried to kill you because you broke into her house."

The workers stood around us, their faces grim. Nobody made any move to help their boss.

I looked at them. "Anything you reclaim here is contaminated. Being here is a crime. Taking anything out of this zone is a crime. You need to know this."

Kyle stayed down, until I grabbed him by his shirt and pulled him up, his face two inches from mine. "I will ask this only once. What was in the vault under the Blue Heron?"

"What vault?"

"You answer her," Felipe said. "You tell her everything now."

"I don't know what the hell this bitch is talking about."

"If you don't answer me, I'll kill you." I shook him, my bloody claws staining his shirt with the behemoth's gore. "What was in the vault?"

"I don't know!" he screamed. "I don't know anything about any vault! I swear!"

"Did you have something to do with the murders at the Blue Heron site? Answer me!"

His pupils dilated and he was hanging in my hands, completely limp, paralyzed by fear. He wasn't lying. People in a state of complete panic freeze or run. Mother Nature turns off their mental faculties, so her favorite children don't think themselves to death. Kyle was too terrified to formulate a lie. He truly had no idea what I was talking about.

I dropped him and looked at his crew. "He's all yours. You need to clear out. I'm reporting this site to the first cop I see."

I found my bow and quiver and walked away. Ascanio jumped off the beast and joined me. His voice was a deep growl, shredded by his teeth. "It. Wash. Aweshome."

"This was a tragedy." People came before animals. I knew that, but when you turn into an animal, your perspective is a little different.

"Yesh. But aweshome."

He was a boy. What did he know?

"Sho, we didn't learrrn anyshing?"

"That's not true. We established that Kyle Bell had nothing to do with the murders. We can eliminate him from our suspect pool. Are you hungry?"

"Shhtarrrving."

"Good. Let's go find something to eat."

CHAPTER 5

✳

The best thing about Big Papaw's Cookout was their brine. Big Papaw guarded its secret like it was weaponized plague, but there is very little you could keep from a shape-shifter's taste buds. That brine had root beer, paprika, garlic, pepper, and salt in it, and after the pork ribs had soaked in it for at least a day, Papaw threw them on the grill with some hickory wood chips. I could smell it a mile off, two if the wind was stronger, and it made me drool.

The restaurant was located in an old abandoned gas station, with smoke grills in the back, outside. I parked the Jeep in the parking lot—my beastkin feet were smaller than Ascanio's huge warrior-form paws, so I had to drive—and Ascanio and I went inside.

Colleen, Big Papaw's oldest daughter, manned the counters. She gave me the evil eye and kept one hand under the counter, which I decided not to hold against her. When two furry, blood-soaked creatures walk into your place, anybody would get alarmed.

I dug in my pants and pulled out two twenties. "Hey, Colleen. We need as many ribs as this will buy."

Colleen raised her eyebrows. "Do I know you?"

"It's me, Andrea. You can quit stroking the shotgun now. We're not a threat to anything except your barbeque."

Colleen blinked. "Andy? I didn't know you're a shape-shifter."

Neither did anybody else. "Surprise, surprise."

"We ish harrrmlesh," Ascanio assured her, smiled, and winked, flashing huge teeth.

Colleen winced, swept my money off the counter, went to

the back, and came back carrying a metal pan with three huge
slabs of ribs piled on it.

Ascanio grabbed the pan.

"Thanks," I said. "We'll eat in the parking lot and bring
you the pan once we're done. Don't want to alarm your regulars."

"Much appreciated."

We headed into the parking lot and sat on the low brick
wall surrounding it, with the pan of ribs between us. Ascanio
stared at the meat. That's right. I was the alpha and even the
devil child had learned that in the Pack one doesn't eat until
his alpha gives him permission.

I ripped one slab in half and gave him one chunk of it. He
took it and tore into the meat, crunching bones. I bit into my
ribs, my hyena teeth crushing the soft bone. The sweet taste
exploded in my mouth. *Mmm. Food. Yummy food. So hungry.*

We went through two slabs before either one of us decided
to slow down enough to talk.

"Can I asssssk a bad quessshtion?" Ascanio asked.

I thought of reminding him that he'd promised to be good,
but after everything he'd been through today, he had earned
some leeway. "Shoot."

"How come you're beasssshtin?"

He would have to ask that question, wouldn't he? I sucked
on a bone, buying time. Telling the kid I was too chicken to
talk about it wasn't an option. "Let's take the Atlanta Pack.
Seven clans, each grouped by the beast. Within the clans you
have structure. At the top of it are the alphas, then the betas,
then other people in charge of different things appointed by
the alphas. The alphas themselves make up the Council, which
is led by the Beast Lord and the Consort. For the individual
shapeshifter, there are all sorts of safeguards in place. If you
have a problem with someone or someone is abusing you, you
can take it up the chain of command all the way to Curran and
you will be treated fairly. You may not like the decision, but it
will be just."

Ascanio nodded.

"Kids like you don't realize it, but this sort of structure is
pretty new. Curran has only been in power for about fifteen

years. Before that, each clan was on its own, and some, like Clan Wolf or Clan Rat, were broken up into individual little packs. Each pack was only as good as its alpha. If the alpha was an abusive asshole, you couldn't do much about it."

I handed him another chunk of ribs. "My mother was a first generation shapeshifter. She grew up on a small ranch in southern Oklahoma with her mom and dad. One day a loup bouda got into their farm. He slaughtered the horses, killed my grandfather, and attacked my mom and my grandmother. My mother was fourteen years old and she had never seen a hyena before, let alone a shapeshifter. My grandmother killed the loup, but then went loup herself. My mother hid in the storm shelter underground. By the time the sheriffs made it out to the farm, my grandmother had dug a hole almost six feet deep, trying to get my mother out to kill her. They put silver bullets through her brain real fast.

"So my mom was fourteen, all alone, a shapeshifter, and not knowing a thing about being one. The sheriffs made some calls and found out that there was a small bouda pack in Eastern Texas. The alpha was female and oh so nice on the phone. She even offered to meet them halfway to take the poor girl off their hands. So they drove out and handed my mother and the twenty thousand dollars left over from my grandparents' life insurance over to Clarissa. Bypassed the whole Child Services mess and delivered her right to her own people. They thought it would be better for everyone that way."

I dropped my bones into the pan. "Clarissa was a sadistic bitch. She wasn't loup but she was damn close. She loved torture. Got off on it. Her own life turned out to be shit, so she made everyone else's miserable. She and her two daughters, Crystal and Candy, ran the pack of two dozen boudas. My mom was small like me. The first day she arrived, Crystal beat the shit out of her and then urinated on her face. It went downhill from there."

Ascanio stared at me, the ribs forgotten in his hands.

"The best we can figure out, my father was an exotic pet. The pack heard rumors of a drug dealer compound where a lot of large predators were being kept for show. Eventually law enforcement got around to raiding it, and three days later my father walked out of the brush. Lyc-V steals pieces of its host

DNA and most of the time the transfer is from animal to human. For my father to exist, the virus had to have infected a human, and then passed from the human back to my father. This almost never happens because people don't run around the wilderness biting animals."

Even when shapeshifters encountered their natural counterparts while in beast form, most wildlife gave us a wide berth. A hundred-pound wolf looked at a two-hundred-and-fifty-pound werewolf and pretty quickly decided to run for the hills.

"Nobody could ever figure out how my father managed to get himself infected. He didn't have enough brain power to explain what happened to him. Clarissa thought that my father was the funniest thing ever. They put a spiked collar on him and would lead him on a leash while he was in his human form. He couldn't really talk, except for a handful of words like 'no' and 'hungry.' He was mentally deficient. Clarissa thought it would be oh so hilarious to have him rape my mother. He didn't know what he was doing. He just knew that there was a female provided for him, so he mated. My mother was barely sixteen. I was born nine months later and they started beating me when I was still a toddler. For my mother, her chief tormentor was Crystal. For me, it was Candy, Clarissa's younger daughter."

"Didn't your mom trrrry to prrrotect you?"

"She tried, but they would gang up on her. She used to bait them when they would start on me, because they would switch over to her instead. They told her that if she left, humans would kill her and me. She had no money and nowhere to go. On my eleventh birthday Candy and her flunkies set me on fire. My mother realized that sooner or later they would kill me. As soon as I healed enough to move, my mother grabbed me and ran. We ran clear across the country. They never came after us."

A memory flashed before me, my mother and I huddling in the bathroom in some hotel room, wrapped in a blanket, both of us shivering because some stray noise outside reminded us of Clarissa's voice.

"I didn't mean to upsshet you."

"I know. Finish your food."

He looked at the ribs. "Not hungrrry anymorre."

"It's okay," I told him. "Don't let it go to waste."

He bit into the rib. "Did you ever go back?"

I smiled at him. "What do you think?"

He blinked.

"Funny thing about that pack," I said. "A few years ago someone went over there and wiped them out. Must've been some sort of marksman, because most of them had been shot from a distance. Very clean shots, with silver bullets." I leaned over and touched a spot at the base of his skull about half an inch below his earlobe. "Apricot. Also known as medulla oblongata. It's an area of the brain that controls involuntary functions: breathing, heart rate, digestion. It is the only place in the shapeshifter body that guarantees instant death when hit by a silver bullet. Very small target." I held my fingers a little over an inch apart. "Tiny. Takes a lot of practice."

Ascanio's eyes were huge on his bouda face.

Not everyone got a clean death. Some were more up close and personal. Not everyone died either. There were four children—all boys—and three adolescents—two girls and a boy—in chains. The next generation, new victims of Clarissa's tender love and care. They made it.

"What happened to yourrr dad?"

"He died about two years after we ran away. He was a hyena and they only live about twelve years or so in the wild. He probably lived twice that. If you're done eating, we need to get a move on."

He hopped off the wall.

We wiped our faces with the towel from the Jeep, returned the pan, and drove out.

"Whereee to now?" Ascanio asked.

"Garcia Construction." I highly doubted that we would even be allowed to enter Anapa's HQ in our current shapes.

Garcia Construction had an address on the east side of the city, in the tangle of newly renamed streets, and it took us a good hour and a half to find it. The building sat in the back of a lot behind a chain-link fence, but the gate stood wide open. We parked on the street and breezed right in. Gravel crunched under my paw-feet. I really hated gravel. It was sharp, it got stuck between your toes, and it didn't exactly provide a stable surface.

Random dirt and refuse littered the gravel lot before the structure. The building itself was nothing special: built post-Shift, with magic in mind. Just a brick box, with barred dusty windows and a barred door, a standard house for a world where monsters spawned out of thin air and tried to break into your house to eat you. Another chain-link gate, on the right of the building and also wide open, led to the back lot.

The place smelled abandoned: squirrels, the musk of a tom-cat on the prowl, dog excrement decomposing in the sun, tree rats. No human odors. Odd.

I ran my fingers along the wooden board nailed tight across the double door. Dirt.

"They arrrre closshed," Ascanio observed.

"It looks that way. Either the Heron building was supposed to be their big comeback and they didn't rehire anyone until they got a contract, or . . ."

"Orrr?"

"Or someone hired them specifically to reclaim the Heron Building and when the deal fell through, the client abandoned them. Come on, we're going to dig in their garbage."

"Oh boy!"

Smartass.

The Dumpster by the fence didn't yield any new information. It wasn't exactly empty either. The moment we lifted the lid, a very upset mama skunk aimed her butt at us, and we dropped the lid pronto. Stupid May, everybody was having babies.

I went to check the mailbox, while Ascanio trotted off to the back.

The metal box was empty. No mail. Hmm.

"I found shomeshing!" Ascanio called.

I made my way to the back. The narrow space between the building and the fence opened into an enormous back lot, filled with random metal junk. Tiny creatures, fuzzy and quick, with long chinchilla tails, skittered over the refuse. The gravel lay unevenly. It looked like something had been dragged out.

Ascanio greeted me in the back, holding up a flat tire, with a jagged chunk of metal embedded in it. He stuck the tire under my nose. The scent of automotive lubricant wafted up. Fresh. Car grease changed its scent in the open. This was a recent blowout.

Someone had driven into this lot probably during the last week, no more than ten days ago for sure. I held up the tire. It wasn't just flat, it must've exploded. The vehicle to which that tire belonged couldn't have gotten very far. I looked back at the drag marks. Someone had been towed out. That was the most likely explanation.

The dirt on the board blocking the door was months old. Magic had killed most of the cell phones—if you had a working one, you were likely in the military. So how did this person get themselves out of their blown tire predicament?

I jogged to the street, with Ascanio at my heels. Two hundred yards down the road, a tall sign announced Downs Motor Care. *Aha.*

I pointed at the sign. "This would be a clue."

Ascanio chortled next to me. It sounded like something out of a nightmare.

We walked to Downs Motor Care, which consisted of a parking lot littered with car parts and filled with random clunkers of both the mechanical and the magical persuasion. A large metal garage sat in the back. Two of the garage's four doors were open. In the first door, a man dug under the hood of a Dodge truck.

"Afternoon!" I called out.

The man spun about, saw us, and hit his head on the Dodge's hood. He was young, in good shape, with a face that looked like something had chewed on the left side of it and spat him out.

The mechanic yanked a large wrench from the nearby table. "What do you want?"

I held up twenty bucks. Six months ago I would've flashed my Order ID. He would have instantly been put at ease and I would have gotten my information. But in the past couple of months of working with Kate I had learned that the private sector paid for the answers to their questions. It chafed me, but I needed to find the killer.

"Looking for some information, sir," I said.

Ascanio showed him the tire.

The mechanic studied us for a long moment. "Put the money on the ground. Pin it with a rock and don't come any closer."

I should probably rethink running around in beastkin shape, especially if I kept getting bloody. All my witnesses seemed to be disturbed by it.

I put the twenty under the rock. "Did you tow someone out of Garcia Construction in the last week or so?"

The mechanic rested the wrench against his chest. "Yeah."

"Who was it?"

"Some woman."

"Was she one of Garcia's regulars?"

He shook his head. "Never seen her before."

"What did she look like?"

He frowned. "About early forties, nice dress, good shoes. Well put together. Looked like a businesswoman to me."

"Did she mention what her name was or what she was doing there?"

"No. I changed the tire, she paid me, that was it."

"How did she pay?"

"Gave me a check."

I blinked at him a couple of times, before I remembered that fluttering my eyelashes didn't exactly go over well in my current shape. "You took a check from some woman you don't know?"

"It was a check from her business. I called it into the bank; they said it was good."

"What sort of business?"

"I don't remember," he said. "Store of some sort or the other. Art something."

Interesting. "Any chance you can find that cancelled check?"

"I have work to do," he said. "I'm busy."

I showed him a card, bent down, and put it under the rock. "If you happen to run across the check, there is another fifty bucks in it for you. The address and phone number are on the card."

"Maybe," he said. "Like I said, I'm busy."

"Thank you for your time."
I walked off.
"Now what?" Ascanio asked.
"Now we go to the office and bathe."

I was sitting in the office, with my beastkin feet on the desk
and a bottle of Georgia Peach Iced Tea, custom-made for me
by Burt's Liquor, where I'd made a strategic stop before arriv-
ing at the office. Outside the barred window, evening had
dimmed the sky to a deep purple. Ascanio was in the back,
trying to scrub himself clean in the office shower. He'd caught
a nap on the way back to the office, so I expected him to
emerge in his human shape and at least semi-conscious.

I sipped my drink. All in all, a productive day. A hell of a
lot of excitement.

Footsteps. I twitched my furry round ear, listening. Light
stride, sure steps . . . Kate.

The door swung open and Kate walked in. Her jeans and
T-shirt were splattered with blood and she was carrying a severed vampire head. The T-shirt had a smiley face on it.

In my natural untanned state I was pale. If you put me into
a pitch-black room, my face would probably light up like the
moon. That's why I cultivated a sun habit that resulted in a
mild pigment formation in my skin. I liked to call this tan
golden brown. My favorite cosmetics company, Sorcière,
which had a slightly cannibalistic tendency to name all their
foundation skin tones after food, liked to call my tan "cream."
Cream was only a couple of shades darker than the palest
"milk." If I really baked myself, I could get all the way to
"vanilla blush," which meant pale beige. Woo-hoo.

Kate would need "dusky honey" at the very least. I knew
this because a few weeks ago I had to explain to her what concealer was and why she couldn't use it by itself on the strange
rash we got after clearing some odd rat-critters from an old
warehouse. Putting concealer and foundation on Kate turned
out to be a losing proposition, because after the first five minutes it bugged her and she kept rubbing her face until she
looked like a clown who got painted up in the dark.

Her hair, put away into a long braid, was chocolate brown

and her eyes were dark too, framed in dense black eyelashes, and oddly cut, large, but slightly elongated with curvy corners. The first time I saw her, I had stared, trying to figure out what the heck she was. There were shades of India there, or maybe Arabia, or possibly a touch of Asia. She could twist it any way she wanted, depending on makeup, which she rarely wore.

At first glance you looked at Kate and thought "fighter," maybe merc. Five inches taller than me, she was all muscle—well, and some boobs—but mostly muscle. She moved like a predator and when she got pissed off, she exhaled aggression, like hot breath on a winter evening. Still, men looked, until they saw her eyes. Kate's eyes were crazy. It was that hidden-deep crazy that told you that you had no idea what the hell she would do next but whatever it was, the bad guys wouldn't like it.

Kate looked at me for a long second. "Hey."

I saluted her with my bottle. "Hey."

Kate went into the kitchen, pulled a ceramic dish from under the sink, sat the vamp's head into it, put it in the fridge, and washed her hands. She came back, slipped the sheath off her back with her sword still in it, hung it on my client chair, and plopped into it.

"What are you drinking?"

"Georgia Peach Iced Tea. Want some?" I offered it to her with my claws.

"Sure." She took a sip, and coughed with a grimace. "What the hell is in this?"

Heh-heh. Lightweight. "Vodka, gin, rum, sweet and sour, and peach schnapps. Lots of peach schnapps."

"Do you actually get a buzz from this?"

"Sort of." Lyc-V made it very difficult to get drunk. "It lasts for about thirty seconds or so and then I need another gulp."

Kate leaned back against her chair. "Where is the bane of my existence?"

"In the shower, freshening up."

"Oh God, who did Ascanio screw now?"

"No, no, he's covered in blood."

"Oh good." She sighed and stopped. "The kid is covered in blood and we're relieved. There is something wrong with us."

"Tell me about it." I took another swig. "Not going to mention my beastkin appearance?"

"I like it," she said. "The torn pants and gore-stained T-shirt is a nice touch."

I wiggled my toes. "I was thinking of painting my claws a nice shade of pink."

Kate glanced at my feet. "That would take a lot of nail polish. What about some golden hoops in your ears instead?"

I grinned. "It's a definite possibility."

"What happened?" Kate asked.

"I saw Raphael this morning. I'd called him last night, because Jim put me on some shapeshifter murders and I needed to interview him. I wanted a chance to apologize."

Kate took my bottle and drank from it. "How did it go?"

"He replaced me."

The bottle stopped in Kate's hand, three inches above the table. "He what?"

"He found another girl. She is seven feet tall, with breasts the size of honeydew melons, legs that start at her neck, bleached blond hair down to her ass, and her waist is this big around." I touched my index and thumb claws. "They are engaged to be engaged."

"He brought her *here*?"

"She sat in that chair right there." I pointed at the other client chair. "I'm thinking of burning it."

Kate put the bottle down. "Did you punch him?"

"Nope." I took a long swig. The alcohol burned my tongue. "After he told me that his new sweetheart's best quality is that she isn't me, it didn't seem like it would make any difference."

"Is she a shapeshifter?"

I shook my head. "A human. Not a fighter. Not that bright either. I know what you'll say—it's my own fault."

"Well, you did check out of his life," Kate said. "You checked out of my life for a while."

"Yeah, yeah." I took a deep breath. There was no action to displace the pain now. No escape. The ache settled in my chest and scraped at me with sharp little claws.

"Are you going to fight for him?" Kate asked.

I looked at her. "What?"

"Are you going to fight for him, or are you going to roll over on your back and take it?"

"Look who's talking. How long did it take you and Curran

to have a conversation after that whole dinner mess? Was it three weeks or more like a month?"

Kate arched her left eyebrow. "That's different. That was a misunderstanding."

"Aha."

"He brought his new main squeeze here after you called him with a peace offering. That's a slap in the face."

"You don't have to tell me that. I know." I growled, deep in my throat.

"So what are you going to do about it?"

"I haven't decided yet."

"Nothing is free," Kate said. "If you want it, you have to fight for it."

Coming from a woman who had fought off twenty-two shapeshifters to stay by Curran's side, that was a statement based on experience.

"I'm thinking about it." Thinking if I wanted to fight for Raphael. What he did to me was cruel. I hurt and I wanted revenge more than anything else. But at the same time, who was I to stand in the way of his new happiness? Whatever Rebecca was giving him, he clearly needed it, otherwise he wouldn't have made plans for their engagement. "How did your day go?"

"I got some head. It was vamp, but still."

I stared at her. Kate was the last person I would have expected to make that joke. Well, someone had loosened up since mating. "That good, huh."

"Yup."

"I have a glass monster corpse for you. It's in the freezer." Kate grinned a deranged smile. "You shouldn't have."

"It's a bribe for putting up with my psychotic break."

A car engine roared outside.

"That's my ride," Kate said.

The door swung open, and Curran shouldered his way in. Muscular, built like he fought for his life every day—which wasn't too far from the truth—Curran moved like a beast who knew he was at the top of the food chain. When he walked into a room, he owned it and you knew that if you disagreed, he would prove it to you. Judging by the blood spatter on his T-shirt, he had done it today already.

I rose. It's polite to afford monarchy its due. If you don't, they get royally pissy.

Curran's thick blond eyebrows furrowed. We didn't really get along that well, mainly because I complicated his life. A good portion of the older shapeshifters believed in killing beastkin, and my existence meant he would have to resolve this prejudice sooner or later. On top of that I was a shape-shifter and I wasn't in the Pack. He managed to ignore this fact, probably because Kate and I were best friends. However, I had spent the whole day galloping around the city in my beastkin shape. Ignoring me was no longer an option.

Kate stepped next to him and kissed him. He turned to her, focusing on her completely, as if they were alone in the room. That's what mating meant. It stabbed at me a little. There was a time I'd had that, too.

"Hold on, let me grab the vamp head." Kate went into the back.

The Beast Lord looked at me. "I see you've decided who you want to be."

"I'm working on it."

"I'll see you in a couple of days, then."

If I didn't present myself in three days or make some sort of arrangement to do so, he would take it as an open challenge. To present myself, I would have to swallow my pride, put aside the memories of my tormented childhood, and go back to Aunt B, a bouda and the woman I had slapped. The woman who had sent two boudas to thrash me. I would have to bow my head and apologize and ask to be admitted into her clan.

I'd rather eat dirt.

"I hope so," I said.

"The Pack isn't so bad, Andrea," he said quietly. "And loyalty goes both ways."

"I know," I said. "I just . . . I feel like I failed." What the hell was I doing having a heart-to-heart with the Beast Lord? "I worked so hard at my previous life. Joining the Pack is the last nail in that coffin."

"The only thing you failed at was pretending to be something you're not. And you got away with it for a very long time." Curran shrugged his shoulders. "Nobody in the Pack

will judge you for what you are or whose daughter you are.
You have my word on it."

Ascanio emerged into the room and bowed his head. Normally either Kate or Derek gave Ascanio a ride. He couldn't be trusted with his own vehicle. Today he had the privilege of Curran's company. I didn't envy him the car ride home.

Kate came out of the kitchen, carrying a plastic sack. She waved at me and the three of them went into the night, closing the door behind them. The car pulled away.

I was all alone.

I sat down and drained half a bottle of my Georgia Peach Tea in a single long swallow.

To rewrite my life, I had to own all of the choices I'd made and deal with their consequences. I could take off and start over somewhere else. It would be easier. So much easier than bending my knee to my new bitch alpha and seeing Raphael and his happy bride at every clan gathering.

I laughed at the thought. It sounded too bitter and I stopped and headed to the shower instead. The night was still young. It was barely past six-thirty. I could get cleaned and sift through my evidence some more.

From the moment I was born, I learned that I had two choices: to fight or die. I wasn't the dying type. Atlanta would respect me. The Pack would value me. And Raphael . . . Well, Raphael would come to regret replacing me, because I would prove to him that I was a much better choice.

CHAPTER 6

❖

I awoke in the closet again.

I kicked off my blanket in disgust. I'd dreamt of being beaten. The memory of the dream fluttered in front of me, still vivid. It was my eleventh birthday, and the older boudas had chased me into an old farm equipment store. I'd hid in a metal drum trough, the kind used to feed the pigs. They'd found me, poured kerosene into the drum, and set me on fire.

I remembered the smell of my hair burning.

I pulled my knees to my chest. My dream wasn't just a nightmare; it was an actual memory. I had spent years trying to suppress it, but the stress and all the talking with Ascanio must've caused it to resurface in my subconscious. I reached over and touched the closet wall to remind myself the dream was over. The sleek paint felt cold to my fingers. Since I made such frequent visits here, maybe I should just move in. Install a toilet, a sink, build myself a nest . . . heh.

The day was starting outside. It was time to get on with it. I needed to get dressed and visit Anapa's office. In my human shape. At least the magic was down. If I got irritated, I'd shoot my way out of it.

I left the closet. Outside my window, past the bars, thick gray clouds clogged the sky, promising rain. Against that faded backdrop, the crumpled husks of once-tall buildings hunkered down, dark and twisted, tinseled with green plants stubbornly trying to conquer the crumbling city. On the fringes of the business district graveyard, new construction sprouted, stout buildings of wood and stone, no more than four stories high and built by skilled masons. Human hands, no machines.

In the distance, police sirens wailed. Just another fun morning in post-Shift Atlanta.

I stood in front of the mirror in the bathroom. The woman who looked back at me seemed sharper than she'd been yesterday. Meaner. Stronger. Too rough around the edges for most of the things in my wardrobe. Normally I wore jeans, khakis, off-white shirts. Neat professional attire, meant to inspire confidence and communicate safety to prospective petitioners for the Order's assistance. The motto was confident but nonthreatening.

I was done with being nonthreatening. There had to be something in my closet that fit the new me.

Input Enterprises had a southeast address, on Phoenix Street. Despite the ruined condition of the neighboring blocks, this street was clean of garbage and refuse, brand-new houses lining both sides like soldiers on parade. There must've been some serious money behind that rebuilding project, because the houses had been tastefully embellished with cornices and decorative brackets. Even the bars on the bay windows were stylishly ornamental, with metal squiggly shapes. The area clearly was making an attempt at becoming a respectable business district.

I parked the Jeep in a small lot and walked, looking at the building numbers. The overcast sky finally decided to cry on my shoulder. The rainwater turned the asphalt dark. It was good that I wore a hat.

When I found the right number, instead of a building I saw a stone arch with a sign that read INPUT ENTERPRISES on the wall, complete with an arrow pointing inside the arch. Fine.

I walked through the long narrow tunnel and emerged into a wide space. A large patio stretched in front of me, all sand-colored stone, with vegetation confined to narrow rectangular flower beds, running in two lines toward the building in the back. The structure rose three stories high, but the three floors were oversized, pushing the height of the building to a dangerous level. Another foot or two and magic would take notice of it.

The main part of the structure was all modern office: glass, steel, and pristine white stone combined into a sleek elegant whole. The top of the building suddenly broke with the plan and turned into a cupola of glass and crisscrossing metal beams with a golden sheen.

I walked through the front doors. A polished tile floor rolled from where I stood to the marble counter, manned by a receptionist. She was in her early twenties, her makeup was heavy, her suit powder blue, and her pale brown hair was arranged in a picture-perfect French twist. Behind her a large banner affixed to the wall, golden letters on black, read, HAPPY BIRTHDAY, BOSS!

I walked across the tiled floor. The receptionist looked up and did a double take. I wore a light brown duster. I had left it open in the front, and it showed off my blue jeans, combat boots, black T-shirt, and twin Sigs in the hip holsters. An old cowboy hat sat on my hair.

I stopped by the counter, tipped my hat, and drawled in my native tongue. "Howdy, ma'am."

The receptionist blinked. "Ehhh, hello."

"I'm here to see Mr. Anapa."

"Do you have an appointment?"

"No. I'm investigating a murder on behalf of the Pack." I handed her my PI ID.

The receptionist gave me a practiced smile and nodded at the low couches on the right. "Please take a seat."

"Sure. So boss is having a birthday? Is he throwing a party?" Raphael had mentioned getting an invitation. It nagged at me so I thought I'd check it out.

"It's tonight," the secretary informed me.

Ha. Either my guns had made an impression, or nobody had explained to her that she was not supposed to give strange women confidential information. Most receptionists would've told me to shove off. "Wonderful. How old is he?"

"Forty-two."

I went to the couches and sat. Minutes trickled by, slow and boring.

A quiet creaking of plastic wheels rolling came from the hallway. A man emerged—Latino, late fifties, early sixties. He pushed a bright yellow industrial mop bucket and he walked slowly, his eyes tired, his shoulders sloping forward. Probably part of the night cleaning crew, wrapping up his shift. As he passed the counter, the receptionist cleared her throat.

He glanced at her.

"There is a mess in the second-floor kitchenette," she said. "Someone spilled coffee."

"My shift was over half an hour ago," the man said.

She stared at him. My opinion of Anapa's reception staff plummeted. How difficult was it to clean up your own coffee spill? Get a rag and mop it up. If the man's shift was over, let him go home.

He heaved his shoulders. "Fine. I'll get it."

I watched him roll away. The building lay quiet again.

I studied the stone tile: golden brown with slight charcoal and russet undertones. Beautiful. Raphael had a similar type of tile installed in his place. I could never understand the man's aversion to carpet. His house looked like a castle: stone tile on the floor, beige and gray wall paint, Azul Aran gray granite countertops. He'd actually hired an artist to come in and paint stone blocks on the foyer's walls. Cost him an arm and a leg, but it looked awesome, especially once I bought him a pothos vine and installed some tiny hooks to keep it growing in the right direction. He also hung bladed weapons on the walls.

I could picture him as a hidalgo, ruling some grand castle like Alcazar, dressed all in black. My imagination conjured up Raphael, his muscular body hugged by a black doublet, leaning against a stone balcony, a long rapier on his waist . . . with a seven-foot-tall blond bimbo by his side.

I had to stop obsessing. It was like my mind was stuck on him—every moment I wasn't actively thinking about the case, my thoughts went right back to Raphael. Sometimes I plotted revenge, sometimes I felt like hitting my head against the wall. These bouts of feeling sorry for myself and daydreaming ways of making him regret he was ever born had to stop.

My ears caught the sound of distant footsteps. I rose. Three people strode out of the hallway, a trim woman in a beige business suit in the lead. She wore glasses and her light brown hair had been braided away from her face. Her clothes and hair said "business." Her posture and eyes said "combat operative." A man and a woman in tactical gear and dark clothes brought up the rear, holding cop batons. Each sported a sidearm on the hip.

"Good morning, Ms. Nash," the woman said, her voice crisp. "Mr. Anapa sends his regrets. His schedule is full and he's unable to see you."

"I'm investigating murders on behalf of the Pack," I said. "I only have a few questions."

"Mr. Anapa will be very busy this entire week," the woman said.

"He isn't a suspect."

"Whether you suspect him or not is irrelevant. You're no longer a member of law enforcement. You're here as a private citizen. Please leave our premises." She turned, squaring off with me.

If I'd still had my Order ID, I'd have made her swallow those words. I considered my options. I could go through the two guards, but the faux secretary would provide a problem. The way she kept measuring the distance between the two of us telegraphed some sort of martial arts training, and her stance, square and straight on, said law enforcement experience. She was trained to wear body armor. Most shooters would *blade* their body sideways, minimizing the target area. People in bulletproof vests tended to face the danger.

Law enforcement meant she knew the rules and understood exactly what I could and couldn't get away with. If I made a scene and got in to see Anapa, she'd sound the alarms and the cops would be on me like wolves on a lame deer. I could see the headline now: "Shapeshifter terrorizes local businessman."

A part of me, the bouda part, wanted to do it.

I had to back off. She knew it and I knew it. "I'll be back," I told her.

"Bring a cop with a warrant," she said.

I reached the door.

"Ms. Nash!" she called.

I turned. The "secretary" smiled. "This lobby isn't big enough for the two of us, Ms. Nash."

I shot her with my index finger. "I'll remember you said that."

Outside, the cloud cover had broken. I squinted at the sunlight and turned to examine the building. Anapa didn't want to be questioned, but that didn't make him guilty. It might just make him an ass. Except that I'd questioned hundreds of suspects over the years and this was far from a typical reaction. Usually when you walked up to a place of business and told the employees that you were investigating a murder, natural curiosity took over and everyone gathered around to find out more. People are voyeurs and most of us are fascinated by morbid things. You tell someone, "I'm investigating a murder," the next question is usually, "Who died?" Anapa's receptionist had asked no questions. Neither had Anapa's knight in beige business armor.

The beige business suit woman must've taken the time to research my background to punch me with that "you're no longer a member of law enforcement" bit. True, the Order had retired me, but before that my career was distinguished and nothing in my resume indicated that I gave up easily. She didn't strike me as the type who missed details. It would have been so simple for Anapa to chat with me for ten minutes and clear his name. He would be off my suspect list and I would go away and stop bothering him. But he used his security people to chase me off instead. All sorts of alarming flags popped right up. Why all the secrecy?

When I was training, my instructor, a grizzled and scarred ex-detective named Shawna, taught me to eliminate suspects rather than look for them. Look at your suspect pool, pick a most likely one, and try to prove that he didn't do it.

Right now that process of elimination had excluded only Bell. Anapa still remained on my possible perp roster, and now he had managed to bump himself right to the top of my suspect list.

I surveyed the building. Barred windows, surveillance cameras—which would work only during tech—and, if the rest of the security was anything to go by, probably really good wards on the windows. As a shapeshifter, I had a natural resistance to wards, but breaking one would really hurt and create enough magic resonance to make anyone in the building with an iota of magic sensitivity scream bloody murder.

I circled the building. On the north side, a small window three floors up had no bars. The security cameras were also conveniently positioned to cover other approaches. I stood for a while and watched them turn. Sure enough, the pattern of the cameras offered about twenty seconds of undetectable approach to the building. They'd built a trap into their defenses. I chuckled to myself. Clever. Not clever enough, but it would fool your average idiot.

I had to get close to Anapa. He refused to see me, his building was well defended and likely booby-trapped, and I didn't have the legal leverage to force him to meet with me.

The door opened and the older Latino man exited, minus his mop bucket. He squinted at the sky, a long-suffering look on his face, sighed, and started toward the street. I followed him at a discreet distance. We passed through the stone arch, turned onto the sidewalk, and I sped up, catching up with him.

"You need something?"

I held up a twenty. Stuck in your investigation? Don't have a badge? Offer people money. That's just how we roll.

"Tell me about Anapa and his office?"

The man looked at my twenty. "I'd take your money, but there isn't much to tell."

I nodded at the small restaurant on the other side of the street, with a sign that said RISE & SHINE. "It's raining. Let me buy you a breakfast and a cup of coffee."

We got inside and sat in a booth. The waitress brought us hot coffee. I ordered four eggs and my new friend ordered some doughnuts. We both stayed away from sausage. Unless you knew the restaurant well and trusted the cook, ordering ground meat was a bad idea, because for some places "beef" was a code for rat meat.

The coffee was fresh, at least.

"So tell me about Anapa."

The man shrugged. "He isn't there much. He comes in and out when he feels like it. I only seen him three or four times. Good suit."

"Where's his office?"

"Third floor, north side. There isn't much there. I clean dust from his desk once a week."

Interesting. "What about his employees?"

The man shrugged. "There are about twenty or so of them. It's a sham."

"What do you mean?"

"The company is a sham. It's like a bunch of kids got together, bought good clothes, and pretend to play at being businesspeople. They sit, they talk, they drink coffee and have lunches. Once a week, when the boss shows up, they all line up by his office to make him feel important. But not that much work is getting done."

The waitress brought our food and left. It started raining again outside our window.

"How do you know?" I asked.

He bit his doughnut. "Paper. They don't use any. A working business like that makes paper waste. You know, copies, notes, shredded documents, empty boxes from office supplies they order. I work for a janitorial company. I have other clients on my route that have staff half Input's size. They make three, four times Input's paper waste. I go into Input's copy room, their waste bins are empty. Two-thirds of the time I don't have to touch them. This week was my biggest trash haul to date for them, and that's because they sent a memo out about Anapa's birthday." He finished his doughnut. "They do send packages to his house sometimes by a personal courier. I've seen receipts from it in the receptionist's trash. Thanks for the food."

"Thank you for the information."

He left. I ate all the yolks out of my eggs and poked the eggs whites with my fork. If the man was right, then whatever business Anapa actually did took place from his house. Well, there was one way to check on that.

I waited until the waitress came by with the check, paid for my meal, and let her see that I was leaving a nice tip. "Got an odd question for you."

"Sure."

"What day do garbage men empty the Dumpsters on this street?"

"Friday."

"Thanks."

It was Wednesday. The Input Dumpster should be almost full. I took myself and my duster out into the rain, walked back to the Input building, and circled it. A narrow alley led from the back of the building's lot to a larger street. Two Dumpsters sat in the alley, against a brick wall, one blue, one green. I flipped open the lids. Since the intrusion of magic made the mass production of plastic a thing of the past, all trash had to be divided and sorted. Food garbage was packed into wooden barrels or recycled metal drums, set in the green Dumpster, and picked up by composters. The recyclable waste—wood and metal—was simply thrown into the blue Dumpster, together with paper waste packed into burlap sacks.

Input's green Dumpster had a single drum, half-filled with remnants of rotting lunches. The blue Dumpster contained a sad, half-deflated burlap sack. I ruffled through it. Lots of copies of the memo about Anapa's party, some crumpled doodles, most featuring boobs of various sizes and an ugly but exceptionally endowed man doing X-rated things to said boobs, and a legal pad half soaked with coffee.

I abandoned the garbage and headed back to Rise & Shine.

I had to get into Anapa's house.

The solution to the dilemma appeared in my mind.

No. No, there had to be some other way. Any other way.

Any way at all.

Anything would do.

I clenched my teeth. It didn't help me produce any brilliant alternatives.

Fine.

I walked into the restaurant, offered them ten bucks to use their phone, and called the office. Ascanio answered.

"Cutting Edge Investigations."

"It's me."

"You didn't take me with you this morning," he said. "I was good yesterday."

Oh bother. "Ascanio, you can't come with me every time. Any news for me?"

"There's an autopsy report from Doolittle," he said. "Raphael called."

Think of the devil. "What did he want?"

"He asked when you're going to release the building site crime scene to his crew, because 'that damn cat' won't let him do anything until you say it's okay and he isn't 'made of money.' Could've fooled me. I told him you were out, and he asked who with, and I told him that I wasn't at liberty to say. Then he chewed me out."

Christ. Just what I needed. "Did he leave a number?"

"He said he's at his main office. Also that guy from the service station yesterday found the check he received for towing that woman's car. He says if you come by his place after five, he'll give it to you. He said to bring the money."

Well, it was thin but at least it was something. "Please open Doolittle's report and look for the estimated time of death."

The phone went silent. I tapped my fingers on the counter.

"Between two and four a.m.," Ascanio said.

"And the cause of death?"

"Death resulted from anaphylactic shock due to a snake-bite. Symptoms included respiratory failure, multisystem organ failure, and acute renal failure . . . What does severe ecchymosis mean?"

"It means subcutaneous accumulation of blood. Thanks." I hung up and dialed Raphael's number.

"Raphael."

His voice took me to all sorts of places I didn't want to go. "It's not enough you brought your floozy to my office, now you're hassling my intern."

"Intern, huh. Just what is he learning under you?"

Really? He really went there? "Are you alright? First, you replace me with a bimbo, now you're feeling threatened by a fifteen-year-old boy? Did something happen to give you an inferiority complex?"

"That boy has a long resume of sleeping with adult women and you looked a bit desperate the last time I saw you."

I pictured myself reaching through the phone and slapping him off his chair. "Thank you for your concern, but have no fear. I prefer men, not boys. That's why I'm not with you anymore."

He snarled into the phone.

"Temper, temper, sweet pea." Sweet pea? Where did that one even come from? "I understand that your upcoming engagement will set you back quite a bit and you are in dire need of money, so you need me to release the crime scene."

"I have money! I need the site released because it's a waste of everyone's time for it to sit there."

"Two conditions," I said. "One, all items from the vault are to be stored in the Keep until the end of this investigation. I've catalogued them."

"Done," Raphael said. "Will send them in under an armed convoy during tech. Two?"

"You still have that invitation to Anapa's birthday bash tonight?"

"Yes."

"Is the invitation for you and a friend?"

"Yes."

"I need to be that friend."

Raphael paused. "You like Anapa for the murders?"

"Possibly. I tried his office. They wouldn't let me through the door. He's got a bulldog in a business suit on staff and she didn't buy my sweet smile."

"You mean you showed her your guns and she didn't faint?"

Ha-ha-ha. "No, honey, you're the only one who does that."

"As I recall, it was usually the other way around."

"I've seen plenty of guns. You have a nice one, but it didn't make me faint."

"That's what you say now."

"Raphael, I don't own this phone. Don't make me break it, because I just gave up my last ten bucks to use it."

His voice was sweet as honey. "Darling, do you need me to loan you some money?"

"I have never in my life needed you to loan me money. If I was dead, and the ferryman needed a coin to take me across the river to the afterlife, and you had the only quarter in existence, I'd tell you to stick it up your ass."

People looked at me. This wasn't going well.

"Andrea . . ."

"The next words out of your mouth better be work-related or I'll drive to your office and shoot you in the gut. Repeatedly."

"Why in the gut?"

"Because it's painful and not life threatening." He was a shapeshifter; he'd heal the bullet wounds.

He laughed. He actually laughed at me on the phone. My head was about to explode.

"Why do you want to meet Anapa?" Raphael asked.

"Meeting him is secondary to sneaking into his office and looking through whatever dirty laundry he might be keeping in there. Someone had to have known about that vault, because it wasn't a random robbery."

"Really? And here I was thinking random robbers strolled by a deep dark hole guarded by people who grow four-inch claws and decided, 'Hey, I think I'll go in there and steal things.'"

Bastard. "It's a good thing that you are so pretty, because you sure aren't smart."

"I run a clan and a God damn business," he growled. "I'm smart enough."

"Yes, yes." Raphael's outrageous hotness was his downfall. People rarely took him seriously at first glance. Instead of listening to the smart things coming out of his mouth, men dismissed him as a pretty face and women concentrated on not drooling. I heard many things said out of his earshot: a player, high-maintenance, beefcake, yummy, and so on. Ruthless businessman and lethal fighter weren't usually the labels people arrived at until they got to know him better. It was a costly mistake to make. A few weeks ago one of Aunt B's enforcers forgot that and decided to insult him. Raphael retaliated in kind and she lost her head and attacked him. He landed three killing wounds before she even hit the ground.

Raphael was silent. Probably seething on the other end. This wasn't getting us anywhere.

"I don't want to fight," I said, keeping my voice professional. "I just want to solve this murder. I know this is difficult for us both. Let's go back to the killers. They came in prepared, they killed your people, and they knew how to open the vault. All that implies prior knowledge and resources. It is very likely that one of the three reclamation companies who bid on that building had something to do with it. I've eliminated Bell as a suspect. The Garcias are a dead end for now— something might pan out there and I'll know more by tonight, but as of this moment, their work site is abandoned and has been for a few weeks. That leaves Anapa. How much paper waste does Medrano Reclamations generate?"

"Enough for the city to charge us for commercial pickup," Raphael growled.

"Input produces almost nothing. Tomorrow is their garbage

day and their Dumpster has half a sack of paper trash, most of it lewd drawings. I talked to a janitor, and he thinks their business is a sham. Apparently Anapa operates out of the office in his house. I don't like this any more than you do, but his party is my chance to take a look at him and search his office. Believe me, I would rather eat broken glass than go with you anywhere."

"Thanks," he said, his voice dry.

"You're welcome."

"It's a black-tie affair."

Of course it was. "Black-tie like my blue dress?"

"We ruined the blue dress, remember?" he said. "We were having sex on the bed and knocked the bottle of cabernet onto it?"

I flashed back right to that sunny afternoon. We had wanted to go to dinner, and I had laid the blue dress on the bed, and then Raphael brought a bottle of wine to the bedroom and did his Raphael thing, and we ended up on the bed ourselves, with the dress on the floor.

Anger bubbled up inside me, mixing with sadness, and a sick feeling that I was falling and falling, and somewhere below, a hard bottom waited for me. I was angry with Raphael. I was angry with myself. I wanted to bite someone or something.

"That's right." Damn it. "Okay, I'll come up with something."

"I'll pick you up at seven," he said.

"Much obliged," I drawled.

"Don't do your Texas thing on me; it won't work."

"I've done my thing on you and you quite liked it at the time."

"Not nearly as much as you liked what we did after."

I didn't answer and neither did he. We just sat there, with the phone line between us. We had to stop doing this to each other.

"Raphael, there is something else I wanted to mention. I meant to tell you this yesterday morning, but the appearance of your *fiancée* knocked me off my stride. From talking to Stefan, I understand there were six people besides you who were there when the vault was discovered."

"I know where you're going," Raphael said, "and I can tell you right now, none of them would betray me."

"Then this will be very easy. Help me eliminate them. I need to account for every moment of their time from the instant they left the site until four a.m. If they made phone calls, we need to know. If they went to a bar and talked to someone, we need to know. You know them best and I would rather you do it, because my hands are full."

"I'll take care of it."

"Stefan needs to be checked out, too."

"I said I would take care of it."

He would. Raphael was infuriatingly thorough when he wanted to be. "I'll see you tonight, then."

"Maybe."

Bastard. "Seven o'clock. Be there or your site will stay closed."

"You do understand that if we get caught, the Pack will be blamed. The PAD isn't going to bother with subtleties like you not being an official member of the Pack or that we're investigating a murder. They'll see it as two shapeshifters burglarizing the house. We're disenfranchised enough as is."

"I'm aware of that, thank you."

"Just thought I'd remind you," he said.

"I appreciate your concern."

"Fine."

"Perfect."

I hung up. I felt like taking a cold shower. The clock on the wall behind the counter showed twelve minutes past ten. I had until three p.m. to find a dress and read through Doolittle's report. Then I'd go to see the mechanic with a check from the mysterious woman and her towed car.

Since I was near a shopping district, I tackled the dress first. When you are short and curvy, your choice of dresses is limited. I had decent breasts, muscular calves, and strong, pretty legs. There was a magic point about two to three inches above my knee, where dresses and skirts looked great on me. Anything else had to be floor length, because people generally looked at me from above, and lengths in between made my legs look shorter and wider. Styles that made my neck look shorter than it already was, like bateau and collar necklines, were right out. On top of that, dresses with a bold pattern or bright mix of colors completely swallowed me, overwhelming my pale face and blond hair.

When I needed formal wear, I usually shopped at Deasia's, a family-owned shop ran by Deasia Randall. The owner, a stern-looking black woman in her mid-fifties, had impeccable taste.

After an hour at Deasia's, I'd tried all of the usual suspects: teal, peach, blue . . . I even tried a chartreuse, which made me look like a barrel dyed in pea soup. Things that should have looked good on me, because they always had, suddenly didn't.

Deasia examined me with the critical eye honed by thirty years of fashion experience. "What is the dress for?"

"For a formal birthday party at a millionaire's house." And I had to look presentable enough to get through the door.

"Who's escorting you?"

"My ex-boyfriend."

Deasia's eyebrows rose. "Ah. Mystery solved. Has he moved on?"

"Yes."

"And you want to make an impression?"

"I want to knock his socks off. I want him to see that I'm just fine on my own. I want to be vibrant."

"Vibrant or shocking?" Deasia asked.

"I'll take shocking."

"Wait here."

She disappeared between the racks of clothes. I surveyed my latest attempt. A violet, high-waisted number should have been flattering, but it wasn't. My face had changed, too. I used to be able to pull off fresh and even sweet. The woman who looked at me now looked good in a duster and a pair of guns. Draping pretty purple fabric on me was like coating a razor blade in a Skittles candy shell.

Deasia reappeared, carrying a hanger with something black and lacy.

"I appreciate it, but black is not me," I said. "It washes me out."

Deasia fixed a junkyard dog stare on me. "Try it."

I took the dress and went to the dressing room. I took the purple monstrosity off and pulled the black dress off the hanger. Black lace over black fabric. Not me. I slipped the black dress on, stepped out, and looked into the three-paneled full-length mirror.

The black dress hugged me like a glove, stopping about three inches above my knee. Solid black below the waist, the asymmetric gown climbed up diagonally across my chest, over my left shoulder. The left side had a tiny sleeve, but the right shoulder was shockingly bare. A long serpentine shape of a Chinese dragon was cut into the black fabric of the dress. Its head rested on the left side of my chest, its long body slithering between my breasts, just a hair too narrow to be indecent, curving to the right, and sliding down my right thigh. Black, jagged lace overlaid the dragon's outline, its pattern mimicking the dragon's scales, giving a sexy glimpse of my bare skin. A single red stone marked the dragon's eye and as I turned, it shone with the pure ruby glow of a bouda's eyes.

Black had never been my color, but it was today.

Deasia set a pair of black pumps in front of me. I stepped into them, picking up four inches of height.

Holy shit. I looked aggressive. "This is an evil dress."

"Evil can be beautiful," Deasia said. "Don't over-accessorize. Pair of earrings, nothing too large, and maybe a bracelet. That's it. Oh, and this dress calls for a red mouth, Andrea. Scarlet red."

"I'll take it."

"Of course you will. Knock him dead."

Raphael wouldn't know what hit him. Neither would Anapa. And if any evidence of Anapa's connection to the deaths of the shapeshifters existed, I would do my best to find it.

When I walked into Cutting Edge's offices, a man was sitting in my client chair. He was bent over, doing something with his feet, and as he turned his head at my approach, I saw a car seat. A baby lay in it, a little spot of white and pink against the green fabric patterned with cartoon dinosaurs. The man's face seemed familiar. It took me a second, and then I placed it. Nick Moreau.

The last time I'd seen him, in June, he'd looked ten years younger. The man who sat in front of me now seemed old and tired, and when he gazed at me, his eyes were devoid of life, as if they had been covered with ash.

"I told him you were out," Ascanio said, from the storeroom doorway. "He said he didn't mind waiting."

I sat in the other chair next to Nick. He ran his hand through his light brown hair.

"That's my son," he said.

"He's beautiful," I told him.

"Would you like to hold him?"

"May I?"

Nick picked the baby up and put him in my arms. Baby Rory looked at me with dark gray eyes, puzzled and fascinated, his mouth slightly open. He was nearly bald, his hair a soft peach fuzz on his head. His eyelashes were a happy, sunny blond.

So tiny. Such a fragile little life.

"Hey there," I whispered.

Baby Rory looked at me and I could see no fear in his eyes. No sadness, no bitterness, nothing jaded. The world was a big wonderful toy and Baby Rory had no idea how badly it had hurt him. I wanted to wrap him in my arms and make it all be okay. I wanted to give him his mother back.

"He's beautiful," I told Nick again.

"His mother was, too," he said. "He can't even talk. He'll never remember her."

Baby Rory cooed and I hugged him to me, gently. How do you tell a baby his mother died? How do you even begin to explain why?

Nick reached inside his jacket, took out his wallet, and handed me a photograph. On it a woman smiled. Her hair was a mass of cinnamon curls around her face. Here was a pretty girl with freckles on her nose. Her file said she was twenty-six, only two years younger than me. She'd had no idea, but Rianna Moreau had been living my dream. She had a husband who loved her without reservation. She had a fulfilling job she loved. She had Baby Rory. They were a family together and their future looked bright until some asshole came over and robbed them of it.

Nick's eyes watered. He squeezed his hand into a fist. "He

won't know that she was kind. He'll know that she loved him because I'll tell him, but he will never feel that love. My son is barely born, and his life is already broken."

I wished I could say something, but nothing that would come out of my mouth would make his loss easier to bear.

Baby Rory made little noises, oblivious to his father's grief.

"I'll never see my wife again." Nick's voice faltered. He pulled himself back. "I want you to understand. I want you to know what they took from me. To me, she was everything. I can't even say her name anymore."

I reached over and rested my fingers on his clenched fist.

"Raphael said you're the best. He said you would find them." Nick's gaze searched my face. If only I had the right words . . .

"You're a carpenter," I said. "You build beautiful things because that's what you do. Investigation is what I do. I live it and breathe it, I'm trained for it, and I'm damn good at it. Your wife is not a name on the report, Nick. You and your son, you aren't some meaningless statistic. Rianna is real, and so are the two of you. I know what you had and I know what it's like to lose it. I understand."

I saw the split second when Nick broke down: something in his eyes snapped, the line of his mouth sagged, and he cried. I set Rory back into his car seat and hugged Nick. He shuddered in my arms, not sobbing but spasming, as if the pain inside him was breaking out in short bursts.

"I can't promise you success," I told him, patting his back. "But I promise you I won't stop looking. I'll never stop looking. I'll do everything I can to get you and your son your answers and your justice."

In the corner Ascanio stared at us, his eyes freaked out.

Nick shook, rigid, his voice a low guttural growl with bits and pieces of words coming through. ". . . Take her from me . . ."

"I promise you that when I find them, they will suffer," I told him. "It won't bring your wife back, but when we're done with them, they will never rob anyone else of their life again. You must stay strong, Nick. You must be strong for your son. He still has a father, a tough, fierce father who loves him, who will be there for him."

Gradually the shudders stopped. Nick pulled away from me, suddenly, as if just realizing that he had been crying. He picked up the child carrier. Baby Rory yawned.

"You'll tell me when you know?" Nick asked.

"I will."

He went out the door. I slumped in my chair.

Ascanio came over and sat on my desk. "Man, that was heavy."

"That's the other half of the job," I told him. "You are accountable to the victims of the crime you're investigating. You accept responsibility for it. They place their trust in you and they expect you to bring them justice. You must never forget that it's about people. It's about suffering and loss."

"That sucks."

"Congratulations—you're catching on."

He frowned. "But I thought you were supposed to be detached. So it's not personal."

I sighed. "You can't let it get to you, because you still need to focus. You need some distance to be objective. But it's personal. It's always personal. You can't ever forget that there are people involved. You also can't let your compassion for the wronged cloud your judgment, because there are more important things at stake than getting Nick his vengeance."

Ascanio studied me. "What can be more important than that?"

"Making sure that the guilty never do it again. The people who killed Rianna and the other shapeshifters broke the most sacred of laws—they murdered. Since they did it once, they will probably do it again. First and foremost, we have to make sure we keep them from destroying another life."

Ascanio pondered it. "Nick doesn't see it this way."

"Nick doesn't need to. It's our job to worry about that, not his."

"I think he wanted you to tell him you would find the killer and solve the whole thing."

"Yes he did."

"So why didn't you?"

"Because I don't make promises I can't keep. Now get off my desk and bring me Doolittle's report."

CHAPTER 7

---❋---

The good doctor's report confirmed what I'd already known: the four shapeshifters, including Nick's wife, had died of snake poison. I had noted four different bite sizes on the bodies and Doolittle had found one more, which meant five sets of fangs and probably five assailants, unless our killer was a hydra. Or a gorgon. Not that anyone had ever seen a gorgon, but you never knew what fun atrocities magic would commit next.

The snakes were some sort of vipers, and based on Doolittle's learned opinion, the largest bite belonged to something with a head the size of a coconut and its poison was lethal to humans in tiny doses and shapeshifters in slightly larger ones. Besides the official report, the envelope contained a small scrap of paper that said, "If you find it, call me immediately. Do not attempt to confront the snake."

I wouldn't confront it. I would shoot it. Repeatedly.

Jim had run the fingerprints I took off the vault's door through the database. Out of eight sets, seven belonged to Raphael's crew. The eighth was a mystery. None of the databases had any hits.

The trace analysis wasn't much better. No smoking guns.

I sifted through the files. Raphael's crew was a tight-knit bunch, all Clan Bouda and their relatives. Family men and women, they stuck together. They visited the same places, they went to the same barbecues, and they babysat each other's children. Raphael was very selective in his hiring habits and he hadn't hired anyone new for eleven months, long before the Heron Building ever came on sale.

Of the fourteen people currently on the crew, six were

mated, with both husband and wife working for Medrano Reclamations; three others were mated to someone else; two were
children of other members of the crew; and the three remaining shapeshifters had worked with Raphael for years. They led
quiet lives—they worked, they came home, they spent time
with their kids.

Jim's background check had found zip. This type of envi-
ronment didn't exactly provide fertile ground for secret sins.
Nobody was a degenerate gambler. Nobody borrowed money
from unsavory sources. Nobody seemed to have room in their
lives for blackmail, murder, and torrid affairs. And if an affair
had occurred, their biggest worry would've been their bouda
spouses. Boudas were wild until they mated, but once the mating occurred, they went right into possessive, fiercely jealous
territory. And their scandals were notoriously public. We
loved drama.

I called around to the local MSDU to a buddy of mine.
During my time with the Order, Ted had loaned me to the military a couple of times, and I had earned enough respect there
to cash in a favor or two. Lena, my MSDU contact, ran a quick
check on Anapa's criminal history for me. He had none. Either
both he and his corporation were disgustingly law-abiding or
he knew how to cover his tracks.

Finally I looked up and nodded at Ascanio. "Get your
gear."

He grabbed his knife. "Where are we going?"

"To the library."

His enthusiasm visibly deflated and he emitted a tragic
sigh. "But 'library' and 'kick-ass' are two concepts that don't
usually go together."

"That's the nature of the business. Five percent of the time
you are killing monsters. The rest of the time, we're digging
through the dirt for a tiny piece of the perpetrator's pubic
hair."

"Ugh."

I was fighting on two fronts. One, he was a fifteen-year-old
boy equipped with the body of a monster and flooded with
hormones. He was desperate for an opportunity to let some
steam out. Two, he was a bouda. We were an easily bored species. In nature hyenas relied on sight more than scent in their

hunting. We didn't do dogged wolflike pursuit, we didn't travel single file, and we didn't typically track. Following the trail of breadcrumbs went against Ascanio's natural instinct. But as I've pointed out to him before, the human part of him was doing the driving. I would prevail.

"You can always stay here and practice broom drills."

"No, thank you," he said and produced a dazzling smile. The kid was something else. "May I drive?"

"Yes, you may." I had to give him something as a consolation prize.

We locked the office and went on our way.

"So why are we going to the library?" Ascanio asked.

I leaned back against my seat. "Don't take Magnolia. Take Redberry instead."

"Why?"

"Redberry has some sort of weird yellow vines growing on the buildings. I want to check it out. To answer your question, we are going to the library because it's the only place accessible to the public where we can tap into the Library of Alexandria project."

"What's that?"

"Years ago—before you were born—people had access to a network of data called the Internet. If you needed an address, for example, you could type it into your computer and it would pop right up, with directions of how to get there. If you needed to look up something like the boiling point of hydrochloric acid, you could do that. Instant knowledge at your fingertips."

"Wow."

"Yeah. Well, when it became obvious that magic was going to wreck the computer networks, people tried to preserve portions of the Internet. They took snapshots of their servers and sent the data to a central database at the Library of Congress. The project became known as the Library of Alexandria, because in ancient times Alexandria's library was said to contain all human knowledge, before some jackass burned it to the ground. Since the tech is up, we're going to dig through that database."

"What are we digging for?"

"Facts. Let's look at what we have. First, Raphael buys a highly contested building, leaving all other bidders in the dust.

Then Raphael's crew finds a secret vault that wasn't in any of
the documents they had. Someone went to Raphael's site,
attacked the shapeshifters guarding it, and opened the vault.
Then they left the site, leaving most of the vault's contents
untouched. What does that tell you?"

Ascanio frowned. "It wasn't random."

"Right. There are easier places to rob and a guarded tunnel
isn't like a bank. It doesn't automatically look like something
valuable is hidden in it. Also a random robber would've emptied the vault."

Ascanio looked at me. "So the thief had to know about the
vault and what was in it."

There was hope for him yet. "Exactly. We have two ave-
nues of investigation: one, find out who knew about the vault
and could've accessed it, and two?"

"Find out what they were after," Ascanio said.

I smiled at him. "Good. We know that the building was
owned by Jamar Groves. If the Blue Heron had a secret vault,
Jamar had to know about it, because he was the one who had
put it there. We know that Jamar Groves collected art and
antiques. It's logical to suppose that the secret vault contained
Jamar's personal stash. We also have the catalog of the vault's
contents, which I made at the scene. We're going to search the
archives for any mention of Jamar and his collection and compare it against the list of items in the.vault."

Ascanio arranged his pretty face into a martyred expression.

"The Central Library sits on the edge of Centennial Park,"
I told him. Over the years the park had exploded in size, swallowing additional city blocks, and the library was one of its
victims.

"So?" Ascanio asked.

"Centennial Park is owned by the witch covens. They provide security for the library, because it is a depository of
knowledge."

Ascanio came alive. "Female witches?"

"Most of them, yes. If you work hard, I'll let you flirt."

The teenage bouda grinned.

"Don't get your hopes up," I told him. "The witch girls are
pretty pragmatic."

* * *

Ever since the Shift, the moment when our slow apocalypse in progress began, the plants had decided it was time to wage full-on assault on all things human. Magic fueled the tree growth, and Centennial Park was a shining example of that. In the decade since the Shift the park had tripled in size, taking over the neighboring city blocks. Once the Atlanta witch covens had purchased it from the city as their meeting place, the park had stopped expanding sideways, directing all of its growth upward instead. As we drove up, a dense wall of green greeted us, the tree trunks bound together with thorny vines, as if a three-hundred-year-old forest had somehow sprouted in the middle of the city.

The brown square building of the Central Library sat recessed in the green. A pair of massive ash trees hugged it on both sides, their branches and roots braiding together, sliding over the walls and sometimes through them, as if the library itself was some odd mushroom growing from their twin trunks. The trees sheltered the library and while its neighbors had long-ago fallen and crumbled, the library looked intact.

We parked in a large parking lot, which used to be Forsyth Street, and went to the doors. Inside, a young dark-haired girl, barely fifteen if that, stepped in our way. She carried a staff, wore jeans and a frilly white T-shirt, and the left side of her face sported a tattoo of some arcane symbols above her eyebrow and down over her cheekbone.

"Please surrender your weapons!" she chirped in a high voice and nodded at the cart full of plastic bins.

Ascanio's eyes lit up.

I removed my Sig-Sauers and put them into a plastic bin. The two knives followed. I put my wolfsbane and a small flask of my silver powder into it.

"Thank you!" the witch said and looked at Ascanio.

The boy offered her his knife with a charming smile. "Hi! What's your name?"

"My name is Put the Knife into the Bin, Please!"

Ascanio deposited the knife into the bin and followed me. "Giving up?" I asked.

"She isn't interested," he said. "Cute, but not interested."

That was one thing I could honestly say about the Atlanta boudas: the men always understood the difference between no and maybe.

We crossed the floor to a heavy desk manned by a female librarian. She smiled at me. "May I help you?"

"We need access to the Library of Alexandria."

"Are you a member?"

"No, but I would like to be."

"Andrea?" a familiar male voice said.

I turned. A tall, broad-shouldered man stood on the right, by the reference bookshelves, looking at me. He wore a black robe with silver embroidery along the hem and sleeves, fastened by a leather belt around his narrow waist. His jet-black hair was shaved on the sides of his head into a semblance of a horse's mane. His features were bold and harshly cut: he had a large aquiline nose, a square jaw, prominent cheekbones, and a full mouth that could be either sensual or cruel.

His eyebrows were black, and his eyes, full of humor, were black, too. He seemed to really like that color, which was understandable since he was a volhv, which was kind of like a Russian druid, and he worshipped Chernobog, a Slavic god of "Everything Bad and Evil," as Kate once put it. If you looked in a dictionary under "dark wizard," you'd get his picture. Except he would be standing on a pile of skulls and holding a staff with magic fire shooting from it.

"Hi, Roman."

The volhv put his book down and walked over to us. I had to admit, the robe, the hair, and his height combined into a pretty menacing whole. He smiled, showing even white teeth. "You remembered my name."

He had one of the best male voices I'd ever heard. Rich and resonant and just a touch suggestive. Or maybe I was reading too much into it. The first time I ever saw him, he was in a loup cage in our office, because he'd attacked Kate and she didn't like it. He'd made some comments to me, which could have been construed as flirting. In a dark, terrible wizard way.

I also remembered him having a Russian accent. Not a big one, but now he was talking like he'd been born and raised in Atlanta. Maybe he had been.

"Still the same outfit, I see. Do you ever change it up?"

"In private," he said. "Must maintain the whole 'knitted from darkness and shadow' image."

"Aren't darkness and shadow the same thing?" I asked.

He wagged his eyebrows at me. "Aaah, you'd think so, but no. Shadow implies the presence of light. I am not all bad, you see. Parts of me are good. In fact, parts of me are excellent."

Ascanio rolled his eyes behind him.

"So," Roman said. "What brings you here?"

"We're trying to get access to the Library of Alexandria."

"I can help you. I've got this, Rachel." Roman waved at us. "Follow me."

We followed him up a tall gray and brown staircase. "Do you come here often?" I asked.

He rolled his dark eyes. "I live in this bloody place. Dad's making me track down some obscure legend. The Witch Oracle foresaw some things a couple of weeks ago, and I've been digging in ever since."

"Could you just tell him no?" Ascanio asked from behind.

Roman glanced at him and heaved a dramatic sigh. "My father is the Black Volhv. My mother is one of the Witch Oracles. In my place, you have to ask yourself, is saying no worth the problems, the nagging, the accusations of not being a good son, the lectures from both of my parents, and the story of how my mother was in labor for forty hours, which I can recite from memory. It's easier to just do what they want. Besides, if the prophecy is the sign of something dreadful happening, we might as well be prepared."

"What sort of prophecy was it?" Ascanio asked.

"That's classified." Roman winked at him. "I could tell you, of course. But then I would have to kill you and chain your soul, so you would be my shadow servant for all eternity. Come on, it's right this way."

Roman turned left, between the bookcases, going deeper into the library's second floor.

Ascanio's eyes widened. He turned to me. "Can he do that?"

I shrugged my shoulders. "I have no idea. Why don't you try bugging him, so we'll find out?"

"No thanks."

Roman led us through the narrow tunnel between book-

shelves all the way to the back of the library, where five terminals glowed weakly. He pulled a card out of his pocket and
swiped it through the card reader of the two closest terminals.
The Library of Alexandria logo—a book encased in flame—
came on the screens.

"Here you go."

"Thank you. Much obliged." It was really nice of him.

"Say, can I ask you a question? In private?"

"Sure." I pointed at the left terminal. "Ascanio, search for
our boy. Remember, anything that has to do with his art collection."

We walked along the wall outside of Ascanio's hearing distance, which took us almost all the way to the end of the
section.

Roman's dark eyes turned serious. "You have ties with the
Pack, yes?"

"Some."

He frowned, looming next to me, all tall and dark. "Did
you hear anything . . . alarming? Anything about them taking
over the city, for example?"

"No. It wouldn't happen anyway. Curran is a separatist," I
told him. "He believes in maintaining a distance between the
shapeshifters and everyone else. The Pack worships his footsteps. They wouldn't do anything without his say-so. Even if
they did, how would they hold the place? Everyone else would
unite and crush them and that's leaving aside any action the
government would take."

Roman stroked his chin. "True, true . . ."

"Why do you ask?"

"The prophecy. Some prophecies are distinct. This one
wasn't. The witches saw a shadow falling on the city and then
there was howling. Deafening, scary howling. They aren't sure
if it's a dog or a wolf or something else. Also they saw a spiral
of clay."

"So what does it mean?"

Roman shook his head. "No way to tell. It must've felt terrifying, because my mother was rattled after it."

I had met Evdokia. Anything that managed to rattle her had
to be treated as a serious threat.

"Are you free tomorrow night?" Roman asked. "I'd love your perspective on things."

"Are you asking me on a date?" Flirting or not flirting?

Roman leaned one arm against the bookcase. "Who, me? I don't date. I only steal virgins to sacrifice."

Flirting. Shamelessly flirting. "Hmm, then I'm not of any interest to you. I'm not a virgin."

He grinned. "This would be a professional meeting."

"Aha."

"Kompletely profeshonal," Roman said, turning the Russian accent back on.

He was charming and funny and a bit scary, which was always a draw in my book. But every nerve in me still hurt. If there was one thing I'd learned, it was that jumping from one relationship into another was a bad idea.

Still . . . my life didn't have to be tied with Raphael's. The world wasn't limited to one bouda jerk. Here was a guy, a funny, handsome guy, who probably thought I was hot. It could be someone like him. It could be no one, for that matter. I could be perfectly fine by myself.

"I'm investigating four shapeshifter murders," I told him. "Have you heard anything?"

"No. But I can ask."

"Well, see, I'm no good to you, because I'm not a virgin and you are no good to me because you know nothing about the murders. Maybe some other time?"

He reached out to me. One second his hand was empty and the next a small black card with a white phone number appeared as if by magic. "Take a card?" he asked, winking. "Come on, take one."

"Will it sprout fangs when the magic hits?"

"You won't find out unless you take it. Or are you chicken?"

I swiped the card. "Just a warning, if it turns into something nasty, I'll shoot it."

Roman laughed quietly.

"You want one of mine?"

"Five-five-five, twenty-one thirteen."

The number to the office. He must've gotten it from Kate.

"Well, I've got to go," I said.

Roman glanced up and said in a conspiratorial voice. "If I disappear in a dramatic pillar of black smoke, do you think the sprinklers will go off?"

I leaned over to him and kept my voice low. "Probably. But I'm willing to close my eyes for a second and pretend you did anyway."

I closed my eyes for a long moment and when I opened them, he was gone.

When I returned to the terminal, Ascanio handed me a notepad with notes. "I found some articles. Also the volhv likes you," he said, his gaze fixed on the screen.

"Yes, he does." I scanned his notes. He'd made a list of the art auctions Jamar had visited.

"Does this mean you're done with Raphael?"

I gave him my sniper stare. "If you ever want to set foot out of the office again, you will stop taking an interest in my love life. It doesn't concern you."

He turned to me with an expression of remorse that could've made the angels weep. "Yes, ma'am."

How do you go from Baby Rory to Ascanio? To think that one day I might have kids, and given that I was half-bouda they would probably turn out just like him. The mind boggled.

"It says here Jamar bought a toilet seat for fifty thousand dollars," Ascanio said.

I looked on the screen. "It says it's from Amarna, from the eighteenth dynasty of ancient Egypt."

"It's a toilet seat," Ascanio said.

"It's four thousand years old."

He looked at me, incredulous. "Some ancient Egyptians sat on it and took a dump."

"I assume so."

"He paid fifty thousand dollars for a used toilet seat."

"Maybe it was gold-plated," I told him.

"No, it says here it's made of limestone, so if you were to use it, you'd freeze your ass off when you sat on it."

"It's not cold in Egypt. It's hot. Your grasp of geography is shaky, my friend." I sat down at a terminal next to him and typed "Jamar Groves" into the search window.

"You could buy a car for fifty thousand dollars. A really

nice car." Ascanio's eyes lit up. "A Hummer. You could buy a converted Hummer."

"You don't need a Hummer," I said.

"Chicks dig the Hummer."

"You don't need any chicks either."

He gave me an injured look. "I have needs."

"I have needs too and right now I need you to concentrate on tracking down Jamar's antique collection. Get to it."

We'd been in the library for three hours when the magic hit, cutting our research short. We'd identified thirty-seven items. Considering that my list of the vault's contents included only twenty-nine, that gave us at least eight artifacts for which we couldn't account. A knife from Crete; two necklaces from the Etruscan civilization, which was apparently some sort of pre-Roman culture in Italy; a cat-headed statue from the Kingdom of Kush; a bronze head of Sargon the Great, who was some sort of king in Akkadia; a spear from the same country; and two stone tablets with ancient Hebrew writings. None of those lit up with Christmas lights and sirens when we found them. Whether I liked it or not, it was time to quit and head home.

"That mechanic said he'd found the check from the woman he towed," Ascanio said.

"Yes?" He was going to be my next stop.

"I can pick up that check for you," Ascanio offered.

I eyed him. "Promise not to get yourself killed."

"I promise."

"And if there is any threat, you will run like a scared bunny."

He nodded.

"Okay." I gave him the money. "Do not kill, do not get killed, do not mess up. Go, faithful apprentice!"

He flashed me a grin and took off. Well, it would keep him out of trouble for a little while. Hopefully.

I stared at the now-dead computer terminal. Tonight Raphael and I would go to Anapa's house.

If all went well, we wouldn't kill each other.

CHAPTER 8

Raphael was on time. He was always on time. At seven, a small rock hit my bedroom window and bounced off the bars with a loud clink. I glanced through the glass. Raphael stood below, wearing a tuxedo.

Like we were kids going to the prom.

I swiped my oversized clutch off the bed and checked myself for the last time in the mirror. The evil dress was still stunning and badass. My blond hair floated around my head in a beautifully disarrayed cloud that had taken half an hour to arrange and coax into place. I'd tweezed my eyebrows into a perfect shape, applied a narrow line of eyeliner around my eyes to make them stand out, brushed a light dusting of bronze onto my eyelids, and finished off with a double coat of mascara. My lips were a shimmering, intense red, matching the ruby of the dragon's eye.

I slipped a bracelet on my wrist: red garnets mixed with white sapphires. It was the only noncostume piece of jewelry I owned. My mother bought it for me when I graduated from the Order's Academy. I always thought it brought me luck.

I checked my clutch to see if the outline of my Ruger SP101 showed through the black leather. Nope. All good. With the magic up it wouldn't even fire, but it comforted me to have it with me. I didn't bring a knife. I could count on Raphael having several.

For some reason, when a typical weresomething got into a fight, nature flipped a switch in its head that dictated it grow claws and fangs and rip things apart instead of shooting them from a distance or cutting them with knives like smart people do. I always thought it was to Raphael's credit that he was the exception to this rule.

He was waiting. No more stalling. I was as hot as I was going to get.

I shrugged my shoulders and walked out of the apartment in my four-inch black heels. *Click-click-click* down the stairs and out the door.

The evening breeze swirled around me, flinging scents into my face. Raphael waited for me on the sidewalk. My brain took a second to process what I was seeing and got stuck. My coordination unraveled. I stopped.

Raphael wore a black tuxedo. The light of the early evening played on his face, painting the left side golden, while the right remained in cool shadow. He looked perfectly poised between darkness and light. The elegant jacket mapped the strength of his broad shoulders and the supple resilience of his narrow waist, bringing to the forefront both the natural beauty of his body and its dangerous edge. His blue eyes looked hard and focused, hammering home the point—crossing him would be extremely unwise.

He didn't wear his tuxedo like a relaxed gentleman would wear a dinner jacket, nor did he wear it the way a knight wore his armor. Raphael wore it the way an assassin wears his leathers and cloak. He was a dagger in a black sheath. I wanted to reach for him, even knowing he would slice my flesh to pieces.

My heart hammered in my chest. This was such a bad idea. But it was my only chance at Anapa and his office, and I owed it to Nick and the families of four dead shapeshifters to take it.

Raphael was looking at me and I just stood there, unable to move. I had to do something. Say something.

Sad, sad Andrea cradling her pitiful broken heart. Pathetic.

The vitriol did its job. The world stopped spinning, my mind snapped into gear, and I finally registered the significance of Raphael's expression. He looked blank. Completely blank, as if he was gazing at something that had broken his brain.

"Raphael?"

He opened his mouth. Nothing came out.

"Are you okay?"

Raphael's lips moved. He swore.

Ha! I got him! Drink it in, darling. Where's your seven-foot-tall fiancée now?

"Is there something wrong with my dress?" Rub it in, rub it in . . .

Raphael finally managed to formulate a word. "No. Just wondering where you hid your gun."

I showed him my giant clutch.

"Ah," he said. "Didn't see that."

Of course he didn't. He was too busy looking at me. It was a small revenge, but it tasted so sweet.

Raphael led me to his Pack Jeep that spat and roared, belching magic. He opened the door for me. As I got in, his scent slid along my skin, singing to me.

Maaate. Mate-mate-mate.

Damn it.

I sat in my seat. Instead of closing the door, he leaned toward me, a look of intense concentration on his face as if he were about to say or do something rash.

My breath caught in my throat. If he bent down to kiss me, I would punch him right in the face. I wouldn't be able to help myself.

Raphael pushed himself away from me and closed the door.

Good. It was better this way. Really.

Raphael got into the Jeep, shut the door, muting the roar of the water engine, and we took off.

He reached to the side compartment in his door, pulled out a folder, and dropped it on my lap. I opened it. A time line of his workers' movements on the night of the murder. "Great. Thanks."

"You're welcome."

I dug into the time line.

Twenty minutes later it was clear that none of Raphael's people had had time to double back to the site and murder their friends and colleagues. Raphael was the only man without a solid alibi. According to his schedule, he'd gone home, apparently without his fiancée. Knowing him, I had expected them to be at it like rabbits, but I guess even rabbits had an off day once in a while.

I tapped the paper. "What about Colin? Jim's file said he's in debt."

"He's in debt because his house caught fire. He took out an emergency loan from the Pack. He works hard and he knows that if he's ever in trouble, he can come to me."

I leaned my head back, but not too hard—wouldn't do to mess up my hair against the headrest.

"We agreed to share information," Raphael said.

"I don't have much to share. Spent all day at the library trying to pin down Jamar's art collection. Found eight items that weren't in the vault, some with pictures. Nothing stood out. Got a set of prints that doesn't belong to anyone on your payroll, but there are no hits in any of the databases. Analyzed a metric ton of trace evidence without any conclusive leads."

"You will solve it," he said. "If Jim hadn't assigned you to this, I would've asked for you."

"Thank you for the vote of confidence. So nobody can confirm that you went home?"

Raphael shrugged. "No. Had I known I'd have to provide an alibi, I would've made sure not to spend the night alone."

"I'm surprised you did."

He didn't rise to the bait. "It's been forty-eight hours and we have no leads."

His tone told me he wasn't criticizing. His people were dead. Raphael was angry, frustrated, and hurting. "I wouldn't say that. You know how it goes—slow and steady wins the race."

"I know." He looked at the road. "I had to sign the death benefit papers today."

That had to have sucked. "Nick came to see me. He's having a rough time."

"He isn't the only one," Raphael said. "I should've known about the vault. I should've known it was there."

"Don't beat yourself up," I told him. "I pored over Jamar's press releases all day and I never once saw the vault mentioned. You didn't miss it. The information just wasn't there to begin with."

"You really think Anapa had something to do with it?"

"I don't know if he did. He has no criminal record. He has

no parking tickets. His company is squeaky clean, although I didn't have time to dig too deep. In addition, I spent an hour on him in the library today and I found zip. He wouldn't see me, but he knows he's under scrutiny. His people know who I am, too."

Raphael glanced at me.

"His mouthpiece made sure to remind me that I no longer had the Order on my side."

"Ah."

Ah what? Ah—too bad? Ah—I understand? Ah—serves you right? "They know who I am; they know I'm tenacious. Why not spend ten minutes answering my questions? Then I go away, and everyone's happy."

"You think he's hiding something?"

I sighed. "I don't know. I'm collecting information and I've run into a roadblock. Short of staging a break-in, this party is my best bet."

Raphael snorted. "A break-in. You?"

"I thought about it," I said. "I think he has the roof heavily warded and there are a lot of surveillance cameras. He did leave a very nice route open for me, with cameras not covering it even, so I'm pretty sure it's trapped six ways to Sunday. I'd probably go through the basement instead. But again, since he isn't in the office much, there's not much point."

Raphael stared at me. I wished he would stop doing that. Every time he turned to me, my heart kept trying to pirouette out of my chest in a futile attempt to flop itself at his feet. Meanwhile my hands wanted to wrap around his throat and strangle him. It was good that my brain was in charge.

"Who are you and what have you done with Andrea?"

"I'm the new and more-screwed-up version. Or much improved, depending on the way one looks at it."

He stared straight ahead. "I thought being screwed up was something we had in common."

"No, I was always the fucked-up one. You were the spoiled one."

The line of Raphael's jaw hardened. "I've worked since I was sixteen, six days a week. I've built my company from nothing with ten thousand dollars of seed money I borrowed from the Pack, just like everyone else, and I've paid back five times that. I am supporting the entire Clan Bouda now. Nobody gave me any special treatment. How exactly am I spoiled?"

I blinked at him. "Seriously?"

"Yes. Please, enlighten me."

"You remember last year you wanted to take that vacation in the Keys for a week?"

He glanced at me. "You're going to hold our vacation against me? You loved it."

I did. It was just me and him and the ocean. "Do you remember that bouda family wanted to join the clan about the same time? The De La Torre family?"

An individual shapeshifter joining the Pack was a relatively simple affair. He presented himself to the alphas of his clan, and if they said yes, they would then in turn sponsor the shapeshifter before the Pack. With families and small packs, the process became complicated. Multiple background checks and individual interviews later, a special date had to be set, and alphas or betas of other clans had to be present.

Raphael shrugged. "What about the De La Torres?"

"Aunt B had the date set and you had to be there to sponsor them with her."

"Yes."

"And you told your mother that she was welcome to do whatever she wanted but you were going on your vacation."

"I'd worked seven-day weeks for two months nonstop."

I bared my teeth at him. "Are you going to let me make my point or do I have to bite you to keep you from interrupting?"

"If you bite me, I'll bite back. And I grow bigger teeth."

Oh, it's like that, then. "But I'm much more motivated."

He snarled. I snarled back and snapped my human teeth at him. A little crazy light sparked in Raphael's eyes, but I couldn't figure out what it meant. I used to be able to read him better. I used to know exactly what he was thinking—it registered on his face and if it didn't, he would tell me. He was more closed in now, self-contained and hidden. There was a steely resolve there, and a hint of danger under the surface. Raphael had become unpredictable. It was exciting. Exciting was so not the emotion I was looking for.

"What, nothing to say?" he asked.

"I'm waiting to see if you're going to do something or just flash your pretty teeth."

"Don't tempt me."

I gave a mocking sigh. "Oh, I would. But then I would have to bring your battered body to your fiancée and I hate hysterics. Or did you mean the other sort of tempting?"

Raphael laughed. It was a wild laugh that promised all sorts of evil things. Fun evil things.

Something loomed in front of us.

"Bus!" I barked.

He looked at the windshield and swerved, avoiding an overturned bus by a couple of inches.

Tiny needles of adrenaline prickled my skin. I shuddered, trying to shake them off. The hairs on the back of my neck stood on end. Spots ghosted just under my skin, making faint stains on my arms.

"What was the point of bringing up the vacation?" Raphael asked.

"Your mother rescheduled everything. She traded a favor to Curran for a special dispensation so the family could stay for another week in the Pack's territory. She convinced Valencia to bump her ballet recital—forty students had to change their schedule to match the new date. B schemed and shuffled things around. It didn't matter how many people were going to be inconvenienced, but her baby boy would have his vacation, by God." I laughed. "I'd walked in on her fighting with Valencia. It almost came to blood. I offered to move the vacation. She looked at me like I had grown a Christmas tree on my head."

I imitated Aunt B's voice. "Oh no, dear. You know how hard Raphael works. You two go down there and have a good time."

Raphael stared grimly through the windshield, steering around potholes in the magic-pitted pavement with surgical precision.

No comment, huh?

"You grew up sheltered and you don't even know how lucky you are. Your mother loves you more than life itself. She celebrates the fact that you exist." Considering that both of Raphael's brothers had gone loup in childhood and B had had to kill them, I couldn't hold that against her. "You're smart, handsome, and respected. You're a dangerous fighter and you've made yourself wealthy—"

"Comfortable," he said through clenched teeth.

"Okay, comfortable. Women throw themselves in your path. I bet when you brought your fiancée to Aunt B, she didn't even blink an eye, when anybody else would have gotten tossed out of the Bouda House."

"Is there a point to you stroking my ego?"

"It's not stroking. These are plain facts, darling. Raphael, you are adored. You have everything."

"Not everything," he said.

"Everything," I repeated. "If you aren't spoiled, I don't know who is. That's why you can never put yourself in my shoes. All this good fortune gave you blinders. To you, 'bouda' means people who think you are a demigod. To me 'bouda' means people who break your bones for fun."

He turned to me again, his blue eyes dark. "This bouda clan never abused you. This Pack offered to protect you and take you in. You betrayed them."

And we were back to square one.

"We're here." Raphael nodded ahead. At the end of the street, a spacious mansion rose against the sky, all carved white stone and gold accents. Beautiful.

A gated parking lot waited for us, complete with an attendant in a small booth, armed with an arbalest. If we parked in that lot, we would be trapped.

"Not in the lot," I murmured.

"Yeah. Might have to leave fast." Raphael turned off onto the side street. Good idea. If we had to leave in a hurry, it would be quicker than maneuvering out of a parking lot.

I pointed at the half-ruined building. "That looks nice and shadowy."

He parked behind the ruin and shut off the engine, killing the constant noise that had provided background to our conversation. We sat steeped in the sudden quiet.

I faced him. "We keep coming back to this again and again, so let's just do this once and for all, because I don't want to talk about it anymore. Let's say the Bouda House got attacked and set on fire, and then some knight of the Order called asking for my help. Your mother forbids you to leave, because she needs you here. Your clan house is in ruins. I want you to come with me to help the Order. Would you?"

"This is exactly what you don't understand." Raphael's face was resolute. "If my mother put that sort of condition on me, I would've told her to fuck herself. Anyone who gives you an ultimatum of 'pick me' or 'save your friend' isn't worth your loyalty."

He had a point. "You're right. But my question stands. The Order was everything to me, Raphael. It was my pack, my family. Every day I got up and went to work, I took pride in being me, because I was a knight. I helped people. I wasn't a pathetic little freak creature that everyone kicked and punched whenever they felt like it. I didn't want to be that creature. Maybe it was cowardly to reject being a shapeshifter and pretend I was a human. I don't know. I do know that as long as I was a knight, I wasn't a victim. I mattered, do you understand that?"

"Yes," he said.

"Do you think it was easy for me? Because it wasn't. Sometimes no matter what I did, I had shitty choices to make, and I made mine the best I could. So tell me, Raphael, would you have walked away from your mother and your clan to help the Order?"

"No," he said. His tone told me he finally understood. He didn't like it, but he got it. The Order had been my family. It mistreated me, but you don't abandon your family just because they do something you don't like. We had finally reached an understanding. Sadly, it was too late for both of us.

"Then I consider this matter closed." I opened my car door and stepped out into the cooling air. A moment later he joined me. We walked down the street toward the mansion.

"I'm sorry about the way things went down in the office," Raphael said. "I shouldn't have brought Rebecca. It was petty."

"Water under the bridge." I waved my hand at him and gave him a sweet smile. "But if you do it again, I'll kill you both."

He laughed under his breath. It was the delicious seductive laugh I remembered. "Be careful, someone might mistake you for a filthy bouda."

"I like boudas. They're fun in bed."

"They?" A sudden edge crept into Raphael's voice.

"They. Since you are now officially a taken man, you won't mind if I test-drive someone else from the clan."

"Like who?"

We strolled through the gates. The guard in the booth checked out my dress and stared. I gave him a friendly smile.

Raphael held up his invitation. The guard examined it and waved us on.

"Enjoy the party."

"We will," Raphael answered in a voice that suggested hell would freeze over before he would enjoy anything.

We strolled up the sidewalk.

"Who?" Raphael demanded.

For a man a hair away from mating to another woman, he was very interested in my sexual adventures.

"I haven't decided yet. I always wanted to have a three-some."

Raphael stopped.

"Two guys or maybe a guy and a girl. Since you're more experienced than me, you must've had both? Which one was more fun?"

"Why stop at two partners?" Raphael said, enunciating the words very clearly. "Why not have half a dozen? You could hand out numbers to keep order. Get a little cute sign that says, 'Now serving.'"

Oh, the spoiled bouda didn't like that. Not one bit. "Don't be silly. That would be tacky." I paused by the glass and wrought-iron door, waiting for him to open it.

"Tacky?"

"Yes."

Raphael swung the door open. Inside, a tiled lobby waited for us, bathed in the bright glow of electric lamps made to look like old gaslight lanterns. I stepped through and nodded to an older woman standing by the door. She wore a dress the color of red wine and her makeup was flawless. Two men stood near her. Both looked like they chewed up bricks and spat out gravel for a living.

"Your invitation," the woman said.

Raphael handed her the invitation and unleashed a smile. Wow. Ascanio didn't know it, but he had a long way to go.

The woman's face softened. She brushed the invitation with her manicured fingers and smiled back. "Welcome to the party."

Sixteen or sixty, it didn't matter. Raphael smiled and they sighed. And he wondered why I thought he was spoiled.

Raphael put his hand on my back, gently escorting me to the next room. A spacious chamber stretched in front of us. Its cream walls rose high, supporting a twenty-foot ceiling. The granite floor was polished to an almost mirror gleam. Enormous, twelve-foot-tall windows, framed with gauzy white curtains and thicker golden draperies, spilled the weak evening light into the room. Matching accents ran along the molding. To our right a curved white staircase led upstairs. The entire place felt like a palace, graceful and somehow timeless.

The air smelled of wine, cinnamon, and another odd, but familiar aroma . . . oregano . . . no, marjoram, mixing with the lush, smoky sweetness of myrrh. "Interesting choice for potpourri."

"Spicy." Raphael leaned to me, that dashing smile still on his face. "I can't tell if he's covering up the scent of something bad with this perfume or not."

We stood for a long second, our nostrils fluttering, taking shallow breaths and trying to break the fragrance down to individual scents.

"I'm a bust," I said. If there were any hidden odors under that amalgam of herbs and resins, I couldn't find them.

Raphael furrowed his eyebrows. "Me too."

All around us people glided across the floor, men in tuxedos and tailored suits, women in expensive dresses and shiny rocks, looking like attendants to some ancient tyrant. Music emanated from somewhere above, gentle, exotic, and unobtrusive, like a hint of an intriguing perfume.

"Why do I get the feeling I'm at court?" I murmured.

"And there's the king himself," Raphael said.

The guests parted and I saw a man. Of average height, he had a wealth of wavy hair the color of pale amber. An expensive suit of light gray sketched his lean figure. He turned.

Huh. Anapa was beautiful.

He was in his late thirties, closing in on forty. His narrow face, with pronounced cheekbones and a strong chin, was masculine but it was a civilized masculinity, refined, aristocratic, and very carefully groomed. Some wealthy men carried grooming too far, trimming their eyebrows and shaving their chins until they looked slightly feminine. Anapa stopped on the right side of that. His hair was perfectly cut but slightly tousled. His eyebrows still retained some shagginess. His lips were full and crisply drawn, but his cheeks and chin suggested the future possibility of stubble. His large blue eyes, with hooded eyelashes, betrayed a lively intellect and a spark of humor. His skin, sun-painted and dark for a blond, spoke of the South, bright sun, and blue water. He didn't seem Nordic in the least. More like Mediterranean.

He saw us and smiled, making laugh lines at the corners of his eyes stand out. It was a warm, friendly smile, as if he found something about us incredibly amusing and couldn't wait to share.

"We've been seen," Raphael said, starting toward Anapa.

We strolled through the crowd toward our host. "How are we playing this?" I asked.

"I'm a businessman and you are my brainless delicious arm candy."

Delicious arm candy? "It's good Rebecca isn't here or she'd think I was poaching."

"She wouldn't know the meaning of the word," Raphael said, his face flat.

"Oh, she isn't a jealous type?"

"No, she actually wouldn't know what the word meant."

Ha!

The woman in the blue dress in front of us stepped aside and Anapa approached us.

"Mr. Medrano." Anapa offered his hand.

Raphael shook it. "Happy birthday."

I batted my eyelashes and did my best to appear dumb as a board.

"Thank you, thank you." Anapa looked at me, still smiling, an appreciation in his eyes. There was nothing at all sexual in his gaze. He examined me more the way one would examine a rare good-looking dog. Or a horse. "And you would be his lovely companion."

I slipped into my Texas twang and offered him my hand.
"Good evenin'. Such a pleasure to meet you."

Anapa took my fingers into his. He raised my hand, as if to
kiss it, and paused, inhaling the scent instead, savoring it.
"Mmm." He chuckled softly. "You have the most intriguing
body."

Okay, that was freaky.

Raphael moved, subtly inserting himself between me and
Anapa. His hand covered mine and the other man let go.
"Dear, say good-bye to Mr. Anapa. He has other guests to
meet."

"Bye." I wiggled my fingers at him.

Anapa grinned at us again. "For now."

Raphael steered me into the crowd.

"What the hell was that?"

"I don't know," he growled. "He seemed normal before."

Apparently I had a special gift for bringing out the crazy
in men.

We moved to the refreshments table and turned, scanning
the room. A man on the staircase to our right. Two guys by the
exit, a woman by the balcony, but no guards in the hallways
radiating from the main room. I plucked a small piece of toast
with pine nuts and mushrooms heaped on it from the appetizer
tray and took a bite. Hmm. Yummy.

"Second floor," I murmured.

"Mhm," Raphael agreed.

If the office had been on the first floor, it would have a
guard restricting access to it.

"Ready?" Raphael asked.

"Sure."

We stepped to the right in unison and began weaving our
way from one group of people to the next. The second floor
would have to wait. We had just come in and the guards were
still watching us, and if they were good, they had probably
nailed my identity by now. We had to circulate until they
focused on someone else.

Forty minutes later, we had made a complete circuit of the
room. The old Raphael used to be expert at small talk. He

spoke to men about business, paid women subtle compliments, and everyone loved him. The new Raphael at my side seemed grimmer and less willing to chitchat. Despite his looming at my side like a dark but gorgeous shadow, we managed to ferret out the location of the office from a clueless older couple who had been invited there before. Anapa's lair of doom was on the second floor on the south side of the house. Coincidentally one of the first-floor bathrooms was on the south side too, a fact I discovered when I went to fix my hair.

The music grew louder. Couples were dancing, in the middle of the floor, swaying back and forth. The alcohol was going as fast as the waiters brought it out. A few people looked good and sauced on Anapa's superior grog. The small talk went from weather and harmless gossip to spicier topics and meaningful stares as the booze lowered inhibitions.

Raphael took my hand and led me to the middle of the floor.

"What are you doing?" I asked through my smile.

"If I have to listen to another recount of how Malisha from Accounting hooked up with Clayton from Legal, I'll lose my mind." He turned me, still holding on to my hand, maneuvering me into a classic dance pose. His arm slid around my waist and I shivered.

"So you thought dancing would be better?"

"Yes." He began swaying. "Pretend to enjoy it."

"A handsome man, a great party, lovely food. What's not to enjoy? Oh wait, the man is you." I began swaying, too. I was really good at swaying. He would regret ever pulling me on this floor. "You like screwing with me, don't you?"

"Well, since we decided not to screw each other anymore, I have to get my fun somehow."

Since we're playing that game . . . I tilted my face up to his and gave him a lovesick gaze.

"Do you have to sneeze?" he asked.

"Be quiet. I'm pretending to enjoy your company, just as you said."

"Try not to strain anything."

"Oh, I won't. I'm very good at faking it."

That shut him up.

We kept swaying. Standing close to him like this, all but

wrapped up in his arms, was pure torture. I leaned closer to
him and made a small noise, not quite a growl, not quite a
purr, made from desire and lust. Raphael focused on me, like
a hungry cat on a mouse.

"You should take me to the bathroom to make out," I
told him.

A flash of ruby fire exploded in his irises and melted. He
leaned closer, pulling me to him. "What?"

"You should take me to the bathroom to make out," I
repeated into his ear. "There is no way we can make it up that
staircase. We can use the bathroom window to get to the second floor."

Raphael's hand slipped from my waist to cup my ass. A
little electric zing dashed through me.

"Wow, straight for the goods, huh?"

"Can't just make out right out of the blue." Raphael's grin
was pure evil.

We swayed for a bit more.

Raphael squeezed my butt.

"Seriously?"

He shrugged a little. "Faking it, honey, you remember."

I wrapped my arms around his neck, stretched against him,
like a lazy cat wanting a stroke.

At the other end of the room someone shattered a glass. The
room collectively turned toward the sound. Raphael took my
hand and we quietly slipped away into the left hallway. It was
mostly deserted. Two guys milled about at the wall, engrossed
in a discussion that involved phrases like "asshole" and "like
he runs the damn place." They didn't pay us any mind.

A small sign on the door to the right said, BATHROOM.

Raphael tried the door. The handle didn't turn in his hand.
Occupied.

A security guy stepped out from the room down the hallway, a severe unsmiling block of a black suit complete with an
earpiece.

Raphael pushed me against the wall and braced my body
with his, catching my right arm above my head and pinning it
against the wall with his left. The oldest cliché in the playbook.

He studied my face for a tiniest second, bent down . . . His
lips touched mine.

I wanted to kiss him. I wanted him so badly and that need blocked out everything else. And why the hell couldn't I kiss him? So what if he had a fiancée-to-be? I didn't owe her anything. Being good was overrated.

Raphael licked my lips, demanding, seducing. His teeth caught my lower lip, pulled lightly. I had him all to myself. In this moment he was entirely, completely mine.

I opened my mouth.

He lingered, kissing my lips, slowly, surely, as if we had all the time in the world and there was no need to hurry. Little electric shocks shot from my heart all the way to my fingertips.

His tongue slid into my mouth and touched the tip of mine. He tasted like Raphael: spice, fire, and need wrapped into one. I licked him, inviting him in. We kissed, every stroke of his tongue, every touch of his hands caressing my body, magnified to an almost painfully intense sensation. Warmth spread through me, my body ready for more. I wanted him to touch me. I wanted his hands on my breasts. I wanted to pull his clothes off and run my fingers down the hard muscle of his chest. I teased him, enticing him, then pulling back, letting him think he could reclaim my mouth and taking his instead.

It felt like coming home. It felt like medicine soothing a raw wound. I loved him so much, and I kissed him, drinking in the cocktail of sweet memories and bitter future.

The bathroom door opened next to us, the sound too loud in my ears.

I stopped and instantly Raphael straightened. A short man who had come out of the bathroom gave him a thumbs-up with a "Go you!" smile and headed down the hall. The security man was nowhere in sight.

The kiss had torn a gaping hole inside me. I wanted Raphael. I wanted to hold him and to know that he was all mine. I wanted to make love. I needed a cold shower.

I had to get myself together and I needed to decide how bad I was going to be, because making love to him in this bathroom right now would be really, really bad.

Raphael held the bathroom door open for me. I stepped inside. He followed and locked it.

Get a hold of yourself. You can do it. It was just a stupid ruse anyway.

He had the most self-satisfied look on his face. He'd wanted me to melt right there and now he felt all smug because he'd gotten under my skin. Apparently I was a toy.

You bastard. Okay, let's see how you like this.

I pushed him against the door and kissed him again, sliding my body against his, nibbling, licking, purring in his arms. He went for it, hook, line, and sinker. I let him start stripping his jacket off and broke away.

"I think the bars on the window have silver in them, don't you?"

He stopped, his tuxedo halfway off his shoulders.

"It's good that I brought gloves."

"Andrea!"

"What? Oh, you mean the kiss? I'm sorry, I wasn't quite finished. I'm all done now, no worries." I patted his chest. "Your virtue is intact. You won't have to confess anything to Rebecca. It was just one kiss. It didn't mean anything."

His snarl was music to my ears.

I turned to the window. It was near the ceiling that it was just wide enough for us to get through. The bars formed a rectangular grate that gleamed weakly in the light of the moon, too pale not to be a silver alloy. Silver meant burned hands. I'd handled silver bars with bare hands before. It felt like grabbing something dipped in acid.

I opened my clutch and took out my glass cutter and my gun, a black shirt, and a pair of cloth gloves. Behind me Raphael paced the length of the bathroom like a caged tiger.

All my hormones were still in overdrive, and my whole body was humming. My hands shook a little.

Inside the bag was a carefully concealed zipper. I unzipped it, and where a normal clutch would have had a lining, this one had thin shoulder straps and extra material that allowed it to be unfolded into a larger backpack. I'd had it custom-made some time ago.

"Fancy." Raphael commented.

"Glad you like it. Now I know what to get you for your birthday."

"I want mine in blue," he said. "To match my eyes."

"Whatever you say." I slipped on the gloves. "The window is barred. Could you lift me, please?"

He wrapped his hands around my legs and picked me up without a word. He didn't just lift me, he embraced me, caressing me without moving his hands. I was still keyed up, and when he touched me, I almost groaned.

Oh, it was on now. We were playing a sadistic little game, and I wouldn't lose to him.

I grabbed the grate. Solid. I braced one knee against the wall, and yanked it hard, pushing against Raphael. The grate came free. Raphael lowered me to the floor. I slid the grate behind the vanity, next to the trash can, slipped off my shoes, and turned my back to him.

"Could you unzip me?"

He touched my neck and drew my zipper down, slowly. A delicious little thrill ran through me. I had no idea I had so much bouda in me.

I stepped out of the dress. Underneath I wore a tiny black bra and spandex bike shorts. I slipped the shirt on, rolled my dress up, packed it, my shoes, my lucky bracelet, and my clutch into the backpack, and buckled the belt diagonally across my chest.

"Swiss Army Purse," Raphael observed. I heard the familiar playful notes in his voice. The kiss must've thrown him off balance, but he'd recovered now, and he was up to something. "Any handcuffs in there?"

"No, why, do you think I'll need some?"

"Depends on what you're planning to be doing and with whom."

And he went there. The Old Andrea would have given him a look. I leaned over to him with a sweet smile. "I don't need handcuffs to keep a man in my bed. I think we both know that. If I really wanted to take you away from your fiancée, I would. Lucky for her, I'm not a glutton for punishment."

I put the glass cutter into my mouth, jumped up, and slid through the window, holding on to the bricks with my fingertips before he called my bluff. I heard Raphael unlock the bathroom. A moment later he pulled himself through the window with easy grace.

We climbed up like two lizards, hurrying up the wall. Raphael reached the second-floor window and ripped the grate off with a casual tug. I cut a semicircle of the window's glass, popped it out, slid my hand through the opening and unhooked the latch. The second latch followed, and I slid the window up and dived in, legs first. Raphael followed, setting the grate back in place.

I looked around the dim room. The contours of a large canopy bed rose from the gloom to the right.

Raphael brushed against my back. My body stood at attention. Sex? Yes, please. My mind said, "Not until hell freezes over."

"You're touching me," I chided him.

He caressed my back, sliding his hand down, hitting every sensitive point I hadn't even known I had. "No, this is touching you. That was just accidental contact."

"Oh? Good to know. If you touch me again and I break your arm off, you can be sure it will be completely accidental."

He stepped close, his thigh brushing my butt. I elbowed him in the ribs. It was hardly a gentle nudge.

He laughed.

"I know it's difficult, since I have a shapely butt and all, but try to focus on our illegal burglary."

"As opposed to legal burglary?"

Argh.

I snuck to the door and edged it open. The hallway was empty. Ahhh. Finally things were looking up. I padded out of the door and down to the end of the hallway, where a massive wooden door loomed. Supposedly the office waited behind it. I left the bedroom and jogged to the door. Raphael followed me.

I tried the handle. Unlocked.

"Too easy," Raphael murmured.

If we got caught, the Pack would have hell to pay.

"No choice now." I stepped into the office.

The scent of myrrh spiced the air. Rows of brown shelves looked at me, filled with assorted volumes and objects. A brigantine cast in pewter with startling detail. An ancient vase, a statue of a muscular man kneeling. Next to the shelves, a heavy rectangular desk sat on a spare rug, its corners trimmed with golden accents. Three chairs waited for someone to sit down, one behind the desk and two in the corners of the room. Shimmering golden curtains framed the two windows. Decorations of twisted metal hung on the black walls, the most prominent being metal scales with a moon above them, on the wall directly opposite the desk. The moon's stylized eyes were closed to mere slits and her mouth smiled.

The place was empty.

Raphael moved past me and checked the windows. I locked the door and slipped behind the desk. From this vantage point, the room took on a new light. Every object within the office had been placed into a precise position oriented with the person behind the desk in mind. The desk was the center of this little cosmos, and the moment I sat behind it, I became the focal point of the room, as if I had assumed a place in the center of some invisible convergence of power. If inanimate objects could worship, the trappings of Anapa's office would have knelt before me, because I sat in the place of their god.

The tiny hairs on the back of my neck stood up. Whatever intelligence was at work here, it couldn't possibly be human. People did not think like this.

Raphael peeled himself from the window and stood by me. "What?"

I beckoned him with my hand. He approached and I took him by the shoulder and tugged him down to my level. "Look at the room."

He surveyed the office. His eyes widened.

"It's not just me, is it?" I whispered.

"No." He bared his teeth. "The sooner we get out of here, the better."

I tried the bottom drawer. It opened easily. I rummaged through it. Papers, monthly business statements from the bank . . . nothing interesting. I tried the top one. Locked.

Raphael pulled a pick from his pocket and threaded it into the lock. He twisted and the lock clicked. Raphael slid the drawer open. A brown leather folder. I plucked it out, put it on the desk and opened it. A clear plastic sleeve shielded a photograph: an ivory bowl carved with figures of people engaged in combat and long vessels with little cabins sailing over the sea of drowned men.

"What do you think the country of origin for this is?"

Raphael was watching the office. "Hell if I know."

I wished I had Kate with me. She would've told me when and where it was made and for what god.

I turned to the next plastic page. This photograph showed an ancient jug made of brown clay with a long conical spout. The tip of the spout had broken off.

"What do you think this is?"

"A piss-pot."

"That is not a piss-pot. Will you take this seriously?"

"I'm taking this very seriously," he said under his breath.

I flipped the plastic. A beat up–looking dagger with an ivory handle . . . Wait a minute.

"I know this." I tapped the plastic. "I saw it today in the library. Jamar had bought that knife. It's from Crete and I didn't see it in the vault."

I stared at the knife. It was very plain, with a foot-long, curved blade and a simple ivory handle in surprisingly good condition.

Raphael focused on the blade. "It's ceremonial."

"How do you know?"

"The blade has never been sharpened." He drew his finger along the knife's curved edge. "See? No marks on the metal. Also the profile is wrong. It's too curved to stab in a forward motion, but if I slashed with this, I couldn't draw it through the wound all the way. It almost looks like a tourné knife."

"What's that?"

"It's a cooking knife for peeling. You remember, we have the set in our butcher block."

He would have to stop saying "our" sometime. Pointing it out to him now would stop the flow of knife information, though, and I needed his expertise. I knew guns, but Raphael knew knives.

He kept going. "If it was sharpened and shorter, it might be a variation of a karambit, a curved knife from the Philippines. Shaped like a tiger's claw. I never really saw much use in it— too small and my own claws are bigger. Where was this found, did you say?"

"Crete."

Raphael frowned. "Cretan knives and swords were typically narrow and tapered, like the Greek kopis." He turned the picture. Turned it again. "Hmm."

"What?"

He lifted the picture with the knife pointing down. "Pickaxe. That's what it reminds me of. The only way to get the maximum effect of this blade is to stab someone with it straight down." He raised her fist and made a hammering motion. "Like with an ice pick."

"Like if someone was tied down and you stabbed them in the heart?"

"Possibly. And Anapa killed four people for that?" Raphael's voice dripped with derision and rage.

"We don't know that." I couldn't keep the excitement out of my voice. "All we know is that Anapa knew about the knife and it's important. We don't know why." And there was no convenient description of it either. A little card listing its name and special powers would've been nice. "It's a place to start looking."

I flipped to the end of the book. More artifacts. Nothing else I recognized. The knife had to be the key.

"You matter to me," Raphael said. "You always did, and not because you were a knight or a shapeshifter."

Suddenly the game wasn't funny anymore. "I mattered so much that rather than waiting for me to get my shit together, you found another woman. Let's be honest, Raphael, get a blowup doll, put a blond wig on her, and she and I would matter about the same to you. Hell, the blowup doll might be better. She won't talk." Christ, I sounded bitter.

"I don't want to play anymore," he said. "I love you."

It hurt. You'd think I'd be numb by now.

"Too late. You are about to be engaged."

"Rebecca doesn't matter," he said.

"Raphael, she's a living, breathing woman. Someone you felt strongly about. Of course, she matters."

"Rebecca isn't my fiancée."

I froze. "Come again?"

"I said, Rebecca is not my fiancée," he repeated.

"What do you mean, she isn't 'my fiancée'? I mean, your fiancée."

Raphael shrugged. "She's some gold digger I picked up at a business engagement. Someone must've pointed me out to her as a good catch, so she attached herself to me. My mother has been getting on my last nerve with her machinations, and since I had to go to the Bouda House for a barbecue, I took

Rebecca there. After she told Mom that it was very exciting that we all turned into wolves, I explained to my mother that if she didn't lay off me, someone like Rebecca would be my next mate. Rebecca must've overheard me."

This was not happening.

"You left me," Raphael said. "No explanation. We had a fight, then we all went to battle Erra, and after she set all of us on fire you disappeared. I thought you were dead. I went to every hospital. I sat in waiting rooms. Every time they would bring in a new charred body, I'd stop breathing because I thought it might be you under all that crusted meat. And what do I get after all that? A note in the mail. Five days later. Five fucking days later, Andrea! 'Don't look for me, I have to do something for the Order, I will be back soon.' A fucking note. No explanation, nothing. You dismissed me from your life and went on your crusade. Now, weeks later, you suddenly decide to call me, like I'm just some mutt who will always be waiting for you."

I opened my mouth.

"I brought her because I wanted you to know what it felt like. You go through life so hung up on helping people you barely know that you hurt people who actually give a damn. You want the truth about Rebecca? Fine. I barely know her. She was a means to an end. I haven't even slept with her. I thought about it."

There were too many words I wanted to say at once.

"Out of spite," Raphael said. "She kissed me and it didn't do anything."

The correct response finally accreted in my mind. I made my mouth move.

"I hate you."

He spread his arms. "What else is new?"

Everything that churned inside me, everything that hurt and twisted, like a whirlwind of shattered glass in my chest, tore out, shredding through my brave front. "You broke my heart, Raphael!" I snapped. "I cried for hours when I got home last night. It felt like my life was over, you egoistical sonovabitch. And you, you put me through this just to teach me a lesson? Who the hell do you think you are? Do you have any idea how much that hurt?"

"Yeah," he said. "I know exactly how much."

"There is a difference! I *was* one of those charred bodies in a hospital bed. I was out for three days and woke up in a military hospital, chained to my bed. There was an Order's advocate sitting by my side. I had no choice: either I came with him or I would be taken into custody by the Order and brought to headquarters in leg irons. I got to write two notes, stop by my apartment for ten minutes to grab my clothes, and we were gone. I didn't even have a chance to make arrangements for Grendel. I had to take the dog with me and they agreed to it only because I would rather fight the lot of them than let the dog starve to death inside my place. I didn't hurt you on purpose, but you hurt me deliberately. Am I a toy to you?"

His eyes sparked with red. "I could ask you the same thing."

"You . . . you asshole! You spoiled baby!"

"Self-centered idiot."

"Momma's boy!"

"Stuck-up, self-righteous harpy."

"I'm so done with you," I told him through clenched teeth.

"I think I'm tired of doing things your way," Raphael said lazily. "Don't expect me to go meekly into the night just because you said so."

My voice could've cut through steel. "If you don't, I'll shoot you."

He snapped his teeth. "You better make it count. One shot will be all you get."

That challenge burned right through the last of my defenses. My other self spilled out of my human body in a mess of fur and claws, exhaling fury. I snapped my monster teeth at him, my beastkin voice a ragged snarl. "I'll carve your heart out. You'll regret the day you were ever born. Of all the selfish, egoistical bastards—"

"And you want me." He grinned. "You can't wait to climb back in my bed."

"Grow up!"

"Look who's talking."

The magic slammed into us, like a massive deluge. Wards spilled from the top of the door frame and windows in shimmering curtains of translucent orange. Blue symbols ignited in the corners of the room.

The moon on the wall opened its eyes with a metallic screech.

I dived under the desk and Raphael flattened himself against the wall, under the scales.

"Boudas," the moon said in Anapa's amusement-saturated voice. "So predictable. Couldn't resist snooping around, could you?"

Crap! Crap, crap, crap.

Raphael jerked a curtain off the window and tossed it over the moon.

"That won't help you," Anapa said. "Don't leave. I'll be right there."

I lunged out from under the desk and hit the ward on the closest window. Pain burned through me, I blinked, and Raphael pulled me off the floor. My teeth rattled in my skull.

"Ah-ah-ah," Anapa-Moon said. "I told you not to leave."

Raphael hurled himself at the window ward. His resistance to magical wards was higher than mine. The defensive spell clutched at him, sharp whips of orange lightning stinging his skin. His body jerked, rigid. His eyes rolled back in his skull.

I grabbed him and pulled him back. The orange lightning kissed me, and I almost blacked out again. We crashed to the floor.

"Fi-fi-fo-fum," the moon sang. "I smell the blood of hyena man and I'm coming up the staaaairs."

Raphael's eyes snapped open. He surged off the floor and looked up.

If we busted through the floor, we'd fall right into the welcoming embrace of his security. Going through the ceiling was our best bet.

"Pick me up!" I called.

He grabbed me and thrust me upward. I punched the ceiling, putting all of my strength into it. The panel broke from the impact of my fist, and I hit the wood beam underneath it.

"What are the two of you up to?" the moon wondered.

I hammered the ceiling with my fist again and again, widening the hole. The wood cracked, then broke under the barrage of my punches. I tore the broken section of the beam out, hurling it aside, and punched the darkness. It tore and the night sky winked at me through the narrow gap. No attic. We would break out straight onto the roof above. Raphael set me down on my feet, took a running start, and jumped, flipping in midair, kicking at the opening I had made. He landed in a roll as a shower of wooden boards hit the floor. "Go."

I crossed my arms over my head and jumped. Wood and shingles hit my forearms, and I grabbed onto the roof and pulled myself up. The edge of the roof glowed with magic. On the ground below, huge orange symbols stretched across the luminescent lawn, a pale yellow glow coating every single blade of grass in a sheath of magic. The entire yard around the house was warded and it was a hell of a ward. Great.

Raphael forced his way through the hole behind me.

Landing on the lawn wasn't an option. The magic could fry us or do something worse. I spun around looking for a tree, a tower, a wall, anything close enough to jump to from the roof.

At the far end of the roof a long cable dived down to the wall that surrounded Anapa's home.

"Power line," we barked at each other at the same time.

We dashed along the roof. I danced onto the power line and ran along it, balancing on my oversized feet. One, two, three, tilt, tilt . . . I leaped on the low stone wall that separated Anapa's home and yard from the street. Raphael pulled off his shoes, hurled them into the night, took a running start and jumped, catching the power line with his arms. He swung himself back up on it and walked slowly, arms out, suspended between the glowing orange lawn and the black sky.

I held my breath.

The side door of the mansion sprang open. A deep rumbling roar reverberated through the night, made by a cavernous mouth. My hackles rose.

Raphael swayed, ran the next ten feet, and jumped, clearing the remaining distance in one powerful leap. He sailed through the air and landed on the wall, next to me.

A bright, unnaturally yellow flash of light exploded on the lawn. I didn't wait to see what it was. We jumped down off the wall into the street and ran.

The roar chased us. Out of the corner of my eyes, I caught a glimpse of a huge shadow leaping over the wall like it was nothing. The creature landed on the street behind us, as big as a rhino, its head with a huge mane armed with long crocodilian jaws. Its odor hit me, a pungent oily odor, reminiscent of rotten fish, old blood, and decomposing sweat, shot through with an unnatural stench. Revolting, violent, terrible, it lashed at me, promising death. Fear squirmed through my body. My instincts whipped me into a sprint.

We raced down the street.

The thing behind us roared again and gave chase. It pounded after us, huge, but freakishly fast.

I glanced back. The distance between us was shrinking.

The air turned to fire in my throat. A stitch pricked my side.

Run. Run faster. Faster!

I glanced over my shoulder again. The beast was gaining. We were sprinting full-out, and it was gaining.

We took a corner at breakneck speed. A ruined building loomed in front of us, a big, dark wreck with a gaping black hole in its bottom floor. Raphael pointed at it. We veered right and leaped through the gap into the darkness.

Inside, the building was vast and empty, a shell bordered by outer walls. Tall support columns rose up, supporting nothing—the top floors had crumbled long ago, and the moon shone through the holes in the dusty glass roof, painting the floor in random patches of blue light. We flew across it like two phantoms, silent and quick, and sank into the deep inky shadows against the opposite wall. Raphael reached over and squeezed my hand. I squeezed back.

Maybe the beast would pass.

A dark silhouette loomed in the gap in the wall through which we had entered. No such luck.

The beast took a step forward. Half of its body swung down—it lowered its head. I heard it sniff. Tiny puffs of dust slid across the floor. It was tracking us. If we fled, it would outrun us. If we took to the rooftops, we'd eventually run into ruins and have to land, and it would be waiting. We had to kill it.

Next to me Raphael shrugged off his tuxedo jacket. He wore twin leather sheaths underneath. He drew two foot-long knives out and passed them to me. I held them while he pulled off his shirt. His pants followed. He took the knives back and I eased my backpack off my shoulders.

The beast took a step forward. Claws screeched on the concrete. Step—scratch. Step—scratch. Its revolting scent drifted toward us, washing over me like a shower of cold slime.

I gathered myself into a tight clump.

The beast moved into a patch of light and my pulse sped up. What I had mistaken for a mane of coarse hair was a mane of tiny brown tentacles. They wriggled and twisted, stretching and coiling, like a nest of three-foot-long, thin earthworms. Scratch the neck from the list of possible targets. Cutting or clawing through the mass of writhing flesh would take too long.

The beast dipped its head again, bracing on powerful legs sheathed in sandy fur. The long claws on its front paws scratched the dust. Its sturdy frame looked built for ramming. If it took a running start, it would smash straight through the wall and not even slow down. I could see no weakness. Why did things like this always happen to me when I didn't have an assault rifle handy?

The beast raised its head. Large yellow owl eyes peered straight at us.

We'd have to go for the gut and eyes. Those were our only options.

I touched Raphael and pointed to my eyes. He nodded, hunched down, muscles contracting, and leaped. His skin burst in midjump as his body snapped into a new, stronger form. A man had started the leap, but a bouda in warrior form finished it: a seven-foot-tall lethal hybrid of animal and man, armed with deadly claws and wicked teeth set into oversized jaws that could crush a cow's femur like it was a peanut shell.

I dashed to the side.

Raphael landed on top of the beast and raked its back with his blades. Blood drenched the gashes. The creature bellowed and dropped to the ground, rolling. Raphael leaped off, into the gloom. The beast sprang to his feet and whirled, trying to lunge after him.

I struck from the side, slicing across its forehead with my claws. The creature whipped back, too fast. Teeth grazed my skin. I jumped back and the beast lunged at me, snapping its teeth. I leaped backward again and again, zigzagging as it chased me. Damn, it was fast.

Raphael shot out of the gloom and cut at the beast's side with his knives.

The beast paid him no mind. The tentacles on its head sparked with deep orange. The orange light pulsed outward and caught my arm. An intense ache seared my shoulder, a cold burn, like someone had skinned my arm open and poured liquid nitrogen over the muscle.

I cried out and raked its snout with my claws, gouging the sensitive flesh.

The beast lunged at me. The glow pulsed and clutched me. Pain exploded in my head. I couldn't move; I couldn't make a sound. I just shuddered in the magic's grip, the agony so intense, it felt like my bones were splintering.

Someone cut my legs off, the walls somersaulted, and I crashed into the dirt.

Behind the beast Raphael turned into a whirlwind of steel, flinging blood into the night.

The beast howled.

I tried to get up, but I still couldn't move my legs. I could see them right there in the dirt, but they didn't obey.

Raphael hammered a massive kick into the creature's ribs.

The abomination spun toward him, its mane sparking.

Raphael ran.

The creature bellowed, an otherworldly, terrible sound. Blood from the cuts I'd caused dripped into its eyes, rendering it half-blind. It raised its snout, inhaled, and charged after Raphael.

I just had to get up. I had to pull myself upright.

Raphael sprinted along the wall, leaping over the piles of refuse. The creature raced after him, devouring the distance between them in huge leaps. The floor shook with each thud of its paws.

I rolled up to my knees, clumsy like a drunk, and forced myself upright.

The creature's mane turned bright orange.

"Magic!" I yelled.

Raphael glanced over his shoulder.

The orange glow around the beast's mane coalesced and whipped from the creature in twin bolts of bright lightning. Raphael zigzagged, but it was too late. The left bolt caught his ankle, splintering into a dozen small forks that bit into Raphael's flesh. It jerked him off the ground.

The world stopped. All I could see was Raphael's face, twisted by pain. Fear clamped onto me and spurred me into a desperate sprint.

For a second he seemed to float weightlessly, suspended a foot above the ground, and then he crashed down, rolling in the dirt.

Please don't die. Please, please, don't die.

There were fifty yards between me and the beast. It felt like I was running for an eternity, stuck in some sort of hell, watching the man I loved die in slow motion.

The beast snorted in vicious glee.

I'll get there, honey. Hang on another half a second.

The giant jaws opened wide, teeth ready to rend.

I smashed into the beast from the side, thrust my claws under it, and sank them into the creature's gut. Blood drenched me. Slippery innards slid against my fingers. I grabbed them and yanked.

The beast spun, trying to bite me. I sank my claws into the wound and hung on. The orange lightning bit into me, fire and ice wrapped in pain. The moonlight dimmed.

Raphael loomed on the other side of the beast and clawed it. He was alive. I almost cried from the relief.

The magic stung us again.

Oh my God. It hurt.

The magic wouldn't kill us. It just hurt.

Hurt.

Raphael and I stared at each other over the beast's spine through the haze of pain and laughed. Our eerie hyena cackles echoed through the ruin.

It wanted to play the hurting game against two boudas. It had no chance.

We mauled the beast.

It raked us with its hind legs and shocked us with its magic, and we clawed it and clawed it, hanging on and laughing through the pain. I tasted blood in my mouth and clawed even harder, digging into the beast's stomach, wrenching innards and bone out. We carved and gouged, blacking out and coming to, throwing blood and wet entrails.

The beast shuddered.

We ripped into it. It was the creature or us, do or die.

The beast stumbled, careened to the side, and crashed down.

I looked up, breathing hard. Across from me Raphael stood, covered in gore. His muscular furry chest heaved. Between us the beast lay, the bones of its rib cage bare. We had nearly stripped its carcass. It should've died ages ago, but the magic must've kept it alive.

I sank to the floor. My body was red with blood, some of it the beast's, some my own. Long scratches marked my side and right leg from the hip down—gouges from the beast's claws. The cuts burned. If I were human, I'd have needed hundreds of stitches.

We won. Somehow we had won and both of us had survived. It was some sort of miracle. I was bone tired. The floor looked so nice. Maybe if I just lay down here for a minute and closed my eyes . . .

"Andrea."

Raphael's eyes glowed with ruby fire. His face, a meld of human and hyena, didn't mirror emotions well but his eyes stared at me with a chilling determination.

"What is it?" I asked.

"I'm taking you home."

My mind chewed on his words, trying to break them into chunks. Take me home? Take me home . . . Home. With him.

My fatigue evaporated in an instant. "No."

"Yes. You're coming home with me. We'll take a bath and eat and make love, and everything will be fine."

I got my ass off the floor. "I don't think so."

"I'm done doing things your way. Your way means we don't talk for months. You're coming home with me."

"You hurt me, on purpose, but everything is cool now, because you didn't sleep with Rebecca and we can go home."

"Yes!"

"It doesn't work this way. I'm not going home with you. You and I are done."

"You're mine," he snarled.

What the hell. Maybe the fight had knocked some screw loose in his brain.

"You'll always be mine." He stepped on the carcass and started toward me. I looked into his eyes and saw bouda insanity glaring back. The fighting had tipped the balance between rational thought and crazy passion. Raphael's emergency brake was malfunctioning and he and I were on a collision course. "You know it and I know it. We love each other."

"We're bad for each other."

"You're not leaving me again!" he growled.

The adrenaline still coursing through me surged up. He was challenging me! I marched toward him, put my muzzle as close to his as I could, and said slowly, clearly pronouncing every word, "I *am* leaving you. You don't get to play with me. I'm not your pet and you don't get to hurt me because you think I should be punished."

Baiting him was stupid. I knew that, but I couldn't help myself. The crazy cocktail of biochemicals and magic that got me through this fight drove me on. I knew I should stop, but it was as if there were two of me—the rational Andrea and the emotion-crazy beastkin—and right now the rational Andrea was being dragged off by a raging river of hormones, while the beastkin Andrea waved good-bye from a cliff nearby.

I bit off words. "You broke my heart and now I'm walking away from you. Watch me."

He'd hurt me. He would pay.

"This is me walking away." I turned and took a couple of steps. "Are you watching?"

He lunged at me, and we went down, rolling in the dirt, arm over leg. My back hit the floor and Raphael pinned me in a classic schoolyard bully mount, sitting on my stomach. One of the worst positions you can be trapped in. Great.

"Not walking away now," he said.

I bent my knees, planted my heels in the ground, and bridged under him. He pitched forward, his right hand coming down on the ground. *Got you.* I dropped my hips, caught his right arm, pulling it snug against my chest, stepped my right foot over his, capturing him, and bridged sharply to the right. Raphael pitched over and I rolled up on top of him. He clamped my shoulders with his hands.

"I'm getting up and walking out of here. You'll have to fight me to stop me. Your call."

Raphael opened his arms. He was letting me go. I had known he would.

I jumped to my feet and walked away. A part of me was screaming, *What are you doing, stupid? Run back.* I kept walking, holding on to the memory of Raphael telling me, "I know exactly how much it hurt." This thing between us was too complicated and it hurt too fucking much. I had nothing left in me now and I couldn't deal with it.

Behind me Raphael roared, shaking the ruin. I kept walking. The sound of his frustration chased me until I finally broke into a run. My body hurt. Fever heated my face from the inside—the Lyc-V was trying to mend my battered body. If only mending other things were that easy.

I ran faster, scurried up the wall, through the opening, and out into the moonlit night. I leaped onto the nearest roof and ran and ran, the air burning in my lungs, droplets of the beast's blood falling off my body, leaving a grisly trail.

I kept going until the fatigue built into an ache in my limbs. I was on a roof . . . somewhere. The buildings around me no longer looked familiar. I slowed, then stopped. Behind me the city stretched, steeping in magic. In front, a river flowed, like a silvery serpent glinting in the moonlight. Tall trees stood guard on the distant bank. Tiny points of light, green and turquoise, drifted gently between their branches. I had run all the way across the city to Sibley Forest, one of the new post-Shift woods, supercharged by magic and filled with hungry things that viewed humans as tasty, fun-to-catch snacks.

The trees beckoned me. They looked so peaceful and even though I knew they weren't, I couldn't resist.

I dived off the building into the river. Cool water foamed around me with a million bubbles. I surfaced and swam, gliding through the cool depths as if I were flying. The river ended too soon, and I emerged onto the opposite bank, dripping wet but no longer bloody. I climbed up and made my way through the underbrush. The forest sang to me in a dozen different voices and teased me with a myriad of smells. I inhaled the spicy scent of forest herbs, the musk of a raccoon, and the slightly bitter scent of opossum. My ears twitched, catching the sounds of mice scurrying in the underbrush, the distant hooting of an owl, and the chirping of cicadas, fiddling away in the soothing darkness.

As I walked, the grasses rubbed against my legs, tickling my fur. Above me a dense vine covered with tiny white flowers shivered in the night breeze. The tiny flowers detached, glowing with pale green, and floated past me, like fairy lights. Fascinated, I crouched in the grass and watched one of the glowing blossoms settle on a leaf. So pretty.

I walked the woods, thinking of nothing at all. If I could've shifted into a hyena, I would've. I just wanted to cool down, smell things, watch animals move about, and pretend that I was part of this world, rather than the place across the river. My choices were simpler here. Lay in the grass or on a fallen log. Watch the mice or try to catch one. Listen to the owl hooting or listen to the frogs singing. Simple and easy.

Finally I climbed a large tree, curled up in its branches, and fell asleep.

CHAPTER 9

❖

Sleeping in a tree seemed like a great idea in theory. In practice, I woke up just before sunrise, all achy, my fur damp with morning dew, and reeking of decomposing blood. Apparently not all of it had washed off in the river. The magic had fallen, with tech once again holding on to the planet's reins, and the magical forest of yesterday was a soggy, muddy, and unpleasant place. Faced with the lovely choice of remaining in my beastkin shape or trotting across the city butt-naked, I decided that fur was preferable. I cleared the river and stuck to the rooftops.

I had conspired to break the law with my ex-boyfriend, who I professed to hate, broken said law, destroyed the victim's attack dog/magic creature in a fit of murderous frenzy, and then run away across the city, wandered around some woods, and fallen asleep in a tree in my beastkin shape.

When I went off the rails, I didn't do it halfway. No, I flipped a few times, caught a lot of air, and then exploded in a fiery crash.

I made it to my building, walked up the stairs to my apartment, and stared at my door. My keys were in my backpack, which I had dropped before we fought the monster in the warehouse. The bars on my windows were welded to a metal frame built into the brick wall. I could probably bend them, if I strained hard enough and wrapped something around my hands, since the bars had silver in them, but I'd take out some of the wall with them. How the hell was I going to get inside without busting the door?

Footsteps came from below. A moment and Mrs. Haffey walked up the stairs, carrying something wrapped in a kitchen towel.

Awesome.

Mrs. Haffey saw my furry butt and stopped. For a long second we stared at each other, she in a pink bathrobe and I, six feet tall, furry, bloody, and smelling like a wet dog who had rolled in a swamp.

Don't scream. Please don't scream.

Mrs. Haffey cleared her throat. "Andrea? Is that you?"

"Yes, ma'am. Good morning."

"Good morning. Here, I made you a carrot cake last night." She held the toweled object out to me.

I took it and sniffed, wrinkling my black nose. "Thank you. Smells wonderful."

"I just wanted to thank you for Darin. We've been together for so long. I just don't know what I would do without him." She stepped toward me and hugged me.

Oh my God, what do I do?

I hugged her back, as gently as I could, with one arm.

"You take care now," Mrs. Haffey said, smiled, and went downstairs.

She'd hugged my furry, smelly, bloodstained self. She had no idea, but I would run back into that basement and fight off a hundred of those bugs just because she hadn't screamed when she'd seen me.

I needed to get inside and change into my human shape, pronto. Before any neighbors decided to call the cops because there was a monster breaking into that "nice Texas girl's" apartment.

I gripped the handle of my door. It turned in my hand, but my brain didn't process it right away and I slammed my shoulder into it. The door flew open with a thunderous thump and I rolled into the apartment, springing into a crouch.

My apartment smelled of Raphael. If he was still here, there was no way he wouldn't have heard me.

I kicked the door shut, snarled a little to let him know I meant business, and set out to search. A quick glance told me that my living room was Raphael-free. My bedroom was also empty, and so was my closet. I made a full circle, came to the kitchen, and stopped. My nylon mesh backpack sat in the middle of my kitchen table, with my dress and shoes still in it. My tablecloth was missing in action and long, jagged scratches covered the table's surface. The scratches looked suspiciously like letters.

I climbed on a chair and looked at it from above.

MINE.

Oh, that's great. Fantastic. So mature. Perhaps he would pull my pigtails next or stick a tack on my seat.

I shoved the table. Who did he think he was, breaking into my apartment and vandalizing my furniture? I had never done that to him. I had never ruined any of his things.

I went to shower and scrubbed myself clean.

I mean, what the hell was I even supposed to do with this MINE thing? One moment he was shoving another woman under my nose, the next he'd decided we were back on and couldn't understand why I wasn't getting with the program. An old song surfaced in my memories. *Love is all you need.* Maybe, but in real life love was rarely all you got. Raphael and I also had pride, and guilt, and anger, jealousy and hurt feelings, and all of it was mixed into this giant Gordian knot. Untangling it seemed impossible.

Smelly, ugly, stupid bouda moron. I should've emptied a jar of fleas in his car. It would've been good for a laugh. It wouldn't solve anything, but it would make me feel better.

I put on my clothes, sat down at the kitchen table, tried my carrot cake—it was delicious—and looked at MINE some more. This was so unlike Raphael. The echoes of his roar floated up from my memory. Raphael was subtle. He seduced and enticed, and he was really good at it. So good that I had fallen for him even though I had sworn that hell would freeze over before I let a bouda touch me. This was very much unlike him. Was he really that desperate to get me back?

I wished I had been born in a different time. Somewhere in the past, before the magic, before the shapeshifters, when I could have just been a cop and done my job. When Raphael would have been a regular guy and I would have been a regular girl, and none of the complicated shapeshifter things would have gotten in the way. Or better yet, I wished the magic had never come. But that would mean that I wouldn't have experienced the magic forest. I would be slower, blinder, deafer. Weaker. No, the magic was here to stay and so was the other me. I had suppressed her for so long, and now she had taken the wheel and was giggling maniacally as she drove me off the cliff.

* * *

When I got to the office, Ascanio opened the door with an expression of profound alarm on his face. "Take me with you. Please. I'll do anything."

I stepped inside the office and saw the source of his panic. It sat behind Kate's desk. It had blond hair two shades lighter than mine, wore a blue T-shirt and a black skirt with layered ruffles, and looked to an outside observer like a cute teenage girl. And she was—at fourteen years old, Julie was cute and very much conscious of her position as Curran and Kate's adopted child. Most of the time she was a perfect Pack princess, polite and poised—except when Derek, Kate's sidekick, or Ascanio were in the room. Derek got frosty replies studded with spikes and if Ascanio was present, she turned into a foul-mouthed sarcastic devil.

It was hard to be a teenage girl. I had been one and I didn't care to repeat the experience.

"Take me with you," Ascanio begged.

"He can't go. He failed the test on the 'Epic of Gilgamesh,' " Julie said, her voice iced over. "Kate told him to sit here and study it."

Ascanio turned to her and said a single derision-soaked word. "Snitch."

"Crybaby," Julie said.

"Harpy," Ascanio said.

Julie gave him a look of concentrated scorn. "Pussy."

Ascanio glared at her.

Julie crossed her arms.

"Where did Kate go?" I asked.

"To the Mercenary Guild," Julie said.

Probably still trying to settle the dispute over who was going to be running the Guild. They had a bit of a power vacuum and Kate, as one of the veteran mercs, had seniority.

"Did you pick up that check from the mechanic?" I asked. "For that woman's vehicle?"

"It's on your desk." Ascanio turned to Julie and mouthed, "Bitch."

Just couldn't let it alone, could he?

"Is it me or does it smell in here?" Julie waved her hand in front of her nose.

Oh no, she didn't. Accusing a shapeshifter of reeking was the ultimate insult.

"You're so dirty, Ascanio." Julie grimaced. "Be careful, you might get fleas if you keep going this way."

Ascanio bared his teeth at her. "Be careful you don't get lice. They'll shave you bald."

Julie rolled her eyes. "It's not necessary to shave your head if you have lice. You simply use a solution containing an extract of pyrethrin or any other of the wide variety of antilice herbal compounds and then comb the lice out. Your ignorance is staggering. I sometimes wonder how you survived to sixteen years of age. I'm curious, did you live most of them in Bubble Wrap?"

That kid sounded more and more like Kate every day.

"I had no idea you knew so much about lice," Ascanio bit back. "Speaking from experience?"

"Yes, I am. I lived on the street for a year. Remind me, where did you live?" Julie tapped her finger to her lips, pretending to think. "Ah yes, you lived in a religious commune, sheltered and coddled, where you spent your time trying to nail anything that moved—"

That's enough of that. "Quiet!" I barked.

Two mouths clicked shut.

I looked at the check. It was a business check from "Gloria's Art and Antiques." Antiques. Why would an antique dealer visit a reclamation company unless she knew that they were bidding on a building that contained a vault full of antiques? Reclamation companies didn't deal in antiques; they dealt in metal and stone. Not much else survived a fallen building.

"Here's the address." Ascanio handed me a piece of paper. "I looked it up."

"Thank you. Very nice of you." I looked at the address. White Street, Julie's old neighborhood. Right on the edge of the Warren, a poor part of Atlanta where beggars, gangs of homeless kids, and small-time criminals of opportunity made their home. Most of them wouldn't know what "antiques" meant, let alone buy them. This case was getting stranger and stranger.

"Please don't leave me here with her," Ascanio murmured.

I looked at him. "Did Kate tell you to stay put?"
"Yes."
"Then stay put. Study your epic, get yourself straightened out, and I'll take you with me next time."

I turned and walked out of there before he did any more begging.

White Street received its name when an unnatural snowfall covered it with two feet of pristine powder. The snow refused to melt for a couple of years and most residents had decided that discretion was the better part of valor. If a street's magic could sustain two feet of snow in the middle of the scorching Atlanta summer, there was no telling what else it could do. By the time the snow finally melted, most of the people living in its buildings had fled. As I drove down the crumbling pavement, the abandoned houses stared at me with dark rectangles of empty windows, like the black holes of a skull's orbits. If I wasn't a seasoned former member of law enforcement, I'd admit that the place gave me the creeps, turn my vehicle around, and drive away screaming like a little girl.

Gloria's Art and Antiques occupied a large rectangular building. The front facade was a typical two-story brick affair, but the structure extended from the street, over a city-block deep. Enough space there to warehouse a lot of antiques. Or a small herd of tanks. Or some vicious magical elephants . . .

I checked my Sig-Sauers and tried the door. Unlocked. I swung it open. A little bell chimed with a silvery tone as I stepped inside. In front of me, a narrow room stretched, framed by twin glass counters. The floor was polished wood, the counters glass and steel, the walls a silvery gray. The whole place was the exact antithesis of antique.

The air smelled of jasmine, not the purified scent of the perfume, but real jasmine: dark, slightly narcotic, with a hint of indole. There was something ancient and savage in that scent and it set my teeth on edge.

I walked over to the counter on the right and examined the contents of the glass case. A magnifying glass with an ornate metal handle. A metal toy car with faded, half-peeled-off green paint. A small round box filled with blue and white glass beads. A cheap pocket watch. Some coins, an assortment of beat-up knives, a set of antique glasses, dark red at the bottom and gold-yellow on top, a glass punch bowl with a grape pattern on the side and an odd yellow patina . . . This was crap. You could find pricier stuff at a flea market. Did she have a warehouse full of this junk?

A tall woman strode from the depths of the store. She wore a brown and beige suit. Her light brown hair was coiled into a complex arrangement on her head. Her eyes behind black-rimmed glasses were dark and calm. Neat, trim, professional.

"Hello," she said. "Can I help you find anything?"

"Hi. Are you Gloria?"

"Yes." The woman nodded.

"My name is Andrea Nash," I said. "I'm investigating a multiple homicide on one of the Pack's business sites."

Gloria stepped behind the left counter and walked toward the door. I had to turn to keep facing her.

"Multiple homicides?"

She was up to something. "Yes."

"Who was killed?" Gloria set a large plastic bin onto the counter.

"Some shapeshifters. They were employees of a reclamation company."

"That sounds tragic." Gloria offered me a smile. "But I don't know what it has to do with me."

She stood, one hand on the bin, her muscles tense. Normally I'd make slow circles around her, pulling the evidence out of her a little at a time, but she was too keyed up for that. Strategic decision time. Anapa was likely after the ceremonial knife. She could be, too. She could be working for him even.

I took a gamble. "Give me the knife, Gloria."

She hurled the contents of the bin at me. I ducked right, but not fast enough. A clump of ribbons hit me in the chest and fell apart into two dozen slithering cords around my feet.

Snakes.

The blistered bodies of Raphael's crew flashed before me. Getting bitten meant death. I jumped up and to the right, trying to put some distance between me and the knot of terrified snakes, landed on the clear floor, and drew my Sigs. Behind me a heavy metal grate slammed in place over the door.

Trapped.

I spun and saw Gloria crouching on the counter. What the hell now?

Gloria opened her mouth. Her jaws unhinged and the mandible split in half, opening even wider. Her lips curled back, baring her teeth and turning her face into a grotesque mask. Twin fangs slid from the recesses in her gums, above her human canines.

Whoa.

Gloria crouched down.

"Don't!" I barked. I couldn't get bitten and I needed her alive, because whatever she knew would die with her.

Gloria jumped. It wasn't a martial arts kick. She just leaped at me like there were springs in her legs, mouth open, fangs exposed.

I fired. Two shots bit into her stomach, the third and fourth took her in the chest, and then she crashed into me. Her hands crushed my arms, pinning them to my sides. Four bullets and she hadn't even slowed down. She should've been dead or bleeding.

I tried to rip my arms free, but she clamped me down, her hands like steel pinchers, and bit down, aiming for my throat. Hell, no. I smashed my forehead into her face. She reeled back, her nose a broken mess of red tissue. I ripped my left arm out of her grip, the second Sig still in my fingers. Gloria bit my right arm, puncturing the skin straight through my shirt, and I put the Sig to her ear and pumped three rounds into her skull.

Blood sprayed the floor, littering it with chunks of brain tissue and shattered skull bone. Gloria sagged down and crumpled by my feet.

Well, that had gone great. Gloria and her secrets were dead, and I'd gotten myself bitten and was about to join her. How in the world had this gone wrong?

My arm burned. I ripped my sleeve off carefully, keeping my right arm still. A single puncture marked my arm near the elbow—she had only gotten one fang in, but one was enough. The tissue around the bite had turned bright red. The beginning of a swelling stretched the skin to hot hardness.

If Raphael's people were any indication, I had minutes before the venom killed me.

The best method to prevent the spread of snake venom came from Australia and involved applying a broad tight bandage, complete with a sling and a splint to my arm. The venom had to move through the body through the lymphatic system before entering the bloodstream. The idea was to compress the tissue, preventing the lymph from moving to and from an injured limb.

I couldn't bandage myself without moving my affected arm, and even then I couldn't do it right and tight enough. All I could do was apply a tourniquet and hope my arm and I survived.

I pulled gauze from my pocket and bound my arm above the bite site, cutting off the flow of blood and lymph to my arm. It would have to do.

Gloria was still very dead on the floor. The rational, collected part of me took over. One, Gloria had giant fangs. Two, she was venomous. Three, she was connected to a reclamation company that bid on Raphael's building. If she wasn't part of the posse that had killed Raphael's people, she'd definitely met them for brunch. I finally had my lead, except I was dying. If the venom finished me off, the cops would never release the crime scene to the Pack. I wasn't an official member, and I wasn't registered as a shapeshifter with the city, which made this crime scene fall into the jurisdiction of PAD. The Pack, and whoever would take over the investigation after me, would not get a crack at any evidence Gloria's body offered. I had to preserve whatever evidence I could.

I took out the Polaroid camera from the pocket on my belt, pulled the woman's lip back, and took a shot. The camera printed the photograph. I flipped it over, wrote "Property of Jim Shrapshire" on it, stuck it inside my shirt, and slid the camera back. If I died, the cops would find it and ask Jim about it, which would mean he would see it and make his own conclusions. Here's hoping I hadn't just killed myself.

I walked across the floor toward the phone. A couple of snakes struck at my combat boots as I walked past, but none of them connected. I reached over and pressed the lever on the wall, raising the metal grate over the door, climbed up on the counter to get out of their range, picked up the phone, and dialed the office.

"Cutting Edge!" Julie chirped into the phone.

"Give that to me," Ascanio growled.

"This is Andrea. Put me on speaker."

"Done," Julie said.

"Listen to me very carefully. I'm at Gloria's Antiques on White Street. I've been bitten by a poisonous snake, probably a viper, the same kind that killed Raphael's people. I'm dying. Call the paramedics, give them Gloria's address, tell them to bring antivenom. Next, call Doolittle and repeat what I just told you. Then call Jim and tell him the same thing. Tell him the paramedics have been called. Do not open the door of the office to anyone except Kate. Do you understand me?"

"Yes," Julie said, her voice flat.

"Good." I hung up.

My metabolism was probably twice as fast as that of a normal human. The faster the metabolism, the faster the spread of venom through the body. I had to keep calm. The more I worried, the more I moved and the faster I would die.

I lay flat. Below me snakes slid around on the floor, their scales making the faintest of whispers against the floorboards. My arm burned. My forehead felt clammy. Sweat broke out along my hairline. Nausea came, squirming from my stomach into my throat.

I concentrated on breathing. In and out. Calm.

In.

Out.

I would survive this. No final thoughts, no regrets, no worrying about things I should've said and done. I would survive this.

In.

Out.

I wanted to run outside, to jump into my car, and drive myself to the emergency room. I would be riding to my death.

In.

Out.

I tasted metal in my mouth.

In.

Out.

A fever started, burning slowly just under my skin.

In.

Out.

I can do this. I will survive this. I will get justice for the four families. I will resolve things with Raphael. I have too much to live for.

I just had to not move.

My breath was coming in short gasps. So much for my calm breathing. I didn't want to die.

The pain pierced my chest. My heart fluttered. I was hot, so very hot . . .

A man in firefighter yellow busted through the door and swore. "Snakes! There are fucking snakes in here!"

I closed my eyes.

"Run that by me again?" Detective Collins, a tall, fit, Caucasian man in his early forties, leaned toward me. "She jumped at you and you shot her four times in half a second?"

"Yes." I shifted inside the blanket the paramedics had wrapped me in. I was sitting in the chair, by the counter from which Gloria had leaped at me. The first responders sank fifteen vials of antivenom into my body and when that didn't quite do the trick gave me five more. My head swam and I felt cold and clammy. Any other time I'd be miserable, but now being sick and woozy just confirmed that I was alive.

"What happened next?"

"She grew fangs and bit me."

"With her fangs?"

"Yes."

Detective Tsoi, a dark-haired Asian female in her late thirties, arched her pretty eyebrows at me. "So would you say she was like a snake?"

I looked at her. Behind Tsoi, Animal Control packed the last of the snakes into bins.

"I just want to be sure that we're on the same page," Tsoi said. "Are we talking about snake people?"

"Yes."

Tsoi and Collins looked at each other.

"Everybody knows there is no such thing as reptilian shapeshifters," Collins said.

"I didn't say she was a shapeshifter." And that wasn't strictly true either. There were reptilian shapeshifters; they just weren't the product of Lyc-V.

Tsoi pondered me. "Your file says you were discharged from the Order due to post-traumatic stress. You failed your psych eval?"

"I'm not crazy." My head hurt and I still wanted to vomit. Every word was like a hammer to my head.

"Nobody says you are," Collins said. "Nobody even mentioned the c-word."

I took a deep breath, trying to keep what little liquid was left in my stomach from geysering out. They knew I was weak and they were trying to squeeze everything they could out of me, hoping I'd slip up. I didn't blame them. In their place, I would've done the same thing. Get as much as you can while you can. They'd Mirandized me the moment I was conscious, which meant I was detained and this wasn't a routine conversation.

"She isn't crazy," the ME said, straightening from where he was examining the corpse. "Got two retractable fangs here. Also something going on with her temporomandibular joint. Look at this." He pulled Gloria's lower jaw down. Her mouth gaped, not quite as wide as the maw of a snake, but far wider than any human skull had a right to open.

"Snake people." Collins stared at him. "You've got to be shitting me."

The ME spread his arms. "Hey, I call them like I see them. I tell you fangs and a jaw that opens one hundred degrees. You can draw your own conclusions from there."

"Isn't there some sort of a cult who thinks there are secret snake people?" Tsoi said.

"No, those are Reptilians," the ME said. "They're supposed to be more like lizards."

"I shot her four times," I said. "It didn't even faze her."

"EnGarde Deluxe," the ME said. "Tactical concealed bulletproof vest. She was wearing one under her jacket."

Well. That explained a few things.

Collins heaved a sigh and turned to me. "What are you doing here?"

Three days ago I would have cooperated, out of habit, and because I was hardwired by the Order to play nice with the PAD. But now I was playing for the Pack's team and I would sit here and keep my mouth shut, until they sent in my backup, hopefully in the form of a lawyer. "No comment."

Collins fixed me with a heavy stare. "Don't tell me you drove all the way to White Street to go shopping."

"No comment."

"Seriously? You're seriously going to do this?" He sounded personally offended.

"Yes."

Collins shook his head. Tsoi arranged her face into a sympathetic expression. "Listen, all of us here know that this is connected to the four murders on your ex-boyfriend's reclamation site. Level with us. We're all good guys here. We're all on the same side."

These two were good. It had been less than two hours since the PAD uniformed cops, who had shown up right after the paramedics, had detained me at the crime scene. Collins and Tsoi, who had appeared half an hour ago, already knew who I was. They knew my job history, they knew my connection to Raphael, and they were obviously sore about losing the case of Raphael's crew to the Pack's jurisdiction. I bet they were the responding detectives to that crime scene.

I understood their frustration. Four murders in the middle of the city—of shapeshifters, no less, who were stronger and faster than most—didn't sit well with the general public. It's not that we were popular, but if this unknown threat could take on four shapeshifters at once, an average Joe didn't stand a chance. People tended to panic easily nowadays, and the PAD was feeling less than pleased about being locked out of the investigation.

"Come on, Nash," Collins said. "Help us out here. What were you doing here?"

"No comment."

They stared at me. I knew that stare. I had given it myself a few times. It said, "We got you and you're not leaving, but we're willing to listen and if you just talk to us, all of this will go away."

Laymen think cops are stupid. They see some guy with a bulldog face and assume that he's dumb and they can talk their way out of whatever trouble they got themselves into. But that bulldog-faced cop has a degree, three hundred homicide investigations under his belt, and over three thousand hours in the interrogation room. You're not winning that fight. If you just stopped and thought about it, you'd keep your mouth shut.

But when you're put on the spot, you want to explain your side of the story. You want someone to understand, you want sympathy, and you want to get out from under that stare.

Explaining yourself is a powerful urge. I'd seen people who knew better, attorneys, experienced cops, and even knights of the Order crack under pressure and say stupid things just to explain themselves. I would not be following their example.

"Nash, don't bullshit me. Do I need to define obstruction of justice to you?"

"No comment."

"Andrea, not another word." A lithe, muscular man shouldered his way to us, moving like an acrobat: graceful, sure, and weightless. He was on the near side of thirty, handsome, with green eyes and sharp features. His short hair, bright orange-red, had been brushed straight up and spiked, standing up like needles on a frightened hedgehog. Barabas. Technically, he was a member of Clan Nimble, but he'd grown up in Clan Bouda. He was Kate's adviser on the Pack's law and from what Raphael had told me, nasty and vicious in a fight.

"Perhaps I need to define obstruction of justice for you, Detective." Barabas's face took on a dangerously focused expression. "'Obstruction of justice' is an attempt to interfere with administration and due process of the law. To be guilty of obstruction of justice, a person must knowingly and willfully obstruct or hinder a law enforcement officer in the lawful discharge of his official duties by violence, destruction of evidence, bribery, corruption, or *deceit*. Note the emphasis on deceit. Therefore, to charge my client with 'obstruction,' you must prove that my client has been deceitful. My client isn't lying. She's refusing to answer, as is her right under the Constitution, which, the last time I checked, was still the supreme law of this land. But nice try."

Wow. I had hoped for some backup, but Jim had sent the big guns and Air Support.

The ME waved at Barabas. Barabas waved back. "Hey, Mitchell. Long time, no see."

"Who are you?" Tsoi demanded.

"Barabas Gilliam." A business card materialized in Barabas's long elegant fingers. "I'm her attorney."

Tsoi glanced at the card. "You're a Pack lawyer. What are you doing here?"

"Working." Barabas grinned, displaying sharp white teeth. "You see, even us dirty Pack lawyers have to pass the bar just like everyone else. If you check, you'll find that I'm a member in good standing. I'm licensed to practice law in the lovely State of Georgia and several of her illustrious neighbor states, which means Ms. Nash can hire me to represent her."

Tsoi pointed at me. "Is she a member of the Pack?"

"No, Ms. Nash is a private citizen, who has retained my services. Now I do make it a point to keep up with current legislation, but perhaps I missed something—is there a new law that states a Pack attorney can't practice outside the Pack? If so, thank you ever so much for bringing it to my attention, Detective."

"You think this is some sort of comedy going on here?" Collins gave him his tough stare.

A little red spark flared in Barabas's eyes. "Excuse me."

He struck with preternatural quickness and yanked a five-foot snake from the counter, an inch away from Tsoi's elbow. Tsoi jumped, clearing half the room in a single bound.

The snake body flailed in my lawyer's fist. Barabas jerked the snake to his mouth and bit its neck.

"Jesus Christ!" Collins took a step back.

Tsoi clamped her hand over her mouth.

Barabas spat the head onto the counter. "Pit viper—my favorite. Where were we? Ah, yes. You were trying to intimidate me. I apologize for the interruption. Please, resume your staring."

"That snake is evidence," Collins growled.

"I would be happy to surrender it to you. Considering that I just saved your partner from being bitten, I had expected more gratitude."

Barabas offered the headless snake back to Collins. The detective grimaced and took it.

"What sort of shapeshifter are you?" Tsoi demanded.

"He's a weremongoose," the ME told them.

Barabas smiled at me. "We're leaving."

"No, you're not!" Tsoi said.

"You can't hold her. All of us here know that. But just to be sure, let's review the facts," Barabas said. "My client, a poor defenseless woman . . ."

Collins almost choked on his own spit.

". . . who came here to browse the merchandise of this shop, was attacked by a monster and killed her in self-defense. She will not be speaking to you any further, because, as we all know, anything she says to you can and will be used against her in a court of law; however, as 801(d)(2)(a) tells us, none of it can be used to help her, because anything she utters to you is hearsay. So speaking to you is of no benefit to her, whatsoever." Barabas turned to me. "Can you walk?"

"Maybe," I told him. "I haven't tried."

Barabas picked me up, like I weighed nothing. "Will there be anything else, Detectives?"

"She isn't Pack, so don't even think of claiming this is a Pack scene," Tsoi growled.

"Wouldn't dream of it." Barabas strode out of the door and into the sunshine.

He walked down the street. "I parked on the side so they couldn't block me in. It's a fun tactic they use—they'll park behind you and try to grill you while they take their sweet time moving their vehicle. Are you okay?"

I nodded. I was so happy to be out of there. "Barabas, if you weren't batting for the other team, I'd marry you."

He grinned. "If I weren't batting for the other team, I would accept your proposal. You had me at 'No comment.' If all my clients were this smart, my life would be much easier. Much, much easier."

He paused by a Pack Jeep, opened the passenger door, and carefully loaded me inside.

"Where are we going?"

"To your office. It's closer than your apartment and better fortified. Doolittle is already there and he's awaiting your arrival with all sorts of needles and torture devices."

"Great," I murmured.

"He's very excited. It will be fun," Barabas promised and started the engine.

As we pulled out of the parking lot, my stomach pirouetted inside me. "You won't tell anyone about carrying me, will you?"

"It'll be our special secret," he said.

"Thanks."

CHAPTER 10

❖

Doolittle was a very nice man. He looked to be in his early fifties, although he was probably older—shapeshifters lived longer and looked younger than most regular people. His skin was dark, almost blue-black; silvery gray salted his short dark hair; he spoke in a soft voice with a soothing Southern accent; and the glasses he insisted on wearing combined with a slightly absent-minded look in his eyes made him resemble a kindly college professor, someone who specialized in history or anthropology and spent his life in an office full of books. You half expected him to sit you down to have a heart-to-heart about some long-forgotten civilization and reassure you that really a B on your paper wasn't so bad.

However, the moment any kind of injury, no matter how trivial, manifested itself, Doolittle turned into a stubborn, disagreeable tyrant, who treated you like you were six years old. He served as the Pack's medmage. He set broken bones, he removed silver and other foreign objects, he sewed up wounds, and generally spent his every waking minute making sure that the shapeshifters of the Pack remained breathing. And he went about it with the dogged persistence that made his animal counterpart so famous. If there were any laws of nature, one of them surely said that arguing with a honeybadger was futile.

The second I stepped across the threshold, Doolittle placed me into a chair. He drew my blood and examined the bite site on my foot and the bigger one on my shoulder, which had acquired a plum-purple swelling. Barabas recounted the scene, while Julie and Ascanio hovered in the background, quiet like two mice.

"Pit vipers?" Doolittle asked, checking my eyes.

"Appears so. At least the one I caught was. Not a rattle-snake, though." Barabas shrugged. "Three-inch fangs."

"Nauseous?" Doolittle asked me.

"Yes." I was still sweating, too. The sweat drenched my face and my back, clammy and cold, and my heart was beating too fast. The bite on my arm hadn't sealed itself either. That was a bad sign. Lyc-V closed most wounds in minutes.

Someone pounded on the office door. Barabas moved to the door, slid aside the metal shutter covering the narrow spy window, and looked through it.

"It's your lover man."

"Barabas, open the damn door," Raphael snarled.

Barabas slid the shutter closed. "Do you want me to let him in?"

"I'm thinking about it."

Barabas slid the shutter open. "She's thinking about it."

"Andrea," Raphael called. "Let me in."

"The last time I saw you two together, you were so happy," Barabas said. "Just out of curiosity, Raphael, how the hell did you manage to fuck that up?"

Raphael's voice gained that dangerous, I'm-about-to-go-nuts quality. "Remind me, how are things with you and Ethan?"

"None of your business," Barabas said.

"Let me in and I won't rip your head off."

"You won't rip my head off anyway," Barabas said. "We're friends."

"Let him in," I said. If we didn't let him in, he wouldn't go away. He would just stand by the door and him and Barabas would yell obscenities at each other. My head hurt enough as it was.

Barabas swung the door open, and Raphael marched in. He saw me and turned pale.

"Don't agitate her," Doolittle warned.

"Wouldn't dream of it." Raphael pulled up a chair and sat next to me.

Doolittle shined a light into my eyes, listened to my heart-beat, and thrust a glass of some murky liquid into my hand. "Drink this."

I took a tiny sip. It tasted like someone had mixed kerosene with turpentine. "This is awful."

Doolittle peered at me through his glasses. "Now, young lady, you will drain that glass. If I can drop everything and rush over here, at the very least you can repay me for my kindness by taking your medicine."

I gulped the drink. It burned my throat and I coughed. "Doc, you're trying to kill me . . ."

"Drink a bit more," Raphael said.

I pointed at him. "You heard what the medic said. Don't agitate me."

I bravely took another swallow of the nasty stuff, trying to force it down and keep it there.

"Very good," Doolittle approved. "I seem to recall that I warned you not to confront that snake."

"The snake confronted me. That is, the woman with snake fangs confronted me."

"If you finish the whole glass, I'll give you a lollipop."

There was something deeply absurd about this entire conversation. "Stop treating me like a child."

"I will if you take ownership of your predicament and take your medicine." Doolittle looked at Barabas. "I don't suppose you saw the snake woman in question?"

Barabas shook his head. "The second I walked in, the ME blocked her head."

"Such a shame."

I took another gulp—I'd never tasted anything more vile; I'd drink warm milk with baking soda before this stuff—and pulled the Polaroid out of my bra.

"Here."

Raphael took the Polaroid out of my fingers and handed it to Barabas without a word.

My lawyer's eyes widened. "Why does it say 'Property of Jim Shrapshire' on it?"

"Because that's Jim's real name."

"That doesn't explain anything," Barabas said.

"If I died, the PAD would claim the scene and the Pack would be locked out of the investigation. There was a good chance that they wouldn't let the Pack examine Gloria's body. But when they found the Polaroid on my body, they would show it to Jim and ask him about it. He would know to look for her known associates with retractable fangs."

"You were bitten and your priority was to take pictures?" Barabas said.

"Don't agitate her," Raphael told him.

"It seemed important at the time."

Barabas looked at Raphael. "How do you put up with that?"

"Job first. That's the way she's wired," Raphael told him.

Doolittle emitted a long-suffering sigh. "You know snake-bite emergency procedures. You can't even claim ignorance. This was just willful disregard of your life, that's exactly what that was."

The weremongoose and the werehoneybadger peered at the photograph.

"Folded fangs," Barabas said. "Like a rattlesnake."

"Or a saw-scaled viper." Doolittle frowned. "What is this world coming to?"

"What's so special about a saw-scaled viper?" I asked.

"It's a fun little snake," Barabas said. "Small, bad-tempered, active after dark. You walk by it, it bites you, you think nothing of it. Twenty-four hours later you develop spontaneous internal bleeding. Kills more people than any other snake species in Africa. It's also delicious and has a tangy aftertaste."

I drank my nasty medicine and connected the dots for them: Garcia Construction, drag marks of a towed vehicle, mechanic, check with Gloria's name on it, and Gloria attacking me when I mentioned the knife.

"So it is the knife we saw when we broke in to Anapa's office," Raphael said.

Barabas stuck his fingers in his ears. "Lalalala, I'm not hearing anything about any break-in."

"Yes," I told Raphael. "They're all after it."

He frowned.

I finished the last of the medicine and put the glass on the table. "I want my lollipop. I've earned it."

Doolittle reached into his bag and offered me a choice: grape, watermelon, or orange. No-brainer. I took the watermelon and stuck it in my mouth. "So why does she have fangs?"

"It's some sort of magic augmentation," Doolittle said. "Perhaps it's a creature we've never seen before."

"Her fang span is similar to the bite wounds on Raphael's employees."

Doolittle nodded. "Similar, but unfortunately we can't know for sure, because we don't have her head."

"Also, there were multiple bites of varying sizes on their bodies," I said.

"Which means her friends are still at large," Raphael finished.

"People walking around with venomous fangs," I interrupted. "How is that even possible?"

Doolittle glanced at me with a wry smile. "How is it possible that we grow fur, fangs, and claws?"

Touché.

Doolittle checked my blood in the test tube and took a fat leather roll from his bag. "The blood coagulation is still abnormal." He unrolled the leather kit on my desk. Odd metal instruments gleamed, each in a neat leather pocket. It looked like the kind of toolkit a medieval torturer would carry around. Doolittle's hand paused over the scalpel.

"You're going to cut me, aren't you?"

Doolittle nodded. "That purple swelling on your arm is the accumulation of dead Lyc-V combined with trapped venom. We must purge it from your system. Do you remember how to push silver from your body?"

"Yes." Not something you'd forget.

Doolittle pulled up a chair and sat next to me so our eyes were level. "I need to make a cut on your arm and insert a needle into the muscle affected by the bite. The needle is made of a silver alloy."

It would hurt. Oh yes. It would hurt like hell.

Raphael reached over and covered my hand with his.

"We must give it a few minutes for your body to react," Doolittle said. "Then I want you to concentrate on pushing the needle out. This will stimulate blood and lymph flow to the wound and expel the poison. If we purge the poison, your chances of survival will be significantly higher."

The tiny hairs on the back of my neck stood on their ends. I was tired, so tired, and my body felt like it had been beaten with a sack of rocks. The mere thought of silver needles made me want to cringe.

"You can do it," Raphael said. "Stop being a baby about it."

"Screw you."

"That's right," he said. "Come on, tough guy. Show me what you've got."

I clenched the chair's armrests. "Do it."

Raphael put his hands on my right shoulder, pinning me to the chair. Barabas clamped me from the left.

Doolittle took a scalpel. His hand flashed, too quickly to see. Pain stung me, quick and sharp. Black blood gushed from the wound, and Doolittle wiped it with gauze. "This will sting."

A white-hot needle thrust into my arm. My entire body screamed in alarm. It felt like someone had bored a hole in my muscle and poured molten metal into it.

"Hold it in," Doolittle told me, his voice gentle. "You're doing wonderful. Wonderful. Hold it. A little longer . . ."

I growled and clawed at the armrest with my left hand. Barabas held me tight.

"Did you like my message on the table?" Raphael asked.

"Loved it," I ground out through clenched teeth. "I'll have to repay the favor later."

The pain grew and grew, inflaming my arm. I shuddered, my limbs shaking.

"Don't change shape," Doolittle said. "You're doing fine. You're doing very well. Just a little bit more. Hold on for me, Andrea."

The pain ate its way through my muscle all the way to the bone and scraped it with sharp serrated teeth. I snarled.

"Aaalmost there," Doolittle crooned. "Almost."

"We got you," Barabas told me. "We got you."

I couldn't take it. I couldn't take another second. My body twisted, looking for a way to escape. Faint spots appeared on my skin.

"Don't change shape," Raphael snapped.

"Shut up."

"Be good or I'll kiss you in front of everybody."

"Hell no," I snarled. I had to hold on and live through this so I could punch him in the face. It was a great goal.

"Hold on," Doolittle told me. "Ten more seconds."

Aaah. It hurts. It hurts, hurrts, hurrrrrts . . .

"Expel," Doolittle's voice snapped.

I concentrated every ounce of my will on the pain.

Heat spread through me, combing through my flesh with spiked fingers.

Get out of my body. Get the hell out!

The needle shivered.

I cried out.

"Expel it," Doolittle urged.

"You can do it," Barabas told me.

I pushed. The needle slid free and scalding-hot blood gushed down my arm. It ran gray, purple, and then finally bright red. Raphael let go of my arm and I punched him in the chest. It was the closest part of him.

"Good girl." Doolittle exhaled. "Well done."

I wiped tears from my eyes and saw Ascanio. He stared at me. His eyes were huge and terrified.

"Let that be a lesson to you," Doolittle told him. "Don't get bitten. Bring the meat from the refrigerator. Andrea needs to eat."

It's amazing how much good a sandwich, or three, can do for you. My head had stopped spinning and I no longer felt like my legs wouldn't support me. I eyed the dwindling ham, from which Julie had carved the meat for my sandwiches. No more food would physically fit into my stomach, but I was still hungry.

Doolittle set a small plastic box down in front of me and flipped open the top. Six small ampoules in a neat row.

"Antivenom," he said and showed me a gun-looking object. "One ampoule goes in here. Once you hear a click, press it against the skin and pull the trigger. Not for use on humans. It is in the form of a gun, so you should have no difficulties using it."

An antivenom gun—load, press, squeeze the trigger. Okay, I could do that.

"Unfortunately, that is all I can do until I know more," Doolittle said. He leaned closer and looked into my eyes. "I strongly advise against any physical activity for the next twenty-four to forty-eight hours. Nothing strenuous. No sexual relations, no running, and no fighting. Do you understand me?"

"Perfectly."

"I'm not naive enough to think that you'll heed my advice."

"I solemnly swear to heed at least one-third of it. No sexual relations won't be a problem."

Barabas laughed under his breath.

Doolittle shook his head. "Should you feel faint, you *will* take another dose of antivenom and you *will* lie down."

"Yes, sir."

Doolittle shook his head again and went to pack up his tools. Barabas stepped into his place and leaned against my desk, his arms folded over his chest. "As your attorney, I'm forced to advise you to stay away from that crime scene. We both know you won't, but if you get caught, there will be repercussions."

"Thank you for the warning." Now I had advice from both a doctor and a lawyer. I tried to fight a yawn, but it won. "I'll definitely take it under consideration."

I had to go back to the scene. Everyone in the room knew it.

"Also, you won't like hearing this, but as a lawyer, I'm used to that. Your position with the Pack is muddy. This makes things a hell of a lot more complicated than they have to be. Sort yourself out."

Settle things with the woman who sent two boudas to beat the crap out of me. Right.

Barabas looked at Julie. "Please get your bag. We're going back to the Keep."

Julie crossed her arms. "But . . ."

"Julia," Barabas said calmly. "Please get your bag."

Julie stomped to the kitchen and returned with her backpack.

My eyes were apparently producing glue instead of moisture, because I had trouble keeping them open. "Take Ascanio with you, too," I said. The boy was looking really rattled.

"No," Raphael said.

I turned to him. "You don't get to give orders here."

"I'm still his alpha. Ascanio or me, one of us will stay here with you and stand guard while you sleep. Gloria is dead and now her friends and relations might be looking for you. You can barely keep your eyes open. I don't care how good this door is, you need someone awake and alert in case they show up. That can be Ascanio if you prefer, but I'm more than happy to lie in the bed with you and hold you while you sleep. It's your choice."

There came a point in everyone's life when they were just too tired to argue. I opened my mouth and realized I had hit that point. If they weren't gone in the next half minute, I'd fall asleep sitting up. "I'll take the kid."

Ascanio blinked. Julie stomped on his foot as she passed him and he elbowed her in the ribs.

"Call me if anything," Barabas told me.

"Sure."

A moment later and both the lawyer and the doctor were gone. Raphael and I looked at each other.

"Go away," I told him.

"For now," he said. "I'll be back."

"I won't let you through the door."

"We'll see about that." Raphael turned to Ascanio. "Guard her."

"Yes, Alpha."

He walked out. Ascanio locked and barred the door behind him.

I pondered whether it was worth it to force myself upstairs to the bed or if I should just lie down on the nice comfortable wooden floor. My dignity won. I was a badass, God damn it. I could take twelve stairs. I'd kick their ass.

I dragged myself to the upstairs cot and collapsed face-down. I tried to take my shoes off, but the world slipped through my fingers before I had a chance to raise my head from my pillow.

"Andrea?" Ascanio whispered next to me.

I opened my eyes.

He was crouching by my cot. "I'm sorry to wake you up. My mother is outside the door. Can I let her in?"

"Of course you can let her in."

"Thanks."

He took off. I rubbed my eyes and sat up. The windup clock on the night table by the cot said seven p.m. Every cell in my body ached. Below, the bar clanged—Ascanio was opening the door. I forced myself upright, crossed the loft, and sat down on top of the stairs.

Ascanio swung the door open and stood aside. Martina came in. She had a rare look to her, a kind of regal beauty on the crossroads of severe and sensual, but not really leaning toward either. Her dark hair crowned her head in a braided updo coil. Her tan skin was flawless. Her features were large and boldly cut, and she held herself with great poise, so self-possessed with quiet confidence that people gravitated to her. Barabas called her Queen Martina. She wore jeans and an olive-colored blouse, but the nickname still fit.

Ascanio closed the door, locked it, and stood there awkwardly. I'd never seen him awkward before.

"How are you?" Martina reached over to touch his cheek, but stopped before the actual contact, as if she'd thought better of it.

"I'm good . . . Thank you."

"I brought you your favorite," she said, handing him a basket.

Ascanio took the towel off the basket and smiled. It was a shy little kid smile, so at odds with his teenage Don Juan persona, I almost did a double take.

"You should eat those," she said.

Ascanio glanced at me.

"It's okay," Martina said. "Go on. I'll visit with Andrea."

Ascanio took the basket, leaned over, and kissed his mother on the cheek. Then he turned and went into the kitchen.

Martina climbed the stairs and sat next to me.

"What's in the basket?" I asked.

"Cannoli," she said. "He really likes them."

And she had come all the way here, an hour from the Keep, just to bring them. Something wasn't quite right.

"Did Raphael ever tell you our story?" she asked.

"No." I knew that for some reason Ascanio hadn't lived with the clan for a while, but that was about it.

She nodded. "I was young and living in the Midwest. I wasn't bitten—I was born a bouda. My mother was a bouda also, my father was a werewolf. I had the best family, Andrea. I was so loved."

"What happened?" I asked. Funny, I thought that all her

self-assurance would create a distance, but she seemed so nice. Her voice just put me at ease.

"We had a flood," she said. "One of those insane freak floods that sometimes hits states like Iowa. The river swelled and took down our town. We were sitting on the roof, and my mother saw our neighbors floating by in the car, their kids in the backseat. The car was sinking and everyone was screaming. The car went under. My mother was stronger than my father, so she went in after it. She didn't come back. My dad dived in to get her out. He didn't come back either. I sat there on the roof and cried and screamed and screamed and begged God to let them come back, but there was nothing but muddy river."

I could picture her sitting on the roof, crying her eyes out. "That's awful."

"Thank you. My grandparents took me in, but it wasn't the same. I left as soon as I could and traveled around, doing odd jobs here and there, bouncing at bars, waitressing in diners. I was kind of wild. If a guy had nice eyes and nice biceps, I was game." She smiled, a little spark in her eyes. "Looking for love in all the wrong places. I had fun."

"Did you find Mr. Right?"

"I found many Misters Right-for-Now. None of them lasted very long. I didn't know it back then, because I was young and stupid, but the kind of great love I was looking for couldn't happen for me back then. I didn't even know what kind of person I wanted to be, let alone what I needed from a guy. But I wanted that love I lost, so I had this bright idea: I would get pregnant and have a baby. A baby would love me no matter what, because I'd be her mommy. We would be a little family together. It would be just like it was before."

"It's never like it was before."

"I know that now, but back then I was selfish and damaged, and very young. About that time I met Ascanio's father. John was gorgeous. Beautiful man. And a bouda like me. A little on the passive side, but he was kind and very proper. Seducing him was so much fun and once I did, he just did whatever I said. I was okay with being in charge. We were together for two months when I got pregnant. I was so happy. I told him and he cried."

"He cried? Like in joy?"

"More like in horror."

"Oh no."

Martina nodded. "Yes, that should have been a clue. Apparently John grew up in this religious cult worshipping some made-up god, and he had been sent out in the world for a year-long pilgrimage. He came to terms about 'sinning' with me—probably because I was very good at sinning and he liked it—but a child threw him for a loop. We couldn't have a child in sin, and he refused to marry me unless we went back and had his prophet do it. The catch was I'd have to sleep with said prophet to have my body purified."

"No," I said. "Screw that."

"That was my reaction. It's my body and I wouldn't be abused in this manner. It also let me know real quick that John wasn't good husband/father material. I told him he was free to hit the road. Me and my baby would be just fine. But John had a change of heart and stuck around. I should've twisted his head off right then, but silly me, I thought he had come about because he loved me. I went into labor. The hospital had never had a shapeshifter give birth before and mine was a long and terrible thing. Then I got to hold Ascanio and it was all worth it. He was so beautiful, I was reading this French book at the time about a sculptor and he had this ridiculously good-looking apprentice, whose name was Ascanio. I knew exactly what to name my baby. The hospital sedated me after that to let me rest. When I woke up, my beautiful baby was gone. John took him."

"He what?"

"He took him back to his cult. He left me a note, the slime. It said that he couldn't let his son be raised in sin, and since Ascanio was an innocent, he'd be taking him away, but I couldn't come, because I was tainted by our sin."

"I would have killed him. I would've murdered him right there."

"I tried," Martina said. "I looked for him for years. I was bitter and broken by then, and that's when Aunt B came across me. She was on a trip of some sort. I was, well, the proper term is fucked up. I hadn't shifted into my animal shape for years. Didn't seem like there was any point to it. It only brought me misery. She went after me. 'Come be with your own kind. You don't have to do anything. Just come, live with us for a bit, and if you don't like it, you're free to go.' Eventually I went with her. It didn't matter one way or another. So I came here and slowly, little by little, I thawed out. Then the call came. The cult's prophet decided my boy was too much competition and was mucking up his harem plans, so he called us to come and get him. We did."

"And John?"

"He'd died a while back. A good thing too, because I would've killed him. So you see it's difficult for us both," Martina said. "Ascanio never had a mother and I never had a son. We try the best we can and when we find something that can make one of us happy, we both sigh a little in relief. I make him cannoli and he buys me scented soap with his Cutting Edge money. I have two drawers full of it." A small happy smile lit up her face. "If you ever run out, you let me know. I've got enough to keep the whole Pack clean for a week."

I really liked her. I hadn't known I would, but I did. Still, things had to be said. "You didn't come here to tell me this story, did you?"

"No. I came here to talk about the clan and Aunt B."

"I don't mean to be rude," I said. "But there is nothing you can say to make me play ball with Aunt B. I won't go over there and I won't beg and scrape to be admitted into the clan, so I can be one of her girls and run her errands. That won't be happening. And I think it's cowardly of her to send you in for this talk. Enforcers didn't work, neither will you, so I wonder what her next move is going to be. How many will she send?"

"She didn't send me," Martina said. "My son did."

"Oh."

"Do you know what I do for the clan?" she asked.

"No."

"I'm a licensed therapist," she said. "I specialize in the areas of family therapy, anger and stress management, adolescent adjustment, and loss and grief counseling. I'm one of ten Pack counselors."

"I'm not in the Pack," I told her.

"I know." She smiled. "This is a freebie."

"I don't need therapy." It sounded hypocritical the moment

it left my mouth. "Okay, so maybe I do, but I don't . . . I don't know."

"This doesn't have to be a therapy session," she said. "This could be just the two of us talking. We could talk about Deb and Carrie and their conduct in your parking lot."

I stared at her. "How much did Ascanio tell you?"

"He didn't say anything about your past," she said. "Except that you have had a hard time, and there was abuse and it was bouda-related. He did want me to go to Aunt B and explain to her that boudas couldn't keep trespassing in your territory, because they would push you too far. In his words, 'They're trying to punk her in her own place.' He's worried you'll kill someone."

"He's right," I told her.

Martina took out a small recorder. "I made this for you."

She pressed the button. Aunt B's voice sounded from the tiny speaker.

". . . I said to go over there and find out what they talked about. I said to be slick about it. Did I say to rough anybody up?"

"No, ma'am," Carrie said quietly.

"So why would you take it upon yourselves to improvise?"

"We thought . . ." Deb started and fell silent.

"I wouldn't do so much of that, if I were you, dear. When you think, you end up with broken bones. Besides, it makes me so happy when you let me do your thinking for you. You do want to make me happy, don't you?"

"Yes ma'am," two female voices chorused.

"I'll explain things to you now, because I don't want you to feel left out. You thought that because Andrea is beastkin, you could easily dominate her. Andrea is a survivor. Never underestimate that. She learned to kill, she trained for it, and she's had practice. You fight for fun and dominance. She fights every battle as if it's for her life. If you attack her, she will pull you apart like a badly sewn dress. Andrea also understands how the forces that uphold human law work. And we all know how important that is, don't we?"

Another chorus. "Yes, ma'am."

"Do you understand now why she would be an asset to the clan?"

"Yes, ma'am."

I was an asset. That was news to me.

"I don't care if she is beastkin, elephant, or platypus, we need her. She's like a pine. She won't bend, she will only break. I've spent months trying to convince her that joining us was in her best interests and the two of you decided to throw a wrench into my plans."

"I'm so sorry," Carrie said.

"Me, too," Deb echoed.

"Go away and do try to stay away from me for a day or two, yes?"

"Yes ma'am."

The door closed. A terrible screech followed, the sound of metal being tortured.

"It was a very nice bookend," Martina's voice said.

"Well, now it's a very nice piece of junk," Aunt B said.

I glanced at Martina. "Was that an owl?" It was one of a gorgeous pair of bookends, metal and finished in pale bronze, with large amber Swarovski crystals for the eyes. Aunt B used them on her desk to keep the files from falling out of the file holder.

Martina stopped the recording and nodded. "She squeezed one in her hand. If you crushed a jelly doughnut in your fist, and the filling spilled out? That's what it looked like." She pushed the button.

"Did Ascanio say what Andrea and Raphael spoke about?" Aunt B asked.

"No. He did bring Rebecca there."

The recorder fell silent.

Aunt B sighed. "Why is it that we sacrifice and work so hard to keep our children from making our mistakes, and they insist on ignoring everything we say?"

"Probably because they are our children and at their age we ignored our parents also."

Aunt B sighed again. "Are you going to see her?"

"Yes."

"Will you tell me how it goes?"

"You know that anything she says to me is confidential," Martina said.

"I know. Just tell me if it's salvageable or not. We need her."

Martina shut off the recorder and put it down between us.

"This doesn't change anything," I told her.

Martina looked at me. "What's the alternative, Andrea? Where do you see this situation going? You slapped her, in public."

"She backhanded me down the stairs."

"That was a gentle love tap compared to what she could've done. You challenged her. She can't ignore you. You wouldn't, in her place."

No, I wouldn't. I would've gone after me. Quick, too.

"You can leave," Martina said.

"I'm not leaving. This is my home now. Why should I leave?"

"Then joining the Pack is your only choice. You can't be unattached, Andrea. It is our law and you are subject to it, because you are a shapeshifter. You are one of us."

I clenched my teeth. "I could fight her."

"You would lose. But suppose you won," Martina said. "Then what? I won't follow you, Andrea. You didn't fight beside me; you didn't prove to me that you deserve to lead. I don't know you and I don't trust you. If you succeeded and killed Aunt B, we would all gang up on you. I don't know where Raphael's allegiances would lie, but he would have to choose between the woman he loves and his family. It is a lousy choice to make."

"Raphael and I are at a complicated place."

"I don't doubt it. We're boudas, after all." Martina shrugged. "If a woman sees her boyfriend in a restaurant with another woman, she may march over and confront him there. She may wait and confront him later. But if a bouda sees another woman with her mate, she would throw her drink in his face, and then the table, and then perhaps an unlucky member of the restaurant staff if one happened to be nearby. We make dramatic statements, in fight and in love."

"Life would be easier without the drama," I told her.

"Not for us. We have to vent, Andrea. That's the way we're wired. But back to the clan. B's current second isn't fit to be in charge of the clan. She is beta, because nobody else wants the job and responsibility. We would be left leaderless and have to fight it out. Would you really be that selfish, Andrea?"

She was right. I wouldn't be. I didn't want to be governed by shapeshifter laws, and some long-forgotten teenage part of me wanted to stomp my feet and scream that it wasn't fair. But it was. A citizen of the country was subject to its laws, and while some people thought it was unfair, they still had to obey them. When they didn't, people like me arrested them.

I didn't want to be treated special because I was beastkin. But I was, because I had forced the situation into a corner, and now everyone was making special allowances for me.

What did I really have to lose by joining the clan? B was right, I did have the proper tools. I could join, take a position of responsibility, prove myself, and when the time came, I would take the boudas away from Aunt B.

I puzzled over this thought, turning it this way and that in my mind. "Logically I know you are right. Everything you said makes sense. But it feels like giving up somehow."

Martina nodded. "You feel like your hand is being forced, and you have to join the Pack not because you want to, but because you must to do it to survive. This is your home and you want to live here on your terms, not the Pack's."

"Yes."

"What is it you want to do in life, Andrea?"

I looked at her. I had no idea how to answer.

"Each of us selects a purpose," Martina said. "Mine is to help people heal themselves. What's yours?"

"I'm not sure," I told her.

Martina smiled. "Something to think about."

I was a shapeshifter. Nobody could take it away from me. Nobody could force me into early retirement and the boudas needed me. But I had no idea what my goal in life was. I had never thought about it in grand terms.

"Thank you for coming by," I said. "Will you tell Aunt B I will be visiting her in a day or two?"

Martina nodded. "I'll let her know."

I catnapped after Martina and Ascanio left and heard the phone ring through my sleep. By the time I made it downstairs, the answering machine had kicked in.

"Andi, it's me," Raphael said.

I stepped away from the phone.

"I went to see Garcia Senior," he said. "He says that they were approached by Gloria Dahl and asked to bid on Blue Heron. I thought maybe Gloria and Anapa were working together. It would make sense: he would put in a bid and she would put in the second-highest bid, so in case something went wrong with his bid, he'd still get the building. But Garcia said that Gloria's bid was almost eighty grand below mine, which would make it one hundred and fifteen thousand below Anapa's. Basically, she had no chance. If they were working together, their bids would be closer together. Anapa bid way too high and she bid way too low."

Huh. I could've sworn Gloria was Anapa's flunky. Well, showed what I knew.

"I hope you went home," Raphael said. "I'll be driving by later. Don't do anything stupid without me."

Don't do anything stupid without him. I wouldn't be doing anything with him, stupid or otherwise.

I checked the world outside the window. It was a few minutes past nine and the evening sky was vast and dark. Perfect.

I had to go back to Gloria's crime scene. It was highly likely that Gloria, whoever or whatever she was, and her pals must have murdered Raphael's people. That explained both the wide fang spawn and the location of the bite wounds. But I had no concrete proof. I didn't have access to Gloria's corpse, so I couldn't measure the exact distance between her fangs and I still didn't know where her associates were or what she was after.

I had a good suspicion that the knife in the photo that I'd seen in Anapa's office was involved. In fact, I was sure of it, but again I had to obtain evidence of that. I had to figure out what the knife was and what it was for, and the only way to shed light on this situation would be to break into the crime scene and I would have to do it alone. If I got caught, I'd be detained, but I was just a private citizen. If anyone from the Pack was detained with me, the matter would take on a completely different light.

Everything inside me hurt. I felt like I'd been chewed up by a beast with small sharp teeth. My bones felt so heavy, you'd think they were made of lead.

I didn't want to go anywhere. I just wanted to lie there and fall asleep so I wouldn't hurt anymore. But there were people dependent on me for answers and I wouldn't get those answers by taking time out to rest. Besides, with the magic down, now was the best time to search the room. Who knew how long technology would last?

Come on, Ms. Nash. Get your ass in gear.

I forced myself to sit up. Doolittle had said no physical activity, but time was of the essence. I'd just have to take it easy.

I drove to Pucker Alley two blocks from White Street and hid the car in the shadow of a ruin. A vast, cloudless sky stretched above me, and the night was gauzy with curtains of silvery moonlight. Just my luck. I grabbed my duffel bag out of the backseat and pulled it open. It held my emergency kit: matches in a plastic bag, gauze, antibiotic ointment, Band-Aids, knife, roll of duct tape, flask of alcohol, bottle of water, an MRE—a Meal Ready to Eat courtesy of the United States Army—spare knife, rope, gloves, hat, and a towel. I had once read a book that said a traveler should always have one and it made a lot of sense.

I slipped on the gloves, hid my hair under the hat, zipped the duffel, and set off.

My forehead immediately began to sweat under the cotton hat. Hats and muggy Atlanta spring didn't exactly play nice. But I'd suffer a little sweat to keep from leaving stray hairs at the scene to be found by PAD crime techs.

The street in front of Gloria's Antiques looked very much the same, deserted and foreboding. No sign of the cops' presence remained. I had figured as much. Atlanta was a busy city and the PAD was stretched thin. They'd likely resume processing the scene tomorrow.

My ears caught no close noises. White Street lay empty.

I approached the door. A large paper seal was plastered across the door and part of the door frame with a big red DO NOT ENTER on it. Most police departments didn't have the budget for the infamous yellow crime scene tape. Ninety percent of the time, a sticker was the only indication of sealed premises. It wasn't meant to physically prevent anyone from entering the scene. It was meant to give the cops proof of your intent to enter despite the seal.

I pulled my lock pick ring out of my vest pocket, sliced the sticker with the thicker pick, and slid it and its thinner twin into the lock.

One, two, three . . . *Click.*

I edged the door open, slipped through, and locked it behind me. The moonlight spilled through the windows, giving more than enough illumination to examine the scene where I had almost died. The snake woman was gone and so were the snakes. The dark smears of Gloria's blood still painted the floor. Beyond them, the back door waited for me. I walked past the stains along the counter. The cops had probably swept the scene, but I didn't want to contaminate it if they hadn't yet.

The back door had a serious look about it. I rapped my knuckles on the door. Steel. Large lock, with a few fresh-looking scratches across the metal. The PAD must've gotten a locksmith to pop it open. I tried the door handle. It turned easily in my hand. The door swung open, revealing darkness. I stepped inside, shut the door behind me, and slid my hand along the wall, groping for the light switch. My eyes did fine with little light, but this was complete blackness. No moonlight meant no windows, so nobody would see me.

The air smelled of jasmine, that same dark, entrancing, menacing scent I'd smelled before. My ears caught nothing. No sound troubled the silence except for my own breathing.

My fingers brushed the light switch. A row of recessed lights ignited in the ceiling. I stood in a long rectangular room. In front of me four rows of heavy-duty shelves stretched the length of the space, almost all the way to another door in the opposite wall. Odds and ends filled the shelves. A collection of beige stone spheres, ranging from the size of a grapefruit to as big as a basketball. A strange metal contraption with a tall metal rod in the center and two-feet-wide rings of metal threaded onto it. A dozen empty bottles, green, yellow, brown, and clear, were thrust through holes in rings, suspended upside down at an angle. A spear with a stylized metal flower for a guard. A lantern wrapped in chains. A fishing net hanging off a hook in the shelf. Clocks, a bust of a monkey carved from some dark wood, an ancient underwater helmet, a violin, an Egyptian cat next to brass scales, a Catholic priest's vestments with a purple stole . . . There was no rhyme or reason to it. No organization by type, no markings on the shelf.

A smorgasbord of junk, protected by an inch-thick metal door. That meant the junk was likely magic.

I squinted at the door in the opposite wall. A metal chain sealed it, locked with a heavy padlock. The PAD must've run out of time or experts, because from where I stood, the padlock didn't look touched. I tiptoed through the gap between two shelves toward the back room.

The padlock featured a little black wheel. Combination-based. Great.

I grasped the chain and pulled. Little black dots swam in front of my eyes. My nose felt wet, as if I was bleeding.

The metal gave with a tortured screech, and the links of the chain snapped.

I wiped my nose on my sleeve. No blood.

I pulled the chain out of the loops on the door and eased it open. A small office waited inside: a writing desk with a computer and a phone on it, shelves filled with files, and a tall glass cabinet. Inside the cabinet, a staff rested, caught between two metal hooks. It stood at least six and a half feet tall, its shaft of brown, aged wood polished to a smooth sheen. At about five feet high, the wood gave way to ivory that flared into a complex shape that seemed oddly familiar. A ferocious male face with a long mustache had been carved into the ivory, followed by rows of Cyrillic characters etched into the wood.

Cyrillic. I wondered how Roman was doing.

I moved to the desk and turned the computer on. It started with a quiet whirring. Code scrolled up on the screen, some sort of mathematical nonsense, and the log-in screen came on, requesting a password.

Let's see. "123456."

The PC beeped and the log-in refreshed with a warning in red. Denied.

"12345678"?

Another beep.

"Password."

Beep.

Okay, fine. How about "password1"?

The screen blinked and Windows booted up.

Heh. One of the most common passwords, right up there with "Jesus," "letmein," and "Iloveyou." I bet she'd thought she was brilliant.

I pulled up the recent documents. Two clicks and I stared at the picture of the knife from the photograph in Anapa's study.

I leaned back. Something was vitally important about this knife. If Raphael was right and Gloria and Anapa were two independent players, that knife had to be truly something special. It looked so simple, time-worn, and almost brittle.

I sifted through the contents of the folder. PDF files. Yellowed clippings of news articles about Jamar's collection. An interview with the building's architect and next of kin after the Blue Heron fell. I hadn't seen that one before.

> When asked for comment, Samuel Lewinston, who has authenticated most of the artifacts Jamar Groves had acquired, stated, "It's a great loss. The city lost one of its best sons and the people of Atlanta lost a collection that was a true treasure. The objects that were once our link to the past now lay buried with Jamar in his vault. Perhaps, one day history will repeat itself and they will be once again uncovered."

They were uncovered, alright.

Magic punched me, strong and sudden. The world blossomed in an explosion of sharper scents and brighter colors. The computer screen turned dark. I raised my head to the sky and swore. There were times I really hated magic. This was one of them.

A small silvery web flared on top of the ceiling directly above me. *Uh-oh.*

I jumped to my feet and moved away. Another web blossomed on the brick wall, expanding. A third bloomed to the right and above, yet another to the left and below . . . All around me glistening webs sprouted like wildflowers, stretching and growing. Within seconds the entire office was sheathed in a network of pearly slime, drawn in gossamer patterns across the walls and ceiling.

I moved toward the doorway and glanced through, into the

main warehouse. Iridescent webs hung in layers from ceiling to floor, forming curtains over the shelves, the walls, and the other door.

The office was sealed tight and I was trapped in the middle of it.

Staying trapped here wasn't an option. Tomorrow the PAD would show up, and I would be arrested. They would be disinclined to take it easy. If I was arrested, I would be jailed and I'd go away for a while, and Jim would have a hell of a time trying to pick up my investigation where I left off. Killers would go unpunished, justice wouldn't be served, and Nick would not get closure for the murder of his wife.

I needed to get the hell out of Dodge.

I took a pack of wooden pencils off the shelf and hefted it in my hand. If that stuff exploded, I'd have to duck and cover.

I hurled the pencils into the web. For a second, the small package stuck to the slime, and then the web around it shivered and wrapped over it, twisting and winding, over and over, until the pencils disappeared from view and only a thick cocoon of slime remained. The rest of the pearly curtain flowed, replacing the web that had been used up by the cocoon.

If I tried to bust my way through the walls or run through the slime, I'd be wrapped up like a mummy ready for burial faster than I could blink.

New plan. I pulled out my knife and worked a square of the parquet floor aside. Concrete. Great. Just great. That's the second time I had gotten trapped after breaking and entering. Maybe God was trying to tell me that I should give up my life of crime.

I dug in my duffel bag and pulled out the small flask of alcohol. The chair yielded a leg, the medkit gave me the gauze, and once I soaked it in alcohol, I had myself a torch. I set it on fire and carried the torch up to the wall. The flame licked the slime. The web bit at the torch, jerking it, and I let go a fraction of a second before the slime touched my fingers.

The torch stuck to the wall, cocooned in webbing. Fire didn't work. Fire pretty much always worked.

I looked around. Throwing something heavy at it wouldn't do either—there was too much web and the walls were solid enough that I'd have trouble breaking through.

Think, think, think . . .

My gaze snagged on the staff.

I walked up to the desk and grabbed the phone. Phones were strange. Sometimes they worked during magic and sometimes they didn't. The phone clicked, once, twice, and I got a dial tone. I fished a card out of my wallet and dialed the number.

"Ullo," a familiar Russian voice said, dripping fatigue. *"Yesli ehto ne catastropha . . ."*

Well, it looked like a catastrophe from my end. "Hi," I said. "This is Andrea."

"Oh, hello." A new life came into the voice. "How are you?"

"I'm great. Never better. Hey, listen, I have a staff here I thought you might be interested in. It's about six and a half feet tall, part wood and part bone. There is writing on the shaft and a face with a mustache. Interested?"

Roman fell silent for a second. When he came back on the line his voice was calm. "Can you read the writing?"

"Some of it looks like runes and some of it is Cyrillic. Let's see, the top one under the face looks like backward number four, then e, then p, then something that looks like capital H except it's lower case . . ."

"Are you holding the staff now?" Roman's voice was still very calm.

"No, it's in a case."

"Do not touch the staff. It's a very bad staff."

"Noted."

"Where are you?"

"I'm in the back of a warehouse. I broke into it illegally, and I'm now trapped by some strange ward. Looks like spiderwebs made out of slime. If you were to come and help me with the web, the staff is yours."

"Give me the address."

I recited the address.

"I'll be right there. Don't touch the staff. Don't touch the web. Don't touch anything until I get there."

I hung up. The dark scary servant of all evil was on his way to rescue me. Somehow that thought failed to make me warm and fuzzy.

* * *

I had just finished going through the last box of documents, when the door across the warehouse opened, and Roman called out, "Andrea?"

"In here," I yelled. "Don't touch the webs!"

I got up and walked to the office doorway. The large warehouse space with the shelves stretched before me, shrouded in the curtains of the web. I could barely see him. From where I stood, he was merely a gray silhouette in the opposite doorway.

"Okay, okay, I got this." The silhouette muttered something in Russian. A dull roar issued from Roman's direction.

Roman's voice rose, chanting, mixing with the roar.

The webs shuddered. The curtains bent toward Roman, turning concave, as if pulled backward.

Roman's chant gained power, preternaturally loud, words pouring out, whipping and twisting through the roar like a live current of power.

The curtain of webs snapped taut and broke. Roman stood in the gap, arms spread wide, his black robe flaring as if caught by a ghostly wind. He grasped a wooden staff topped with the head of a monster bird in his right hand. The bird's beak gaped wide open, filled with darkness and grotesque, so big a watermelon could have fit through it. The pearl-colored web twisted into a knot, sucked into that cavernous mouth.

The floor of the warehouse shuddered. Roman stared straight up, the chant bubbling from his mouth, each word vibrating with power. Splashes of pure darkness swirled around his black boots. Something peered at me through that darkness. Something ancient, malevolent, and cold.

The temperature in the room dropped. I shivered and watched a cloud of vapor escape my mouth.

A choir of deep male voices sang in tune to Roman's chant. The web kept hurtling into the staff's mouth.

My hands itched, wanting to release claws. Every hair on my body stood on end.

The warehouse shook.

An enormous bell tolled, a menacing bass note to the choir and the chant. Despair rolled over me like a thick viscous wave. Images fluttered before my eyes: a hill of corpses against the dusk, bright red blood painted over by feathery frost, and a primal dark figure atop the corpse mound . . .

Out of the corner of my eye, I saw the web on the wall flutter behind me, stretching toward Roman.

I dropped down and hugged the floor.

The web tore off the wall and flew over my head. For a second it stuck to the doorway of the office, billowing like a sail in a strong wind, and then it was pulled toward the staff.

The last of the web vanished into the dark beak. Roman's chant changed, receding from overpowering to soothing. The darkness melted, taking with it the somber choir and the bell. The top of Roman's staff closed its beak and shrank.

I sat up slowly.

Roman raised his arms, as if accepting an ovation, and grinned at me, flashing white teeth. "Huh? Am I good or what?"

I clapped. Roman bowed.

I got up off the floor and walked to the dark wizard.

"Do I get a hug for being a hero?" He wagged his black eyebrows at me. "Maybe a kiss?"

For being an evil priest of an evil dark god, Roman seemed surprisingly normal. Either he was hiding his evilness really well, or it really was just a job for him. Priest of darkness, nine to five. It's just the family business.

"No kiss?" Roman looked sad.

Why not? It's not like Raphael owned me or we were together. It could be much simpler with someone like Roman. We could start fresh and clean. I looked at the dark wizard. Really looked at him. He had the most wicked eyes, dark and full of a strange fire. *Here goes.*

I leaned over and kissed him. His lips covered mine. He was good at kissing, not really claiming or demanding, but enticing, almost charming. And I felt nothing. Zip, zilch, nada. No heat, no spark. Nothing.

Stupid Raphael. I wished so badly I could be rid of him, but when he kissed me, I wanted to throw him on the bed and make him nuts. When Roman kissed me on the mouth, it felt like a peck on the cheek.

We broke apart. Roman grinned. Well, one of us had enjoyed it.

Roman's gaze fixed on something over my shoulder. I glanced back and saw the fishing net hanging off the hook.

"That can kill you," he said. "You better stand closer to me."

"Any closer and we'll be rubbing against each other."

"Now that's an idea . . . This can kill you, too." He pointed at the monkey bust. "Also that." The sandglass. "And those"—he pointed at the stone spheres—"those can kill everyone if used properly. This is like an armory for a mage."

Roman pushed himself from the shelf, one arm protectively around my shoulder. "I think I need to see that staff now."

I led him down to the office. "It's in a glass case here. I didn't touch it." I realized he wasn't next to me and turned. Roman stood in the doorway, his gaze fixed on the staff, his mouth slack.

"Kostyanoi posokh," he whispered.

"What?"

"The Bone Staff. Here, hold this!" Roman thrust his stick at me.

I shook my head. "No. It bites things. I've seen it do it."

"He will behave," Roman promised.

I gripped the staff. It turned and stared at me with its vicious raptor eyes. Its beak opened a fraction of an inch. I bared my teeth and pantomimed breaking it. The beak snapped shut.

Roman dug in the pouch at his waist, pulled out a handful of moist black soil, and tossed it at the floor in front of the case. He knelt on the dirt, said something in Russian, and squeezed his eyes shut.

Nothing happened.

Roman cautiously opened one eye, then the other.

"No big kaboom," I assured him.

The black volhv rose. "You got any more of those gloves?"

I pulled a pair out of my duffel and passed them to him. He slipped the gloves on, opened the case, and carefully took the staff out. The top of the staff flowed like molten wax forming an outline of a serpent mouth with two glistening fangs. The Bone Staff hissed. The bird staff in my hand screeched.

"Shhh," Roman murmured. *"Tiho, tiho,* easy."

The serpent melted back into the bone. A moment later the bird realized it was screaming by itself and shut its beak.

"We've been looking for this for eight hundred years." Roman shook his head. "How did it even get here? When you described it, I thought it might have been a duplicate someone made to show off, but this? This is the real thing. I can feel the power through the gloves even."

"So this is some sort of artifact?" I asked. I felt so tired all of a sudden. I had to make sure not to get bitten again. The snake venom was turning me into an old decrepit woman.

"The Bone Staff belonged to the Black Volhv, the head priest of our god," he said. "It's been missing for centuries, since the Mongols invaded Russia. Eventually the Horde came to the town of Kitezh on Lake Svetloyar. It was the last of the great pagan strongholds. But the magic was already weak, and the Mongols were too many, so the volhvi decided to work one last spell to keep the holy relics from the Horde. They sank the city."

"What do you mean, sank?" I asked.

"Buried it in the lake. The whole thing. The Bone Staff was supposed to have been lost with the city, but then years later a respected old volhv, who was just a boy when Kitezh sank, claimed on his deathbed that the staff and other relics had been smuggled out of the city by him and two others before the place went under."

"So this is a holy relic?"

"Yep. The bones are supposed to belong to a Black Serpent Guhd. My dad will shit himself."

He was a walking encyclopedia of magic expertise. Just what I needed, except the picture of my knife was stuck in a nonfunctioning computer. I grabbed a piece of paper and a pen off the desk and sketched the knife one-handed, still holding on to the staff. "Do you know anything about a knife? Looks somewhat like this?"

Roman squinted at my drawing. "Is that a walrus tusk?"

"No." Obviously my drawing skills were lacking.

"Then no. Not off the top of my head, no. Magic knives aren't exactly scarce."

Drat.

"You better let me have that." Roman reached for the bird

staff and I let go. The volhv took it and grinned. "Two staves. It's like having two women."

I rolled my eyes. Men.

"Thank you for your help."

"You're welcome. Are you done here? If not, I'll wait."

I didn't find anything useful in the papers. The only thing that had any valuable information was the computer. I crouched down, disconnected the tower, and picked it up. "I'm done."

Outside, the night was pleasantly warm. We turned the corner and I pulled my hat off. *Phew.* The night breeze cooled my sweat-dampened hair.

Now I just had to get to the car. Get to the car and hopefully not pass out while I was driving. The exhaustion settled deep into my bones. It felt like I was dragging a cement block chained to my feet with every step and carrying another one in my arms. Look at the big bad shapeshifter. It was good that night had fallen and butterflies fluttered around. If one of them landed on me, it would score a perfect knockout.

Roman walked next to me, his stride brisk, looking fresh as a daisy. A very menacing black daisy.

"I can make it from here," I told him. *I hope.*

"Please," he said, as if I offended him. "I'll walk you to your car. Streets are not safe at night."

I shifted the tower in my arms. "You do realize I turn into a monster?"

"When you turn into one, we'll talk. Right now you're not a monster. You're a lady. A very attractive one. And this is a bad neighborhood."

Heh. Ever the gentleman. "So if someone were to make trouble, would you turn him into a frog?"

"I don't do frogs. That's my mother's thing. The transmogrification never works completely. Changing the shape of something against its will requires a lot of energy, so you change someone into a frog and then it fails and he turns back into a human and comes after you with a gun."

"Speaking from personal experience?"

"No, but I've seen it happen."

We turned another corner. Roman cleared his throat. "So. You come here often?"

I cracked up.

"I like it when you laugh," he said. "It's hot."

Woo! "Thank you, Mr. Wizard."

"Oh no, not a wizard." He shook his head. "Magus maybe. I could live with that, but the proper term is volhv, really. We are priests."

I ducked through the gap in the ruin and stopped. My Jeep sat on four wooden blocks. Someone had taken my tires. They jacked my Jeep and stole my tires, the rims, and everything.

Screw you, Pucker Alley.

Roman shook his head. "Something tells me this is not a safe neighborhood."

I exhaled rage through my nose, like a pissed-off bull. It would take me thirty minutes to reach the office at a fast run on a good day. On a bad day like today, I'd be walking for a couple of hours.

"It's okay." Roman let out a shrill whistle.

A rapid staccato of hoofbeats approached from a distance. The night parted and an enormous horse trotted toward us. Massive, its coat slick and soft, like midnight sable, the horse approached, pounding the asphalt with every step. She stopped by Roman and nuzzled his shoulder, her long luxurious mane falling in a black wave down one side.

Wow.

Roman shifted his bird staff into the crook of his elbow and petted her nose. "Good girl. See, we can ride."

"Together on one horse?"

He grinned.

"You're a dirty volhv," I told him.

"Okay, okay, I'll walk."

"No, it's your horse. Besides, I'm a big girl. I can make it home on my own."

"No." He shook his head. "If you walk away, I'll just follow you. I'm going to see you home safe."

His jaw muscles were set, giving his face that telltale stubborn expression. Great. My dark volhv turned out to be a Southern gentleman. I had struck some sort of uniquely male chord in his soul. In his head, abandoning me alone on a night street clearly did not compute.

"There are some women who'd be offended in my place," I told him. "I'm not helpless and I turn into a monster."

"Maybe I'm afraid and I want company." He pretended to shiver. "I may need a big strong monster to protect me. You wouldn't leave a defenseless attractive man out on the streets alone, would you?"

I laughed. "Okay. You win."

Soon the two staves rested securely in a leather holder attached to the saddle and my tower was packed into a saddle-bag. We walked, Roman with his hand on the horse's black leather reins embroidered with silver thread and I next to him, carrying a compound bow and a quiver of arrows I had gotten out of the car.

"So why the Chernobog?" I asked. "I'm sure Russians have other gods, besides the deity of cold, evil, and death."

"It's the family trade. Our pantheon is all about balance. Where there is light, there must be darkness. Life is followed by death and the decay nourishes new life. Belobog, the white god, and Chernobog, they are brother gods, you see. My uncle is a white volhv, one of his sons will likely be a white volhv, too, and our side is the black volhvs. So that's why I'm Chernobog's priest." He turned to me and grinned. "And also for the chicks."

Ha! "The chicks?"

"Mhm." He nodded, completely serious. "Women like a man in black."

I laughed.

"Admit you were impressed," he said.

I kept laughing.

"A little bit?" He held up his index finger and his thumb about an inch away from each other. "Not even a little bit?"

"I was impressed."

"See?"

"It's just you seem really funny and easygoing."

"I do enough bad shit to keep ten city blocks awake at night wrapped up in nightmares. I don't need to maintain an image. At least not all the time." He glanced at me. "I'm really quite a nice fellow in my time off. I even cook."

The street ended. Below us a vast graveyard of broken buildings stretched, some little more than heaps of concrete dust, some still faintly recognizable as their former selves. The moonlight gleamed on a million shards of glass. Wooden bridges spanned the wreckage. To the left, behind the empty shells of the buildings, turquoise and orange fog rose, like a faint aurora borealis that had fallen from the sky. Unicorn Lane, the place where magic raged and bucked like an infuriated wild horse. We would be keeping clear. Only fools visited the Unicorn when the magic was up.

We started on the long bridge.

"So what about you?" Roman asked. "You seem different."

"How?"

"You were all clenched up before." He drew his hand over his face, turning his expression somber. "Very serious. Robot Andrea."

Robot, huh? I showed him the edge of my teeth. "You liked me anyway."

"Well, how can you not like this?" He indicated me with his hands. "I'm only a man."

"You are shameless."

He grinned. "But no, seriously. Something happened? Or is it just because Katya was there?"

"Katya?"

"Kate. Your friend."

"Oh. No, it's not her." I shrugged. "I spent a long time locking up a part of myself. I thought it was best that I suppress my animal side. You know, the bad part."

He nodded.

"But it wasn't bad. Turned out I had been smothering something essential inside myself. Maimed it. I hobbled myself like a prisoner in leg irons and then heroically limped through life. When I think about all of the fun I could've had, all the chances I could've taken, it makes me a little sick. But now I'm free. Maybe a little too free, but I'm enjoying it."

"Enjoying is good," he said.

"You understand about letting go, don't you?" I asked. He probably didn't get to let himself off the chain that often either.

His face turned grim. "I let go, lives end. People like me have many names. Volhv, *kudesnik*, which means 'magician,' *charodei*, which means 'enchanter,' but the most common term in history was *mudrets*. A wise man. People say that wisdom is bought with experience, which is just a polite way of saying that you'll fuck up a lot, people will get hurt, and your guilt will gnaw on you in your dreams. Well, I've earned my wisdom, every drop of it. Let's talk of something else. Let's talk of how when we get to your office, you will offer me a cup of tea. You drink tea, right?"

I nodded. Maybe I would offer him a cup of tea. Why not?

"What kind of tea?"

"Earl Grey, if I can get it."

"You put sugar in it?"

"No."

He stopped, a shocked expression on his face. "No sugar?"

"No."

"You have to have sugar. And lemon."

The night breeze swirled about me and I caught a weak hint of jasmine, followed by the exact same layered scent I'd smelled in Gloria's office. I notched an arrow and spun, scanning the ruins.

"What is it?"

"We're about to get jumped."

"By whom?"

"Venomous people with snake fangs in their heads."

The ruins lay deserted, no movement. A least half a mile separated us from the street and another mile or two of the bridge remained.

Roman pulled the bird staff out of its leather holder. "Where are they coming from?"

"I don't know."

"How many?"

"I don't know."

Behind us, something clanked against the wood. I whirled. A woman climbed over the edge and rolled onto the bridge coming to a crouch, holding a tactical combat blade. A man pulled himself up behind her.

No physical strain. No fighting, no running . . . Well, I was screwed.

A dry pop, like glass cracking, punched my eardrums. A cloud of black smoke exploded on the other side of the bridge, cutting us off.

"Teleportation, huh. Okay. I got this," Roman muttered and dug in the pouches on his belt.

The woman hissed at me, baring fangs.

Okay. Enough of that.

I fired. The bowstring twanged and the arrow sprouted from the woman's left eye.

The man charged at me.

Arrow, sight, draw, fire, all in the space of a second.

The second shaft sliced through the man's throat, ripping a satisfying scream. He faltered, stumbled, and pitched over the side.

The black smoke coalesced into a bald man. He wore a strange pleated robe of brick-red fabric and an odd-looking apron. He held a short staff in his hand. Several small clay spheres hung from the staff, suspended by a string like a bunch of grapes. Another wizard. Great.

Roman yanked a pouch off his belt and hurled reddish powder into the air. The tiny dust granules hung, unmoving, shook, turning black, and sprouted wings. A swarm of black flies streamed toward the man.

More people scrambled onto the bridge.

Arrow—fire. Arrow—fire.

Two fell but they kept coming.

Fire, fire, fire.

The man howled a single word. Magic slapped me, nearly ripping the bow from my fingers. The flies rained down in a cloud of ash.

The man waved his staff around, tore a small pot off of it, and hurled it at the ground. The bridge shivered and white scorpions skittered over the boards, heading for us.

I sent another man flying off the bridge with my arrow in his chest. Two more crawled up to take his place. Were they cloning these guys under the bridge?

"It's like that, then? Okay." Roman barked out something vicious and drew a line with his staff, and spat. The scorpions reached the line and melted into boiling goo.

The man let loose a string of unfamiliar syllables and pulled out a strange-looking knife. The moonlight gleamed off the roughly hewn blade and the man sliced himself across his chest. Blood poured. He ripped the entire bunch of spheres off his staff and smashed them on the ground.

Dark wavy lines formed upon the bridge boards and coalesced into snakes. Hundreds of snakes.

Not again.

"I can command snakes, too," Roman yelled. "This won't help you."

"We'll see!" the man yelled back.

The snakes slithered to us.

"Imenem Chernoboga!" Roman thrust his staff into the boards and planted his legs, gripping the staff directly in front of him with both hands. The bridge quaked. The staff opened its beak and screeched. Wind spun around Roman, stirring his robe. The snakes halted, unsure.

The other wizard shook his staff. The snakes attempted their best to slither forward, but hit an invisible wall of Roman's magic.

The black volhv clenched his teeth. The muscles of his face shook from the strain. Sweat broke out at his hairline.

The snakes reversed their course but made it only a few feet before slamming into the other wizard's magic. The reptiles began piling onto each other. Heads reared, and the snakes bit each other in a frenzy.

I had five arrows left.

Four.

The swarm built on itself. The injured snakes split in half, growing extra heads and tails and multiplying with shocking speed.

Roman shoved the three-foot-tall knot of snakes back at the other wizard.

The wizard ripped the wound on his chest and flung his blood at the swarm, pushing it back.

Two arrows.

"You will not pass!" Roman thundered.

Great. Now he had decided he was Gandalf.

The five-foot snake swarm teetered toward the wizard. They just kept shoving the snakes back and forth with their magic, and meanwhile the swarm was growing bigger and bigger. It was a tower now, a boiling, slithering tower of reptile flesh.

"I'll eat your guts!" the wizard yelled. The snake tower careened back toward Roman.

Last arrow. I had to make it count.

"If I tell you that yours is bigger, will you kill him?" I snarled.

"I'm trying," Roman squeezed the words out through clenched teeth. Blood poured from his nose.

I spun to the heap of dripping snakes, ran to the side of the bridge, and leaped onto the wooden rail, balancing on my toes. The snake tower rocked this way and that and through the gap I glimpsed the wizard's strained face.

I fired.

The arrow punched through the left half of his chest. He gasped, clamping his fingers to the arrow's shaft.

Roman groaned and the snake tower spilled over, burying the wizard.

I turned around. There were seven people on the bridge and they had stopped advancing, gaping at the writhing knot of reptilian bodies.

The knot showed no signs of getting smaller. In fact it was growing bigger, expanding like a snake tornado.

"Uh-oh," Roman said.

"What do you mean, 'Uh-oh'?"

He glanced at me. "Run!" And then he turned and sprinted down the length of the bridge, leading his horse by the reins.

It's never a good thing when the black volhv says "Uh-oh" and then runs for his life. I dashed after him, ignoring the black specks fluttering before my eyes and the pain returning to my muscles.

We ran past our attackers. A moment later, they saw the writing on the wall and followed us. We pounded down the bridge. Behind me something roared. I didn't look back.

The air turned to fire in my lungs. My stomach lurched. Nausea came, followed by vertigo.

We cleared the bridge. Roman dropped to one knee, breathing like there was an anvil on his chest. I turned around.

A thirty-foot tower of snakes rose behind us. It swayed, rocking back and forth, dripping wriggling snake bodies, and exploded. Reptiles rained onto the ruins, revealing a single creature. Its long serpentine body was coiled into a tight spring. Brilliant gold and amber feathers flanked its triangular snake head. I had seen winged snakes before. They were tiny. Three feet was considered to be a large specimen.

The serpent raised its fanged maw to the skies. Scarlet

wings snapped open along its chest. It sprung up, uncoiling its ten-foot-long body, and took to the sky.

"Well, that's not good," a woman said behind me.

"Did Martinez turn into this, or did they eat him?" a man asked.

"How am I supposed to know? He was the priest."

I spun around. The nine of us looked at each other. Roman pushed off the ground.

No arrows, I felt half-dead, and my volhv was all used up. There was only one thing I could do.

A large, blond woman jerked her sword up and charged me. I met her halfway, changing shape as I moved. My claws sliced into her stomach, cutting through the fragile muscle. Her slippery entrails slid against my fingers. I grasped a handful of intestines, ripped the sodden mass out, and flung it at the rest of her crew. A blood-curdling hyena cackle broke free from my fanged, black-lipped mouth. I charged.

A man stepped in my way. His blade cut my side, but I didn't care. I gripped his right arm, wrenched it out of the socket, and tore it off.

The mist of blood lingered in the area like an exotic, entrancing perfume. I danced through it, drunk, but crystal clear, maiming, killing, carving the pliant flesh into hot, juicy morsels. They fell before me and I loved it. Rage sang through my veins, fuel to my internal inferno. Inside me a distant small voice squeaked a warning—I was using up the last of my fragile reserves—but it felt so good and I didn't want to stop.

Another man stepped in front of me. I backhanded him out of the way. He flew and fell. Fun! I chased him and pinned him to the ground. My teeth snapped a hair from his throat. *Hello, prey!*

A familiar scent zinged through my nose. I knew this scent. I puzzled over it, holding the man down.

A name floated up to the surface of my memory: *Roman.*

Reality slammed into me, sudden and hard. I pulled myself back from the brink. My mind registered the strained expression on Roman's face and my claws puncturing his shoulders.

Oh God.

I rocked back, releasing him, slipped on something slick, and slumped against a ruined building. The street was filled with bodies. Blood pooled in the recesses of the uneven pavement, its scent like the cut of a razor on my tongue. A thing that used to be a woman lay only a few feet away. Half of her stomach was missing and her skull was a mess of crushed bone. I had done that.

"You okay?" I asked softly. My voice was hoarse.

"Yeah." Roman slowly rolled up. "What the fuck was that?"

"Bouda rage. It happens sometimes when we're at our limit. We get a few minutes of berserker rage." It was the last-ditch defensive mechanism of a body out of options. "I was bitten by a viper earlier. The Pack medmage pumped me full of antivenom. It made me weak, so when I turned, my body reacted. I didn't mean to hurt you."

Roman brushed his robe and got up. "No worries. Black doesn't show blood at all."

"I'm sorry." He had no idea how close I had come to killing him.

"No worries. Look." He raised his arms, indicating the scene with the dismembered bodies, blood, and his black horse at the beginning of the bridge. "All our enemies are dead, we survived, the horse survived, the staff survived. I even get to say the best line from my favorite book. All is well."

I pushed away from the building. Roman opened his mouth to say something and didn't close it.

"What is it?"

"Breasts."

"Oh for the love of God!"

Roman squeezed his eyes shut and turned away from me. "I have a cloak in my bag."

"I'm comfortable with my body the way it is," I growled.

He turned toward me a little and opened one eye, then turned and looked at me. Or rather at my chest.

"Don't stare."

"You said you were comfortable."

Comfortable was one thing. Being on the receiving end of a very male stare was another.

"How about we find some gauze and bandage your shoulders," I suggested.

"It really isn't that bad."

We walked toward the horse.

"What were you doing in front of me anyway?" I asked.

"You had that dark-haired bitch by the throat and kept beating her head against the wall for almost three minutes," he said. "I became concerned . . ."

A red and gold silhouette plummeted from the sky. It dived at the horse, bit the Bone Staff, ripping it from the leather, and shot up to the clouds.

Holy shit.

Roman fell to his knees. He opened his mouth and let out a wordless scream of pure rage. "Aaaaaaaaaaaaaaaaaaaaaa!"

"It will be okay," I told him.

"I had it! It was in my hands!" He showed me his hands, as if expecting the staff to materialize in his fingers. "In my hands! Eight hundred years!"

"I know," I told him. "I know."

He slumped forward. "I had it and I lost it. I lost it!"

"Come on," I told him. "Let's get ourselves home before we both pass out."

We climbed the stairs to my apartment. I had collapsed on the street, my body finally giving out, and we had ended up riding Roman's horse after all. Roman moved like a zombie. Despondent didn't even begin to describe him. If despair was liquid, he'd be dripping buckets of it with every step.

"I had it in my hands," he told me mournfully, halfway up the stairs.

"I'm sure I have some honey in my pantry," I told him. "And lemon juice. We can have a nice cup of hot tea."

The landing smelled like fresh banana bread. Mrs. Haffey had been baking again. I slid the key into the lock and swung the door open.

A pair of familiar black boots sat in the shoe rack in my foyer, between my black pumps and my yellow work boots.

You've got to be kidding me. He didn't.

"Something wrong?" Roman asked.

On the right, a row of hooks was attached to the wall—I usually hung my rain-dampened jackets there to dry out before taking them to the closet. A large black leather jacket hung on the middle hook.

I marched into my apartment. What must be a spare set of Raphael's keys was in the round plastic dish where I normally left mine. In the kitchen a hanging pot rack had been installed over my dining room table. Raphael's copper-bottomed pots hung from it, and in the corner, his wine cabinet sat next to my spice shelves.

I dashed out of the kitchen, almost knocking Roman over. In the living room three prized swords from Raphael's collection hung on the walls. A picture of Aunt B in a dark frame was on the bookshelf next to the picture of my mother. Raphael's beige and brown Jaipur rug covered the floor. He had double-stacked my DVDs in the media case and added his own, all pre-Shift movies he loved: the entire Rocky collection, the *Godfather I* and *II*, *Commando*, *Tropic Thunder* . . .

I tore into the spare bedroom. I had used it for weapon storage. A new desk sat by the window with a computer on it and a tall filing cabinet next to it. He'd made himself an office! In my spare room! A picture of Raphael and I sat on the desk next to the keyboard. He had his arms around me. I was smiling.

"Do you have a boyfriend?" Roman asked.

"No," I snarled.

"A male roommate?"

I shoved the door to my bedroom open. A second night table stood on the other side of my bed, the perfect match to the one I had. With the same lamp. And his spy novels in a stack on top. I yanked open the closet door. Raphael's clothes hung on the left side, with his shoes in a row. I pulled open the dresser. His underwear. Condoms. His socks.

He had moved into my apartment. He'd snuck in and made it look like he'd lived here for the last ten years. His scent was everywhere, floating through my territory.

Words failed me. I just stood in the middle of my place, shaking with rage.

Breaking and entering was an essential part of the shapeshifter courtship. The idea was to break into your prospective mate's territory and get out undetected, proving that you were sleek enough to mate. Some clans left gifts. Boudas played practical jokes. But this? This was going too far.

He'd punked me. Did he expect that after everything that had happened I would think this was charming? Did he think challenging me was funny? I would rip his head off.

"I think you have a boyfriend."

I inhaled and exhaled slowly. "No, I just know somebody with a really sick sense of humor."

"Really? Because there is a picture of you and him back in the office." Roman pointed his thumb back over his shoulder.

"He's an ex-boyfriend. He is having trouble understanding the word 'over.' "

"So what, he just moved his stuff in while you were gone?"

"Yes," I ground out.

"Ballsy."

No, that wasn't ballsy. That wasn't even in the mile radius of ballsy. It was in its own little universe with the word "lunatic" stamped on it. He should be locked in a padded room and never let out.

"Should I leave?" Roman asked.

"No. I promised you a cup of tea; we will drink that tea, God damn it."

I made a pot of tea in the kitchen. We sat at my kitchen table with MINE scratched on it and drank one cup each, before Roman couldn't stand it any longer and bailed.

The second he was out the door, I grabbed my phone and dialed Raphael's number.

"Hey, babycakes," he said into the phone.

Babycakes? Babycakes! "You want to act psycho? You haven't seen psycho yet."

"I'm not worried," he said. "To go psycho, you'd have to pull that stick out of your ass and we both know that won't be happening."

I unclenched my teeth. "You will regret this."

"Love you, babe."

The plastic receiver crunched in my hand and the phone went dead. I looked at it. Crushed electronic guts peeked out through the gaps in the broken plastic. I dropped the mangled wreck of the phone on my table and went into the bathroom.

A razor and shaving cream rested on the sink next to my lotion. A second toothbrush greeted me, a twin to mine, except mine was green and this one was blue. He had invaded my territory. He had put his stuff into it. He, he, he . . . Aaaaargh! He'd made my place smell like him!

I grabbed the toothbrush. I wanted to break it into tiny pieces and then feed it into the garbage disposal.

No. I wouldn't give him the satisfaction. I wouldn't gather all of his things into a large metal trash can, I wouldn't pour gasoline on it, and I wouldn't set it on fire. No, nothing so pedestrian.

This, this deserved a special retaliation.

I would have to think of something. Oh yes. He would regret this. He would wish he'd gotten run over by a PAD tank instead.

CHAPTER 11

———✦———

I woke up early and lay in bed for a few minutes, looking at the ceiling, before my brain finally registered that there was a new chandelier on it. I must not have noticed it last night, when I finally fell into bed, exhausted and enraged. A glossy silver disk of about eighteen inches in diameter was attached directly to the ceiling. Long wavy crystal leaves patterned with ribs of varying textures cascaded from it, suspended by chains hidden within crystal beads. Thin tendrils of crystal, like the curved shoots of a grape vine, hung between the leaves, translucent with light, and between them, on longer gleaming chains, textured crystal spheres, frosted with silver, clinked gently in the light breeze from the open windows. It was beautifully romantic, yet modern, a kind of chandelier a twenty-first-century mermaid might have in her underwater cave or an Ice Queen from an Andersen fairy tale might hang in her palace of ice.

It was exactly the kind of chandelier I would've loved to have. Elegant, feminine, romantic, but without a trace of corny cuteness. And I wanted to rip it out of my ceiling. He made me so angry.

I pushed myself out of the bed. The fatigue still napped deep in my bones, but it was growing weaker. No nausea. No ache. My body must've won the war with snake venom. Now if I could only win the war with myself.

The magic was down and I was deeply grateful for not having to resort to the kerosene cooker. I went into the office, confiscated Raphael's monitor, and hooked up Gloria's tower at my kitchen table. While the computer booted up, I made myself two pieces of Texas toast—a slice of thick bread, buttered on both sides and fried a bit in the pan, and a small steak, barely seared on both sides. I needed the calories. I boiled some shockingly strong coffee in an ibrik, a little Turkish coffeepot Kate had given me as a gift, and sat down to my breakfast. Mmm, coffee, the breakfast of champions. Delicious and nutritious.

I was halfway through my first cup and knee-deep in Gloria's files, when someone knocked on my door. The peephole revealed a scowling black man in his early thirties, dressed in black and looking like he wanted to bite someone's head off. Jim. There were other people in the hallway behind him. What the hell?

I opened the door. Jim stood in my doorway. He was over six feet tall, with short hair, and the kind of muscular build that resulted when you fought for your life a lot. He looked like a thug, and he worked very hard to keep looking like that. Jim liked to be underestimated.

When I first came to Atlanta, I made it a point to read through the background files the Order kept on the shapeshifters. Before Jim's father went to prison and died there, shanked by an inmate, Jim was taking advanced classes and skipping grades. Jim could've been anything he wanted. A doctor, like his father. A scientist. An engineer. But life got in his way. He was the alpha of Clan Cat now and he oversaw the entirety of the Pack's security, which meant every day he got to spy, discover, and eliminate threats to the Pack. Jim loved his job.

Behind him eight people crowded into the landing: Sandra and Lucrezia from Clan Bouda, both combat operatives; Russell and Amanda from Clan Wolf; two guys I didn't know; Derek, the third employee of Cutting Edge; and my lawyer, Barabas.

"If this is a lynch mob, you didn't bring enough people," I said.

"You don't answer your phone," Jim said. His voice was at odds with his face: his face said "bone-breaker," but his voice said "romantic ballad singer."

"I crushed it."

"Why?" Barabas asked.

"I was having relationship issues," I told him.

Derek grinned. He used to work with Jim before joining Cutting Edge. At nineteen, he had been almost arrestingly handsome, but then some monsters poured molten metal on his face. We had killed the fuckers, but Derek's face never healed quite right. He wasn't disfigured, but he was scarred, and he looked like the type of man you would not want to meet in a dark alley. I've seen him walk into a bar and stop the chatter with his face alone.

Jim, Derek, Barabas, and two combat boudas, not counting the other guys. Either they expected me to put up a hell of a fight, or something heavy was about to happen.

"Can we come in?" Jim asked.

And see Raphael's handiwork? Unfortunately, telling the Pack's chief of security to shove off would have been extremely unwise, not to mention counterproductive to my investigation. Great. The shapeshifters gossiped worse than bored church ladies. Before tonight the whole Pack would know about Raphael's stunt. "Of course."

I watched them file into my apartment. The two boudas nodded at me in passing. This was interesting.

The eight shapeshifters spread through my living room and kitchen and suddenly my apartment seemed too small.

"I thought Raphael had moved out," Barabas said.

Remain calm. "Actually, we never lived together in my place. I lived at his," I said. I would not bite Barabas. It wouldn't be right.

"He was back here last night while she was out," Jim said. "Him, and a large moving truck."

"Oh." Barabas thought about it. His eyes lit up. "Oh!"

Slapping my lawyer was not in my best interests either. I turned to Jim. "You put a detail on my apartment?"

"The second you became a target," he said.

Well, that just took the cake. I tilted my head. "So good of you to let me know, cat. I'd hate to mistake my babysitter for a threat and accidentally shoot him."

Jim blinked. *Ha!* I had managed to surprise the spy master.

"So these are new furnishings?" Barabas said, his face pure innocence.

"Don't tempt me, Barabas."

The two bouda women made big eyes at the portrait of Aunt B on my shelf.

"Lovely decorations," Sandra offered and bit her lip, obviously straining not to laugh.

"Yes, the way the light here plays on Aunt B's face is very nice," Lucrezia added.

"Fuck you, Lucrezia," I told her.

Sandra groaned and the laughter burst out of her mouth. She doubled over. Lucrezia dissolved into giggles.

By tonight, not just the Pack, but the shapeshifters in Canada would know what Raphael had done to my apartment. I would murder him.

I crossed my arms on my chest and turned to Jim. "Is there a reason for all of you coming here?"

"Yes," Jim said. "Why do you have your computer on the kitchen table?"

"This is a long conversation."

"I have time."

We sat down at the kitchen table and I briefed him on last night while Derek made more coffee for everyone. I explained Anapa in broad terms, the Bone Staff, the volhv, and the knife. At the end, Jim nodded at the computer. "Kyle, see what you can do with that?"

A beefy guy who looked like he bent steel rods for a living sat down at the computer, opened a small briefcase, hooked up some box with blinking lights to the tower, and his fingers started flying over the keyboard. He winked at me, still typing without looking at the keyboard.

"Gloria has no fingerprints on file," Jim said. "No driver's license, no city permit for her shop, nothing. She just showed up one day and set up her trinket bazaar."

"And nobody cared because it was White Street?" How did he know all this?

Jim nodded. "How can I make your life easier?"

If we didn't have an audience, I might have hugged him. "Gloria and her friends likely murdered Raphael's people. First, I need to canvas White Street and the Warren and shake some information out. How often was she at the shop, who came to visit her, when did she leave, what did she drive, where she went, and so on. Basic legwork. Second, I need to establish Anapa's whereabouts."

"You still like him for this?" Jim asked.

"There's something weird about him. I have a gut feeling that he is up to his ass in this mess, but he probably wasn't working with Gloria. Third, I need a ritual knife expert. I left a message for Kate, so that should be taken care of if I can tear her away from Curran's side for five minutes."

"I'll take care of it," Jim said. "I'll check in with you as soon as we know something."

Someone knocked. This was my day for visitors apparently.

"Hold on," Jim said and nodded at the door.

Derek walked to my door. I heard it open and then Derek's voice said, "Come in, Detectives."

Barabas hid behind the wall in the kitchen.

Collins and Tsoi entered my living room. Two uniformed officers followed and Derek brought up the rear. The cops stared at the shapeshifters. Jim and Company stared back.

"What are all of you doing here?" Collins finally asked.

"I could ask you the same thing." Jim kept his voice calm.

"We need to speak to Nash," Tsoi said.

"By all means," Jim said. "We won't be in the way."

"We'd rather do this down at the station," Collins said.

"Is my client under arrest?" Barabas said, stepping out in plain view.

Collins grimaced. Tsoi rolled her eyes.

"You didn't have to jump out like a jack-in-the-box," Collins said.

"But I know how much the two of you love surprises. I'd like to see the warrant, please," Barabas said.

Collins locked the muscles on his jaw.

"No warrant?" Barabas smiled.

Tsoi was looking around the room, doing the math. Ten shapeshifters vs. four cops. Suddenly everyone's face turned grim.

"All this would go away if you cooperated," Collins said.

"We're willing to cooperate, if we get full disclosure on the antique dealer case with access to evidence," Jim said.

"Not happening," Tsoi said.

"Your call." Jim shrugged.

Collins turned and walked out.

"This isn't over," Tsoi said and left, the two uniforms in tow.

Nobody said anything until Sandra at the window announced, "They are getting into their cars."

"I told you," Jim said to Barabas. "I know Collins, he's a reasonable man."

Barabas sighed. "But I was looking forward to a fight."

Suddenly things made sense: somehow Jim had discovered the cops were coming to pick me up, and he'd brought his posse over to keep them from taking me off.

"How did you know they were coming?" I asked Jim.

"I have my ways."

"You bugged the PAD station." Sonovabitch. If he got caught, there would be hell to pay.

Jim smiled without showing his teeth. "Something like that."

"They are under heavy-duty pressure from above to solve the case," Barabas said. "People with snake fangs made somebody in the mayor's office really nervous. Almost makes me wonder if they know something that we don't and they want to put a lid on this whole thing as fast as they can. The plan was to pick you up and sweat you a little for information. We can't let them do that—you have things to do and there is no reason you should be wasting time in their interrogation room. Since your phone was out, we decided to show up before they did."

"We take care of our own," Lucrezia said.

But I wasn't their own. Well, not officially. And yet they had come here to back me up. I looked from face to face and realized they would do it again and I would do the same. In their heads, I already belonged.

Wow.

For once in my life I didn't have to hide who I was. They had my back and that was that.

Half an hour later everyone filed out of my apartment. Kyle took the computer with him. On the way out, Sandra stopped by me. "Aunt B wants a word. Today at ten at Highland Bakery. She said not to be late."

The gentle paw of the Bouda alpha. "I'll be there."

Jim was the last to exit. He paused at the door. "I've got the

legwork. My people will do the background and they'll dig up
whatever dirt Anapa has."

"Aha."

"I know Collins. He is competent and thorough. When you
leave your apartment, you'll have a tail. I need you to do nothing for twenty-four hours or so. You know how the game is
played: you're the lightning rod. Lead them around, don't lose
them, go have lunch with Aunt B, visit a market or something.
Be anywhere but near Anapa or White Street. Let the cops
concentrate on you, so my people can work in peace. You can
use a day off anyway. You look like hell."

"You'll spend your life a bachelor, Jim."

"Stay away from White Street."

"Fine, I got it."

I hustled him out the door and locked it. I had phone calls
to make.

At eleven o'clock I walked through the door of Highland Bakery wearing black pants, a black shirt, my steel-toed combat
boots, and crimson lipstick. It matched the new me much better. My clandestine police escort conveniently parked right
across the street.

Located on Highland Avenue, the low brick building that
housed Highland Bakery had survived magic's jaws mostly
intact. This area was called the Old Fourth Ward. Before the
magic took Atlanta apart, the Fourth Ward was a happening
place with historic buildings from the beginning of the previous century, defunct factories converted to loft apartments,
and renovated shotgun shacks—long, narrow, rectangular
structures, once reminders of poverty transformed into trendy
housing. Supposedly the name came from the structure of the
house: if you fired a shotgun through the front door, the pellets
would fly through the whole house and out the back door.

The Old Fourth Ward was home to the Boulevard—a place
where more drugs passed hands than in most other areas of the
city combined—and Edgewood Avenue—where dozens of
bars and restaurants had offered drinks, music, and other plea-
sures of the nocturnal variety.

Now with Downtown in ruins to the west and Midtown

equally ravaged, the Old Fourth Ward had quieted down. The bars and restaurants were still there, but they catered to working-class patrons. It was a place where carpenters, masons, and city employees came for lunch, and Highland Bakery was the place where they stopped on the way home when a craving for sweets struck them.

I had checked the outdoor area, but Aunt B wasn't at any of the black wrought-iron tables, so I went inside, past the counter filled with confections of chocolate, berry, and cream, through the narrow room with a bench to the back. The restaurant was near empty—lunch was a good hour away. Aunt B sat in the corner, with her back to the wall. She looked to be in her early fifties, slightly plump, with a kind face and chestnut hair she put up in a bun. She wore a nice green blouse and khaki capris and looked just like a grandmother about to serve you some cookies.

Looks were deceiving. Most people were terrified of Aunt B. Hell, I was terrified of Aunt B. Even other alphas steered clear, including my best friend, the Beast Lord's Consort. Whenever Aunt B was mentioned, Kate got this odd look on her face. Not alarm exactly, but definite concern.

On her right sat Lika, her beta. Tall, well built, Lika had short dark hair and a harsh face, the kind you would expect from a female soldier who spent too much time on active duty. Clan Bouda had a few women who were older, more experienced, and could take Lika out, but none of them wanted the hassle of the beta job. Betas had busy lives and a lot of responsibility. Alphas made decisions, betas saw them implemented.

Here was my chance. I would join Clan Bouda, just like everyone wanted. But I would do it on my terms.

I paused before the table and stared at Lika. "You're in my seat."

Aunt B's face remained perfectly placid.

"Is that so?" Lika's eyebrows came together.

"Move," I told her.

"Move me," she said.

I looked at Aunt B. Normally public challenges were to the death, but there were only three of us here.

"To submission," she said. "I don't want to lose either of you. There aren't many of us."

Lika got up from behind the table. She had about six inches on me and maybe forty pounds, all of it lean, hard muscle. But she had never seen me fight, while I knew her moves.

I pushed the nearest table back, clearing some space. Lika did the same.

Lika rolled her head to the left, cracking her neck, then again to the right. I rolled my eyes and pretended to look bored.

She lunged. It was a fast, deadly lunge. Her right fist snapped out like a hammer.

I ducked low under the lunge, smashed my shoulder under her rib cage, grabbed her legs a couple of inches under her butt, and heaved. My lunge had knocked her off her center of gravity and she had nowhere to go but up. I flipped her in the air and drove her down with all my strength, crouching to control her fall. Lika's back hit the floor—boom! Before she had a chance to catch her breath, I drew a line with my fingers across her throat and stepped back.

Lika took two seconds to shrug off the daze and rolled to her feet. "Again?"

I looked at Aunt B, like a good little bouda. I knew about the chain of command. In fact, the chain of command made me feel secure and comfy.

Aunt B nodded.

Lika shifted her stance and rocked back and forth on her toes. Okay. I tensed, as if to advance. She took a step with her left foot and kicked out with her right in a roundhouse, aiming for my ribs with her shin. It was a hell of a kick. Had I stayed still, it would've shattered my ribs, crippling me. Can't do much with shattered ribs, except bend over to one side and moan.

I caught her leg just under the knee, wrapping it with my left arm, took a step forward, pushing Lika back and off balance, and swept her other leg from under her. She went down hard. I crouched long enough to pretend-slice her side— marking her internal organs as my target. If I had claws, I could've shoved my hand into her, under and into the rib cage, and ripped her heart out. I took a few steps back.

Lika rolled to her feet. Her lip trembled in the beginnings of a snarl.

"No fur," Aunt B said. "Ladies, in a public place, we wear our public face."

"Again?" I asked and looked at Aunt B.

She nodded.

Lika charged. Her hands closed over my arms. A grappling move. She was banking on her superior strength. But no amount of strength could change simple physics.

I clamped my hands on her forearms, planted my left foot in the middle of her stomach, and rolled back. She didn't expect it and the momentum pulled her down. I rocked forward, slamming my ankle onto her throat and forcing her back, and rolled up into a sitting position with both legs across Lika's chest and her arm clenched to me. Before she had a chance to get her bearings, I leaned back, stretching her arm across my body. With my thighs as an anchor, all I had to do was pull a little and her elbow would be toast.

"Dislocate," Aunt B said.

I pulled the elbow. The joint popped with a dry crunch.

Lika growled through her clenched teeth.

"There will be no rematch," Aunt B said. "She has better technique and more education. She's also faster than you are. Are we clear, dear?"

"Yes, ma'am," Lika squeezed out.

"Let her go."

I released Lika's arm, rose, and offered her my hand. The bouda looked at it for a second, sighed, and gripped my fingers with her uninjured hand. I pulled her up. "Good fight."

"Whatever." Her voice didn't hold any real hostility. "I was tired of being a beta anyway. You can have all the hassle."

Lika looked at her limp arm. "I'm going to the bathroom to fix this."

"Don't be too long," Aunt B said. "I'm ordering your favorite red velvet cupcakes."

"Yes, Alpha." Lika walked away toward the bathroom.

Aunt B turned to me and smiled. I could've sworn there was pride in it. It couldn't be. I was deluding myself.

"Sit down, dear," Aunt B said. "Love the lipstick, by the way."

"Thank you." I took Lika's spot and waited until the bathroom door closed behind her. "Why hurt her?"

"If you gave her half a chance, we would be here till sundown." Aunt B shrugged. "Lika is stubborn. Nothing short of a decisive victory would stop her. Remember that. You'll deal with her as my beta and she does prove troublesome on occasion."

Aunt B looked at me from across the table. Her irises flashed a bright, ruby red. The weight of the alpha stare pressed on me. I held it for a moment too long and forced myself to look down at the table. "Welcome to the family," Aunt B said.

I was in. For better or worse, I was now a member of Clan Bouda and Aunt B's second.

A waitress came in with a tray of cupcakes, a pot of tea, and three cups.

"You haven't lived until you've had their red velvet cupcakes." Aunt B pushed a plump cupcake toward me. "Have one."

My new alpha was offering me food. Another show of loyalty and submission. Breaking elbows wasn't enough, apparently. I bit the cupcake and licked the creamy icing. Mmm, cream cheese. Fighting made me hungry.

The waitress departed.

"You do know what the beta job entails?" Aunt B asked.

Of course. "Enforcer, gatekeeper, errand girl, bouda nagger."

Aunt B cut a small cupcake in half and bit off a piece. "You forgot babysitter."

"I'm sorry. How silly of me."

"Why the sudden change of heart?" B asked.

"Two things. First, Jim came to visit me this morning. He brought eight people with him. They occupied my apartment and when some cops showed up trying to take me in, they were met with firm resistance."

"And?"

"And I realized that if I was in trouble, the Pack would back me up and I would back up the Pack. All my friends are in the Pack. I like to belong. I need it, need the structure." I licked the icing. "I'm tired of starting over. I'm not likely to stop being a shapeshifter, so I might as well make the best of it. I will be the best bouda I can be."

"Better than me?" B arched her eyebrows.

"Yep. I plan to eclipse your fame."

Aunt B smiled. "Aiming high."

"Always." I sipped my tea.

"And the second thing?" Aunt B asked.

"I spoke to Martina and realized that to take the clan away from you, I need to earn their loyalty first."

"Oh, so you plan to take over?"

I licked the icing off my lips. "In a few years. Once I am sure they will follow me."

Aunt B leaned back and laughed.

"You've done such a good job for such a long time," I said. "Don't you feel you deserve a nice retirement?"

Aunt B kept laughing. "Very well. I will speak to Curran. In light of the investigation, I'm sure the lion will grant us an extension on having you officially admitted into the ranks. As long as it is known that you and I have an understanding and an application has been made, you won't encounter problems."

Lika returned from the bathroom, rubbing her arm, plopped at the seat next to me and waited until B waved her toward the food. Lika snagged a red velvet cupcake. "Yummy."

"I need you to go to Milton County," B said.

Uh-oh. The sheriff of Milton County and I didn't have the best relationship. He was the one who had locked us up after the hot tub incident.

"Where to?" I asked and sipped my tea. Earl Grey. Tasty.

"To the Milton County Sheriff's office," Aunt B said.

I choked a little on my tea.

"Some of our people got arrested last night," Lika said. "Including your boy."

My boy? Oh. "What did Ascanio do this time? Last I saw him, he was with his mother."

"Nothing," Aunt B said. "Wrong place, wrong time. There was some sort of bar brawl. I could go to Kate with this, but you see, she is spending all her time with Curran. Something to do with the Vikings, not sure what exactly." Aunt B waved her spoon. "Involving her right now means involving the Beast Lord and I don't feel like setting his tail on fire. He'll growl and fuss and I'd rather avoid all that. So I need you to go down there and make this problem go away. I understand you and Beau Clayton have a special relationship."

Yeah, he'd thrown my bikini-clad butt into a jail cell. "I can do that," I said and stole a second cupcake.

"I'm so glad," B told me.

We all drank some tea.

"I know you've spoken with my son," B said to me.

"Yes. He seems to have gone insane."

"The mating frenzy will do that," Aunt B said. "And I'm not talking about the blonde. He has never been dumped before, dear. He has no idea how to handle it."

Lika snickered.

"I told him we were through, and he broke into my place, scratched MINE into my table," I told her. "And then he moved his things into my apartment."

Lika stopped eating. "Seriously?"

I nodded.

Aunt B grinned. "He was always such a clever boy."

There it was, the final proof that Raphael could do no wrong. I had just told her he had gone nuts, vandalized my furniture, and was guilty of breaking and entering, and she was bursting at the seams with pride.

"What would you do in my situation?" I asked.

Aunt B cut another slice off her cupcake. "I was never one to let a man get the better of me, dear. If someone dared to treat me in this manner, I would rub his nose in everything he had lost by his idiotic stunt. I would do something . . . spectacular. Something he would never forget. And I would make sure everyone knew what a fool he was."

"If I spring the boudas out of jail, what are the chances of Raphael spending this evening away from his house?"

Aunt B smiled at me above the rim of her cup. "I would say those chances are very, very good."

I got up. "I'd best get on with it, then."

Aunt B's eyes sparked with an amused ruby light. "Lika will fill you in on the details. Good luck, dear."

I would need every drop of it, too.

"And Andrea?" Aunt B said. "You and I have made a deal today. I trust you to hold up your end of the bargain."

It was like she had looked into my head and seen that inside I was still wobbling. I talked the talk and walked the walk, but somehow she had sensed my hesitation.

"If Curran sets the date for your admittance and you fail to show up, it would be truly disastrous."

"No worries," I told her. "I'll be there."

To say that Beau Clayton was a good old Southern Boy would be an understatement. The man kept a can of green boiled peanuts on his desk, for crying out loud. For some reason, it was half-filled with bullet casings.

Beau looked at me from behind his desk, which was organized to within an inch of its life. He was big as all hell and half of Texas, a massive bear of a man, with lineman's shoulders and power-lifter's arms that strained the sleeves of his crisply-ironed khaki uniform shirt. His dark brown, wide-brimmed sheriff's hat rested on a hook on a wall, within easy reach. Above it a rapier hung, a beautiful sword with an ornate basket hilt. I was pretty sure I had seen it before, but for the life of me I couldn't recall where.

"It's always nice to see you, Ms. Nash," Beau drawled.

I gave him my most dazzling smile. If he thought he could out-Southern me, he was in for a shock. "May I ask why you have bullet casings in that can, Sheriff?"

"Every time someone shoots at me, I put the casings into the can," he said.

Alright then.

"So what brings you to the sunny skies of Milton county?" Beau asked.

"You have some of the Pack's people in lockup." And my first test as a beta was to get them out.

"We're always glad to have guests in our jailhouse," he said. "We almost never get lonely."

I licked my lips, moistening them, and Beau's gaze slid down. *Well, how about that? Hehehe.*

"I understand you have three of our boys," I said. "How would I go about getting them released?"

Beau leaned against his chair. "Well, this is where we run

into a problem. From what I understand, your boys caused a disturbance at the Steel Horse, assaulted two men, and damaged some property there."

I crossed my legs. "As I recollect, the Steel Horse is in Fulton County."

"You recollect correctly, but you see, your boys were out for a hell of a night. Not satisfied with that bit of fun in Fulton, they continued their brawl down Gawker Alley, which put them twenty feet inside Milton County when they were subsequently apprehended."

Drat.

Beau's eyes sparkled a bit. "Eyewitness accounts indicate a female was involved."

I smiled at him. "A female is always involved. So how does your version go?"

Beau clicked the recorder on his desk. A young man's voice filled the room. "So we were just sitting there and then there was a girl and she was looking at Chad and me."

Slurring his words a bit. Not quite sober. Not by a long shot.

"And Chad said, 'Hey, pretty, come hang with us,' and the big black dude said, 'Shut your mouth, white boy.'"

I arched my eyebrows at Beau. The big black dude would be Kamal, who had never said a nasty word to anyone in his entire life.

"And he said, 'Shut your mouth,' and I said, 'We just talking' and the other black guy said, 'We gonna beat your ass if you keep running your mouth.' And then he made one of those hand signs. You know, one of those gang things."

Oh, this was just getting better and better. Beau was making a valiant effort to remain stoic, but his face betrayed the long-suffering look of someone who had to listen to something patently idiotic.

"What happened next?" an older female voice asked.

"We got up to leave, and the girl wanted to come with us, and the first black guy, he, like, got up and he was all, 'You're not leaving!' and we were all like, 'Yes we are,' and then I threw some chicken at them so they'd know we meant business, and the white kid who was with them, he picked up Chad and threw him through the window."

Drunk knights in shining armor, protecting the hapless female from the clutches of scary black guys. Give me a break.

"Then what happened?" the older female asked.

"Then they left and went up the street. And Chad was like, 'We can't let them get away with this shit,' so we followed them. And I said, 'Hey! What do you think you're doing with that throwing people through windows and shit.' And the white guy said, 'You must like going through windows.' And I told him 'Fuck you' in a polite voice and he threw me through the window."

Beau clicked the recorder off.

"It's good that he used his polite voice," I said. "Otherwise no telling what would've happened."

Beau grimaced. "They aren't the sharpest tools in the shed and booze didn't improve their IQ any."

"And what do the Big Scary Black Guys say?" I asked.

"They say that the kids were drunk and kept hitting on the girl who was with them. One of them wandered over, and threw some buffalo wings at them, and got thrown through the window. The girl took off and they decided to leave. The two geniuses followed them and got thrown through the front window of Chuck's Hardware."

"Tossing chicken at people constitutes an assault," I said. "By their own admission, they threw the first punch."

"In the instance of the situation at the Steel Horse, correct. However, your people are not being held for the incident at the Steel Horse; they are being held because during a verbal altercation in Gawker Alley, they took it upon themselves to put two people through Chuck's window."

He had me there. "With all due respect, that's a continuation of the same incident."

"I can see why you might think that, but it took Mike and Chad ten minutes to stagger their drunken way up Gawker. It's two different incidents and you know it."

Argh. "I beg to differ."

"I respect your right to differ, but that doesn't change reality. I cannot have people thrown through windows willy-nilly in my county."

We stared at each other. The level of politeness had risen to dangerous levels.

"We would be delighted to pay restitution to Chuck's Hardware and to restore his window," I said. "We are happy to set it right. Would he be willing to drop charges?"

"He's a reasonable man," Beau said. "It will cost you."

I shrugged. "Boys will be boys, Sheriff. You know how it is, they have fun and we pay the bills."

"You also have Jeff Cooper to deal with," Beau said. "Mike's dad. He's in my front lobby fuming and making an ass of himself. He wants assault charges to be brought up."

I pulled a small plastic case from my pocket and showed him the disk inside it.

"What's this?"

"Surveillance footage."

"The Steel Horse has surveillance cameras?" Beau came to life like a hungry wolf sighting a juicy, crippled rabbit.

"The owner installed them after that scare they had with the pandemic." A pandemic Kate had stopped before it could kill him and his wife. The Steel Horse welcomed Pack members with open arms, which was why they did nothing to help law enforcement when the Pack kids got in trouble. "He doesn't advertise this fact. Besides, they only work half of the time, when the tech is up." I flipped the disk between my fingers. "Shall we?"

Beau took the disk out of its case and slid it into the computer on a small desk in the corner. Black-and-white images filled the screen. Three shapeshifters sitting at a table, with the girl next to Kamal. Two young guys at a table nearby with a collection of empty beer bottles said something. The shapeshifters ignored them. More taunts, this time with the waving of arms. The shorter of the two human teens picked up a basket of chicken bones and dumped it on Kamal's head. Ascanio got up, picked the guy up, and hurled him through the window. Kamal smacked him upside the head. Ascanio shrugged. The third shapeshifter, Ian, dropped some bills on the table and the group left.

"If Mr. Cooper chooses to press charges, we will do the same," I said. "Please feel free to retain the disk. I've made copies. I do have to ask you to release the boys. I'd be in your debt and they aren't a flight risk. You know where to find us: the big stone fortress just a few miles outside of town."

Beau walked to the door and stuck his head out. "Rifsky, get our shapeshifter guests processed out for me, will you? Also, Ms. Nash here is going to leave her information with you for Chuck's to get his window squared away."

I suddenly remembered where I had seen the sword. It used to hang in Kate's apartment. It was her guardian's sword. Pieces of the puzzle clicked together in my head. She'd used it to get me out of jail. I felt ashamed.

Beau turned to me. "Don't leave town and all that, Ms. Nash."

"Wouldn't dream of it." Now I owed Beau a favor. Wonderful.

Ten minutes later three guilty-looking shapeshifters met me on the steps. Kamal saw me and did a double take. "I thought Lika was coming."

I gave him my thousand-yard stare. He shifted uncomfortably in place.

"Let's try this again, from the beginning. You say, 'Hello, Beta. Thank you for coming all the way here and subjecting yourself and the Clan to public embarrassment because of my stupidity.' And I don't break your arms off."

"Thank you, Beta," Kamal and Ian chorused.

I looked at Ascanio. He dropped his gaze to the stairs. "I'm sorry."

"Yes, you are." I started down the street to the parking lot. The three boudas followed me.

A man shoved the door open behind us. Beefy, in his late forties. His face had a lovely red color that probably meant he was about to blow his gasket. "Hey! Hey, you! I want to talk to you!"

I kept walking. "You threw two humans through two different store windows. Enlighten me, what happens when a shapeshifter goes through a sheet of glass?"

"Nothing," Ian volunteered.

"Stop," the man snarled. "Stop, God damn it."

"What happens when a human goes through a sheet of glass?"

Nobody wanted to answer.

"I'll enlighten you, then: they get bruises, possible broken bones, and multiple lacerations. And because they don't have the benefit of Lyc-V, their broken bones will take weeks to heal and the lacerations can kill them if the broken glass happens to slice them at the right place. You almost killed them over a bucket of chicken. What in the world were you thinking?"

We turned the corner, hidden from the building by the stone wall.

"We just wanted to intimidate them," Ascanio said.

The man behind us took the corner at high speed. "You fucking bitch, I said stop!"

The beastkin-crazy Andrea was about to surface. I could feel it.

I looked at him. "Jeff Cooper, I presume?"

"That's right. You degenerates think you can just come here and push people around." He stabbed his finger into my chest.

The three boudas went from chastised to baring their teeth in a blink.

"Don't put your hand on me again," I said.

He poked his finger into my chest again. "Well, I have something to tell you: don't let the sun set on you in this county, because . . ."

I grabbed his wrist and yanked him forward, tripping him with my foot. He went down back first and I caught him by his throat, three feet above the ground, lifted him up a bit and bent down to his face. My eyes glowed with murderous red. My voice turned rough with an animal growl. "Listen well, because I won't be repeating myself, you racist prick. If you make any trouble for me or my people, I'll hunt you down like the pig you are and carve a second mouth across your gut. They'll find you hanging by your own intestines. The next time you hear something laugh and howl in the night, hug your family, because you won't see the sunrise."

I opened my fingers. He crashed on the ground, his face white as a sheet. He scrambled backward, rolled to his feet, and took off.

The three shapeshifters stared at me, openmouthed.

"That's how you intimidate people. No witnesses and not a mark on him. Get your asses to the car."

CHAPTER 12

It was close to noon when I finally walked through the doors of the office. Kate sat at her desk. Grendel sprawled by her feet, an enormous black monstrosity that had more in common with the hound of the Baskervilles than with any poodle I had ever seen. He saw me and wagged his tail.

I paused to pet his head. "The Consort in the flesh. You grace us with your presence, Your Majesty. I'm so honored." I pressed my hand to my chest, hyperventilating. "I shall alert the media posthaste!"

She grimaced. "Har-de-har-har. Did you have lunch yet?"

"No, and I'm starving. I could eat a small horse."

"Acropolis?" Kate asked, rising.

"Way ahead of you." I grabbed the file off my desk and went out the door. "By the way, we have a nice police tail that we aren't supposed to lose."

"The more, the merrier."

When we had both worked at the Order, Parthenon had been our favorite lunch joint. It served the best gyros. Unfortunately, now we were about forty-five minutes away from Parthenon, but we had found Acropolis, half a mile away, which was just as good if not better. It didn't have Parthenon's outdoor garden, but we made do with a secluded booth near the window in the back.

We ordered a heap of gyros, tzatziki sauce, a plate of bones for Grendel, and yummy pink-drop fruity drinks. Even with my shapeshifter senses, I had no idea what was in them and we both had decided it wasn't prudent to ask. Our police escorts, an older woman and a man in his twenties, were seated all the way across the room, by the window. For now we had privacy, at least.

I took the picture of the knife from the file and pushed it toward her. "Ancient knife."

She pondered it. "This is not battle-ready."

"Raphael thought it was ceremonial."

She nodded. "It's a fang."

"What?"

"It's a fang." She turned the picture toward me. "Wolf, maybe. Here, look."

She reached down and pulled Grendel's upper lip up, revealing huge canines. "Exactly the same."

She was right. The knife was shaped just like a canine tooth. "How did I miss this?"

Kate wiped her hands on the cloth napkin. "I wouldn't have connected it either, except Curran gave Grendel a pork chop last night and this doofus wolfed it down and got a bone shard stuck in his gum. I had to pull it out and got a close look at his teeth. I can't seem to impress on the Beast Lord that giving him pork chops is not a good idea. He says wolves eat boars. I say that wolves never had a boar sliced into chops, which makes pork bones very sharp."

I unloaded the whole story on her, sparing no details. Kate's eyes kept getting bigger and bigger.

"And here we are," I finished.

"The place smelled of jasmine and myrrh?"

I nodded.

Kate thought for a long moment. "You said the millionaire's name was Anapa?"

I nodded. "I checked on it. It's some sort of small town on the Black Sea in Russia."

"It's also in the Tell el-Amarna Tablets," she said. "In the late 1880s clay tablets were found on the site of an old Egyptian city. The tablets dated to about the fourteenth century BCE. They were probably part of some royal archive, because most of it was pharaohs' correspondence with foreign rulers."

"How do you even remember this stuff?"

"Most of the tablets are from Palestine and Babylon," she said. "It was part of my required education. Anyhow, the tablets are written in Akkadian, and the name Bel Anapa is mentioned. 'Bel' meant 'master' or 'lord' in Akkadian, similar to the Semitic Ba'al."

"Like the demon Baal?"

Kate grimaced. "Yes. They had this thing where only priests were allowed to say the god's name, so they just ba'aled their gods. Similar to the way Christians use 'Lord' now. So some Greeks ended up thinking that Bel or Ba'al meant a specific god, but it doesn't: Bel Marduk, Bel Hadad, Bel Anapa, and so on."

Great. "Which god is Anapa?"

"The Greeks called him Anubis, God of the Dead."

Whoa.

"The one with the jackal head?" I asked, raising my hands to my head to indicate ears.

Kate nodded.

Okay. No god that had "of the Dead" attached to it could be taken lightly. Hades, Hel, none of them were cuddly puppies.

"He can't be a god," I said. "There isn't enough magic for gods. We've established that." Gods ran on the faith of their worshippers like cars on fuel. The moment the magic receded, their flow of faith was cut off and the gods dematerialized.

"He could be just using the name," Kate said. "He could be the child of a god."

I stared at her.

"Saiman is the grandchild of a god," Kate said. "Anapa could be also."

I thought of the office in Anapa's mansion. That otherworldly office no human being could've made. "Do you think the knife might be modeled after his fangs?"

"It's possible."

"Does Anubis have any sort of helper animals?" I asked. "Like something about five feet tall with the jaws of a crocodile and . . ."

"Body of a lion? With a mane?" Kate asked.

Damn it. "Okay. Drop it on me."

"Demon Ammit, the Devourer of the Dead, the Eater of Hearts, the Destroyer of Souls."

I put my hand over my face.

"Supposedly after receiving the soul of a recently deceased, Anubis weighs the heart against the feather of Ma'at, the Goddess of Truth. If the heart is heavier, it's not pure and Ammit gets a delicious treat. The soul doesn't go to Osiris, doesn't receive immortality, and generally doesn't get to collect its two hundred dollars. Instead, it is condemned to be forever restless." Kate squinted at me. "Let me guess, you nuked the Devourer of Souls."

"Yup. And since he was guarding Anapa—"

"She." Kate drank.

"Ammit is a girl demon?"

"Mhmm."

I sighed. "Well, in any case, Anapa definitely isn't just using the name."

And if Anapa was Anubis, that meant I had officially pissed off a deity. I had never done that before.

I tapped the picture of the knife. "It could be an Egyptian knife. Ancient Crete and ancient Egypt traded. Even I know that."

"It could be Greek, too," Kate said. "The worship of Anubis actually spread through Greece and Rome."

"So I have an Anubis of some sort, a possibly Egyptian knife, and snakes. Lots of snakes: snake people, vipers, flying snakes . . . and a Russian staff with a serpentlike head. How does this all fit together?"

We stared at each other.

"No clue," Kate said. "But it's not good."

The gyros arrived. Kate pushed the plate toward me. "Eat."

"Why?"

"You've lost at least ten pounds since I last saw you."

"I'm getting fashionably slender from all the exercise," I told her.

"That last time was three days ago. You're not slender, you're starving. Eat the damn food."

For ten minutes we did nothing but eat.

"How did it go with Aunt B?" Kate asked.

"I caved in," I said. "I went to see her, sat real calm by her feet, and let her put a collar on me. She was surprisingly gracious about it." My cup was empty. I raised my glass. A waiter appeared and refilled it. "Thanks." I looked back at Kate. "I'm not actually all that bitter about it. It cost me a big chunk of my pride, but I'm not bitter. I'm now a Bouda beta."

"Congratulations."

We clinked our glasses.

"Why the hell not? I decided that's what I want and if I have to wear Aunt B's collar for a few years to get it, so be it. I'll learn everything she knows. I'll figure out how she thinks, and then I'll use it against her. That's the bouda way."

"And Raphael?"

I shrugged. "I haven't decided. Anyway, Roman mentioned that the witches were all upset over a vision of the Witch Oracle. They heard howling and saw a spiral of clay. I'm thinking since Anubis is involved, maybe that was a jackal howling. Would Anubis have any sort of influence over werejackals?"

"I don't know."

I'd have to call Jim and warn him to pull any jackals he was using out of the team working on Anapa. No need to tempt fate.

"Don't change the subject." Kate fixed me with her stare.

"What subject is that?"

"Raphael."

"Ah, that subject." I popped a piece of gyro into my mouth. "I said I haven't decided. It's complicated."

Kate put her fork down, leaned her elbow on the table, and rested her cheek on her fist. "I've got time."

It wasn't right to lie to your best friend. Even if it was lying by omission. I chronicled my wonderful romantic adventures.

"I can't believe you kissed the black volhv," Kate said.

"It was tepid."

"Tepid?"

"You know, not hot, not cold, just kind of moderately warm. I feel guilty about it, actually. Roman is a good kisser. I should've enjoyed it more. Besides, locking lips with him was the least of my problems." I counted things off on my fingers. "Going to an IM-1 zone, breaking and entering into Anapa's office, killing Anapa's demon, breaking and entering into a crime scene, stealing evidence from the crime scene, threatening a human civilian with being hung by his intestines . . . I'm afraid your friend is gone and she's never coming back. You've got a crazy bouda instead."

"What are you talking about, you moron? My friend never left."

That was Kate in a nutshell. Once she became your friend,

she remained your friend. Always. I bared my teeth at her. "Who are you calling a moron?"

"You. Let me summarize: so you and Raphael had a fight and didn't talk because you hurt each other's feelings, then both of you got your feelings hurt again, because neither one of you apologized, then Raphael pretended to have a fiancée who didn't do anything for him, and your feelings got further hurt, so you got him back by telling him that you were done, after which he went nuts and scratched MINE into your table, so you kissed a black volhv, who didn't do anything for you, and now Raphael has moved his things into your apartment."

"Yes." That about summed it up.

Kate leaned toward me. "When I was little, Voron took me to Latin America. TV still ran regular programming back then, and they had this really dramatic love story on during the week. It was full of very pretty people . . ."

I pointed my fork at her. "Are you implying that our relationship is like a Spanish soap opera?"

"I'm not implying. I'm saying it."

"You're crazy."

Kate grinned. "Have you traded any significant, tormented glances lately?"

"Eat dirt, Kate."

"Perhaps he has a twin brother . . ."

"Not another word."

She cackled over in her seat. I tried to smile back, but my smile must've been frightening, because Kate stopped laughing. "What is it?"

"I'm all fucked up." I didn't mean to say it. It just came out. "I fought and fought against joining the Pack, and now I'm in. I'm not dumb. I'm smart. I knew it would come to this, and joining the shapeshifters is to my benefit. I don't understand why I resisted it for so long. Now there is Raphael. He's behaving like an irrational lunatic, yet I'm even more obsessed with him. It's like an addiction, Kate. I could just give in and make up with him, but I can't. What is wrong with me?"

"You hate being forced," Kate said.

"You're wrong. I have no problem with authority."

"You have no problem with authority when you voluntarily choose to accept it. You accepted the Order's right to give you commands. If someone had come and tried to force you into the Order, you would've fought them tooth and nail. Aunt B tried to force you to join the Pack, so you balked. But now you've joined on your terms, voluntarily accepted her authority, and you're okay with it because it was your decision, not hers."

"And Raphael?"

"Raphael is an asshole, no doubt about it. Spoiled, irrational, difficult. And you love him and feel pressure to fix things because the two of you had something great and you helped to screw it up and now you feel guilty. It's kind of up to both of you to put it back together, but you'd have to forgive each other first."

"When did you get so wise?"

Kate sighed. "I spend all my Wednesdays listening to the shapeshifter court issues. You wouldn't believe how often they try to use the Pack court to settle their love problems. Look, Andi, whatever you decide, I'm on your side. If you want help, I will help. Just tell me what to do. If you want to sit here and mope, I will find you a hanky."

A hanky, huh? "Just for that, you're going to come with me."

"Where?"

"To Raphael's house. It's payback time."

"Oh no. Another case of breaking and entering?" A mischievous light sparked in Kate's eyes.

"I don't have to break and enter." I pulled Raphael's spare set of keys out of my pocket and jingled them. "He left me this lovely set of keys. Seems a shame not use them."

Kate laughed.

I had already made the calls before I left for my meeting with Aunt B. My evil plan was already set in motion.

I raised my pink drink. "To revenge!"

Kate raised her glass and we clinked.

"It has to be really good," she said.

"Trust me on this. It will be epic."

The front door of Raphael's house swung open. A moment later Kate appeared in the doorway of the master suite's bathroom. She was wrapped in a plastic biohazard suit.

"Still clear," she reported. "It's twenty past midnight. He'll be home soon."

"Almost done," I told her.

"We would be finished already if you hadn't insisted on doing the tub."

I wiped the sweat off my forehead. I had put in nearly twelve hours of work, using every iota of my shapeshifter strength and speed. Kate had helped, especially with cutting things, but I wanted my scent all over this place, not hers, which was why she was wrapped in plastic, and I wore a tank top and a pair of capris, sweating and leaving my scent signature on everything.

"Almost done," I promised again.

Kate turned. A moment later I heard it too, some sort of rumble at the front door.

"I got this," Kate said and went out with a determined look on her face.

A moment later I glued the last strip in place and stuck my head out.

Kate stood by the door with her arms crossed.

That was an anti-Curran pose. What the hell was the Beast Lord doing here?

I padded to the door.

"First, you didn't come home." Curran's voice held zero humor. "Second, I'm told that my mate is lingering in Raphael's house. There can't be any good reason for you to be here."

"Are you spying on me, Your Furriness?" Kate asked.

"No," I said, stepping into the doorway. "Jim has Raphael's house under surveillance."

Curran looked at me, then looked at Kate.

"Revenge," Kate said. "I'll explain later."

Something hissed. The three of us looked up. A dark shadow rose on the neighboring roof, and I recognized Shawn, one of Jim's people. Speak of the devil. "He's coming," Shawn hissed. "Raphael's coming."

Oh shit.

"Help!" Kate held her arms out.

Curran grabbed the biohazard suit and ripped it in half, stripping it from her. Kate thrust the suit into the nearest trash can.

I ran inside the house, locked the front door, ran upstairs, lowered the attic ladder, climbed into the attic, pulled the ladder up behind me, and dashed along the beam to the corner over the living room. My surveillance nest waited for me. I'd bugged the entrance and every room in the house, and now the images from the house filled my tablet. I was going to record this for posterity. I plugged the earpiece in.

Curran and Kate stood by the door.

"I can't believe you decided to come down here and check on me," she said.

"The guy once handed you a fan and told you to fan yourself if the sight of his naked torso was too much."

"That was like a year ago. Will you let it go already?"

"No." Curran grabbed her and pulled her to him, kissing her. "Never."

She kissed him back and smiled.

Awww. Kate and the Beast Lord sitting in a tree . . .

The sound of a car pulling into the parking lot.

I scooted on my pallet of plywood. Showtime.

Raphael approached. My heart skipped a beat. He looked good. He was also carrying something long and wrapped in canvas.

"Hello," Raphael said.

Now that I looked closer, he seemed a little tired. There were slight bags under his intense blue eyes. Yeah, those sleepless nights of breaking into people's apartments and rearranging furniture must be killer.

"Hi," Kate said with a big fake smile.

Don't overdo it, woman. Come on.

Curran just stared. Jesus Christ, those two couldn't lie their way out of a paper bag.

"To what do I owe the pleasure?" he asked.

"We have something important . . . to discuss," Curran said.

I hit my hand on my face. Brilliant, Your Majesty. Not suspicious at all.

"In private. Inside," Kate said.

Raphael looked at Curran then slowly at Kate. "Please come in. I'm sorry I wasn't here sooner. For some reason all of the plumbing in the Clan Bouda House came apart and my mother called me."

"What do you mean, came apart?" Kate asked.

"I mean that every coupling and fitting in the house has been pulled open," Raphael said.

"I didn't know you were in the plumbing repair business," Curran said.

"I'm in the good son business. I couldn't leave my mother in the house with no running water." Raphael opened the door. "Some idiot likely pulled a prank. It's a house full of boudas."

"What's this?" Kate asked pointing at the bundle.

"An apology for being a selfish asshole." Raphael unwrapped the canvas, revealing the instantly identifiable shape of a high-tech compound bow: low-tech bows were bent outward, like a crescent, but this bow's center bent inward, toward the archer. I zoomed in. Lightweight, a hollow carbon fiber riser with the telltale Celtic knot grid pattern, dampers to absorb the recoil vibration, ornate cams, string suppressors . . . Oh Jesus Christ, he was holding an Ifor compound bow. Sleekest, leanest, meanest bow on the market, with pinpoint accuracy and a vibration-free shot delivered in complete silence. It wasn't a bow, it was death wrapped in a dream and twenty-first-century engineering. They were made in Wales by a single artisan family, one at a time. I had been trying to buy one for ages, but there was a waiting list a mile long and UK buyers were given a strong preference. How could he even get one? Where?

"Do you think she'll like it?" Raphael asked.

"She'll love it," Kate said. "But I don't think buying her things will work."

For me! The bow was for me! I dropped my tablet.

Raphael glanced up. "Did you hear something?"

Oh crap.

"No," Curran said. "Can we come in?"

"Of course." Raphael wrapped the bow back up.

I switched to the foyer camera.

The door swung open.

I held my breath.

Raphael stepped inside.

I tapped the screen, splitting it in two and zooming the right half on his face.

Raphael opened his mouth and froze.

The entire house was covered in purple ultra-long shag carpet. It wasn't just purple, it was bright, vivid, psychotic grape-purple. It made my eyes bleed after a mere five seconds. Medrano Reclamations had pulled miles of it out of some warehouse they had reclaimed, and Stefan had sold the entire lot to me dirt cheap, because nobody in their right mind would ever buy it.

I had covered everything: the floor, the walls, the ceiling. The elegant couches, the dark rough-wood coffee table, the swords on the wall, the fireplace. I had wrapped the logs in the fireplace.

Raphael just stood there and stared, his face a mask of utter shock.

Behind him Curran froze in place. Kate put her hand over her mouth, trying not to laugh.

Slowly Raphael walked inside over what once had been his pricy tile and now was just a sea of cushy, hideous purple, and looked at the kitchen.

The island was a block of carpet. I had wrapped his pots and pans hanging from the frame identical to the one he had installed at my place. I had wrapped the frame. The fridge. The stove. The butcher block, each knife handle wrapped lovingly in the purple nightmare.

"Wow," Kate said. "I had no idea you liked carpet so much, Raphael."

"What is it that you wanted to discuss?" Raphael asked, his voice monotone.

"We'll do it later," Curran said. "You're obviously too tired. Come on, Kate."

She hesitated. "But . . ."

"We need to go and do that other thing we need to do." He pulled her away and they went out. The door clicked shut.

Slowly, as if in a dream, Raphael opened the carpet-sheathed cabinet. A stack of carpeted plates looked back at him. I didn't have the time to do absolutely everything, so I had only done the plates. I knew he would open that cabinet. That's where he usually went first.

Raphael drew his hand over his face.

Slowly the shock drained away from his face. He inhaled deeply.

That's right, darling. Drink me in.

He went back into the living room and checked the windows, one by one. Slowly, unhurriedly he made his way upstairs to the master suite.

I switched to a different camera.

The bed was purple, too. He locked the windows and walked into the bathroom. The tub was carpet. The toilet was carpet. I had cut carpet into a long strip and threaded it onto the toilet paper holder.

He turned and finally noticed a mirror, the lonely spot in the synthetic moss that had sprouted all over his apartment. On it I had written in red lipstick, "Your personal padded room."

Raphael raised his head and looked up. An evil smile curved his lips. He was almost unbearably handsome.

"Andreeaaaa," he called, his voice seductive and wicked.

I gulped.

"I know you're here." His voice was like a purr wrapped in a growl. "You could never resist seeing me take this all in."

Bastard knew me too well. I tried to breathe quietly.

His shoes came off. He stretched.

"Andreaaa . . ."

His voice sent tiny caresses all over my skin.

Raphael raised his face and inhaled, sampling the air. He seemed slightly feral.

"I'm going to find you," he promised.

Oh no.

He followed my scent out of the master suite.

"You can't hide from me. I know you, I know how you think. I know you're watching me. Did you wire the house?"

He was hunting me.

Fear dashed through me, mixed with delicious excitement. The tiny hairs on the back of my neck rose.

He reached the attic.

My heart was beating a thousand beats per minute.

He reached for the cord.

Oh my God, oh my God, oh my God.

The attic's ladder slid down.

I took a deep breath.

Raphael put his foot on the first step.

I leaped up, tore my surveillance screen away from the

cables, and tried to hurl myself through the attic window. And ran right into bars. Trapped.

Raphael's head appeared in the attic doorway. He saw me. I dropped my stuff and braced myself.

Slowly, lazily he climbed the stairs. One step, two . . .

"You'll never take me alive," I told him. It felt appropriate.

He stepped into the attic. "You got it all wrong. The plan is for you to take me."

He pulled his shirt off. His scent hit me. He opened his arms . . .

I jumped him.

We collided. The smell of him, the feel of him, the heat of his skin on mine, oh my God, this cannot be happening. He kissed me on the mouth, searing hot. "I love you. I'm so sorry. I'm so sorry I was an ass . . ."

I couldn't even talk. I just kissed him, running my hands over his chest, over his muscled back, touching his hard ridged stomach, wanting him inside me, wanting to be one. He slid his hands under my T-shirt, and I pulled it off, in a desperate hurry. He touched me again, pulling me into his arms, and it felt so right, so good, so sensual that I trembled. I slid my hands into his pants and stroked the hot hardness of his shaft. I wanted to feel him inside me, sliding in and out. I wanted the ultimate proof that he was mine and that I was his, and I was hot and slick and ready. All of my tricks went out the window, and I just rubbed against him, tasting his skin and purring. He kissed my neck, sliding his tongue along the sensitive spots, and then he lost it, too. Somehow, intertwined, we made it down the attic steps into the hallway.

We had had sex hundreds of times. We had tried dozens of positions, we had flirted with our kinks, we had long ago learned how and where to touch to make each other moan and gasp and to delay each other's pleasure until the sweet antici-pation of release became almost torture . . . and we used none of it. We made love in the tried-and-true missionary position right there on the hideous purple carpet in the hallway, awk-ward and impatient, fumbling about like two virgin teenagers caught in a selfless race to make the other happy.

It was the best sex I had ever had.

* * *

My eyes snapped open. I lay in the hallway. Raphael's arm was wrapped around me. The carpet under us smelled like sex and plastic.

The ceiling was steeped in shadows. Raphael's drapes were open and they streamed down on both sides of the window. Moonlight flooded the city and struck the latticework of steel and silver bars on the window, setting them aglow with delicate radiance. The magic was up.

I glanced at the clock. Two a.m. I'd barely had an hour of sleep.

Something had woken me.

A deep rumbling noise rolled through the house.

My body went from drowsy and tired to full alert in half a second. Next to me Raphael sat up.

The sound came again, a low, deep tone like a muted roar of the bull alligator mixed with the bellow of a bull.

The window.

I jumped to my feet and ran to the window. Raphael got there at the same time. We pressed to the wall on the opposite sides of the window frame and edged the curtains aside.

Ammit stood below, its long-jawed, heavy head raised up. Its eyes stared at us. It didn't seem hostile. It simply waited.

Raphael and I traded glances.

He slid the window open. "Hi there."

Ammit stared at us.

"Shoo! Go away, girl!" I said.

"Girl?"

"Kate says it's female."

"What is it?"

"It's an Egyptian demon who devours souls."

Raphael sighed. It was a dejected, *I am so tired of this crap* sigh and it made me want to hug him.

Ammit stared at us.

"If only I had a bow," I murmured. "I could totally shoot it in the eye from here. Boom, arrow to the brain."

"Your bow is on the table downstairs. Do you like it?"

"It's the most beautiful thing in the world." Aside from him and Baby Rory.

"I'm so glad."

"How did you get one?"

He smiled at me, that handsome, slightly evil Raphael smile. "It's a secret."

I ran downstairs to fetch the bow. When I returned, Raphael still stood by the window. "It could go through the door to get to us," Raphael said. "So why doesn't it?"

We peered at Ammit.

"What is it, girl?" Raphael asked, his voice coaxing. "Did Timmy fall down the well?"

Ammit said nothing.

"It would be crazy to go out there," Raphael said.

"We'd have to be insane."

I pulled on my pants, socks, and sneakers. Raphael pulled out two fresh T-shirts from a chest by the basket of clean laundry and tossed one to me. I grabbed my Ifor, he got his knives, and we took off down the stairs.

Outside, the night was bright. Pale bluish vapor rose from the chunks of concrete that made up the low wall around the house—something magic must've been brought out by the moonlight. I drew my bow and we snuck around the building, moving silently, carefully walking on the balls of our feet.

Step.

Another step.

I turned the corner and the tip of my arrow touched Ammit's nose. It's amazing how far you can jump backward, if properly motivated.

Raphael stepped around me and approached the massive beast. We had killed it. I could still picture its corpse in my mind, fresh and vivid, the blood, the dulled eyes, the great maw gaping lifelessly, spilling the tongue on the ground. Yet there it stood.

Raphael reached out.

"Don't," I warned.

He touched its head, petting its cheek. The tentacles of Ammit's mane twisted toward him and slid harmlessly off his hand.

The beast sighed. Two clouds of moist vapor escaped its nostrils.

It didn't open its crocodile mouth and bite Raphael's hand off.

Slowly Ammit turned, trotted forward a few feet, and looked at us over its muscular shoulder.

You've got to be kidding me.

"No."

The jaws gaped open and the roar rolled forth, primal and ancient, so much older than the city around it, so alien that I wondered for a second if the illusion of Atlanta would tear under the force of that primeval call and I would end up standing in the muddy, rich waters of the Nile. I could almost see the tall slender reeds shifting in the night breeze.

The roar sang through my veins, urging me to follow.

Ammit took a step forward and looked at us.

"Should we?" I murmured.

Raphael shrugged. "Alright, Lassie. Lead on."

The great beast started down the slope, and we followed. Ammit built to a fast trot. We ran through the magic-soaked city. My feet were weightless, and we devoured the distance, swallowing mile after mile, tireless and exhilarated.

Tendrils of faint orange vapor curled from the beast, streaming from its mane and back. Its magic enveloped me. It felt so right, running like this, hunting like this, next to Raphael. Lean, muscular, the white T-shirt molded to his body, he ran with grace and power, his long legs in gray Pack sweatpants carrying him forward. His skin almost glowed. Sweat dampened his dark hair. His dark eyes focused on something far ahead.

The compound bow in my hand could be made of horn, wood, and sinew. The oversized white T-shirt Raphael had given me could be a tunic. The asphalt under my feet could be sand or the dry red soil of low hills. The air smelled of lotus and water lily, and sometimes of dew-soaked jasmine, and then of dry desert.

Ammit stopped and I almost cried out. I wanted to keep running.

The reality came back, fading in through the magic. We were in front of the Cutting Edge office.

The magic of Ammit swirled around us, evaporating slowly, like distant notes of perfume dissipating from the skin.

A second Ammit thundered down the street toward us, a huge black horse following it. Roman dismounted next to us, his staff in his hand. He wore a tank top and black pajama pants with an Eeyore pattern.

"I have had it with this shit," he announced. "I got woken up in the middle of the night, didn't get any sleep again, rode across the whole damned city, *nu na cherta mne ato nuzhno.*" He waved his hand in front of his face. "Damn magic everywhere, making me sneeze."

The Ammit next to him opened its mouth. Roman whacked it with the top of his staff on the nose. "You—shut up."

The Ammit looked just like a cat who had gotten popped with a newspaper: half-shocked, half-outraged. Roman surveyed the two of us. "What's the matter with you two? Why do you look all dazed?"

The magic melted, taking the visions of the Nile with it. My mind struggled to formulate a coherent thought, any thought. I opened my mouth. "Your pajamas have Eeyore on them."

"I like Eeyore. He's sensible. A sober outlook on life never hurt anyone."

Raphael shook his head, trying to clear it. "What are you doing here?"

Roman grimaced. "How would I know? Last night I helped Andrea and then a winged *gadina* took my staff, and tonight I woke up with this varmint howling under my window."

Raphael turned to me. "Last night? After I called you?"

"Yeah."

"Why didn't you call me to come and help?"

"Why would I call you? You can't do magic."

The wheels slowly turned in Raphael's head. He looked at Roman. "How long have you been helping her?"

Roman's face took on a dangerous expression. "I'm sorry, since when do I answer to you, exactly?"

The two men squared off. Great. I tried the door of the office. Unlocked.

Raphael stepped forward. Roman did, too. They stood dangerously close.

"I asked you a question," Raphael said, his voice saturated with menace.

Roman's voice turned icy. "And I told you to fuck yourself. Which part wasn't clear?"

"Hey!" I snapped.

They looked at me.

"The door is open," I said. "You can stay out here and compare inches for the entire night, but I'm going inside."

I swung the door open and stepped across the threshold.

The office was bathed in a gentle yellow glow. The air smelled of sweet myrrh, fiery cinnamon, balsam, and the smoky, spicy mix of thyme and marjoram. The pungent aroma didn't seem to drift but saturated the room, hanging in the air, filling the place.

I stepped inside. My desk and Kate's were missing. Four braziers, bronze dishes filled with some sort of fuel on tall metal stems, burned bright, set on both sides of a large chair. In the chair sat Anapa. He rested his cheek on his hand, bent at the elbow and leaning on the chair's armrest, one long leg over the other.

Flames played in his eyes. He looked absurd, sitting there in his makeshift throne room, wearing a three-piece black suit. Thought he owned this place, did he?

I crossed my arms. "Love the makeover. The room has so much more space now. How much do we owe you?"

"Who are you?" Roman asked behind me.

"That's Anubis, God of the Dead," I told him.

"The name is Inepu," Anapa said. It sounded midway between Anapa and Enahpah. "The Greeks didn't bother to pronounce it properly. I always found them very close-minded. Don't follow their suit, you're better than that."

"You aren't a god," Roman said. "Gods can't walk the Earth. Don't have enough juice." He turned to me and Raphael. "Trust me, I've tried to summon one."

"Why the hell would you summon a god?" Raphael asked.

"He was trying to kill his cousin," Anapa said.

"That was a long time ago." Roman waved his hand.

Anapa's lips curved, and he smiled a bright genuine smile, suffused with humor. "No, that was last May."

"Like I said, a long time ago," Roman said.

Anapa laughed and pointed his finger at Roman. "I like you."

"Are you a god?" Raphael asked.

Anapa waved his hand. "Yes and no. The answer is complicated."

Right, we were too stupid to understand it. "I'm sure we can scrape enough brain cells together between the three of us. Indulge us."

"There is no need for such hostility, Andrea Marie. I'm not your enemy. Well, not yet."

So he knew my middle name. So what.

Anapa shrugged. "I suppose I will explain this to you, so you will stop wondering about it. We have important subjects to discuss and I'll need your full attention. When magic began to fade from the world, I took a mortal form and fathered a child, pouring all my essence into it. Then I fell asleep. My child in turn had a child, and he had a child, and on and on, my lineage stretched throughout time, until the returning magic awoke me. As I became aware, I hovered on the verge of existence until my descendant decided to do as most men do and bred with a charming woman. I called to my essence within the bloodline and merged with the beginning life during the moment of conception. In a sense, I fathered myself into being. You could say I am an avatar. Neat trick, huh?" He winked at us.

The human part of him kept him alive during the tech. That also meant he was weak while the magic was gone. Weak was good. "I thought you'd look more Egyptian," I told him.

"And how do you think the original Egyptians looked?" Anapa raised his eyebrows. "What do you know of us? Were you there at the birth of the glory that was Egypt? Were you there to watch as we mixed with Nubians, Hittites, Libyans, Assyrians, Persians, and Greeks, you dumb little puppy? Colors, pigments, texture of skin and hair, those things are mere glaze. The vessel underneath is always clay."

This was above my pay grade. "Roman?"

"He might be a nut job," Roman said. "If he's telling the truth, he isn't at full strength."

Anapa sighed. "So tiresome. Very well."

Wind swept through the office, streaming from behind Anapa—hot, heavy with moisture, streaked with decay, the odor of spiced wine, and heady aromas of resins. The flames bent away from Anapa. A jackal howled, a long eerie wail that gripped my throat in a ghostly fist and squeezed.

The man on the chair leaned forward. A translucent outline shimmered along his skin, expanded, and a different creature sat in Anapa's place. He was tall, long-limbed, and lean. A network of muscle bound his torso, crisply defined, but far from bulky. His skin was a warm, rich brown with a touch of terra-cotta. His face with its wide brown eyes was beautiful, but it wasn't the kind of beauty you wanted to touch—it radiated too much power, too much regal disdain. As he looked at us, the contours of his head flowed like molten wax. His nose and jaw protruded forward and narrowed to a dark nose. Two long ears thrust up. Black and gray fur sheathed his face. The flash of white fangs in his mouth was like lightning.

Magic streamed from him, potent, powerful, over-whelming.

He rose from the chair, an impossibility, a man with a human torso and a jackal head. Outside, the two Ammit roared in unison. The press of his magic was impossible to bear.

The illusion shattered. I realized I had forgotten to breathe and sucked in air in a hoarse gulp.

Anapa smiled at me, sitting in his chair again, languid and mildly amused. "Now, that we have that settled, let's talk. I have a bone to pick with you. All three of you, as a matter of fact."

Raphael took a step forward. "I will reimburse you for the beast."

"The one you killed?" Anapa's animated face turned puzzled. "Oh, there was no need. I resurrected her the moment the magic wave appeared. I did very much enjoy your battle. A stunning display of strategic thinking." He looked at me and then at Raphael. "You and you, you work well together." He turned to Raphael. "Except at the end when both of you went a little mad."

A muscle jerked in Raphael's face.

"Don't worry." Anapa wrinkled his nose. "Happens to the best of us."

Raphael took a step forward. I put my hand on his forearm.

Anapa rubbed his hands together. "Now we'll have our-selves a bit of show-and-tell, shall we?"

The floor of the office between him and us turned lighter.
Stylized figures formed on its surface.

"Neat, isn't it?" Anapa grinned. "I got an idea from an old
movie. So, listen and watch. Please feel free to sit down if you
wish."

Brown figures came down from the hills toward the blue
river.

"That would be the ancient Egyptian cattle herders. The
climate changed, and all of their grass fields are drying out, so
they have to go back to the Nile. Look at them, they are
so sad."

The figures fell to their knees and started drinking from
the Nile. On the other side a second group of figures started
throwing rocks at the newcomers.

"Those are the people who had remained in the valley.
They don't want the poor cattle herders there. See, they are all
upset."

One of the figures held up a crooked staff.

A huge triangular head broke the surface of the water. An
enormous brown and yellow snake slithered out of the Nile
and began to feed on the newcomers.

Anapa leaned forward. "That would Apep. The God of the
River. These guys, the ones who stayed in the valley, they
worshipped him, so he wouldn't eat them. He is a nasty
bugger."

The dismembered bodies of the ancient Egyptians fell in
the water.

"But what's this?"

Four figures appeared, shaking swords and spears. One
had a hawk head, the second had a cat's head, the third a jackal's, and the fourth seemed to be a bizarre cross between a
donkey and aardvark.

"That would be Ra, his daughter Bast, me, and Set."

"I know that myth," Roman said. "It was Ra who killed
him."

Anapa looked at him in mild outrage. "I'm sorry, were you
there? No. Then hush. Of course, myths say that Ra killed
him. That's what you get when you're a sun god and crops
depend on you, my friend. Look, I'll prove it to you." An
ancient mural appeared on the wall, showing a yellow spotted

cat resembling a mountain cat stabbing a snake with a curved blade. "Supposedly this is Ra slaying Apep. Small problem: Ra has a hawk's head on his shoulders. He doesn't turn into a cat, except for this one time. Keep that in mind. Now where were we?"

The four figures attacked the serpent, chopping at him with strange curved swords and poking him with spears. The serpent flailed, knocking them aside, and biting at their bodies. Finally the picture-Anubis turned into a huge jackal and bit Apep's neck, clamping it down. The three other figures rushed him. The snake convulsed, knocking aside everyone except for Bast. The nimble cat jumped over the flailing body and stabbed the serpent in the heart.

"So why do the myths say that Ra killed him?" Roman said.

"Because priests were men and we can't have the big enemy getting killed by a girl, can we now?" Anapa winked at me. "Holy texts are written by committee, and Ra had more priests. His cult was stronger. He is the sun, the life-giver, while Bast was only the protector of Lower Egypt. She used to be a lioness. Very fierce. By the time the priests were done with her, she'd turned into a domestic kitty cat. Took them a thousand years or so, but they crippled the lion."

A bright flash of light exploded from Apep's body, knocking the four figures down.

"Look at us, all knocked out." Anapa smiled. "Lots of magic is released when you kill a god. Look at me there. See, I only have one fang? It broke off in the snake's neck. Took me two days to grow a new one."

The light faded. The four gods still lay prone on the ground. Little figures swarmed Apep, chopping his body to pieces.

"Who are they?" I asked.

"Saii. His priests. They're trying to save parts of him. That one took a scale. And this one got a vertebrae."

"Those four are eating the corpse." Raphael pointed at the four figures on all fours biting Apep's side.

"They are devouring his flesh, so it will live through them. Nasty business."

The final person pried Anubis's fang from Apep's dead body and the figures ran away.

"Of course, we chased them, but they were crafty," Anapa

said. "They scattered to the four winds, hoping to eventually reunite and resurrect their god." Anapa clapped his hands. The mural faded. "And that brings us to our current calamity, gentlemen and the lady, of course."

The god smiled and pointed at Raphael. "You cost me my fang. It was dipped in metal and made to look like a knife, but inside it's still my tooth with the blood of Apep in it. It was in the vault of that damned ruin and you had to buy it out from under me." He turned to Roman. "You lost the staff carved from the vertebrae of Apep and his rib. They hid it in a room full of magical artifacts, so their magic would mask its location from me. You found it, took it out, and instead of taking it someplace safe, you practically served it back to them on a silver platter. Your own holy relic. Here is your award for stupidity. Congratulations."

Roman opened his mouth and clamped it shut.

Anapa turned to me. "And you helped them both, stuck your nose where it didn't belong, set the other furballs on me, and made my life difficult all around. I can't move around the city, because there are two of your kind following me like a tail follows a dog. And half of the time, one of them is a cat. Do you have any idea how much I despise cats?"

Anapa took a long, calming breath. "Right now, Apep's cult has the staff, the fang, and likely at least a few descendants of the Saii, the four priests who engaged in that creative gastronomy. So the question is, what are we going to do about it?"

"What happens if Apep is resurrected?" Raphael asked.

"Well, let us review." Anapa leaned back. "He is the god of darkness, chaos, and evil. Let us agree to put aside philosophical concepts of evil and good, as they are subjective. What is evil for one is good for another. Let's talk instead about chaos. Chaos, as our priest here will tell you, is an extremely powerful force. Do any of you know what a fractal is?"

Roman raised his hand.

Anapa grimaced. "I know you know. Here."

A dark equilateral triangle ignited on the floor.

Anapa waved his hand. A smaller equilateral triangle appeared in the middle of the darker one, its corners touching the sides of the original triangle.

"How many triangles?" Anapa asked.

"Five," I said. "Three dark, one light in the middle, and the big one."

"Again," Anapa said.

A smaller light triangle appeared in the middle of each dark triangle.

"Again. Again. Again."

He stopped, pointing at the filigree of triangles on the floor. "I could go on to infinity. In basic terms, a fractal is a system that doesn't become simpler when analyzed on smaller and smaller levels. Keep that in your head."

A system that can't be broken down to basic components. Okay, got it.

Anapa leaned forward. "To understand chaos, you have to understand mathematics. A lot of your civilization—most of any civilization, really—is built on mathematical analysis, the guiding principle of which is that everything can be explained and understood, if you just break it into small enough chunks. In other words, everything has an end. If you dig deep enough into any complex system, you will eventually unearth its simplest parts, which can't be broken down any further. That sort of thinking works for a great many things, but not all of them. For example, the fractal. It doesn't end."

I felt like I was back in the Order's Academy at some lecture. "This is surreal."

"The fractal?" Anapa asked.

"You. Explaining this."

Anapa gave a long-suffering sigh. "What do you know about me?"

And now I'd been singled out of the class. "You are the deity of funeral rites."

"And what else?"

Umm . . .

"Medicine. The exploration of biology and metaphysics.

Knowledge. This is my primary function. I impart knowledge. I teach. One can't just give man fire. It's like giving a toddler a box of matches—he will burn the house down. You must teach him how to use it." Anapa shook his head. "Back to the fractal. It can't be explained by mathematical analysis, so humanity, as it so often does, declared it to be a mathematical curiosity and swept it under the rug. Except the fractal occurs again and again."

An earthworm appeared on the floor of the office.

"A line," Anapa said. "So simple."

He sliced the air with his finger. The earthworm divided in two. Two became four, four became eight, eight became sixteen, more and more. A swarm of worms roiled and writhed on the floor.

Anapa pondered the knot of bodies. "Left to its own devices, nature defaults to a fractal. A human settlement is a fractal. It is a complex system with randomly interacting components that is adaptive on every level. The pattern of the evolution of a single cell to complex organism is a fractal. The way man approaches his quest for knowledge is a fractal. Think of it: biology, the study of living things. A simple concept."

A straight line appeared on the floor.

"As man accumulates knowledge, the volume of information becomes too much. He feels the need to subdivide it."

The line split into three branches marked with labels: zoology, botany, anatomy, then split again. Botany grew horticulture, forestry, plant morphology, plant systematics. Zoology splintered into zoological morphology and systematics, then into comparative anatomy, systematics, animal physiology, behavioral ecology . . . It kept building and building, splitting, growing, branching, too fast, too much, overwhelming . . .

"Make it stop." I didn't even realize I said it, until I heard my mouth produce the words.

The line disappeared.

"And that's the crux of our problem," Anapa said, his voice contemplative. "Man can't handle the chaos. Oh, you can understand it in abstract, as long as you don't think about it too hard. But at the core of it, whenever humans come against chaos, they deal with it in one of three ways. They hide from it, pretending it isn't there. They dress it up in pretty clothes. The God of the Hebrews is a fractal. He can do anything, he knows everything, he is infinite in his power and complexity. He is a fractal, so humanity felt the need to compartmentalize him. They don't tackle the concept head-on. They tiptoe around it by telling little fables and anecdotes about their deity, and then when push came to shove, they invented a new aspect of him, his son, who comes with a more narrow, definitive message of infinite love."

Anapa fell silent.

"You said there were three ways," Raphael said.

"I did, didn't I? Faced with chaos you will either ignore it, dance around it, or you will go mad. Apep is chaos. He is a primal expression of a fundamental principle, a fractal, a force rather than a deity. The priests of Egypt worshipped against him just to keep him at bay."

"How do you worship against something?" Raphael asked.

"Let me tell you: once a year they got together, made a fake Apep, threw a big party, and burned him with great ceremony. There are actual rules for how to properly defile him. First, we spit on Apep. Then we stomp on him with our left foot. Then we use a lance to stab Apep, and so on. Do you see how they attempted to impose order upon chaos through a complex ritual?"

Anapa leaned forward. "If let loose, Apep will drive humanity insane. You will devolve into primeval barbarism where nothing exists except his worship in its most rudimentary form. You will abandon reason and logic and feed yourselves to him by the thousands like the idiots you are."

The shadow outline of a jackal's head flared around Anapa's head. His dark lips trembled, betraying a glimpse of his fangs. "So you see, I have a vested interest in this venture. In the presence of Apep, no other god can exist. I want to prevent his resurrection, and if he manages to resurrect, I have to murder him again. And the three of you will help me."

Silence descended. My mind struggled to get a grip. Too much information to process. "If Apep is so terrible, why do they want to resurrect him?"

"Because they are outcasts," Anapa said. "They are unlike others. They grow snake fangs in their mouths, they have jaws that open too wide, and they know that others are repulsed by it. They seek to belong. They want to know where they came from and they want to take pride in who they are. They probably think Apep will protect them and he will. It's just the rest of humanity that will be on his menu."

"I want the staff," Roman said suddenly.

"Mmm?" Anapa looked at him.

"I want the staff," the black volhv repeated. "If I do this, you will not harm me and will give me the Bone Staff to take back to my people."

"Fine." Anapa waved his hand.

I stared at Roman. "What are you doing?"

"I'm imposing order on a fractal," Roman said. "If I define the terms of the bargain, he's bound by them. He can't do anything else to me."

Anapa leaned back and laughed.

Raphael stepped forward. His face was grim and I saw determination in the set of his jaw. *Uh-oh.*

"You have a problem with me over the knife. Why didn't you just ask for the knife?" Raphael said.

"Because the less you knew about this mess, the better," Anapa said. "Given half a chance, humans will screw things up, as the three of you have so deftly proven."

"So you deliberately kept me in the dark, and now you want to blame me for my ignorance? That isn't fair."

Anapa's gaze fixed on him. "I am a god. I don't do fair."

Raphael met it. "You have a problem with me, fine. Leave her out of this. She didn't do anything to you."

"No," Anapa said.

Oh, Raphael. Why would you think I would stand for that?

"If you want my help, let her off the hook." Raphael growled.

Anapa shook his head. "No."

"Why?"

The ghostly jackal head appeared around Anubis. "Who are you to question me?"

Raphael's lips trembled, betraying a flash of his teeth. "She goes free with no obligation to participate in your scheme. That's my price."

"Rejected."

They stared at each other. Muscles tensed on Raphael's frame. I smelled a brawl.

A third of me wanted to rip Raphael's head off for the insult. I was perfectly capable of holding my own. I didn't need his help to extricate me, nor did I need his grand sacrifice. Another third was all bursting at the seams with happiness: when facing a god, his first thought wasn't about saving himself but about keeping me safe. He was willing to fight a god of chaos to keep me out of this mess. The final third of me just howled in blind terror, terrified for my safety, and even more terrified for the idiot bouda who was trying to buy my life with his.

And that was my relationship with Raphael in a nutshell: too complicated.

If I didn't do something, the fool would throw himself away. In my head I saw Raphael buried under a pile of snakes. It was like a dagger straight in the heart.

No. No-no-no. Not happening.

I cleared my throat. "Girls, girls, you're both lovely. I appreciate the sentiment, I do. But I will make my own decisions and the two of you will kindly get the hell out of my way."

Raphael looked like he wanted to bite something. A self-satisfied smirk played on Anapa's lips. I didn't like it. Not one little bit.

"Counteroffer," I said. "You take me, let Raphael go." No need for both of us to get killed.

"Denied," the god said. "This is getting tiresome."

Arghhh. "What is it you want from us, exactly?"

"The priests have my fang, the staff, and the descendants of the Saii. They lack the scale. It was made into a shield. I need you to get it before the priests do."

"Why don't you just get it yourself?" Raphael asked.

"Because I am a god. I don't run my own errands."

"Did you know he's a god?" Raphael asked me.

"I had no idea. He hasn't mentioned it," I said.

"So modest and unassuming," Raphael said.

"I will kill you both and make pretty rugs out of your pelts," Anapa said. "Stop being tiresome and get the scale for me."

Simple enough. "Where is it?"

"Ask your friend," Anapa said. "Ask the Beast Lord's Consort."

"Kate?" How the hell was Kate involved in this?

"Yes. Tell her to bring another deer. She will know."

"I'm not going to move a finger unless you give me clear and simple instructions without mystical bullshit."

"That's not my way," Anapa said. "You will take your instructions in whatever form I choose."

"Then I'm out." Chew on that, why don't you.

"Is that your final word?" Anapa said.

"Yes."

"Fine. We'll do it the hard way."

A girl walked out of the back room. She couldn't have been more than seven or eight. She moved slowly, as if unsure where her feet were. Her eyes, dark and opened wide, were blank. Her dark skin had an ashen tint.

I tensed. Next to me Raphael bent his knees slightly, preparing for a leap.

"This is Brandy."

Brandy looked at us with her empty eyes.

"Brandy is a shapeshifter like you. From Clan Jackal. The jackals and I share a certain bond." Anapa studied his nails, looking bored. "I plucked her out at random. Her parents are frantically looking for her by now, I'd imagine. Why don't you tell them how you feel, Brandy?"

The child opened her mouth. "Help," a weak tiny voice said. "Help . . . me."

I yanked the bow off my shoulder and aimed an arrow at Anapa's left eye. Raphael exploded in a riot of fur and muscle, snarling as the monster that was a bouda in a warrior form spilled into existence.

"Let the child go." I sank the promise of death into my voice.

"Every day you do not do as you are told, I'll take another Jackal child at sunset," Anapa said. "If the lion gets involved, the children die. If any of your other Pack friends help you fight, the children die."

I fired. My arrow pierced the wood of the chair a fraction of a second before Raphael's claws scoured it. The child and the god were gone.

CHAPTER 13

❖

The office phone was dead.

Roman took off "to gather supplies."

Anapa said the shapeshifters couldn't help us fight. He said nothing about us telling the Pack what was going on. The Jackals had to be warned. I shifted shape, and Raphael and I ran into the night.

We cut through the decrepit industrial district, moving at the shapeshifter equivalent of a canter. Ruins streamed by us, dark, inky black, like haunted wrecks of ancient ships. Gutted warehouses with steel beams thrusting out, vehicle shells, treacherous caves of concrete hiding hungry things with glowing eyes, born of magic and hungry for a burst of hot blood on their tongues. The beasts looked but didn't venture close. They recognized us for what we were—predators, built to hunt, kill, and devour—and right now neither of us was in the mood to be merciful.

The city ended and we ran along the crumbling highway. Here nature revolted, fueled by magic, and trees had grown with shocking speed, crowding the old road. We kept going, tireless, eating the miles like they were delicious bites. Wolves didn't have a monopoly on marathon chases. We were hyenas. We could run forever.

Raphael moved next to me, so graceful, so lethal, full of fierce beauty. It felt so right, running like this, guarding each other's flank. Together we were a tiny pack . . . a mated couple. Should any threat cross our path, we'd rip into it together. I had forgotten what it felt like.

The road brought us to a group of three oaks. Here a narrow trail branched from the main highway, barely wide

enough for a single vehicle to pass. Blink and you would miss
it. We turned onto it in unison.

The path curled and twisted, veering through the woods.

A wolf howl rose in the distance—a pure, beautiful note
soaring to the clear skies. Another answered. The Keep sentries announcing our approach. A deep voiced whoop followed, a warning and a declaration of ownership in one—a
bouda must've been on duty tonight.

We burst out of the woods into a clearing. A massive structure towered before us, the solid, impenetrable mass of stone
shaped into a semblance of a fortified castle or castlelike fort.
It was the ultimate den, wrapped into a wall of gray stone,
with towers, defenses, a vast underground, and a myriad of
hidden passageways and escape routes. A testament to Curran's paranoia. Even if the Keep were besieged, even if the
siege was lost, the Pack would melt into the woods to reunite
and fight another day.

We cleared the courtyard and kept running, through the
door, through the narrow hallway, up a dozen of stair flights
all the way to the top of the tower, to the floor just below Curran's private quarters. The guard recognized us and stepped
out of the way. Raphael was the male bouda alpha. He sat on
the Council with Aunt B. Nobody would stop him.

We rushed into the spacious room Curran called his office.
The Beast Lord was sitting behind his desk, looking at some
papers. Kate sat on the couch with a tortured look on her face,
holding a copy of the book of Pack law and making notes in a
notebook.

They looked up in unison.

"Clan Jackal is in danger," I said.

We sat in a conference room, both still in our fur, with the
Beast Lord, Kate, Jim, and Colin and Geraldine Mather, the
Jackal alphas. Colin, a muscular, beefy man with a wrestler's
build and pale hair, leaned on the table, his face flat and unreadable. His mate and wife sat next to him. Where Colin was fair,
Geraldine was dark, her skin a deep brown, her hair black, her
body honed to muscular efficiency by constant training.

"Her name is Brandy Kerry," Geraldine said. "She is seven years old. Her parents are on a business trip to Charlotte. They left her here in the Keep in the boarding school in the south wing. She took a nap at five o'clock with the rest of the children in her class. The room is on the seventh floor. The windows are barred. Ruth, the teaching aide, sat by the door, reading a book. At the end of the hour, she came in to wake the children and found Brandy's bed empty. Ruth searched the room. None of the other seven kids saw anything. Brandy just evaporated from her bed and nobody had noticed."

"The rest of the staff searched the floor," Colin continued. "Every room was checked, and to get to the staircase, she would've had to go past the school receptionist and a guard, and Connie swore she did not see a child leave. When it became evident that Brandy wasn't anywhere on the school floor, we were alerted to the situation."

Of all the clans, Jackals were the most paranoid when it came to their children. Where boudas spoiled their kids with too much freedom and cats encouraged offspring to go on solitary wanderings, the jackals always stressed family. In the wild, unlike wolves who formed packs or rats who swarmed, jackals mated for life and lived in pairs, raising their children on their own little slices of territory.

"I yelled at Ruth." Geraldine clenched her hand into a fist. "I thought she walked off or fell asleep, and Brandy had snuck out."

"We checked the bars on the window and did a complete sweep of the wing and the outside," Colin said. "No sign of her."

"He took that baby." A snarl slipped into Geraldine's voice. "He plucked her right out of her bed, that fucking bastard. I will tear his guts out."

"If you confront him, he'll kill you and her," Kate said.

Geraldine whirled to her.

"It's not an insult," Curran said. "She's stating a fact. He has power over jackals."

"So what do we do?" Geraldine raised her hands.

"We do nothing," Curran said.

"But —"

"We do nothing," he repeated. "We don't know where he's

keeping the child, but he won't hesitate to kill her. We will meet his demands. For now."

"He wants Andrea and I to help him," Raphael said. "We will do it."

"We've discussed it," I said. "As long as we play ball, no more children will be taken."

Colin's voice turned into a rough growl. "So you want us to sit on our hands, then?"

"No," Kate said. "Find out everything you can on him. Go to the books, visit experts, get as much information as you can on him. Find out his weaknesses, if he has any. As soon as the moment presents itself, we will hit him with everything we have."

"We've killed wannabe gods before," Curran said. "Hell, we could probably kill him now. But I will not do it at the cost of a child's life. We must be patient and smart. Bring your people into the Keep. The fewer isolated targets the better. Raise the alert. Nobody goes anywhere except in groups of three. Sleep in shifts, with the guards watching over the children."

"I will reinforce the wards on the south wing again," Kate said. "It won't stop him, but it may make it harder for him."

The alpha Jackals looked like they wanted to tear their hair out.

"Patience," Curran said. "We can't pull that chain, because there is a child attached to the other end of it. We'll stalk him like a deer, with all the cunning and calculation we have. Jackals have a reputation as scavengers, but all of us know better. All of us here have seen Clan Jackal families bring down deer and moose. There is honor in taking prey much larger than yourself, especially if that prey is smart and difficult to trap."

There was a reason why Curran was the Beast Lord.

"He may be a god," Curran continued, "but he's in our world now and he's alone. Together we're smarter, more cunning, and more vicious. Patience."

The Jackals switched from agitation to a terrifying steely determination. "Patience," Geraldine repeated, as if tasting it on her tongue to get the full meaning of the word.

Colin nodded. "AJ is a professor of cultural anthropology. He may know an expert."

Five minutes later they had come up with six names and left.

"It won't hold them for long," Jim said, a few moments after the door closed behind them. "When the parents return, they will whip the clan into a frenzy."

"Then we need to resolve it before the parents return." Curran looked at Raphael and me. "What do you need?"

"A deer," I said.

"I'm sorry?" Jim said.

"He said that Kate would know where the shield was and to tell her to bring another deer," Raphael elaborated.

Curran looked at his mate. Something passed between them, some sort of wordless conversation only they understood.

"Hell no," Curran said.

"They can't summon it by themselves and you can't get involved," Kate said.

Curran's eyes turned into molten gold. "Are you out of your mind? It took you, me, and five vampires and we barely got away. He has your scent now. Nobody goes to see him twice."

"Nobody except me." She gave him her psycho look.

The Beast Lord clenched his jaw.

Kate smiled at him.

The tension was so thick you could cut it into slices and serve it on toast. Of all control freaks, Curran was the worst and he existed convinced that Kate was made of fragile glass. I understood it. I completely understood. He was in exactly the same place I had been a couple of hours before: watching someone you love dive headfirst into danger and not being able to do a damn thing about it. It was difficult to watch and harder to live through.

"There are hard battles and there is suicide," Curran said.

"Agreed. I have a plan," Kate said.

Curran raised his hands, inviting the miraculous plan to come forth.

"The volhv serves Chernobog, who presides over the dead and fallen in battle. This is his area of expertise."

"I'd like to be in on this discussion," Raphael said.

"Me, too," I added.

"The shield belongs to a draugr," Curran said. "It's an undead, unkillable giant."

"How unkillable?" I asked.

"We couldn't kill it," Kate said.

"Both of you at the same time?" Raphael asked.

She nodded.

Great.

"We won't be trying to kill him," Kate said. "He's confined by wards, but once we take his shield and carry it past the ward line, the protective spells may fail. We can't let him rampage around, because he eats people. That's where the volhv comes in. Roman will have to rebind the draugr."

"Can he even do this?" Curran asked.

"Well, we'll have to ask him," Kate said.

There was more planning and discussing and talking, and at the end of it, I was so tired, I couldn't see straight. The draugr was really bad news. I said that we needed extra firepower, the kind that would work during magic.

"Galahad warheads," I told them. Strictly speaking it wasn't a warhead, but rather an arrowhead that fit into a custom crossbow and carried a magic charge that would take down an elephant or a giant, for whom it was invented in Wales. In my time with the Order I had managed to order two cases of them from the UK. I even had the new bow to go with them.

Shortly after that, Barabas dragged Raphael off to talk about some sort of important thing that couldn't wait. Kate led me to a room that had a bed, and I collapsed into it, fur and all. The Pack bed was so soft. Like floating on a cloud.

Fatigue weighed me down. I closed my eyes, feeling the ache humming through my legs. Shouldn't have sat down . . . yawn . . . straight after running . . . yawn. Should've walked it off . . . first . . .

I stood in the water. It splashed past my ankles, dark blue-green and warm. Soft mud squished beneath my feet. I made fists with my toes and watched a bright green cloud of powdery silt rise from the river's bottom, swirling around my legs.

Patches of reeds grew, stretching into the river, bending lightly in the wind, as though they were whispering gossip to each other. In the distance, across the vast expanse of water, the sun was setting or rising, a small ball of yellow hovering at the edge of low dark hills, the silver-nacre sky around it painted with pink and yellow.

I looked over my shoulder. A yellow shore greeted me, touched with patches of bright green grass, and beyond it palms stretched upward.

We were definitely not in Kansas anymore.

A slender bird walked past me on long legs. It had a curved neck and a long beak and I realized it was a heron.

A presence brushed against me, saturated with magic. I turned. A jackal the size of a rhino waded into the river downstream from me and lapped the water, watching me with golden eyes.

Right. I was standing in the Nile, watching Anapa, and this was not an ordinary dream. There were rules to this dream. No promises, no striking of bargains, in fact, no talking. Nobody yet had managed to get into a shitty bargain with a god by keeping their mouth shut.

"Beautiful, isn't it?" The Jackal-Anapa raised his head and looked into the distance, at the sun. "Do you like the way it smells?"

It smelled verdant. It smelled like the moisture of the river mixing with the fragrance of dry grasses from the shore, and flowers, and fish, and rich mud. It smelled like the sort of place where life would flourish and hunting would be plentiful.

"It's your father's blood. It calls to you," the Jackal said.

Bullshit. My father was an animal.

"Animals miss their home, too."

Right. He was in my head. No thinking, then.

"Do you know why others fear you? They call you beast-kin, they try to kill you? It is because of this. Of beastly memories you carry in your blood. The Firsts, the pack leaders of your kind, were made in much the same way as you. When primitive man prayed, he prayed for strength. His life was ruled by forces beyond his control: lightning, rain, wind, sun, and things with teeth that sought to eat him in the night. So the primitive man resorted to begging. He prayed to the predators, to those stronger than he, and sometimes, very, very rarely, his prayers were answered and a boon was granted. The Firsts, they are a perfect mix of human and animal. You are not, and thus you do not have the Firsts' strength or control, but you share in their memories. You see the world through your mother's eyes and through your father's."

"I see it through my own eyes." Drat. Shouldn't have said anything. I clamped my mouth shut.

The Jackal chuckled.

The sun had set behind the hills. Dusk claimed the river. Gloom wove its way through the palms. Faint tendrils of steam escaped the river, still warmer than bathwater.

"I want your body," Anapa said.

"That's flattering, but no." I couldn't help it, it just burst out.

"Not in a sexual way, you foolish child. The body I wear in the world is a part of my bloodline. But he is weak. Its magic reserves are meager. Make no mistake, if Apep is resurrected, the assistance I can offer you will be limited at best. Your body is strong. Your blood is rooted in the same place as mine. We're both a mix of beast and man. You're a more suitable host than any of the other shapeshifters I have encountered."

"I'm a hyena. You're a jackal."

"I will make do," Anapa said.

"And what happens to me?"

"You will merge with me."

"You're lying." I knew it. I felt it in my gut.

The Jackal lapped the river. "Perhaps."

"Why would I throw my life away?"

"Because I am a god and I asked for it."

"You are not my god."

The Jackal sighed. "That is the trouble with this age. There was a time when thousands would slit their own throats for my sake."

"No. There was never that time."

The Jackal bared his teeth. "What do you know, whelp?"

"I know human nature. We might sacrifice a few, because we are stupid and hardwired for group survival. But we would never die in the thousands because a god wished it. Those kinds of numbers require material gains, like power, wealth, territory."

The Jackal stared at me. "Give me your body."

"No."

"There may come a time when you will say yes."

"Don't hold your breath."

The Jackal laughed softly. "Look over there."

I glanced up and saw a man. He stood in the river, nude, with the waters lapping at his thighs. The last rays of the setting sun colored his side, throwing orange highlights on his skin, tracing every contour of the etched muscle. He looked so . . . perfect. Except his face was a blur.

"Who is it?"

The man's body arched up, his back bending back at an unnatural angle, the ridges of the stomach muscles stretching and his face came into focus. Raphael.

A figure rose above him, an eight-foot-tall man with the head of a jackal. He raised his hand, a golden staff in it, and passed it over the body. The skin over the Raphael's chest and abdomen split.

I gasped. *No!*

Blood fountained, coloring the waters of the Nile. Raphael's muscles opened like bloody petals. Anubis held his hand with outstretched fingers and a human heart, steaming hot and drenched in blood, tore itself out of my mate's chest and landed in the god's clawed fingers.

My own heart skipped a beat.

Anubis waded through the water toward me, the heart still beating. I tried to back away, but my feet sank into soft mud.

The god bent over me and offered me the heart. It was terrible. Dread pulsed from it in waves. Dread, sorrow, and guilt. It was choking me.

"Take it."

"You bastard! I'll tear you apart!"

Anubis raised the heart, holding the bloody organ just inches from my face and let it go. It hung in the air, terrible, bleeding drop by drop into the Nile.

The river faded. When I awoke, the faint rays of the sunrise, weak and transparent, sifted into the room through my window. I had slept for barely an hour.

I smelled a familiar scent and turned my head. At the other end of the room, near the wall, wrapped in a blanket, with his pillow resting on the floor, lay Raphael. He was back in his human form, and his dark hair fanned across the pillow, his profile perfect against the pale fabric.

He must've let me have the bed, because in our beast forms both of us wouldn't have fit on it.

I looked down and saw myself on the sheets. I had turned human during the night. Olive mud streaks marked my ankles in two smudged rings.

Fear curled in the pit of my stomach, scratching at my insides with icy claws. I wanted to crawl out of my bed, tiptoe across the room, and slide under the blanket with him. He would put his arm around me, and I would lay safe, wrapped in him, breathing in his scent. It would be only an illusion of safety, but I wanted it so, so badly.

I didn't want to die. I didn't want to give my body to any gods. For the first time in my twenty-eight years I was truly living. I wanted to love and to be loved in return. I wanted happiness, and family, and children. I wanted a long life and I wanted Raphael to live it with me. I was terrified that I would fail and little Brandy would pay for my mistakes. Fear gripped me, making it hard to breathe.

I couldn't tell Raphael. He would throw his life away to save me.

I was so scared, and I lay there paralyzed, unable to think of anything but Raphael's heart dripping blood into the Nile.

I crawled out of bed, wrapped my sheet around me, walked across the floor, and crouched by him. "Raphael. Raphael . . . Wake up."

His eyes opened, so blue. He reached out and pulled me down next to him, curving his body around mine.

"Raphael . . ."

He pulled me closer.

The heat radiating from his chest burned my back. "Raphael . . ."

"Just lay with me," he said.

I shut up, stretched against him, trying to banish the gaping hole inside my chest. We didn't have much time. We didn't have any time at all. I cradled that knot of pain and he pulled me close.

If Anapa could invade my dreams and steal children out of

the Keep, there was no telling what else he could do. I had to be careful, because Raphael could die. He could die tonight, tomorrow, the next day, all because a god wanted my body. I had to keep him alive. I would do anything. I would give anything to keep him breathing.

He kissed my neck. It sent an electric shiver down my spine.

"Mmm," he said.

I curled into a tiny ball.

He pulled me closer, wrapping his arms around me. "What is it?"

"You wanted to know why I didn't call you while I was in the Order," I said.

"It isn't important."

"It is. When I woke up after Erra burned, my advocate was there. He took me to my apartment and there were two knights with him. They waited outside. Inside he told me that anyone I contacted while in the Order's custody would come under scrutiny. They would listen in on my calls. Kate has a secret. She trusted me with it and I had an obligation to keep it hidden. I realized then that I had to stay away from her. If she said the wrong thing or, worse, decided to track me down and rescue me, the Order would dig up her past. I couldn't speak to her."

"I understand Kate." He kissed me again. "But why didn't you call me?"

"Because I was scared," I whispered. "My only friend was out of the picture, my mother couldn't help me, and I was all alone. You were all I had left. I was afraid that I would call you and you'd tell me we were done. They put a phone in my room so the temptation to call would be always there. So now you know my dirty secret. I'm a coward."

Raphael turned me over and looked at me, his face close to mine. "You and I will never be done. You're my mate."

He kissed the corner of my mouth. I almost cried.

"I stopped sleeping since you left," he said. "I'll sleep for a couple of hours, wake up, you're not there."

I closed my eyes.

"I need an answer, Andrea," he said.

"An answer?"

"Mate. Yes or no."

"Do you need to ask?" I whispered. "You're my mate."

"If you choose to leave, I will go with you," he said.

I opened my eyes.

"Unless you're just itching to take Curran on," he said. "I suppose we could fight him. We'd lose, but it would be fun while it lasted."

Silly bouda. I hugged him, sliding under him, the weight of his muscular body a reassuring pressure on me. His eyes were so blue. I kissed him, letting his taste wash over my tongue. Every muscle in me shivered in anticipation. "A smelly, stupid bouda once told me that if you make your mate choose between you and his family, you're not worthy of his loyalty. I wouldn't do it to you, Raphael. I love you."

He licked me, nipping on my lower lip. He caressed me. His hand slipped down, stroking, pushing my thighs open. His scent washed over me, and for once, instead of making me hurt in regret, it sang through me. *"Mate . . ."*

I wrapped my legs around him and whispered, "Make love to me."

When I awoke, three hours later, Raphael was gone. The mud from my ankles proved remarkably difficult to remove. It took multiple soapings and scrubbings with a washcloth and even a pumice stone, until finally it was all gone and the skin on my legs was bright red. The Lyc-V would fix it in no time at all, but it aggravated me to no end.

I stalked out into the hallway and smelled English muffins. Crisp, just-out-of-the-toaster, generously buttered English muffins. The aroma grabbed my nose and dragged me down the hall, to a side room, where Kate sat at a long table, drinking coffee. Plates covered the table: heaps of scrambled eggs; hot, crispy hash browns; soft crepes, folded into quarters and drenched with melted butter; bacon, sausage, ham, English muffins.

"Food!"

"Yes!" Kate thrust a plate in my direction.

I loaded my plate, and bit into the ham. Yum, yum, yum. Meat. Meat good. Andrea hungry. Andrea had spent too many calories in the past forty-eight hours. I could do without sleep or food, but not both.

"Have you seen my mate?" I asked.

"He's with his mother."

I rolled my eyes.

"He was in here about half an hour ago, eating up a storm. Aunt B has graced us with her presence and she wanted him to explain things to her."

I ate the English muffin and got another. I could almost feel the energy flooding my body. As a shapeshifter, I could technically go without sleep completely, if I had to, but food was a requirement. I was going to stuff myself until I resembled one of those pigs they served at banquets in old movies.

"Your favorite volhv showed up half an hour ago, complaining about his lack of sleep and stupid gods. He says he brought his Batman belt."

I stopped chewing for a second and caught my reflection in the shiny kettle. I looked like a chipmunk with my cheeks full of food. "So can he bind this draugr?"

"He says so."

"That means we're still on?"

Kate nodded.

Well. My day was finally looking up. About time.

CHAPTER 14

❖

The horses clopped down the dirt path. According to Kate the creature that had our scale-shield lived deep in the lands of Norse Heritage. The neo-Viking territory. The neo-Vikings didn't care for technology within their borders.

Unlike several other Scandinavian organizations, the Norse Heritage wasn't interested in the preservation of Scandinavian culture. They were interested in perpetuating the Viking myth: they wore furs, braided their hair, waved around oversized weapons, started fights with wild abandon, and generally acted in a manner appropriate to people embracing the spirit of a pirating and pillaging barbarian horde. They took in anyone and everyone, regardless of ancestry and criminal history, as long as they demonstrated the "Viking spirit," which apparently amounted to liking violent brawls and drinking lots and lots of beer.

The Norse Heritage Hall was located a good way out of the city. Our small band clopped its way down the road, Kate and I up front, Ascanio driving a wagon with a bound deer on it, and Raphael and Roman bringing up the rear. The two men carried on a quiet conversation, which sounded surprisingly civil.

I patted my horse's neck. Her name was Sugar and she had come from the Keep stables. She was a Tennessee Walker, smart and calm, with high endurance. I liked her color too—she was a red roan of such a pale gentle shade, she almost looked pink.

Kate smirked.

"What?"

"Your horse looks pink."

"So?"

"If you paste some stars on her butt, you'll be riding My Little Pony."

"Bugger off." I patted the mare's neck. "Don't listen to her, Sugar. You are the cutest horsey ever. The correct name for her color is strawberry roan, by the way."

"Strawberry shortcake, more like it. Does Strawberry Shortcake know you stole her horse? She will be berry, berry angry with you."

I looked at her from under half-lowered eyelids. "I can shoot you right here, on this road, and nobody will ever find your body."

Behind us Ascanio chortled.

The road curved, caught between dense, dark forest on the left and an open, low, grass-sheathed hill on the right. Outcroppings of pale rock marked the hills. Norse Heritage Hall sat on the west side of Gainesville, about fifty miles northeast of Atlanta. The massive spread of the Chattahoochee Forest had long ago swallowed Gainesville, turning it into an isolated town, like a small island in a sea of trees.

Kate was riding a dark, nasty-looking gray roan that looked like it couldn't wait to stomp something to death.

"So, do you miss Marygold?"

Marygold used to be her Order mule.

"My aunt killed her," Kate said.

Crap. "I'm so sorry." She had really loved that mule.

Ahead, the top of the largest rock pile shifted. A thick humanoid body pushed from the crest. Its head was wide and equipped with dinosaur jaws armed with narrow teeth. Gray scales shielded its body, protruding from the flesh as if the creature had rolled in gravel. Long strands of emerald-green moss dripped from its back and shoulders. The sun tore through the clouds. A stray ray caught the creature's side and the beast sparkled as if dipped in diamond dust.

"What the hell is that?"

"That's a *landvættir*," Kate said. "They're land spirits that pop up around neo-Norse settlements. He won't bother us unless we turn off the path."

We rode past the creature.

Raphael urged his horse forward and rode up between the

two of us. "Anapa. Powerful enough to snatch a child from the Keep."

"Yes?" I murmured.

"And this is really important to him?"

"Yes?"

"Why doesn't he do it himself?" Raphael grimaced. "Why doesn't he help us? Why keep the Pack out of it?"

I had asked myself these same questions before, so I told him the only answer I could come up with. "I don't know."

He glanced at Kate. She shrugged. "Beats me."

"I asked your volhv," Raphael said to me.

My volhv, huh? "And what did the Russian sugar bear tell you?"

Kate made a strangled noise. Raphael clenched his jaw, then unclenched it.

"He said that Anapa is a god and gods are weird. What kind of a demented answer is that? Isn't he supposed to be some sort of expert on this whole thing, which is why we're bringing him along?"

Gods are vicious, selfish assholes. I shrugged. "Roman is an expert and he gave you his expert opinion. Gods are weird."

"I can hear you," Roman called from behind us. "I'm not deaf."

Raphael shook his head and dropped back.

Anapa wasn't just weird. No, he had a plan. And all his good humor and funny smiles were calculated. They masked his true essence the way soft fur covered a cat's claws. And I would keep his plan to myself. If I told Raphael, he would do something rash to save me. If I told it to Kate, she would worry and try to fix it. There was no way to fix it. It was what it was.

The road turned, forking into two paths ahead. The larger road, marked by an old birch, curved up the hill. The smaller, less traveled path veered right, into some woods.

A man walked out from behind the tree and barred the path. Six and a half feet tall and hulking, he resembled a man-sized tank draped in chain mail. He wore a dramatic cloak of black fur and a polished war helm and carried an enormous single axe on a long wooden handle.

"Good to see you again, Gunnar," Kate said. "We're going to the glade."

The bottom half of Gunnar's face paled. "Again?"

Kate nodded.

"You've been once. You can't go again."

"I've got no choice."

Gunnar rubbed his face. "He's got your scent now. You know what happens to people who go to see him twice."

"I know. I still have to go."

He shook his head and stepped aside. "It's been nice knowing you."

Kate touched the reins and our small procession rolled on.

"What exactly happens to the people who go to see him twice?" I asked.

"He eats them," Kate said.

The old road narrowed, slicing its way into the forest. Tall trees crowded the road, as if protesting its intrusion in their midst. The air smelled of forest: pine sap, the earthy odor of moist soil, the faint harshness of bobcat mark somewhere to the left, and the slightly oily squirrel musk. A bluish fog hung between the trees, obscuring the ground. Spooky.

We came to a stone arch made by tall pillars of gray stone, bound together by vines.

Kate hopped off her horse. "We hoof it now. Raphael, will you take the deer?"

"Sure."

I took the tripod framework out of the cart and pulled it apart into a mount, sighting the path past the pillars. I planted the tripod into the ground and took my huge crossbow off the cart. Dark letters ran along the stock of the bow: THUNDER-HAWK.

"This is new," Kate said.

I snapped the crossbow into the top of the mount, took a canvas bundle from the cart, and unrolled it. Crossbow bolts, tipped with the Galahad warheads.

"This is my baby." I petted the stock.

"You have a strange relationship with your weapons," Roman said.

"You have no idea," Raphael told him.

"This from a man with a living staff and a man who once drove four hours both ways for a sword he then put on his wall," I murmured.

"It was an Angus Trim," Raphael said.

"It's a sharpened strip of metal."

"You have an Angus Trim sword?" Kate's eyes lit up.

"Bought it at an estate auction," Raphael said. "If we get out of this alive, you are invited to come to my house and play with it."

It was good that Curran wasn't here and I was secure in our relationship, because that totally could be taken the wrong way.

I grabbed my backpack. Raphael slung the deer over his shoulder. Kate pulled a leather bundle from the cart. It had a bead pattern along the side that looked very familiar. I'd seen similar designs before on an Oklahoma Cherokee reservation—it was Indian scrollwork.

"Is that a Cherokee design?"

Kate nodded. "I bought this from the Cherokee medicine woman."

I motioned Ascanio over. "Aim like this." I swiveled the tripod, moving the bow. "Sight through here. To fire, flip this lever and squeeze the trigger. Slowly. Don't jerk it."

"Even if he jerks it, he'll hit, trust me," Kate said. "He'll have a large target."

"Don't listen to her, she can't shoot an elephant from ten feet away. She would bash him with her bow and then try to cut his throat with her sword."

Kate chuckled.

"Your turn." I nodded at the bow.

"Aim, sight, flip lever, squeeze the trigger slowly," Ascanio said. "Try not to panic and cry like a little girl."

"Good man." We followed Kate single file up the path, leaving him at the cart.

The forest grew grimmer, the trees growing darker, more twisted, still full of leaves but somehow dead, as if frozen in time. The fog thickened into soup. The usual scents faded. Not even squirrels ventured here, as if life itself was forbidden. These were some screwed-up woods.

I smelled carrion. Strong and recent, butter-sweet.

We came to a clearing—a small stretch of mossy ground slightly larger than a basketball court, bordered by massive trees. In the center of the clearing rose a big stone, tall and flat like a table. A hollowed-out space had been carved into the stone and stained with red. I sniffed. Blood. Only a couple of days old.

"The deer goes on the rock," Kate said.

"So what brought you here the first time?" I asked.

"A dying child," Kate said. "It was me, Curran, and some vampires. He and I were the only ones to get out in one piece. Still time to leave."

"Leave?" Roman rubbed his hands together. "And miss this? Are you fucking crazy?"

He wasn't swearing because he was freaked. He was swearing because he was excited. Wow. For once, I had no words.

"Are you sure about this?" Kate asked me.

I had the most important job in this awesome plan of ours. "Will you get on with it already?"

"She will be fine," Raphael said. "She's the fastest."

To the left some creature screeched, loud and desperate. Another joined it. I fought a shiver.

"The draugr was once a Viking named Håkon from Vinland," Kate said. "The Vikings living there traded with local tribes, who told them that Cherokees were soft. They said that the Southern tribes were farmers, not warriors, and had a lot of gold. So Håkon sailed down on two ships to rape, plunder, and pillage. Except that the Cherokees had good arrows and strong magic. He died in the skirmish. Nobody stopped to bury him, and he was so pissed off by that, that he rose from the dead as a draugr, chased down his remaining men, and ate them."

"Literally?" Roman asked.

Kate nodded. "The Cherokees found him gnawing on their bones. He was too powerful and they couldn't kill him, so they locked him on this hill with their wards to keep him from running loose."

The light gained an odd bluish tint. Somehow the forest had gotten darker.

"This is a bad place," the black volhv said. "We shouldn't be here. Well, I should. But you shouldn't. You see, my god holds dominion over dead things, but this creature belongs to a different pantheon, so I have some protection here, but not too much. Not enough to kill the draugr. Just enough to bind him and survive."

"You're doing wonders for my confidence," I told him.

Kate put the bundle with the Cherokee beadwork on the ground, knelt by it, and untied its cord. Inside lay four sharpened sticks, each about three feet long. She picked the first one up, found a rock and pounded it into the ground by the beginning of the path. That was the way I'd run when it came time to get the hell out of there. The second stick went to the left side of the clearing, the third to the right, and the final exactly opposite the first.

"These are our defenses. They will delay him a little bit. Don't fight him. Just run."

Kate got a pipe out of a box and began smoking it. The tobacco hit her and she coughed.

"Lightweight."

"Whatever." She circled the clearing, waving her pipe around.

"I've never seen this before," Roman said. "It's very difficult to witness Native American rituals these days. So much has been lost due to assimilation and lack of written records. Exciting stuff!"

"Well, so glad we could indulge your intellectual curiosity, Professor," Raphael told him.

"I'm probably making a hash job of it, but the tribe refuses to approach this hill, so I'm all you've got," Kate said.

She completed the circle, sat down, and started pulling things out of her bag: a plastic honey bear, a metal canteen, and a little bag.

I blinked and the forest was full of eyes. Elongated, solid yellow, they peeked at us from under the boulders, from the darkness by the roots of the trees, from the branches . . .

I bared my teeth. "What are these?"

"I'm not sure." Kate kept her voice low. "They came out last time, too. I think they might be *uldra*. Ghastek said they're nature spirits from Lapland. They didn't attack us the last time."

To my right, one of the *uldra* crawled up on the end of the fallen tree trunk, just feet away. An inch or two over a foot tall, it perched on the tree bark, gripping it with avian feet. Dense dark fur covered its humanoid body. Its face vaguely resembled a baboon.

The *uldra* found its spot, moving with slothlike slowness, and froze, oversized hands with long, large-knuckled fingers folded in front of it. Its mouth gaped open, displaying a forest of long, deep-water fish teeth.

"It's just some small *nechist*," Roman said next to me.

"*Nechist?*" I asked.

"Yes. Unclean thing. They're harmless." He dug in his bag. "Hang on . . . Here." Roman pulled out a small pack of crackers and shook one out. "Here, you want a cracker?" He offered the cracker to the creature.

"Roman . . ." A warning crept into my voice. Those teeth didn't look good.

"No worries," he told me. "Here." He clicked his tongue. "Come get a cracker."

The *uldra*'s pale eyes focused on the cracker. Slowly it reached for it and plucked the small square from Roman's fingers. The *uldra* took a bite.

"Good, huh?" Roman clicked his tongue some more. "Come on. Come."

The *uldra* crawled onto his forearm and climbed up the black sleeve to sit on his shoulder.

"Jesus," Raphael said.

Roman made smoochy lips at the *uldra*. "Who's so good? Want another cracker?"

A second *uldra* made its way out of the bushes and sat by Roman's boot, funky arms folded, waiting for a handout. Roman tossed another cracker on the ground. A couple of smaller creatures trudged over and tugged on the hem of his robe.

"There are plenty of crackers for everyone," Roman reassured them.

Raphael leaned forward. The *uldra* bared their teeth. He growled at them.

"No need to bully them." Roman petted the nearest beastie.

The first *uldra* finished its meal and rubbed its head against Roman's cheek.

A low unearthly moan came from the trees. The *uldra* fled. One second they were there and then *whoosh*, only half-eaten crackers were left.

"Here we go." Kate walked up to the stone and the sedated deer lying on it.

The plan was simple. Once the draugr showed up and we obtained the scale, I would take off. Normally I would only have to make it to the stone pillars, which marked the beginning of the Cherokee defenses. But Kate was worried that carrying the scale past the pillars meant we'd be moving a piece of the creature's stash behind the ward line, which may or may not cancel the spells. We had to stop it at those pillars.

"Are you sure you can bind it?" I asked Roman.

"Don't worry," he said. "I've got this."

Suddenly, I was really worried.

Kate opened the pouch, took out rune stones—small squares of worn bone, each with a rune etched on it in black—and tossed them into the basin. They scattered and clinked on the stone, like dice in a plastic cup. She emptied the canteen onto the runes, and I smelled hops and barley. Beer. Kate squeezed the honey bear, squirting a stream of amber-colored honey onto the runes.

Roman leaned toward me. "Those are Norse runes."

I looked at him.

"Not Slavic ones," Roman said. "Just thought I'd point it out."

He looked like he could barely contain all of the excitement.

"Now," Kate said.

I took a deep breath, grabbed the deer by the head, and pulled his throat toward the hollowed out receptacle in the rock. The deer gave me a panicked look. "Sorry, boy." Kate raised her knife and cut its throat. The deer kicked, but I clamped it down. The scent of blood, hot and fresh, washed over me, kicking my senses into high gear.

Kate shook the runes, holding them loosely in her hand, and I saw tiny bursts of lightning between her fingers.

"I call you out, Håkon. Come from your grave. Come taste the blood ale."

A sibilant sound came, made of old bones crunching underfoot, leathery mummified muscles creaking, and eerie evil whisper. I smelled the sickening stench of decomposition, the earth, the dust, and the liquefying flesh, as if someone had thrust my head into a grave. Magic washed over us, dragging freezing cold in its wake. Frost slicked the ground by my feet.

Out from beyond the clearing, the mist streamed at us, thickening as it came. It moaned, like a living thing, its voice full of torment, flowed into a manlike shape, and faded, leaving a *thing* in its wake.

Six feet tall, it was made of dried gristle and that particular, leathery flesh one usually saw on vampires, except his was tinted with blue-gray. Not a cell of fat could be found on its sparse frame. It wore chain mail and metal pauldrons, and neither fit him well—they hung off him, slightly askew, obviously made for a much thicker body. The draugr raised his head and looked at me. Its face could've been used as an anatomy model—each muscle in it so clearly drawn under the thin layer of skin, it looked revoltingly alien. Its cold eyes stared at me, pupil-less and flat.

The undead lowered its head and started licking the blood and beer mixture.

Nausea jerked my stomach. There was something so wrong about this unnatural undead thing sucking up the blood of a creature that had been alive a few moments ago.

"You're done for now," Kate said.

The undead raised his head, its face bloody. His mouth moved, and I saw the leathery cords of his facial muscles slide and contract. Ugh.

Its voice was chilling, hoarse, and ancient. "I know you. I know your scent."

Kate stared it straight in his face. "I brought you blood ale for a boon."

"Foolish meat. Foolish, foolish meat."

The draugr went down for the ale.

"No," Kate snapped.

The draugr leaned on the stone. "I'm Håkon, son of a jarl, scourge of the seas, devourer of flesh. What is it you want, meager meat?"

"I want to see your shield," Kate said.

The draugr turned his head. "My shield?"

"The shield you bore when you sailed here from Vinland to take the gold from the Southern Tribes."

"The *skrælingar*," the draugr said.

"Yes. The *skrælingar*. You took two ships and came looking for it, remember?"

"I remember . . ." The draugr's voice carried. "I remember everything. Birds with wings that covered half the sky. I remember *skrælingar* magic. I remember the arrow in my back. I remember my corpse left to rot."

"Do you remember your shield?" Kate insisted.

The draugr dipped his head toward the ale.

Kate clenched the runes. "If you want the ale, you will let me see your shield."

An evil cold fire flared in the draugr's eyes and dripped from his face in burning tears. "I will devour you. I will lick your bones clean and crush them between my teeth. I will suck the marrow . . ."

"That's nice," Kate said. "The shield."

"Fine, meat. Here it is."

The earth by the stone bulged upward, split, belching roots and smaller rocks. A curved wooden edge emerged, rising higher and higher, until the entire round shield broke free of the ground. In the middle of it sat an oblong, ridged yellow scale, pinned to the wood by metal bars. It was two feet long.

Two feet. What kind of snake had two-foot-long scales?

"Here is my shield, meat."

"Do you remember how I came to you with an honest bargain last time and you broke it?" Kate asked.

The draugr laughed. It was a cold, hollow sound.

"Turnabout is fair play," Kate said.

I grabbed the shield and ran.

The draugr howled, shaking the forest. Roman's voice barked something in Russian. Raphael snarled.

Mist chased me, snaking its way down the mountain, trying to catch my ankles. I flew down the path.

Magic punched my back. I flew a few feet, hit the ground in a tight ball, rolled to my feet, and kept running. Just aftershocks. Kate must've used a power word, her own special brand of magic. It nearly wiped her out—they were her last resort.

You won't escape me, an icy voice whispered in my ear. *Run all you want, meat. Run faster.*

Every hair on my body stood on end.

I leaped over a root. The mist snapped like a whip and wound around my neck in a noose. It jerked me off my feet. I flew back, clawing at the tentacle of magic with one hand, clenching the shield with my right. I hit the ground on my back and the magic pulled me, scraping my skin over the roots.

Oh no, you don't. I growled and grabbed a branch with my left hand.

The magic yanked me backward, crushing my throat. Black circles swam before my eyes.

I planted my feet and forced myself up. Every muscle in my body strained.

The magic pulled.

I pushed forward. Step. Another step. No asshole undead would drag me back. No. Not happening.

The magic tore.

I pitched forward and rolled, head over feet, curving my body around the shield, hitting every obstacle with soft parts of me, as if someone had stuck me into a dryer with a bag of rocks.

I crashed into a tree. The world swam a bit. I scrambled up. The shield lay in shambles at my feet, all except for the scale, which didn't have a scratch on it.

A dark icy shadow fell on the trees next to me.

I grabbed the scale and spun around. Something white was falling, so I thrust the scale up in front of it and crouched underneath.

Foot-long spikes of ice sank into the ground around me, hammering the scale. I held the scale until the impacts stopped and dashed down the slope. Magic exploded all around me in cold bursts, rattling the teeth in my skull. The harsh stench of rot filled my mouth. Around me the trees groaned, as if pulled upright by an invisible hand. My throat burned.

I shot out onto the road.

The stone pillars loomed far in the distance to my right. I sprinted to them. My ribs were screaming in pain.

The trees creaked behind me. The draugr had made it onto the road.

My feet barely touched the ground. The draugr's magic iced my back.

Something whistled through the air and a body hit the road

in front of me, hurled by a supernatural force. Roman. The volhv wasn't moving. I guess the binding didn't work after all.

Between the pillars Ascanio swiveled the crossbow on the tripod, squeezed the trigger, and fired. The oversized bolt sliced through the air above me. *Thank you, kid.*

The world exploded with green. The blast wave slapped my back. I squeezed the last burst of speed from my exhausted body and cleared the pillars. I skidded to a stop and turned around. On the road the draugr stomped forward, an enormous monstrosity, dwarfing the trees, impossibly big. His magic swirled about him in a stormy cloud.

Raphael dashed out of the trees like a fur-sheathed nightmare and charged the giant, ripping into undead flesh.

I pushed Ascanio from the tripod and reloaded.

The undead tried to stomp on him, but Raphael darted back and forth, too fast, stripping dried muscle and gristle from the giant's left leg.

Kate burst from the undergrowth and thrust her sword into the draugr's right foot. I yanked the crossbow up and sighted on Håkon. *Eat this, you undead piece of shit.*

"Hit the deck!" I screamed.

Raphael and Kate dashed away. I fired. The bolt took the undead below the chest, burning it with emerald flames, and exploded. Undead flesh rained, but the draugr remained upright.

Roman staggered to his feet, his face contorted by anger. He screamed something. A flock of crows fell on the giant, ripping rotting flesh from its bones.

"Help the alpha!" I barked, reloading. Ascanio dashed to the draugr.

Raphael picked Kate up and threw her. She sank her sword into the side of the draugr's leg. Magic snapped, and then a car-hood-sized kneecap crashed onto the road. Kate jumped clear. The draugr teetered and dropped to its knees.

"Fire in the hole!" I fired another shot. For half a second the arrowhead buzzed, lodged between the undead's ribs, then it exploded, splashing emerald fire over desiccated flesh. The blast wrenched the draugr's ribs wide open and through it I saw the shriveled sack of its heart.

The crows hurtled into the hole and out of the draugr's back, dragging chunks of bone and tissue with them.

I saw the ravaged remains of the heart and fired. The arrow pierced the tough muscle. Bull's-eye.

The explosion shook the ground. Chunks of rotting corpse pelted the ground and Håkon crashed like a falling skyscraper. His chin hit the dirt, his entire skull reverberating from the impact.

Ha. We killed an unkillable giant. Eat your heart out, Beast Lord.

Kate got up and limped toward us.

Her knee. She had an old injury that kept flaring up. I had completely forgot. Damn it. "Is your knee okay?"

"It's not the knee." Kate limped past the pillar and sagged against the cart. "He backhanded me, the sonovabitch. I hit a tree trunk with my hip. I swear this leg is cursed."

Roman spat on the ground. His face was mournful. "Such a waste. One-of-a-kind and we had to kill it."

It almost tore us to pieces and he had regrets. Wow.

Raphael strode to me. His eyes were on fire.

"Nice shot," he said.

"Thank you. You were . . ." Awesome, brave, fast, amazing. ". . . not so bad yourself."

Roman shook his head. "Such a waste."

"I'll split the teeth with you," Kate said. "If you want them."

He turned to her. "Of course I want the teeth. And the hair."

The two of them started for the head, looking like two starved dogs who had just found a fresh juicy carcass.

Raphael grabbed me into a bear hug. I grinned at him. This wasn't so hard after all.

Ascanio trotted up. "Why are they pulling his teeth out?"

"They're magic," I said.

"Do you want me to help them?"

"Yes," Raphael said.

The kid went off to the giant corpse, where Kate and Roman argued over the teeth.

The draugr's head moved.

"Watch out!" I screamed.

Kate looked at me.

I ran.

The eyes flared with green fire, the great jaws gaped, baring thick teeth. Kate whipped about, slicing with her sword.

I was six feet away when magic erupted out of the draugr's mouth, wound about Kate, and dragged her into the maw, crushing her between those stumpy teeth.

I leaped onto the skull, pulled my knife, and sliced into the tendons holding it together. *Let go of my friend, you fucker!*

The jaws mauled Kate, trying to crack her like a nut.

Grisly flesh tore under my fingers. I caught a glimpse of Kate—she'd curled into a ball, keeping away from the teeth.

The tendons I had severed snapped right back together. I needed to cut faster.

We were rising. I glanced down. The draugr had pulled himself up.

"Raphael!" I yelled, slicing across the flesh. "He's regenerating!" Where was he?

Slayer's blade sliced through the flesh right in the corner of the joint where the mandible fit into the upper jaw. Slayer's blade smoked. Kate was trying to cut her way out.

The draugr chewed, trying to work his massive tongue to shift Kate toward his teeth.

Flies blanketed the undead, turning into maggots, eating his flesh. I sliced and diced, the maggots ate, but the more damage we did, the faster its flesh grew back.

Kate groaned. I had to get her out now.

I went furry. Shreds of my clothes fluttered to the ground. I took a short running start up the draugr's bony shoulder and kicked the temporomandibular joint. The bone popped with a dry crunch, announcing a dislocated jaw. The draugr's mouth fell open and Kate dropped out.

A huge hand swept me off the shoulder and clenched me, squeezing. I snarled and bit. Pressure ground me. My bones whined. He was crushing me as if I were a rag and he were trying to squeeze all the squishy red stuff out.

The scent of gasoline slapped me.

The pain was unbearable now. My eyes watered from pain and fury.

The draugr gripped me harder.

My shoulder gave and I screamed when my arm snapped like a toothpick.

Something sparked. Through my tears I saw the flare of fire and Raphael, his beast face furious, climbing up the draugr a hair above the flames. Raphael leaped up, clawed his way onto the creature's face, and tore an undead eye out of the left socket.

The draugr screamed and dropped me, slapping himself, trying to grab Raphael.

I fell. I tumbled down and suddenly something caught me. I saw Ascanio's face. He dropped me to my feet. Next to me Roman stood, his hands clawing the air, his staff screeching.

Above us the draugr was a pillar of flame.

A furry form jumped off the draugr, hit the tree, and dropped down. *Yes! Go, Raphael!*

The draugr roared and turned toward us.

Roman strained.

The undead took a slow step toward us. Then another.

"He's not burning up," Roman screamed. "I can't hold him."

The flame coated the undead's body, but none of the flesh actually charred. Damn it. Couldn't he just die?

Roman's feet slid backward. Raphael landed next to him.

Kate pulled herself upright. "What do we do?"

"We must break him apart and bury him. He is of the Earth, he belongs to it. The Earth will hold him."

"I can break him if you anchor him for a second," Kate ground out. "But that's all I've got. No more magic left after."

The draugr took another step.

Roman bent backward. His eyes rolled back in his head. Chains coated in dark smoke burst from the ground and bound the draugr's feet and wrists.

Kate opened her mouth and said a word. The magic burst from her in a torrent and smashed into the draugr, barely touching me. Panic splashed me. My fur stood on end and a hysterical hyena cackle tore out of me, echoing Raphael's lunatic laugh and Ascanio's high-pitched giggle.

The draugr jerked back, trying to run, the chains snapped taut, and his body fell apart like a toy coming to pieces at the seams.

Behind me Kate fell to the ground. Roman sobbed once and crashed next to her. It was up to the three of us now.

We ran. I grabbed an enormous arm and pulled it with all my might, into the forest, away from the road, and dug into the soil, yanking the roots out and slicing my furry fingers on jagged rocks. My arms spiked with pain. I ignored it. I dug and dug, throwing fountains of earth, until finally I pushed the piece of the arm into the hole and covered it with dirt. Then I dashed to the road, grabbed the next chunk, and did it again.

The five of us were lying on cots in the Keep's medical wing. When we had limped our way into the Keep with the scale, filthy, covered in blood and dirt, and wearing the delightful perfume of carrion mixed with gasoline and smoke, Doolittle had nearly had an aneurysm.

We had been strong-armed into the hospital wing and made to lie down in our beds. Even Ascanio, who had gotten off scot-free. Doolittle and his assistants examined us and quickly determined that Raphael had second-degree burns, I had a fractured humerus, Roman was dehydrated and had suffered a concussion, and Kate had two cracked ribs, a bruised hip, and her knee had gone out again. And then Curran walked through the doorway.

The rage of the Beast Lord was a terrible thing to behold. Some people stormed, some punched things, but Curran slipped into this icy, bone-chilling calm. His face hardened into a flat mask, and his eyes turned into a molten inferno of pure gold. If you looked at it for longer than two seconds, your muscles locked, your knees shook, and you had to fight to keep from cringing. It was easier to look at the floor, but I didn't. Besides, he wasn't angry with me. He wasn't even angry with Kate. He was angry with Anapa. I had no doubt that if he could've gotten a hold of the god at that moment, he would've broken him in half.

"It's only ribs," Kate told him. "And they're not even broken. They are fractured."

"And the hip," Doolittle said. "And the knee."

There you go. Don't expect mercy from a honeybadger.

"How long do you need to keep her?" Curran looked to Doolittle.

"She can go to her quarters, provided she doesn't leave them," Doolittle said. "I can't do anything else with the magic down. She must stay down until I can patch her up."

"She will." Curran reached for Kate. "Hey, baby. Ready?"

She nodded. Curran slid his hands under her and picked her up, gently, as if she weighed nothing.

"Good?" he asked.

She put her arm around him. "Never better."

And he took her away.

"So young lady, how did you break your arm?" Doolittle asked me.

"She was trying to keep Kate from being crushed," Raphael said.

"A worthy cause." Dolittle peered at me. I waited for the other shoe to drop.

"Did you know your arm was broken?" he asked.

"Yes."

"And did you, by any chance, put said arm into a sling or make an effort to keep it still?"

Oh Christ. "No. I was busy."

"What did you do with said arm?" Doolittle asked.

"I dug." And it hurt like hell, but at that point killing the draugr was more important.

"Were you under stress?" Doolittle asked.

"I was trying to bury pieces of an undead giant to prevent it from rampaging through the countryside and eating any random humans he encountered. This would go a lot easier if you would just tell me where you are heading with this instead of taking the long way around."

Doolittle nodded to one of his assistants. The short, slight woman approached Roman's cot. "We're going to put you in your own private room."

"Is this a code for killing me?" Roman asked. "Because I won't be easy to take down."

She giggled and wheeled his bed out with him on it.

The medmage looked at Ascanio. "You may go, too."

The boy jumped off the bed and took off like he was on fire.

Doolittle pulled up the chair and sat next to me. His face was so gentle. "I once treated a boy," he said. "He was a were-rat, abused by his family. His father beat him repeatedly. He was a hateful waste of a human being and the boy's shape-shifting gave him an excuse to rage."

A lump formed in my throat. "Mhm."

"Lyc-V is a very adaptive virus," Doolittle said. "If the

body is injured the same way repeatedly, it responds. Shapeshifters in colder climates grow denser fur. Shapeshifters in climates with frequent sun exposure develop melanin at accelerated rate."

"Yes." I knew all this.

Doolittle leaned a little toward me. "The boy I mentioned developed his own coping mechanism: his bones healed extremely quickly. His body kept trying to give him tools to run away from the next beating."

"What happened to the boy?" I asked.

"We're not going to worry about it right now," Doolittle said. "I'm going to ask some private questions. Would you like Raphael to stay or to go? Say the word and I will throw him out."

Raphael bared his teeth.

"He can stay," I said.

"Was there physical abuse in your childhood, Andrea?" Doolittle asked gently.

I swallowed. "Yes."

"Over some period of some time?"

"Eleven years."

Doolittle took my hand and squeezed a little. "Your bones heal very rapidly under stress. The body joins them as fast as it can without any regard for whether or not they are aligned. It's simply trying to make you operational again."

I looked at my shoulder. It didn't feel quite right. "You have to rebreak my arm."

"I'm so sorry," Doolittle said. "The arm is crooked. Try raising it all the way."

I lifted my arm. Sharp pain shot through my shoulder right in the center of the bone.

"The longer we delay, the harder it will be to set it right," Doolittle said.

A female shapeshifter wheeled in a cart filled with instruments.

"You're going to use a mallet?" I asked. In my head Doolittle put a crowbar over my shoulder and hit it with a hammer.

"No. I'll use a narrow power saw. You will have to be sedated. I promise you'll feel nothing."

"Okay." What else was there to say?

* * *

The waters of the Nile lapped at my ankles. I strode out of the tepid water onto the shore. The wind brought the razor-sharp stench of blood. A fresh kill waited somewhere nearby.

The dark green bushes rustled. The Jackal walked out, dragging a dead bull by its neck. The Jackal had grown larger since we had last met. It was taller than a horse now, with a massive head and amber eyes the size of dessert plates.

The Jackal dropped the bull in front of me. "Eat."

"No." Food held significance to shapeshifters. Lovers gave it to each other and alphas gave it to their clans. An offer of food was sometimes a declaration of love, but more often an offer of protection in exchange for loyalty, and I wouldn't be accepting any handouts from him.

"Suit yourself." The Jackal bit the bull's soft belly.

"We're helping you. Why not let the child go?"

The Jackal raised its bloody snout from the kill. "Why would I surrender my hostage? She has served me so well."

I sat in the grass. The sun was setting again and the still waters shimmered with faint vapor. The wet sloppy sounds of the large predator eating behind me ruined the beauty of the landscape.

"Why do you do this?" I asked finally.

"Mmm?"

"Why do you play little games? You could've helped us with the draugr, but you didn't. You could've let the Pack join us. It's in your best interests to win."

"No. It's in my best interests to regain my godhood." The Jackal padded over and lay down next to me, a hill of fur and darkness. "Do you know how godhood begins?"

"No."

"With a myth." The Jackal sighed. "It begins with a legend told by the fire. A story of magical deeds and glorious victory over evil. I was there when it began for me, over six thousand years ago. I remember."

"Who were you?" I asked.

"A tribal chief," he said. "I had a wife and many children. Once I saved a litter of jackal pups from a flood and they followed me everywhere I went. They brought others of their kind to the settlement. I was never bitten. I cut my leg while hunting and the pack licked it. It was a true gift."

Pieces clicked in my head. "You were a shapeshifter?"

"I was a First," he said. "The first recipient of the gift, its power undiluted within me. We, the humans, were different then. We were magic. It flowed through us, through our blood, through our bones. We were born soaked in it."

"How did you become a god?"

The Jackal shrugged. "Those memories are murky. My deeds were told in front of the evening fires, my victories, my adventures. They kept me alive. My descendants made me a shrine of bone and stone and prayed for my guidance. My tribe prospered and the more they prayed, the more power I gained, until finally I came to be again."

"Just like that?"

"Just like that. People plead for help to things that are more powerful. They beg the sky for rain year after year, they make a shrine to a image who once brought about rain or to an engineer who irrigated their fields decades ago, and if they pray hard enough, their new deity comes to life and grows in power."

The Jackal gazed at the river. "This new age, it has a saying, 'History is written by the victors.' It is true. Look at the story of Apep. Set, who was there with us fighting as valiantly as any one of us, became the visage of darkness. Bastet was diminished to a vermin killer. And I? I became the tender of corpses, revered, worshipped, but hardly as powerful. Even my brother Sobek, the lord of crocodiles, was more feared than I was. I hate him for that and Sobek reviles me for my knowledge and the reverence it brought. When the time of my people came to its sunset, the Greeks came. They jeered at us. They called me the Barker. The joke was on them—I endured through their time and then through the Romans, but I've never forgotten the insult."

He fell silent.

"The Pack," I prompted.

"Let me tell you how my new myth will go," the Jackal said. "In the new age of magic, when it was young, a vile serpent emerged, threatening the sanity of all people. Mighty God Inepu and his faceless retainers battled him, and slew

him, and triumphed. All those who do not wish to be devoured
by the serpent of madness give thanks to the mighty Inepu.
Ask for his blessing. Ask for his wisdom. Offer your prayers
to him so he may shield you with his might. He is the mighty
warrior, the awe-inspiring slayer."

"That is an ambitious plan." So I was to be a faceless min-
ion and he was to become a warrior god.

The Jackal looked at me. "Don't mock me, pup. Godhood
is like a drug; once you taste it, there is no turning back."

"I still don't understand why you won't let the Pack assist."

"Because they are led by a First," the Jackal said.

"Curran?"

The Jackal nodded. "It is how I began, as a First. What is
more impressive, a jackal or a lion? Which would you fear
more? To whom would you offer your prayers?"

I blinked. "You're afraid Curran will steal your godhood?"

"Afraid is a strong word. I fear nothing." The Jackal laid
his head on his front paws and twitched his ear.

"Except being forgotten," I said.

"There is that."

"And how does my body fit into your scheme? Wouldn't
you be changing gender?"

"I don't care," he said. "A god or a goddess, as long as I
grow in power."

"One small problem," I told him. "For this plan to work,
Apep has to resurrect, and we've got his scale."

"The scale isn't necessary to his resurrection."

"What? So we've done all of this for nothing?"

The Jackal raised his head. "Of course not. The scale is his
armor. Without it, he will be easier to kill. He will be softer."

"Where? Where are they resurrecting him?"

The Jackal laughed under his breath.

I grabbed his ear and sank my nails into the flesh. "Where
are they going to resurrect him? When?"

"I don't know." The Jackal whirled and bit me, taking half
of my body into his huge mouth from the side. Teeth pierced
my stomach and my back. "You're the detective. Figure it out."

The world snapped back at me in a rush of blinding pain,
and I saw Doolittle's eyes above a surgical mask. Agony
gripped my arm. Raphael snarled, "She's bleeding!"

"It will be fine," Doolittle said, his voice calm and steady.

Some female shapeshifter I didn't know pulled the sheet down from me. A curved row of bloody teeth marks gaped in my stomach.

"I'm good," I ground out. "Keep going."

Raphael took my hand in his. I squeezed it and watched the teeth marks knit themselves closed as Doolittle finished sawing through my bone.

Finally Doolittle finished. It didn't hurt once the bone was cut, or at least it didn't hurt too much. Roman sat on my bed for a while and told me funny jokes while everyone cleaned up.

Finally they all left. Darkness had fallen—I had asked for the lights to be turned off, and only moonlight remained. It spilled all around me and I felt completely and utterly alone.

I let out a long breath. It sounded more like a sob.

A shadow detached itself from the bathroom doorway and crossed the floor to me. His scent reached me first, that taunting, comforting, infuriating scent. Raphael knelt on my bed, resting one arm on the headboard, and leaned over me until our eyes were level. "Hi."

"Hi."

"What's going on with you?"

"Nothing. What makes you think there is something going on with me?"

His blue eyes scrutinized me. "You came out of sedation with bite marks on your stomach and mud on your feet."

"Many shapeshifters come out of sedation early."

He shook his head. "This is Doolittle's sedation we're talking about. What's going on?"

I clenched my teeth to keep the words from getting out.

"Andi, I'm right here. Look at me." He leaned closer. "Look at me."

Looking at him was a fatal mistake. The words made a break for it and I couldn't keep them down any longer. I put my arms, the good one and the one in a cast, around him. My cheek brushed his, his skin against mine, and I kissed him. I kissed him with as much tenderness and love as I could, because one way or another I would lose him.

"He wants my body," I whispered into Raphael's ear. "He wants to use it instead of his, because I have better shape-shifter magic."

His arms tightened around me.

"I have to volunteer."

"And if you don't?" he whispered.

"Bad things will happen." I kissed him again, my arms gripping him. "I'll fight him. I'll fight him with everything I have, but if it comes to that, whatever I do once he takes me over, whatever I say, it's not me." I whispered, my voice so quiet, I wasn't sure he heard it. "No matter what happens, I love you. You will always be my mate. I'm so sorry. I'm so sorry we ran out of time."

Raphael squeezed me, pressing me to him. "You listen to me." His whisper was a fierce promise. "He won't have you. We will kill him together. Trust me. I won't let go."

"You may have to," I told him. "You have to promise me that if he gets my body, you will walk away, Raphael. You'll go on, you'll find someone to love, you'll have children . . ."

"Shut up," he told me.

"Promise me."

"I'm not promising shit," he said. "I would die before I lost you."

"Raphael!"

"No."

He slid in the bed next to me, holding me in his arms. His scent enveloped me, and I held on to him, until I fell asleep.

CHAPTER 15

In the morning I awoke alone in the hospital room. Doolittle delivered a huge breakfast to me and stood over me while I ate every last piece of scrambled eggs, sirloin tips, and pancakes. I gobbled it up and escaped the medical ward to go look for Roman.

I found the priest of the Evil God in a corner of the northern courtyard. It was one of those small outside spaces within the Keep, shielded by a tall wall and made to provide relative privacy. To get to it, I had to pass through the stone arch, cut in the bottom of a stocky tower, and midway to it, I heard high-pitched giggles.

The black volhv sat on a bench, surrounded by a gaggle of kids, and was making small things disappear from his hands and reappear behind their ears and in their hair. A female werejackal discreetly watched him from the wall. Visitors to the Keep were never left unsupervised, especially around children.

I leaned against the wall and watched the volhv, too. There was something so joyous about Roman. It was as if part of his life was so bleak and dark that he felt the need to live the rest of it to its fullest, squeezing every bit of fun and happiness out of it. Even his martyred, put-upon sighs had a slightly mocking quality about them, as if he only pretended to be upset.

Roman saw me. "Okay, that's enough magic for today. Scatter now. Scatter, scatter, scatter."

The kids took off. Roman spread his arms. "Can't help it. I'm just popular."

I smiled and sat by him on the bench. "I have a serious question."

"I will give a serious answer."

"Can a god be killed?"

The humor drained from Roman's face. "Well, that depends on if you're a pantheist or Marxist."

"What's the difference?"

"The first believes that divinity is the universe. The two are synonymous and nonexistent without each other. The second believes in anthropocentrism, seeing man in the center of the universe, and god as just an invention of human conscience. Of course, if you follow Nietzsche, you can kill God just by thinking about him."

Ask a priest a question, get an enigmatic answer. Didn't matter what religion . . . "Roman," I said. "Can I kill Anubis?"

"I'm trying to answer. Anubis is a deity, a collection of specific concepts and beliefs. You can't kill a concept, because to do so you must destroy every human being who is aware of it. Your best bet would be to identify everyone who entertained the idea of his existence and shoot them in the head."

"So the answer is a no?"

Roman sighed. "I didn't finish. You want simple answers to very complicated questions. The wrong questions. The question you should be asking isn't whether a god can be killed, but what is Anubis. You must understand the nature of a thing before you can end its existence. In Anubis's case, his divinity is partial. He requires a mortal form to survive the periods of technology. His mortal form is just that—mortal. You know its nature. You know where to cut and how you can break it. You can end Anubis's mortal form. Will it end Anubis? There are no certainties in this world, but I would theorize that no, it will not. As long as there is a cult of Anubis, devoted to veneration of his specific concept with a specific image, he will continue. He will be reborn."

"How quickly?" I asked.

"How quickly will he come back if you nuke him?" Roman frowned. "His grasp on his corporeal form is tenuous. The fact that he could be killed in itself is devastating to his divinity. People don't like to believe in gods who can be murdered and remain dead; they much prefer to believe in rebirth. If I were him, I would've waited a couple hundred years before I decided to get my toes wet in this magic and technology mess. So the simple answer is, he will return. But not in my lifetime and likely not in that of our children or grandchildren. I would prepare anyway, because when he does come back, he'll be pissed off."

"So his mortal body can die?"

"Yes. It's just a body. Unfortunately, it's a body with huge magical potential. I don't know what his reserves are, but he'll use every drop of them to defend himself. He's been very conservative with his shows of power so far, which probably means he's hoarding it for this final battle with Apep in case we fail."

If the mortal body was the most likely target, then fighting him in my dreams would be futile.

Roman patted my back. "Cheer up, deadly girl. Things have a way of working themselves out."

Not this time. But I wouldn't go meekly to the slaughter. No, I would fight him for the lives of the people I loved to the bitter end. Win or lose, Anapa would regret meeting me.

Raphael strode through the arch, followed by Ascanio. Raphael was in black jeans and a black T-shirt that complemented his hair and showed off his carved biceps. Ascanio had somehow managed to copy his outfit so precisely he looked like Raphael's younger brother.

Raphael saw Roman, registered his hand on my back, and focused on him like a shark.

"What are you doing here?"

"I'm sitting and talking to a pretty girl." The volhv regarded him with a slightly mocking air. "We were having a lovely time until you showed up."

"That's nice. How about you go somewhere else," Raphael told him.

"I'm really tired of you telling me what to do," Roman said.

They'd bickered the entire way back from the fight with the draugr. My arm hurt too much to pay attention, but apparently during the battle on the hill, someone had run the wrong way and the two of them had managed to collide, which disrupted Roman's binding. They blamed each other. The fact that Raphael and I had barely gotten back together and he wasn't inclined to tolerate men in my vicinity wasn't helping either.

"Go. Away," Raphael said.

The volhv leaned back, his arms behind his head. "How about you go fuck yourself."

Nice repartee. Not.

Raphael smiled. "Big talk for a man in a dress."

"It's not a dress. It's robes, which are my work clothes. You know, work? The thing real men do?"

Uh-oh.

"Real men, huh?" Raphael was still smiling, and the hint of insanity in his eyes made him look slightly unhinged.

"What was your job again?" Roman frowned, pretending to think. "Ah yes. Don't you stand there and look pretty to impress female visitors? You're really good at that. No real skill involved. Not much of a retirement for that kind of thing, though. Doesn't help to keep a wife and kids fed either. Unless you find a rich old lady and hope she puts you in her will . . ."

He did not just say that.

Raphael froze, momentarily stricken speechless.

"How old would the old lady have to be?" Ascanio asked. "Old like forty?"

"Go back to Aunt B and stay with her," Raphael said. His voice was eerily calm. *Uh-oh.*

"Yes, Alpha." Ascanio spun on his heel and took off.

Raphael had removed him from immediate danger.

"What are you two doing?" I asked them. "Don't we have a bigger fish to fry?"

"Stay out of it," Raphael told me. "This is between him and me."

I knew that look. It was his "I will do this or die trying" look.

"I have to concur," Roman said. "This is an A-B conversation."

Two idiots. "Fine," I said. "Knock yourselves out."

Raphael focused on Roman with the unwavering concentration of a predator sighting his prey. "Right now. Let's go."

Roman grinned. "Sure."

Raphael stretched, rolling his head left to right.

Roman stood, picked up his staff, and spun it like a Shaolin monk bent on a rampage. Raphael squared his shoulders.

Men. Enough said.

Roman leaned forward. Wind swirled around his feet. The black volhv shot forward, as if his black boots had wings. Raphael stepped out of the way, letting Roman pass him, spun, jumped up, and kicked Roman between the shoulder blades.

The wizard flew into the wall, but didn't hit it, because an invisible cushion of air stopped his fall. He dropped down to his feet and turned. "Hmm."

Raphael had a frighteningly grim look on his face.

Roman's lips moved. A cocoon of black threads slid from the ground in twisted streams, wrapping themselves around him, not quite touching.

Raphael lunged, shockingly fast.

The black threads snapped, binding around Raphael's wrist. Roman leaned back and drove a crushing sidekick into the top of Raphael's hip. It sounded like a sledgehammer pounding into a stud. I'd seen it before. It was a sambo kick, part of a personal defense martial art the Russians practiced. *Ow. Ow, ow, ow.*

Raphael grabbed the black threads and pulled. Roman strained, pulling back.

A small boy ran through the stone arch and headed for the two of them. I jumped off the bench, ran, and caught him.

"Hi!" he said.

I lifted him off the ground. My rebroken arm screamed a little and I shifted his weight to the other. "Hi."

"They're fighting!" the boy told me, pointing at the two men.

"Yes, they are. Where are your parents?"

A couple ran through the arch, a tall man and a dark-haired woman in her late thirties, followed by a teenage girl.

"Dylan!" The woman reached for the boy. "I'm so, so sorry. We just wanted to pay our respects to the alpha. We were told he would be here. We didn't mean to interrupt. We're trying to get admitted into Clan Bouda . . ."

I looked at her face, and recognition punched me in the gut. *Michelle.*

Michelle Carver, who put a nail through my hand when I was five, because she thought it was funny to hear me scream. Michelle Carver, who pelted me with bricks, after Candy broke my legs. All I could do was crawl and Michelle chased me and threw bricks and rocks at my head. Michelle, who cheered while the bitch alpha beat my mother to a bloody pulp. Michelle "Hit her again, Candy!"

I had killed every last one of them. Every last one, except

her. She had gone missing a couple of years before I came back and wiped that sadistic clan of bouda bitches off the face of the planet. I had tried to find her, but she had done a good job of covering her tracks.

Raphael let go of the threads. "Andrea?"

I was holding Michelle Carver's child in my hands.

I let go of the boy. He slid to the ground.

"Andrea?" All blood drained from Michelle's face. "Andrea Nash?"

She backed away from me.

Raphael started toward me.

"Do you know what she is?" A hysterical note vibrated in Michelle's voice. "She's beastkin."

The world suddenly became very simple. I moved. Her mate tried to stand in my way. I backhanded him, and he went flying. I grabbed Michelle by her throat and drove her into the wall, pinning her in place. My arm had fur, and my hand had claws, and Michelle's blood squirting under her skin through her jugular tickled my fingers.

"Tell me again what I am." I smashed the back of her head into the brick. "Tell me again."

Michelle croaked in my grip. She made no move to shift. She had no warrior form. She was never the strongest. No, she just liked to yip on the sidelines, picking on someone weaker out of fear. It changed nothing.

"This woman did something bad to you?" Roman asked.

"This woman tortured me and my mother."

Roman shrugged. "If you want to do her, do it quick. I'll go watch the entrance for you."

He was gone. All that was left was me and Michelle's pale, soft throat. The world was red. So, so red, and every time I exhaled, it was growing angrier and redder.

Raphael's hand rested on my shoulder. He stroked me, firm fingers caressing my fur. "You have the right. It would feel good."

It would feel great. He had no fucking idea how great it would be. I wanted to tell him that I finally caught her. I had told Raphael about her before. I wanted to tell him now how much I wanted to rip her apart, but all that came out was a snarl.

"I know you." Raphael put his arms around me, his mouth close to my ear, his voice soothing. "If you kill her in front of her children, it will haunt you for the rest of your life. Let go, babe. Let her go."

No! No, she didn't get to get away with this. No! Everybody else had paid, she would pay, too.

My injured arm hurt. The pain was so raw, so fresh.

She would pay. This weak, cruel waste of a human being. This piece of shit that tormented my childhood. She was the reason I'd woken up holding the fucking butcher knife. She was the reason Doolittle had had to take a saw to my arm. She would pay!

"Let her go, honey. Let her go, Andi. For your own sake. For me. For us." Raphael kissed my fur just below my ear. "Let her go."

I wanted to sink into the red. I wanted to see her blood on my hands. But his voice held me back.

"Stand down," he said. "Her children are watching. Stand down, honey."

I heard a tiny high-pitched sound, wailing at my side, and I realized it was the little boy bawling in hysterical fear. His sister sobbed.

"You are better than this, Andi. Do the right thing. W— away."

As I forced my fingers open, all the pain of my memories and all my frustration tore out of me in a sharp short scream. I spun and walked away, to the other wall, as far away from her as I could.

"She's beastkin," Michelle breathed out. "She's—"

"She's the clan beta and my mate," Raphael said.

Michelle staggered back as if he had hit her.

Raphael's eyes were two burning pools of blood-red fire. "Your application to the clan is denied. Gather your family and leave. If you're in my territory by sundown, I'll hunt you down and drag you before the clans to be tried for torture, abuse of a child, and whatever other charges our lawyers will level against you. You will be found guilty, you will suffer, and you will be executed. Your children will become the wards of the Pack and they'll loathe your name by the time they grow up."

Michelle picked up the prone body of her husband. Her daughter grabbed the boy and they ran out.

Raphael walked to me and wrapped his arms around me.

My anger broke out in tortured sobs. Tears wet my eyes. "I had her."

"I know."

"In my hands."

"I love you," he whispered. "I love you, I'm proud of you. It was the right thing."

"No!" I couldn't stop crying. I wasn't sad, I just couldn't contain it. "She should be dead. That would be the right thing."

"For her, but not for you. It would eat you alive. It's not who you are."

I crumpled down on the ground and cried. I'd learned not to cry back then, because the more I cried, the more excited they would get, but I could cry now. Nobody would stop me, and so I sat there and let it all pour out, while Raphael held me and whispered calm, loving nonsense into my ears.

I could not kill Michelle. I couldn't scar her children the way she had scarred me. But I could join the Pack and make sure that no other little girl had to face my choices. No other little bouda would be hiding, scared and alone, dreading to be found and abused again. Not on my watch. Not as long as I breathed.

Gradually my sobs died down. We sat together, Raphael and I.

"For the record, I had him," Raphael said. I could tell by his voice he was baiting me. There was comfort in the familiar needling, and right now I desperately needed it.

"Didn't look that way from where I stood. He had you all wrapped up."

"That's what you think," he said.

"That is what I think."

"Handling that purple carpet must've done some permanent damage," Raphael said.

"To you."

He leaned over and murmured, "I'm not the one with purple stains on my butt."

Oh, it's like this, then? "Would you like to be?"

He grinned and nodded.

"Maybe you needed backup to help you with Roman," I told him.

"I don't need backup. I can take him with one hand tied behind my back."

"He had one hand tied behind your back."

"Maybe it looked like that from where you were sitting . . ."

That's how Jim's messenger found us, sitting on the ground, bickering and flirting. Jim's teams had returned from the Warren, the poor neighborhood by White Street, and they had brought information about Gloria back with them.

I sat at a large conference table filled with food and reports. Jim sat across from me, and Chandra, Clan Jackal's designated expert on ancient Egypt, sat to my left. Between us teetered small mountains of paperwork—all of the information Jim's team had squeezed out of the inhabitants of the Warren. Derek joined us after the first fifteen minutes. We were looking for clues. Somewhere at this very moment, Gloria's associates were preparing to raise Apep from the dead. We needed to know where that location could be, and Gloria was our only link.

We'd been at it for hours. So far I had made two piles: a big pile of stuff I'd gone through and didn't consider relevant, and a very tiny pile of paper that might be something. I'd covered half a legal pad in notes. I was hungry again. The lunch hour came and went without us finding a smoking gun.

"It would be nice if there was a map," Chandra said. "With a town circled on it."

"And a note that said 'Secret Hideout Here'?" Derek added.

I scrutinized the paper in front of me. Gloria had used a private shipping service, which was faster and more reliable than the post office, but which also forced their customers to declare the exact contents of their packages. In the event your package decided to sprout tentacles when the magic hit, they wanted to be prepared for that eventuality.

This particular operative, whose name was Douglas, had tracked down the shipping company Gloria used and offered their rep an outrageous bribe for the manifest of everything delivered to Gloria's doorstep. Handmade soap, thirty bucks a bar. Expensive perfume. Pricy bath salts. Someone was living high.

Doolittle walked through the door. "Shouldn't you be resting?"

"I'm saving the world," I told him.

Doolittle looked mournful. "I'll make us some hot chocolate."

I went down the list of deliveries: books, blah-blah, more soap, antimosquito cream. Hmm. Georgia was in the grip of a drought. I hadn't seen a mosquito in ages.

"Mosquito cream," I said.

Derek raised his pen. "Boots. She went down to Carlos's Footwear and got herself a pair of rubber boots two days before you killed her. Some kids from the Warren nagged her for change and she told them to piss off."

Fatal mistake. Never upset the street kids.

"So we have water," Jim said.

"In the original myth, Apep lived in the river," Chandra said.

"Could he be somewhere in the Chattahoochee?" Derek asked.

"No." Jim tapped the paper. "Too risky. The Chattahoochee is too shallow and too well patrolled. Half of the city's shipping comes through it. The army would napalm a giant snake the moment they saw it."

"So we either have lakes in the north or . . ." Derek pulled out a map. "Or the Suwanee."

"The Suwanee River would work," Jim said. "It's deep and black water."

I dug through the manifests. "She put in an order with the teamsters for a large crate shipment to be shipped a couple of weeks ago. Supposedly glassware. It's going to . . . Waycross."

"Waycross, Georgia?" Jim asked.

"Yep."

"That's right on the edge of the Okefenokee swamp," Derek said.

"There are also crate orders for Augusta and Tallahassee," I said.

"We need a confirmation." Jim dug through his papers.

Derek and I burrowed into our stacks.

"Pontoon!" Derek announced twenty minutes later. "She bought a pontoon boat."

"When?" I looked through my notes on the shipping records.

"On the fourteenth. Took it off the lot."

"She shipped a large crate of antiques down to Folkston on the fifteenth. Where is Folkston?"

"The east edge of the Okefenokee." Jim rose. "We got her."

"You can't be involved," I reminded him.

"No, we can't help you fight," Jim said. "There is a difference. Nobody says we can't scout the swamp and mark the way for you. You won't go in blind."

"I'll get on the phone," Derek said.

They left the room.

Doolittle put a cup of hot chocolate in front of me. "Drink this before you go."

I sipped it. It had to be half sugar. "It's delicious."

Doolittle patted my arm. "It's good for you. A little sugar goes a long way."

Little, huh?

"Thank you," I told him. "You were always kind to me. Not many people are. I will never forget it."

"You are coming back." Doolittle fixed me with his stare.

"Sure." I got up and hugged him.

Raphael, Roman, and I rode the ley line out of Atlanta. The magic current ran whether the magic was up or down, but when tech ruled, like it did now, the ley line speed dropped to a mere forty miles per hour. It took us several hours to get there. The magic finally spat us and our cargo out right between Waycross and Folkston into the open arms of a shapeshifter woman with a Pack Jeep. She was short, dark-haired, and had a sprinkling of freckles on her nose.

"Here is your ride." She held out the keys. Raphael took them. "Go down that road, take the right fork, then the second left. You'll come to the pier. There are two pontoon boats there. Take them. The way through the swamp is marked with strips of white fabric. Good luck."

She walked away.

We loaded the cargo into the Jeep, and me and my Heckler & Koch UMP submachine gun called shotgun. Roman crawled into the backseat.

Twenty minutes later we pulled up before the wooden pier. In front of us a narrow channel curved into the green wall of trees and underbrush. Two pontoon boats floated on the water the color of black tea.

A crate sat on the pier. On the side someone had written in black marker, "A present from Uncle Jim."

Raphael pulled the top off the crate. Pixilated ACUs—Army Combat Uniforms—in lovely randomized patterns of greens and browns, perfect for the swamp.

"I like this uncle." I found the shortest set and stripped off my jeans.

Roman opened his eyes wide, as if he had never seen a woman in underwear before.

Raphael threw a set at him. "Don't just stand there."

"You want me to wear these?" Roman looked at the ACUs and put his hand over his chest, as if protecting his black robe. "That's not right."

"You have a problem with pants?" Raphael asked.

Roman pulled his robe apart, revealing a pair of black jeans underneath. "I always wear my pants. I just don't want to deal with that retarded outfit. I don't even know how to put it on."

"Wear the fatigues," I told him. "It won't kill you. Not wearing them might."

Roman sighed, rolled his eyes, and stripped off his robe and jeans, revealing a muscled torso. Well. Someone worked out. Roman pulled on the fatigue pants, grabbed the black boots, folded the bottom of the pants in a practiced move, and stuffed his feet into his boots.

Hmmm.

Next he took the ACU top and rolled up both sleeves in a perfectly even summer regulation cuff. Raphael stared at him. Roman pulled the ACU on and flexed. "Makes your arm bigger, see?"

"You asshole," I punched him in the shoulder.

"Gentle! I bruise easily." He rubbed his carved biceps and I caught a glimpse of a tattoo on his arm: a skull wearing a beret. Army Ranger.

Now I had seen everything.

* * *

I stood on the bow of a pontoon boat and held binoculars to my eyes. Raphael sat at the helm. Roman piloted the second vessel behind us. He'd brought some sort of leather harness, which he had fit over his ACUs, and stuck his staff through it. It looked silly protruding over his shoulder.

A river stretched in front of me, its waters blue-black and half hidden by lily pads and water weeds. Strange trees bordered it, couched in the brush and reeds, tall, their trunks bare and bloated at the root where they thrust from the water, then narrowing as they rose to spread in a canopy of fresh bright green. They looked prehistoric. This was not my country.

"Cypresses," Raphael told me, when I had asked about them a minute ago. "They are buttresses against the hurricanes."

We made our way through the labyrinth of waterways and false islands made of floating peat and covered with grass. The air smelled of water, fish, and mud. Somewhere to the left a gator roared, the sound ripping from its throat deep, powerful, and primeval, as if the swamp itself roared into our faces. There was a strange serene beauty in this ancient, wet riot of life, but I wasn't in the mood to appreciate it.

Ahead the river forked, flowing around an island, a dense mess of underbrush and cypresses. A small piece of white cloth dangled from the low-lying bush, dead center of the river. In the past when Jim's people had left markers, they were to the left or to the right, indicating which way we had to turn. This one was straight on.

"Island coming up," I said. "I don't think we're going around this time."

"Got it."

Since last night, Raphael had said exactly sixteen words to me. He was distancing himself. It was probably better this way.

The boat slid into the muddy shore. I jumped out into the soggy soup of mud and water and pulled back the canvas covering the bottom of the boat. Guns stared at me, wrapped lovingly in plastic to keep the moisture out. Two shotguns. A Heckler & Koch UMP submachine gun. And my baby, a

Parker-Hale M-85, my sniper rifle of choice. They didn't make them anymore. She was a gift from my sniper instructor and she let me put a bullet into the center of a man's forehead at nine hundred and sixty meters. She had never failed me.

I took the rifle and one shotgun, Raphael shouldered the backpack filled with ammunition and grabbed the UMP and the other shotgun. A moment later Roman docked and pulled back his own canvas, gathering up a giant rucksack filled with magic paraphernalia, and picked up my compound bow and two quivers filled with arrows. We set off through the swamp, moving as quietly as the wet ground allowed.

The ground climbed up. There must've been an outcropping of rock under all that mud. We kept going up the gently rising hill.

Raphael stopped. A moment later I smelled it, too—smoke. We bent low, moving up the hill in complete silence, until finally we went to ground at its end.

A small city spread out in front of the hill, stretching across the floodplain. Huts and shacks made of wood, tents, premanufactured buildings, all connected by wooden walkways, radiating from a circular channel in the center. Muddy water filled the channel, draining off into the floodplain. In its center a massive structure stretched to the sky. At least three hundred feet tall, it resembled a spiral of smooth coils, wide at the ground and narrow as it twisted about the base again and again, reaching to the flat top.

A clay spiral. Roman's prophecy was coming true.

"They built an enormous dog turd," Raphael murmured.

"It's a snake," Roman said. "Look, see the head is resting on the top, and the snake is curling down around the pyramid. They've made their god out of clay, and then they'll animate him. It's very clever, actually."

The coils at the bottom of the pyramid were at least eighteen feet tall. I put the binoculars to my eyes. The top of the pyramid was flat. The head of a colossal clay snake rested on one side, its eyes closed, Roman's coveted staff thrust through the beginning of the snake's neck. Next to the serpent three clay man-shaped statues sat, their legs crossed, their arms resting on their knees. Behind them a short stubby altar rose. On the altar lay Anubis's fang.

I shifted the view down to the huts and counted, two, five, eight, ten, twelve . . . Thirty-two buildings. People walked to and fro, both men and women. A group of kids carrying fishing rods jumped off the walkway and splashed through the muddy water, heading into the swamp. A woman and a younger girl cleaned fish on a wooden table. A cat sat by their feet, waiting for a handout.

Let's say four people per structure. That's a hundred and twenty-eight people. At least. Some buildings looked significantly larger than others.

They killed four of our people. We had come here with the idea to shoot every cultist in sight. This was a search-and-destroy type of mission. I had no problem killing the adults, but nobody ever said anything about children being present.

An unmistakable wail of an infant in distress tickled my ears. *You've got to be kidding me.*

Roman sighed next to me. "Why? Why do they always bring babies into it?"

"Probably to feed them to the snake," Raphael said.

Our original plan waved good-bye at us, stuck its thumb in its mouth, strained, and exploded. We had to stop the ritual. We had to get revenge for Nick, his son, and the families of other shapeshifters. And we had to make sure not to murder any kids.

"We could try for the knife," I said.

"What? We run all the way to the top in the open?" Roman stared at me.

"The magic is down. Now is the best time to hit them." I glanced at Raphael, looking for support. "No knife, no Apep."

"What did I miss?" Anapa popped out of thin air and crouched down next to Roman, oblivious to mud staining his thousand-dollar suit.

"We're going to get your tooth," Raphael told him.

"Excellent." He lay down on his back and put his arms behind his head. "Go on. Do your thing."

"We need a diversion." Raphael looked at Roman.

The volhv furrowed his eyebrows. "What are you looking at me for? The magic's down."

"I have explosives in my bag," I offered. "If someone sets them off, it would buy us some time."

We looked at Anapa.

"Who me?" He blinked.

"So you're not going to help at all?" Roman chided him.

Anapa sighed.

I pulled the backpack open and took out flash grenades. "Look, this is simple. Pull the pins like this." I pantomimed pulling the pins. "Throw. Run the other way. You're the god of knowledge, you can do it."

Anapa peered at the grenades. "Very well. Where do you want them thrown?"

I pointed to the left strand of trees. "There. In five minutes."

"Very well." Anapa took the grenades and walked off down the hill into the brush, looking absurdly out of place.

"Think he will do it?" Roman asked.

"We'll find out." Raphael was looking at the pyramid with the intense focus of a predator. He slung the shotgun over his shoulder.

I pulled my sniper rifle out of its plastic, chambered a round, and looked through the scope. Two people were guarding the path to the snake pyramid, two more were up on the slope, and then one last one was only a few feet under the snake's head.

I took deep even breaths. Steady.

The man under the snake's head was looking straight at me. He was older, with a careworn face and wrinkles. He looked so ordinary. What the hell was he even doing here on the slope, trying to resurrect an ancient god?

Steady.

The explosion flared on the left, tearing the silence with its thunder. It's funny how a sudden threat separates people: two-thirds of the swamp city ran to their huts like good little civilians in danger, while the remaining third, armed with rifles and bows, dashed toward the explosion, trying to eliminate the danger.

I fired. A wet, red flower blossomed in the middle of the older man's forehead. He pitched back and crumpled onto the clay body of his god.

I sighted the second sentry, midway up, a blond woman, and squeezed the trigger.

Two more shots. Two more people turned into corpses. Minimal casualties. People like to note "minimal" and forget about "casualties," but it's the casualties that wake you up at night.

I picked off another guard, close to the path, and jumped to my feet. We ran straight ahead, single file, Raphael in the lead, his knife out, the wicked curve sharp.

A man noticed us and swung his rifle, blocking our way. Before he could pull the trigger, Raphael sliced and kept moving. The man crumpled down.

We kept going, pounding our way down the wooden walkway. A woman shot into our way, eyes wide and terrified. She opened her mouth, baring twin fangs, and lunged at Raphael. His knife flashed again. The woman fell against the side of a house.

A shout rang from the left—another guard had noticed us. Two rifles snapped up. I fired faster than they did.

The walkway ended. We jumped into the mud, sinking in up to midshin, and waded through toward the pyramid looming ahead.

Bullets whistled past me. I turned around. A woman with a rifle at two o'clock. Aim, squeeze, take half a second to confirm that her body splashed into the mud.

Roman lagged behind. He was moving fast for a human, but not for a shapeshifter.

"Raphael!" I called.

He turned around and doubled back.

"No, I've got this," Roman said.

Raphael picked him up out of the mud and we raced to the pyramid.

The clay body of Apep wound about the structure, and I finally realized why the entire thing wasn't collapsing under its terrible weight—steel beams and the edge of concrete poked out from beneath the clay. The cultists had used some sort of structure as a base. How the hell had they gotten it down into the swamp?

Raphael set Roman down and they began climbing. I lingered. The sentries had done an about-face and were running toward us. I fired. The bullet took the first man in the stomach. He dropped into the mud. I fired again, knocking the second runner out of the lineup. They scattered, taking cover behind the huts.

I turned around and followed the men up the pyramid.

Shots rang out. A bullet bit into my side. *Argh.* Not silver, but it hurt like hell. My body clenched and expelled it. I kept climbing.

Another bullet burrowed into the mud an inch from my head. I shifted sideways, moving along the side of the structure, trying to put the thickness of the pyramid between me and the shooters.

A hail of gunfire tore from one of the huts.

"Honey!" Raphael called. He was above me, shielding Roman with his body.

I turned, pressing my back against the mud, and raised my rifle. The muzzle flash gave the shooter away—third hut on the left, in the window, a faint outline of a man's head. I squeezed the trigger. The rifle barked, and a man's head jerked back. The gunfire died. I turned around and kept climbing.

Above me Raphael and Roman climbed up onto the flat top of the pyramid. I grabbed the edge, pulled myself up, just as Raphael stepped toward the altar . . .

The magic wave drowned us. *Oh no.*

The clay statue of a man in front of me opened its eyes. Its human eyes. The clay figures weren't statues. They were actual people, smeared with a thick layer of mud and left to bake, motionless, under the sun.

Raphael picked up Anubis's fang off the altar.

"Raphael!" I screamed.

The statues jumped, breaking their coats of clay, and grabbed Raphael. He clamped the one in front of him in a death grip. I rushed them from one side, Roman from the other. The clay-covered man in front of me unhinged his jaw and sank his fangs into Raphael's side. My hands closed about his neck. I squeezed, crushing bone and cartilage, and jerked the corpse aside, hurling if off the pyramid. Roman stabbed his staff into the spine of the second man and then Raphael opened his hands and the third cultist fell, lifeless.

Raphael fell. I caught him and lowered him down.

His blue eyes were wide open. "It's hot."

I jerked my knife from my belt, grabbed Raphael's ACU

top and cut it, stripping it off. Two bites, one on the right arm and the other on the torso. I yanked my backpack open, grabbed Doolittle's antivenom gun, and shot it into the first bite.

"Don't move." *Don't die. Don't die, Raphael. Don't die.*

I sank two more shots into him and then three more into the other bite.

"Behind you," Raphael barked.

I whipped around. The fourth statue snapped upright right next to the snake's head, half-hidden by the serpent's skull. Roman charged it.

The clay-smeared man howled something wordless and angry. Roman shoved his staff into the man's chest. The scream turned to a gurgle, as blood spilled from the cultist's mouth. Roman freed the staff with a sharp jerk, stumbled back, and slid down, leaving a bloody smudge on the clay Apep's neck.

"The knife," Raphael squeezed out. His body bucked in my hands, rigid.

I shot more antivenom into him. It was all I could do.

"The knife," he croaked.

I reached for Anubis's fang, which had fallen from his hand. A man's hand snatched it before I could touch it.

"I'll take that, thank you!" Anapa strode to Apep.

Roman blocked his way. The god backhanded him. Roman crashed into the altar. Anapa raised the knife. A jackal howled, loud, deafening.

I lunged at him and hit an invisible wall. It tossed me back and I fell on Raphael.

Anapa plunged the knife into Apep's skull.

The clay serpent shuddered. The pyramid shook under us. Cracks sprang on Apep's blunt nose. The colossal head rose, teetered upright, and fell backward. The clay serpent slid off the pyramid into the mud.

"The show will go on after all!" Anapa spun around, grinning with a mouth full of jackal teeth. "Here we go."

"You fucking bastard!" I snarled.

Raphael shook under my hands. He was going into convulsions.

"I must have my myth." Anapa laughed and vanished.

The swamp shook. A flock of birds rose from the trees, darkening the sky.

"Snakes." Roman pushed himself from the altar.

"What?"

"Flying snakes." He planted the staff into the pyramid and began to chant. Darkness swirled around his feet, flashes of pure black emptiness suffused with silver lightning.

The cloud headed for us. Raphael's limbs shook, gripped by a spasm. I pried his jaws open and forced the handle of the knife into his mouth. I had no more antivenom. I'd injected him with our entire supply.

A deep-voiced bell tolled, echoed by the distant silvery ringing of smaller bells. Eerie male voices chanted in tune to Roman's incantations. The snakes swarmed above us, turning the sky black.

Wind twisted about Roman. I hugged Raphael to me.

The snakes plunged at us . . . and hit an invisible wall, as if a transparent half-sphere shielded us from their onslaught. They touched the wall and slid along the edge of the spell, turning smaller, darker, losing their wings, until they finally landed on the side of the pyramid and slid down into the mud as plain rat snakes.

Raphael gripped my hand, struggling to say something. His eyes rolled back in his head.

I clenched him to me. No, this wasn't the way it was supposed to be. The antivenom had to work. It had to . . .

The last of the snakes fell. Roman dropped to his knees, out of breath, his face pale.

A loud hiss rolled through the swamp as if a thousand snakes opened their mouths in unison. I leaned forward.

Below us a serpent the size of a cargo train circled the pyramid, sliding through the mud. His body shimmered and twisted with a constantly moving mosaic of brown and yellow.

Raphael's heels drummed the ground. He was dying. He was dying and I was out of antivenom.

"Now would be a good time to make some choices," Anapa said next to me.

I grabbed his leg, jerked him down, and locked my hands around his throat. They never touched his skin. A barrier of magic held me back. I squeezed, straining with all my strength. He smiled.

The pyramid shook as the colossal snake curved around it. "You," I snarled. "You!"

A titanic serpent's head rose, hovering above us. A long tongue slivered out of the lipless mouth to taste the air.

"You know what you have to do," Anapa said. His head melted, changing shape, and suddenly my hands touched the thick, furry throat of a Jackal.

I gripped it. "I'll kill you."

"Give me what I want and he will live," the Jackal said.

I didn't hesitate for a second. "Do it and you can have me."

A yellow sheen rolled over the Jackal's eyes.

"Andrea?" Raphael said behind me, his voice almost normal. "Andrea?"

My feet left the ground. I floated up, weightless. The Jackal floated next to me, huge as a three-story house, his head shaggy with fur, his yellow eyes bottomless. Raphael was screaming something down below.

I love you, darling.

I love you.

Forgive me.

The Jackal opened its mouth and gulped me. Magic flowed from me, binding me, anchoring me inside the Jackal, connecting us and circulating out of him into me and back to him. We merged, the monstrous beast and I, and suddenly we were once again solid and the old enemy reared its ugly head in front of us.

Apep hissed and struck.

We dodged, lithe and fast.

The serpent smashed into the corner of the pyramid. The entire pathetic mud pile shook and careened. Humans screamed. Morons. Small pathetic morons wriggling in the mud building their mud-hill temple.

Apep coiled himself, his head swaying back and forth. We ran around him, mashing the mud with our paws and snarling. Apep opened its mouth, the magic roiling inside its dark maw.

We yipped and barked, baiting it.

Apep struck, like a coiled spring, and missed.

We danced around it, so fast, so clever.

Stupid snake. Foolish, foolish, weak snake.

Apep lunged. Fangs struck our paw. We snapped our teeth and it let go.

Little humans cheered. Venom coursed through our veins. No matter. We had enough magic to cleanse our blood easily.

We danced around the serpent. It turned, but not fast enough. We bit its tail and ran, dragging it around the flood-plain, its blood a burning inferno on our tongue.

Look at us pulling your god by its tail. Look at us, little things. *Look at me. I am Inepu. I am the better god.*

Apep coiled back and struck, but I opened my mouth and danced away, too fast for it. Apep gathered itself into a spiral.

I circled it. Bite from the left. The snake mouth met me and I withdrew.

Strike from the right. Again the snake mouth barred my way.

I will win. I will endure.

I will triumph.

I am Inepu.

My magic was weakening. My worshipers were still few. So few. But not as few as Apep's.

I snapped my teeth, lunging low.

Apep shot out. Its fangs pierced my fur and skin. Fire and night rolled into my veins, threatening to end me. I let the serpent bite me and just as it let go, I bit its neck, sinking my teeth deep into its flesh.

Die. Die . . .

Go back into nothing. Dissolve and be forgotten, so I will stand in your place.

Apep writhed in my jaws, whipping its body at me, clenching, coiling, but I held on and bit harder and harder.

The last of my magic was almost spent.

My fangs found bone. I jerked the body of my enemy up and bit down with all my might.

Apep hung limp in my jaws.

I held him high, showing everyone my triumph.

Witness my might. Remember it.

In the mud, small things knelt. I felt the first stirring of devotion, the delicious addictive splashes of their faith.

Worship me. Feed me.

The pliant flesh in my mouth turned to clay. The serpent's body crumbled and I released it. It crashed into the mud in chunks of clay. I howled, announcing my victory.

The small things fled. No matter. They would remember me. Soon, when I recovered, I would find them and add them to my worshippers. The current of faith would flow.

I stood there, exhausted, exhilarated, intoxicated by my power. Invincible.

I was a god.

Weakness flooded me, slowly. The last of my magic was spent. I staggered to their former god's ruined temple. I let go of my form and assumed my new human shape. Healthy. Beautiful. Full of magic and so blissfully easy to heal.

I studied my perfectly formed fingers, my arms, my long, muscled legs.

I was beautiful.

A man walked toward me through the mud. What was the name . . .

Raphael.

Raphael!

I crushed the small voice inside me, smothering it.

The man kept walking. He had a strange look on his face. Humans are curious creatures. This one was . . . angry? No . . . grieving, perhaps, but no, that wasn't quite right either.

Perhaps I should kill—

The magic jerked me back. I had forgotten. I had made the bargain. I had promised he would live.

The human was close now. Determination. That was it. I needed to retreat, to fold myself into the limit of the human mind, but not yet. Not yet. I had just vanquished my enemy. I deserved this, deserved the worship, the taste of power to come.

Perhaps he was coming to kill me. But then any damage he could do, I would heal.

I raised my arms. "What do you think of my body?"

The human attacked. I saw it, saw the glove on his hand with long pale metal claws, and I willed my magic to shield me, but too little was left.

He thrust his metal claws into my chest and scoured my heart.

It burned! It burned like fire. Pain writhed through me, tearing me apart. I'd never felt an agony like this, an all-consuming, terrible pain. I shoved him back, but the pain didn't stop.

The claws had broken off. They ripped my heart apart. My magic streamed past it, unable to remove them. I couldn't heal the damage.

I was dying.

I screamed, and the trees shook from my howl.

I flailed, trying to rip the metal out of me.

No. No, I would not die today. I tore myself from my new form and fled, into the mud, into the sludge, where my old form slumped, discarded.

The world slammed into me in an explosion of pain. Silver burned in my heart.

"I got you," Raphael was holding me. "I've got you."

I was dying.

Suddenly Doolittle was there with the scalpel.

Where had he even come from? Was I hallucinating before death?

"It's okay," Raphael crooned in my ear.

Doolittle sliced my chest open. "Expel this silver if you want to live!"

"Do it, Andrea!" Raphael snarled.

I pushed against the burning points of pain. Doolittle dug in my open chest with forceps. I screamed.

"Expel!"

I couldn't breathe. My chest was on fire, and the unbearable, terrible pain burned inside me like an inferno.

The first shard slid out of me. Doolittle plucked it out with forceps.

The world dimmed, as if someone was blowing out its candles one by one. Doolittle raised his hand. I caught a glimpse of a syringe. Doolittle plunged it down. The needle bit me in the heart.

The darkness tore in a blinding flash of light and adrenaline.

"Silver!" Raphael screamed at me. "Get it out!"

I strained. Another shard slid free.

"Do it, Andrea!" Raphael growled.

"Expel," Doolittle commanded.

It hurt and I was so tired.

Another shard left me.

"Last one," Doolittle barked.

The world went black.

It was so cold and quiet. *Can I please stay here . . .*

I opened my eyes to agony and Doolittle massaging my heart with his fingers.

I screamed, but my voice was just a hoarse croak.

The last point of agony slid out of me. Raphael laid me flat. Doolittle knelt over me. His hands were bloody. He was holding some sort of surgical instrument. A woman handed him gauze. A cooling sensation spread through my insides. I was going numb.

Behind him I saw Anapa stagger to his feet.

Eyes lit up in the swamp. I saw them with shocking clarity, hundreds of eyes.

A flood of furry bodies poured from the underbrush. Jackals. Dozens upon dozens of them, and in the lead were the huge, muscled shapes of shapeshifters in their warrior form. Clan Jackal had arrived.

They circled Anapa.

"We will take the child now," a gray shapeshifter in a warrior shape said.

"Give us the child."

Anapa smiled a lopsided grin that bared his teeth and thrust his arms up. Magic flowed from him in a slow wave.

The Jackals pushed against it.

The enormous alpha in front howled. Hundreds of voices answered in a chorus of howls, barks, and yips.

Anapa pushed.

Clan Jackal gained a foot. Another foot.

Anapa clenched his teeth. There were too many of them and he was too weakened.

"Give us the child," snarling voices demanded.

"Return the child."

"Return!"

"Stop!" Magic pulsed, knocking the first few Jackals back. Others took their place. He didn't have enough juice to disappear. I had been inside him, and I knew. He'd spent everything on that fight.

"Here!" He spat. "Have her."

A little girl materialized in the middle of the Jackal pack. One of the warriors snatched her and ran toward us. The Jackals kept moving, step by step, tightening the ring.

"I gave you what you wanted!"

The Jackals closed in, one step at a time, eyes on fire, fangs gleaming.

"Stop!"

They swarmed him. He screamed, but not for very long.

I sat on a muddy log. My heart was beating inside me. Doolittle had mended it through a gaping hole in my chest, while I screamed, and then he'd repaired my rib cage, and then he had sealed my wounds. He sat next to me now, wiping my blood off his hands with a wet rag. His eyes were red. He had a terrible look on his face.

Raphael knelt by him. "Thank you."

Doolittle shook his head. "I didn't hear that. What did you say?"

Raphael leaned closer. "I said, thank—"

Doolittle grabbed his throat and smashed his head into Raphael's face. It was the most vicious head butt I had ever seen. Raphael fell back. Doolittle snarled something under his breath and walked away.

Raphael shook his head. Blood gushed from his broken nose.

"I think he's mad at you," I told him.

"He'll get over it." Raphael grinned at me.

"How did you know I wouldn't die?"

"I didn't."

"Took a chance, huh?"

He nodded. "We had nothing to lose."

Behind him the Jackals had dismantled one of the huts and dragged Anapa's dismembered corpse onto a pile of wood. Two shapeshifters in warrior form dumped fuel onto the boards and set it on fire.

"How did you know Anapa would panic?" I asked.

"When you told me he had started as a shapeshifter, I went to the Jackals looking for their research on Anubis's weaknesses. They took it very seriously. Half of the Clan was digging up information. They said that in ancient Egypt, when Anubis was still human, silver was virtually unknown. The Egyptians started getting it later, through imports, and even then it was highly prized. There was no reason he would know how silver affected shapeshifters from personal experience. Roman said that he would likely retreat to the old Anapa body if he was threatened. Clan Jackal trailed us. His ego was so colossal, he didn't view them as a threat."

"He didn't even notice them," I told him.

"The hardest part was talking Doolittle into that emergency open-heart surgery. He really didn't want to do it. We argued for hours. He thought you wouldn't survive." Raphael swallowed. He looked sick.

"What's the matter with you? Is it the poison?"

"I just realized you died on me twice." Raphael rolled to his feet and staggered off.

"Where are you going?"

"I need a minute."

He stumbled into the bushes and I heard him vomit.

A shadow came over me. Roman sat on a log next to me. He was carrying something long and wrapped in plastic.

"Nice guy," Roman said. "An asshole, but he loves you."

"I love him, too." I petted his hand. "Thank you for everything. I had fun."

"I had fun, too." He grinned. "Look what I got." He pulled the plastic back. The Bone Staff.

"You got it?"

He nodded. "Spent an hour digging through that clay. Worth every minute." He leaned over and kissed my cheek. "I'll see you around. You call if you need anything, yes?"

"Yes," I agreed. "You call me, too. I owe you some help. As long as I don't have to sacrifice any babies, I'll be there."

"I'll count on it."

He walked off and Raphael took his place, rinsing his mouth with water from a canteen. Around us, the shapeshifters were herding the snake people into a group. I was covered in mud, blood, and swampy muck. Raphael looked even worse, his hair smeared with gore. I really wanted to go back home, take a shower, and sleep for a year.

"Help me off the log?" I asked him.

"No. We're going to get you a nice stretcher and carry you down to the boats."

"I'm okay to walk. My chest hurts a little, but I can make it."

"You are certifiable," he told me. He reached into his pocket and pulled out a plastic bag.

"What's this?"

"I swore that if we made it through today, I would do this." Raphael pulled a small plastic box out of the bag and got down on his knees in the mud.

This was crazy.

He opened the box. A white engagement ring with a band shaped like a beast's paw lay on a small velvet pillow, with a beautiful sapphire clasped in its tiny white claws.

"I'm fucked up," he said. "I have many faults. But I promise if you marry me, I will love you and take care of you for the rest of our lives."

I stared at him.

"If you put up with me, I will put up with whatever you can throw my way," he said. "Bad days, good days, 'I'll cut you if you look at me the wrong way' days. I'll take them all."

I knew I had to say something.

"If you kill her with this after everything I've done," Doolittle said behind me. "You will never leave this swamp."

Raphael searched my face, anxious. "Andi?"

"Yes," I told him. "In sickness and in health, poor, rich, I don't care."

He was still looking at me, as if he hadn't heard.

"Yes, Raphael." I laughed or cried, I wasn't sure. "Yes."

"Put the ring on her, you fool," Doolittle said.

Raphael slipped the ring on my finger and I hugged him.

"I'd kiss you," Raphael said. "But I need to brush my teeth and I'm covered in blood."

"I don't care," I told him. "Kiss me anyway."

EPILOGUE

❋

My Pack admittance ceremony was held on Tuesday in the Pack's main gathering place, a large room deep below the Keep, where the terraced ground sloped in "steps" toward the stage with the metal fire pit. I'd heard Kate describe it before, but I had never seen it. I thought about dressing up, but it seemed kind of pointless. Whichever outfit I wore, I would still be me and that's what really counted.

A few minutes before ten p.m., Martina knocked on the door to the small room where I was asked to wait. "It's time."

I followed her down the stairs, lower and lower. I had no idea the Keep went that deep underground.

Finally she stopped before a solid door. "Nervous?"

"Not really." I had spent the morning sitting in a small room with Raphael and the families of the four murdered shapeshifters, telling them the whole long story. The Pack had rounded up the snake people. It didn't take long for the truth to come out: Raphael's crew was murdered by Saii, the priests. They were the only ones with poison glands. The rest of the snake people had fangs, but their bites were hardly fatal. All six of the Saii were dead. I took out Gloria, Roman and I had killed Sanchez on the bridge, and the four remaining perished before our battle with Apep. The Pack loaded the remaining cultists and what little baggage they had onto the boats and shipped them under armed escort out of the Pack's territory. They were forbidden to return. Derek oversaw the convoy and said that most of them seemed relieved. The Saii had worked them like slaves.

I got to hold Baby Rory again. We made a pact, he and I. He would grow up to be kind and strong, and I would make sure that his clansmen would never mistreat him or break his bones.

I was able to look Nick in the eye when I told him that the

people who had murdered his wife would never again hurt anyone else. He thanked me. This ceremony paled in comparison.

"Last chance to turn back," Martina said.

I knew what waited behind the door. Raphael and his mother. A few members of Clan Bouda. Kate and Curran. My friends, my alpha, my mate, and the new future. For once, I wouldn't have to hide who I was.

I opened the door.

The vast chamber stretched in front of me, dipping down to the stage, on which a metal fire pit stood. Flames danced inside it.

Behind the pit stood Aunt B. To the left, Curran and Kate sat, together with the other alphas and betas. Shapeshifters occupied the terraced steps surrounding them. Hundreds of shapeshifters. Suddenly I was nervous.

There was no turning back. I raised my head and marched down the stairs toward the fire, looking straight at Raphael for support. The stairs lasted for an eternity. Finally I stopped next to Aunt B.

"We gather here to invite Andrea Nash to the Pack," Aunt B said, her voice carrying through the room. "You know her. She has fought for us. She has given her blood and used her skills for the good of the Pack. Today we honor her sacrifice and accept her as one of our own. If any of you have a problem with that, rise and challenge me."

"No, thank you!" someone quipped from the right.

Light laughter ran through the room. I tried to keep still, but the giggles bubbled up out of me.

Aunt B grinned. "It's your turn, dear. Your moment."

I stepped to the fire and pulled my sleeve back. The flames crackled and burned in the fire pit. I thrust my forearm into the fire. The flames licked, searing my flesh. The smell of burned hair from my arm whiffed up. I held it for another second to prove that I was in control. No loup could touch the flames. It inspired strong instinctual terror in them.

I lowered my arm, trying not to wince at the pain, and said the first words of my oath. "I, Andrea Nash, a human and a shapeshifter, swear to abide by the laws of the Pack and my clan. I swear to obey my alphas and honor my clan's traditions. I swear to be loyal to my Pack brothers and sisters, to guard them from harm, and should the need arise, to fight to my death at their side . . ."

MAGIC
GIFTS

A Kate Daniels Novella

CHAPTER 1

❖

I was ten feet from the office door of Cutting Edge Investigations when I heard the phone ring inside. Unfortunately, the key to the office was in my sweatshirt pocket, which at the moment was also full of pale pink slime dripping from the tentacles resting on my shoulders. The tentacles weighed about seventy pounds and my shoulders really didn't like it.

Behind me, Andrea, my best friend and partner in crime solving, shifted the bulbous mass of flesh that was the rest of the creature, rearranging it. "Phone."

"I hear it." I dug in my pocket, all but glued shut by slime. Cold wetness slipped through my fingers. Ew.

"Kate, it could be a client."

"I'm trying to find the key."

Clients meant money, and money was in short supply. Cutting Edge had opened its doors three months ago, and while we were getting a trickle of paying jobs, most of them were lousy. Despite a good recommendation from the Red Guard, the premier bodyguard outfit in Atlanta, clients weren't knocking down our door to hire us.

Our world was beset by magic waves. They flooded us at random, smothering technology and leaving monsters in their wake. One moment you had rogue mages spitting fireballs and lightning, the next the magic would vanish, and the cops would gun down said mages with their now-operational firearms.

Sadly, the consequences of the magic waves didn't always vanish with them, and Atlanta by necessity had spawned many agencies to deal with magic hazmat. All of them had been in business a lot longer than us: the cops, the Mercenary Guild, a slew of private companies, and the big gorilla, the Order of Merciful Aid. The Order and its knights made it their mission to guard humanity against all threats and they did just that— but on their terms. Both Andrea and I had worked for the Order at some point and both of us had left under less than amicable circumstances.

Our reputations weren't stellar, so when we got a job, it was because everyone else in town had already shot it down. We were quickly turning into Atlanta's business of last resort. Still, every successful job was a check mark by our name.

The phone rang, insistent.

Our latest job had come courtesy of the Green Acres Home Owners Association, who had shown up at our door this morning claiming that a giant levitating jellyfish was roaming their suburb and could we please come and get it, because it was eating local cats. Apparently the translucent jellyfish was floating about with half-digested cat bodies inside it, and the neighborhood children were very upset. The cops told them that it wasn't a priority, since the jellyfish hadn't eaten any humans yet, and the Mercenary Guild wouldn't get rid of it for less than a grand. The HOA offered us $200. Nobody in their right mind would do the job for that price.

It took us all damned day. And now we had to properly dispose of the cursed thing, because dealing with the corpses of magical creatures was like playing Russian roulette. Sometimes nothing happened . . . and sometimes the corpse melted into a puddle of sentient carnivorous protoplasm. Or hatched foot-long blood-sucking leeches.

The weight of the jellyfish suddenly vanished from my shoulders. I rummaged in my pocket and my fingertips slid against the cold metal. I yanked the key out, slipped it into the lock, and swung the heavy reinforced door open. Aha! Victory.

I lunged through the door and made a break for the phone. I reached it a second too late and the answering machine came on. "Kate," Jim's voice said. "Pick up the phone."

I backed away from the phone like it was on fire. I knew exactly what this call was about and I didn't want any of it.

"Kate, I know you're there."

"No, I'm not," I said.

"You *will* have to deal with this, sooner or later."

I shook my head. "No, I won't."

"Call me." Jim hung up.

I turned to the door and watched Andrea walk through it. Behind her, the jellyfish squeezed through the doorway on its own. I blinked. The jellyfish kept coming. It cleared the door, turned, and I saw Curran carrying it in his hands, as if the three-hundred-pound mass of flesh was no heavier than a plate of pancakes. It's good to be the Beast Lord.

When had he arrived and what was he doing here, anyway?

"Where to?" he asked.

"Back room," Andrea said. "Here, I'll show you."

I followed them and watched Curran pack the jellyfish into the biohazard container. He slid the lid in place, locked the clamps, and closed the distance between us. I held my slimy arms out to keep him from getting covered in ooze, leaned forward, and kissed the Beast Lord. He tasted like toothpaste and Curran, and the feel of his lips on mine made me forget the lousy day, the bills, the clients, and the two gallons of slime drenching my clothes. The kiss lasted only a couple of seconds, but it might as well have been an hour, because when we broke apart, it felt like I had come home, leaving all my troubles far behind.

"Hey," he said, his gray eyes smiling at me.

"Hey."

Behind him, Andrea rolled her eyes.

"What's up?" I asked him.

Curran almost never came to visit my office, especially not in the evening. He hated Atlanta and its teeming masses with all the fire of a supernova. I didn't have anything against Atlanta in theory—sure, it was half-eroded by the magic waves and it caught on fire with alarming frequency—but I had a thing about crowds. When my workday was over, I didn't linger. I headed straight for the Keep, where the Atlanta shapeshifter Pack and His Furry Majesty resided.

"I thought we'd go to dinner," he said. "It's been a while since we've gone out."

Technically we had never gone out to dinner, just the two of us. Oh, we had eaten together in the city but usually it was accidental and most of those times had involved other people and frequently ended in a violent incident.

"What's the occasion?"

Curran's blond eyebrows came together. "Does there have to be a special occasion for me to take you out to dinner?"

Yes. "No."

He leaned in to me. "I missed you and I got tired of waiting for you to come home. Come grab a bite with me."

Grabbing a bite sounded heavenly, except Andrea would be stuck here by herself. "I have to wait for Biohazard to pick up the jellyfish."

"I've got it," Andrea offered. "Go, there's no reason for both of us to sit here. I have some stuff I need to take care of anyway."

I hesitated.

"I can sign forms just as well as you," Andrea informed me. "And my signature doesn't look like the scratches of a drunken chicken in the dirt."

"My signature is just fine, thank you very much."

"Yeah, yeah. Go have some fun."

"I need a shower," I told Curran. "I'll see you in ten minutes."

It was Friday, eight o'clock on a warm spring night, my hair was brushed, my clothes were clean and slime-free, and I was going out with the Beast Lord. Curran drove. He did it very carefully, concentrating on the road. I had a feeling he'd learned to drive as an adult. I drove carefully too, mostly because I expected the car to fail on me at any second.

I glanced at Curran in the driver's seat. Even at rest, like he was now, relaxed and driving, he emanated a kind of coiled power. He was built to kill, his body a blend of hard, powerful muscle and supple quickness, and something in the way he carried himself telegraphed a shocking potential for violence and a willingness to use it. He seemed to occupy a much larger space than his body actually did and he was impossible to ignore. The promise of violence he carried used to scare me, so I'd bait him until some of it came out, the same way people afraid of heights would rock climb to cure themselves. Now I just accepted him, the way he accepted my need to sleep with a sword under my bed.

Curran caught me looking. He flexed, letting the carved muscles bulge on his arms, and winked. "Hey, baby."

I cracked up. "So where are we going?"

"Arirang," Curran said. "It's a nice Korean place, Kate. They have charcoal grills at the tables. They bring you meat and you cook it any way you want."

It figured. Left to his own devices, Curran consumed only meat, punctuated with an occasional dessert. "That's nice for me, but what will your vegetarian Majesty eat?"

Curran gave me a flat look. "I can always drive to a burger joint instead."

"Oh, so you'd throw a burger down my throat and then expect making out in the backseat?"

He grinned. "We can do it in the front seat instead, if you prefer. Or on the hood of the car."

"I'm not doing it on the hood of the car."

"Is that a dare?"

Why me?

"Kate?"

"Keep your mind on the road, Your Furriness."

The city rolled by, twisted by magic, battered and bruised but still standing. The night swallowed the ruins, hiding the sad husks of once mighty, tall buildings. New houses flanked the street, constructed by hand with wood, stone, and brick to withstand magic's jaws.

I rolled down the window and let the night in. It floated into the car, bringing with it spring and a hint of wood smoke from a distant fire. Somewhere a lone dog barked out of boredom, each woof punctuated by a long pause, probably to see if the owners would let him in.

Ten minutes later we pulled into a long, empty parking lot, guarded by old office buildings that now housed Asian shops. A typical stone building with huge storefront windows sat at the very end, marked by a sign that read ARIRANG.

"This is the place?"

"Mhm," Curran said.

"I thought you said it was a Korean restaurant." For some reason I had expected a *hanok* house with a curved tiled roof and a wide front porch.

"It is."

"It looks like a Western Sizzlin." In fact, it probably used to be a Western Sizzlin.

"Will you just trust me? It's a nice place . . ." Curran braked, and the Pack Jeep screeched to a stop.

Two skeletally thin vampires sat at the front of the restaurant, tethered to the horse rail with chains looped over their heads. Pale, hairless, dried like leathery jerky, the undead stared at us with mad glowing eyes. Death had robbed them of their cognizance and will, leaving behind mindless shells driven only by bloodlust. On their own, the bloodsuckers would slaughter anything alive and keep killing until nothing breathing remained. But their empty minds made a perfect vehicle for necromancers, who telepathically navigated them like remote-controlled cars.

Curran glared at the undead through the windshield. Ninety percent of the vampires belonged to the People, a weird hybrid of a corporation and a research institute. We both despised the People and everything they stood for.

I couldn't resist. "I thought you said this was a nice place."

He leaned back, gripped the steering wheel, and let out a long growling, "Argh."

I chuckled.

"Who the hell stops at a restaurant in the middle of navigating undead?" Curran squeezed the wheel a little. It made a groaning noise.

I shrugged. "Maybe the navigators got hungry."

He gave me an odd look. "This far away from the Casino means they're out on patrol. What, did they suddenly get the munchies?"

"Curran, ignore the damn bloodsuckers. Let's go and have a date anyway."

He looked like he wanted to kill somebody.

The world blinked. Magic flooded us like an invisible tsunami. The neon sign above the restaurant winked out and a larger brilliant blue sign ignited above it, made from hand-blown glass and filled with charged air.

I reached over and squeezed Curran's hand. "Come on, you, me, a platter of barely seared meat . . . it'll be great. If we see the necromancers, we can make fun of the way they hold their forks."

We got out of the car and headed inside. The bloodsuckers glanced at us in unison, their eyes like two smoldering coals buried beneath the ash of a dying fire. I felt their minds, twin hot pinpoints of pain, restrained securely by the navigators' wills. One slipup and those coals would ignite into an all-consuming flame. Vampires never knew satiation. They never got full, they never stopped killing, and if let loose, they would drown the world in blood and die of starvation when there was nothing left to kill.

The chains wouldn't hold them—the links were an eighth of an inch thick at best, good for restraining a large dog. A vamp would snap it and not even notice, but the general public felt better if the bloodsuckers were chained, and so the navigators obliged.

We passed the vampires and entered the restaurant.

The inside of Arirang was dim. Feylanterns glowed with soft light on the walls, as the charged air inside their colored glass tubes reacted with magic. Each feylantern had been handblown into a beautiful shape: a bright blue dragon, an emerald tortoise, a purple fish, a turquoise stocky dog with a unicorn horn . . . Booths lined the walls, their tables plain rectangles of wood. In the center of the floor four larger round tables sported built-in charcoal grills under metal hoods.

The restaurant was about half full. The two booths to our right were occupied, the first by a young couple, a dark-haired man and a blond woman in their twenties, and the second by two middle-aged men. The younger couple chatted quietly. Good clothes, relaxed, casual, well groomed. Ten to one these were the navigators who had parked the bloodsuckers out front. The People's headquarters, known as the Casino, had seven Masters of the Dead and I knew them all by sight. I didn't recognize either the man or the woman. Either these two were visiting from out of town or they were upper-level journeymen.

Both of the older guys in the next booth were armed. The closer one carried a short sword, which he had put on the seat next to him. As his friend reached for the salt shaker, his sweatshirt hugged the gun in his side holster.

Past the men in the far right corner, four women in their thirties laughed too loud—probably tipsy. On the other side a family with two teenage daughters cooked their food on the grill. The older girl looked a bit like Julie, my ward. Two businesswomen, another family with a toddler, and an older couple rounded off the patrons. No threats.

The air swirled with the delicious aroma of meat cooked over an open fire, sautéed garlic, and sweet spices. My mouth watered. I hadn't eaten since grabbing some bread this morning from a street vendor. My stomach actually hurt.

A waiter in plain black pants and a black T-shirt led us to a table in the middle of the floor. Curran and I took chairs opposite one another, where I could see the back door and he had a nice view of the front entrance. We ordered hot tea. Thirty seconds later it arrived with a plate of pot stickers.

"Hungry?" Curran asked.

"Starving."

"Combination platter for four," Curran ordered.

His hungry and my hungry were two completely different things.

The waiter departed.

Curran smiled. It was a happy, genuine smile and it catapulted him from attractive into irresistible territory. He didn't smile very often in public. That intimate smile was usually reserved for private moments when we were alone.

I pulled the band off my still-damp braid and slid my fingers through it, unraveling the hair. Curran's gaze snagged on my hands. He focused on my fingers like a cat on a piece of foil pulled by a string. I shook my head and my hair fell over my shoulders in a long dark wave. There we go. Now we were both private in public.

Tiny gold sparks danced in Curran's gray irises. He was thinking dirty thoughts and the wicked edge in his smile made me want to slide over next to him and touch him.

We had to wait. I was pretty sure that having hot sex on the floor of Arirang would get us banned for life. Then again, it might be worth it.

I raised my tea in a salute. "To our date."

He raised his cup and we clinked them gently against each other.

"So how was your day?" he asked.

"First, I chased a giant jellyfish around through some suburbs. Then I argued with Biohazard about coming and picking it up, because they claimed it was a Fish and Game issue. Then I called Fish and Game and conferenced them in on the Biohazard call, and then I got to listen to the two of them argue and call each other names. They got really creative."

"Then Jim called," Curran said.

I grimaced. "Yes. That, too."

"Is there a particular reason you're avoiding our chief of security?" Curran asked.

"Do you remember how my aunt killed the head of the Mercenary Guild?"

"Not something one forgets," he said.

"The Guild is still squabbling over who should be in charge now."

Curran glanced at me. "That was what, five months ago?"

"My point exactly. On one side there are the older mercs, who have combat experience. The other side is the support staff. Both groups have roughly an equal share of the Guild as a result of Solomon's will and they hate each other. It's getting into death threat territory, so they're having some sort of final arbitration to decide who's in charge."

"Except they are deadlocked," Curran guessed.

"Yes, they are. Apparently Jim thinks I should break that tie."

The Guild's now-dead founder was a closet shapeshifter, and he had left twenty percent of the Guild to the Pack. So as long as the Mercenary Guild remained deadlocked, nobody was getting paid and the Pack alphas wanted that income stream to start flowing again. They put pressure on Jim, and Jim put pressure on me.

I had done enough years in the Guild to be viewed as a veteran. Jim had as well, but unlike me, he had the luxury of having kept his identity semi-private. Most mercs didn't know he was high up in the Pack.

I had no privacy. I was the Beast Lord's Consort. It was the price I paid for being with Curran, but I didn't have to like it.

His Majesty drank his tea. "Not looking forward to settling the dispute?"

"I'd rather eat dirt. It's between Mark, Solomon's longtime assistant, and the veterans led by the Four Horsemen, and they despise each other. They aren't interested in reaching a consensus. They just want to throw mud at each other over a conference table."

An evil light sparked in his eyes. "You could always go for Plan B."

"Pound everyone to a bloody pulp until they shut up and cooperate?"

"Exactly."

It would make me feel better. "I could always do it your way instead."

Curran raised his blond eyebrows.

"Roar until everyone pees themselves."

A shadow of self-satisfaction flickered on his face and vanished, replaced by innocence. "That's bullshit. I'm perfectly reasonable and I almost never roar. I don't even remember what it feels like to knock some heads together."

The Beast Lord of Atlanta, a gentle and enlightened monarch. "How progressive of you, Your Majesty."

He cracked another grin.

The male necromancer in the booth next to us reached under the table and produced a rectangular rosewood box. Ten to one, there was some sort of jewelry inside.

I nodded at Curran. "Your turn. How did your day go?"

"It was busy and full of stupid shit I didn't want to deal with."

The blond woman opened the box. Her eyes lit up.

"The rats are having some sort of internal dispute over some apartments they bought. Took all day to untangle it." Curran shrugged.

The woman plucked a golden necklace from the box. Shaped like an inch-and-a-half-wide segmented collar of pale gold, it gleamed in the feylantern light.

I poured us more tea. "But you prevailed."

"Of course." Curran drank from his cup. "You know, we could stay over in the city tonight."

"Why?"

"Because that way we wouldn't have to drive for an hour back to the Keep before we could fool around."

Heh.

A scream jerked me to my feet. In the booth, the blond

necromancer clawed at the necklace, gasping for breath. The man stared at her, his face a terrified mask. The woman raked her throat, gouging flesh. With a dried pop, her neck snapped, and she crashed to the floor. The man dived down, pulling at the necklace. "Amanda! Oh my God!"

Past him two pairs of red vampire eyes stared at us through the window.

Oh crap. I pulled Slayer from the sheath on my back. Sensing the undead, the pale blade of the enchanted saber glowed, sending wisps of white vapor into the air.

The dull carmine glow of vampire irises flared into vivid scarlet. Shit. The restaurant had just updated its menu with fresh human.

Flesh boiled on Curran's arms. Bone grew, muscle twisted like slick ropes, skin sheathed his new body and sprouted fur. Enormous claws slid from Curran's new fingers.

The vampires rose off their haunches.

Curran stood up next to me in his warrior form, nearly eight feet of steel-hard muscle.

I gripped Slayer's hilt, feeling the familiar comforting texture. Bloodsuckers reacted to sudden movement, bright lights, loud noises, anything that telegraphed prey. Whatever I did had to be fast and flashy. The blood alone wouldn't do it, not when every table was filled with raw meat.

The front window exploded in a cascade of gleaming shards, and the vampires sailed through, like they had wings. The left bloodsucker landed on the table, the remnant of the chain hanging from its neck. The right skidded on the slick parquet floor and bumped into another table, scattering the chairs.

I screamed and dashed to the left, pulling Slayer as I sprinted. Curran snarled and leaped, covering half the distance to the right bloodsucker in a single powerful jump.

My vamp glared at me. I looked into its eyes.

Hunger.

Like staring into an ancient abyss. Behind the eyes, its mind seethed, free of its master's control. I wanted to reach out and crush it, like a bug between my fingernails. But doing that would give me away. I might as well give the People a sample of my blood with a pretty bow on it.

"Here!" I flicked my wrist, making the reflection of fey-lanterns dance along Slayer's surface. Look. Shiny.

The bloodsucker's gaze locked on the blade. The vamp ducked down, like a dog before the strike, front limbs wide, yellow claws digging into the table. The wood groaned. The chain slipped along the table's edge, clinking.

No way to make a neck cut. The chain loop would block the blade.

A high-pitched female scream slashed my eardrums. The vamp hissed, jerking in the direction of the sound.

I jumped on the chair next to the table and thrust sideways and up. Slayer's blade slid between the vamp's ribs. The tip met a tight resistance and then sliced through it. Hit the heart. Banzai!

The bloodsucker screeched. I let go of the saber. The vamp reared, Slayer buried up to the hilt in its rib cage, staggered as if drunk, pitched over, and crashed to the floor, flopping like a fish on dry land.

To the left, Curran thrust his claws through the flesh under his vamp's chin. The bloody tips of the talons emerged from the back of the bloodsucker's neck. The vamp clawed at him. Curran thrust his monstrous hand deeper, gripped the vamp's neck and tore its head off the body.

Show-off.

He tossed the head aside and glanced at me, checking if I was okay. The whole thing had only taken about five seconds, but it felt like an eternity. We were both in one piece. I exhaled.

The restaurant fell silent, except for the male necromancer sobbing on the floor and the hoarse hissing coming from the vampire, convulsing as my saber liquefied its innards, absorbing the nutrients into the blade.

In the far corner a man swiped his toddler from the high chair, grabbed his wife's hand, and ran out. As one, the patrons jumped. Chairs fell, feet pounded, someone gasped. They rushed out of both doors. In a blink the place was empty.

I grasped Slayer and pulled. It slid from the body with ease. The edges of the wound sagged apart and dark brown blood spilled out from the cut. I swung and beheaded the vamp with a single sharp stroke. You should always finish what you started. I wiped Slayer off and put it back in its sheath.

Curran's arms shrank, streamlining, gray fur melting into his skin. A normal shapeshifter would've needed a nap after changing shape twice in such a short time, but Curran didn't exactly play by the regular shapeshifter rules. He walked over to the male necromancer, pulled him upright, and shook him once, an expression of deep contempt on his face. I could almost hear the guy's teeth rattle in his skull.

"Look at me. Focus."

The necromancer stared at him, shocked eyes wide, his mouth slack.

I knelt by the female navigator and touched her wrist, keeping away from her neck and the gold band on it. No pulse. The necklace clamped her throat like a golden noose, its color a dark vivid yellow, almost orange. The skin around it was bright red and quickly turning purple.

I picked up her purse, pulled out a wallet, and snapped it open. A People ID. Amanda Sunny, journeywoman, Second Tier. Twenty years old and now dead.

Curran peered into the journeyman's face. "What happened? What did you do?"

The man sucked in a deep breath and dissolved into tears.

Curran dropped him in disgust. His eyes were pure gold—he was pissed off.

I went to the hostess desk and found the phone. Please work, sometimes even when the magic was up phones would. Dial tone. Yes!

I called the Casino.

"Kate Daniels, for Ghastek. Urgent."

"Please wait," female voice said. The phone went silent. I hummed to myself and looked at the ID. I didn't know which of the Masters of the Dead Amanda answered to, but I knew Ghastek was the best of the seven currently in the city. He was also power hungry and he was making his bid for taking over the People's Atlanta office. He was very much in the limelight at the moment and I could count on a rapid response.

A moment passed. Another.

"What is it, Kate?" Ghastek's voice said into the phone. He must've been doing something, because he failed to keep exasperation from his voice. "Please make this quick, I'm in the middle of something."

"I have one dead journeywoman, one hysterical journeyman, two dead vampires, one pissed-off Beast Lord with
bloody hands, and a half a dozen terrified restaurant staff."
Quick enough for you?

Ghastek's voice snapped into a brisk tone. "Where are
you?"

"Arirang on Greenpine. Bring a decontamination unit and
body bags."

I hung up. Our waiter edged out of the doors and approached
our table, looking green. The rest of the staff was probably
huddled together in the back room, terrified, not knowing if
the danger had passed.

"Is it over?"

Curran turned to him. "Yes, it's over. The People are on
their way to clean up the mess. You can bring everyone out, if
it will make them feel better. We guarantee your safety."

The waiter took off. Someone shouted. A moment later the
front doors opened and people poured out: an older Korean
man, the older woman who had greeted us, a woman who
looked like she could be their daughter, and several men and
women in waiter and chef garb. The younger woman carried
a boy. He couldn't have been more than five.

The owners piled up into the booths around us. The boy
stared at the two vampires with dark eyes, big like two
cherries.

I sat into the chair next to Curran. He reached over and
pulled me close. "I'm sorry about dinner."

"That's okay." I stared at the dead woman. Twenty years
old. She'd barely had a chance to live. I'd seen a lot of death,
but for some reason the sight of Amanda lying there on the
floor, her boyfriend weeping uncontrollably by her body,
chilled me to the bone. I leaned against Curran, feeling the
heat of his body seep through my T-shirt. I was so cold and I
really needed his warmth.

CHAPTER 2

A caravan of black SUVs rolled into the parking lot, their enchanted water engines belching noise. Magic-powered cars didn't move very fast and sounded like a rock avalanche hitting a speeding train, but they were better than nothing.

We watched the SUVs through the broken window, as they parked at the far end, killed the noise, and vomited people, vampires, and body bags. Ghastek emerged from the lead vehicle, ridiculously out of place in a black turtleneck and tailored dark pants. He came through the door, surveyed the scene for a second, and headed to us.

Curran's eyes darkened. "I bet you a dollar he's running over to assure me that we're in no danger."

"That's a sucker's bet."

The Pack and the People existed in a very fragile state of peace. None of us wanted to do anything to jeopardize that.

The People were efficient, I gave them that. One crew went for the vampires, the other headed for the woman's body, the third for the despondent journeyman. Two women and a man in business suits made a beeline for the booth where the owners sat.

Ghastek came close enough to be heard. "I want it to be clear: this was not an attempt to kill either of you. The journeymen weren't supposed to be here and the guilty party will be harshly reprimanded."

Curran shrugged. "Don't worry, Ghastek. If this was an attempt, I know you'd bring more than two vampires."

"What happened?" Ghastek asked.

"They were having dinner," I told him. "They seemed happy together. The boy handed her a necklace and it choked her to death."

"Just so I understand, Lawrence himself wasn't personally injured?"

"No," Curran said. "He's in shock from watching his girlfriend die in front of him."

Ghastek looked over the scene again, looking like he wanted to be anywhere but here. "Once again, we're dreadfully sorry for the inconvenience."

"We'll live," Curran said.

One of the People stepped away from Amanda's body. "The necklace adhered to her skin. There doesn't appear to be any locking mechanism. It's a solid band of gold."

"Leave it," Ghastek said. "We'll remove it later."

If I were them, I'd cut it off during tech and stick it into a hazmat container.

A middle-aged man shouldered his way inside the restaurant, followed by a young woman and a boy who looked about seven. I glanced at the woman and had to click my mouth shut. She looked to be in her late teens, right on the cusp between a girl and a woman. Her body, full in the bust and hips, slimmed to a narrow waist. Her long slender legs carried her with a natural grace. Her hair streamed from her head in a shimmering cascade so precisely matching the color of gold, I would've sworn it was gold if I didn't know better. Her face, a pale oval, was angelic. She glanced at me in passing. Her irises were an intense deep blue and her eyes were decades older than her face.

She was beautiful.

She was also not human. Or she had bargained with something not human for that body.

Curran was watching her. His nostrils flared a little as he inhaled, sampling the scents and I felt a punch of jealousy right in the gut. Well, this was a new and unwelcome development.

Ghastek focused on the woman as well, with the kind of clinical interest usually afforded to an odd insect. "Here come the grieving parents. I've met them before."

"Is that her sister?" I asked.

"No, that's Mrs. Aurellia Sunny, her mother. The boy is Amanda's brother."

Not human.

The middle-aged man saw the female navigator, whose body the People had just loaded on the gurney. "Amanda! Jesus Christ, Amanda! Baby!"

"No!" Aurellia cried out.

He dashed to Amanda. "Oh God. Oh God."

His wife chased after him, the boy in tow. "Don't go near her!"

The man grasped Amanda's hand. The golden band of the necklace popped open. An eerie soft light ignited within the necklace, setting the gold aglow.

"Oh Go––" Amanda's father fell silent in the middle of the word, transfixed by the necklace.

His hand inched toward it.

"Stop!" Curran barked. The man froze, arrested by the unmistakable command in that voice.

I was already moving.

The golden-haired woman pushed past him, yanked the necklace from Amanda's neck, spun, and thrust it at the boy's throat. The gold band locked on the child's neck, adhering to his skin. I missed it by half a second.

The boy gasped but didn't die. His father shook his head, as if awakened from a dream.

Aurellia stared at me with her old eyes and smiled.

"Are you out of your mind?" I snarled. "That necklace just killed your daughter."

"This isn't your affair," she said.

"Take it off. Now." Before it kills again.

She sneered. "I can't."

She knew exactly what that necklace did. She had made a conscious choice between her husband and her son.

The boy dug his fingers into his neck, trying to pry the necklace loose. It remained stuck. The skin around the band of gold was turning pink. We had to get that thing off of him.

The man stared at her. "Aurellia? What's going on? What's the meaning of this?"

"Don't worry about it," the woman told him. "I'll explain it later."

"No, you'll explain it now." Curran moved next to me.

"I have to concur," Ghastek said.

The woman raised her chin. "You have no authority over me."

"Aurellia, what is going on?" her husband asked.

"On the contrary. We have all the authority we need." Ghastek snapped his fingers. A woman in a business suit and glasses popped up by his side as if by magic.

"The necklace caused the death of a journeywoman in our employ," the woman said. "We've expended a considerable amount of money in training her, not to mention the cost of the two vampires that were terminated as a result of her death. That necklace is evidence in our investigation of the incident. If you obstruct our investigation by withholding this evidence from us, we will obtain a court order requiring you to surrender the necklace to us. Should we choose to pursue this matter further, you will find yourself in a very actionable position."

Some people had attack dogs. Ghastek had attack lawyers. If he got his hands on the boy, he'd find a way to remove the necklace. Even if he had to behead the child to get it.

I couldn't let the People get the boy.

"That's nice," I said. "I have a simpler solution. Take the necklace off the child now and I won't kill you."

"Wait a God-damned minute." Amanda's father moved to stand between me and his wife. "Everyone calm down. Just calm down."

"Give me the boy and nobody gets hurt," I told them. "Nobody here will stop me."

"That child is wearing our evidence," Ghastek said.

Curran's eyes lit up with gold. He leveled his alpha stare on the woman. She flinched.

"Give me the child," Curran said, his voice a deep inhuman growl.

"Fine." Aurellia shoved the boy toward us. "Take him."

Curran swept the boy off the floor and picked him up. Ghastek's face fell. We'd won this round.

"Give me back my son!" the man demanded.

Curran just looked at him.

"It's in the boy's best interests that he stay in our custody," Ghastek said. "We have better facilities."

"It's not the quality of your facilities I doubt," Curran said. "It's your ethics and your intentions."

"What is that supposed to mean?" Ghastek narrowed his eyes.

"It means the necklace is more important to you than the boy," I said. "You'll slice the flesh off his neck to get it."

"That's a gross exaggeration." The Master of the Dead crossed his arms. "I've never murdered a child."

"Oh, it's never murder when you do it," I said. "It's a regrettable accidental casualty."

"You can't do this!" Amanda's father thrust himself before Curran. "You can't take my son."

"Yes, I can," Curran said. "We'll keep him safe. If your wife decides to explain what's going on, I'll consider returning him."

"Go fuck yourself," the golden-haired woman said. "Crawl back into whatever dark hole you came out of. I have no care for you or your kind." She turned and walked out of the restaurant.

Her husband froze, caught for a moment between his son and his wife. "This isn't over," he said finally and chased after Aurellia.

"Give us the boy," Ghastek said, his tone reasonable.

"I don't think so," Curran said. "If you want to examine him later, you're welcome to visit the Keep."

Around us the People tensed. In the corner two vampires leaned forward.

I unsheathed Slayer. I had a lot of practice and I did it fast. The lawyer woman jerked back. The opaque blade smoked, sensing the undead. *Come on, Ghastek. Make our night.*

Ghastek sighed. "Fine. I'll make the necessary arrangements later."

Curran headed out through the door. I waited a second and followed, walking backward for the first two steps to make sure that no undead would come leaping out of the darkness at Curran's back.

The door of the restaurant swung shut behind us. Ghastek's voice called out, "Alright, people, back to work. Let's process the scene *tonight*."

"What's your name?" Curran asked.

The boy swallowed. "Roderick."

"Don't be afraid," Curran told him, his voice still laced with snarls. "I'll keep you safe. If anything threatens you, I'll kill it."

The boy gulped.

A giant scary man with glowing eyes and an inhuman voice just took you from your parents, but don't be afraid, because he'll kill anything that moves. *Kick-ass calming strategy, Your Majesty.*

"He might be less scared if you stopped snarling and turned off the headlights," I murmured.

The fire in Curran's eyes died.

"It will be okay," I told Roderick. "We just want to take off that necklace, and then you can go back to your parents. It'll be alright, I promise."

If the necklace snapped his neck, there wasn't a damn thing I or Curran or anybody else could do about it. We had to get him to the Keep's infirmary right away. We drove there in silence.

CHAPTER 3

❖

Doolittle bent over the boy, studying the necklace with a magnifying glass. Dark-skinned, his hair salted with gray, the Pack medic looked to be in his early fifties. Doolittle was the best medmage I had ever met. He had brought me back from the edge of death so many times, we'd stopped joking about it.

There was something so soothing about Doolittle. Whether it was his manner, his kind eyes, or the soft Southern accent, tinted with notes of coastal Georgia, I didn't know. The moment he walked into the room, Roderick relaxed. In thirty seconds they had struck a bargain: if Roderick stayed on his best behavior, he would get ice cream.

Not that Roderick had to be bribed. It took us almost an hour to get to the Keep and the entire ride over, he did not say a single word. He didn't move, didn't fidget, or do any of the normal things a seven-year-old kid would do in the car. He just sat there, quiet, his brown eyes opened wide, like he was a baby owl.

Doolittle pressed his thumb and index finger just above the necklace, stretching the boy's skin. A vein stood out, burrowing from the gold band under his skin into the muscle of his neck like a thin root.

"Does it hurt when I press here?" he asked.

"No," Roderick said. His voice was barely above a whisper.

Doolittle probed a different spot. "And now?"

"No."

The medmage let go and patted Roderick's shoulder. "I do believe we're done for tonight."

"Ice cream now?" Roderick asked, his voice quiet.

"Ice cream now," Doolittle confirmed. "Lena!"

A female shapeshifter stuck her red head into the room.

"This young gentleman is in need of ice cream," Doolittle said. "He's earned it."

"Oh boy!" Lena made big eyes and held out her hand. "I better pay up, then. Come on."

Roderick hopped off the chair and took her hand very carefully.

"What kind of ice cream would you like?" Lena asked, leading him through the doorway.

"Chocolate," the boy said quietly, with a slight hesitation in his voice.

"I've got loads of chocolate . . ."

The door swung shut behind them.

Doolittle looked at the door and sighed. "The necklace is rooted in the sternomastoid. If I try to remove it surgically, he'll bleed out. You said his mother put this atrocity on him?"

"Yes," Curran said.

"The collar glowed when the husband came near," I said. "He was reaching out for it and she yanked it away from him and snapped it on the boy."

"So it was probably intended for her husband," Doolittle said.

"That, or it's an equal opportunity offender," I said. "Any neck will do and the boy was the closest."

"And it killed the girl instantly?" Doolittle asked.

"Pretty much," Curran said.

"Strange. It doesn't seem to be actively harming the boy at the moment beyond rooting in."

"Does it hurt him?" I asked.

"Doesn't appear so." Doolittle leaned against the chair. "I poked and prodded at it a bit. It seems that the 'roots' shift under pressure so any attempt to cut the necklace will likely cause it to contract and strangle him. I don't want to fool with it."

"The woman," Curran said, "she knew better than to touch it."

I thought out loud. "She was unaffected by the glow, so either she's immune or she knows how it works."

"The boy didn't cry when you took him from his mother?" Doolittle asked.

"No," I said.

The medmage glanced at the door again. "The child is very passive and compliant. He doesn't speak unless spoken to. He doesn't take initiative. This boy is doing his best to be invisible. Sometimes this is a sign of a shy nature. Sometimes it's a sign of emotional abuse or neglect." Doolittle crossed his arms. "Such an accusation can't be made lightly. This is just something to keep in mind in dealing with her. If she is emotionally distant, she may not have any attachment to him. Let me run some tests. The sooner we identify what the necklace is, the better."

We left the infirmary and walked down the long hallway, heading toward the stairway leading up to the top of the tower, to our rooms. The Keep's hours were skewed toward the night. For most people ten p.m. meant evening and probably bedtime—both electricity and the charged air that powered feylanterns were expensive and people tended to make the most of daylight. For shapeshifters ten p.m. was closer to four in the afternoon. The hallways were busy. Random shapeshifters ducked their heads as we passed them.

Something had occurred to me. "When the journeyman handed Amanda the necklace, did it seem paler to you?"

Curran frowned. "Yes. Almost white gold."

"And now it's almost orange."

"You think it feeds on the host?"

"It would make sense. Maybe it develops hunger. The girl died instantly, because the necklace was hungry. Now it's satiated, so it's biding its time."

"We'll need to talk to the journeyman," Curran said. "And the boy's mother."

"Yes, the woman. The supernaturally beautiful woman with long flowing hair . . . Can't forget her."

Curran turned his head to look at me.

"What?"

"That's what I'd like to know."

I shrugged. "I'll speak to the journeyman tomorrow."

"I'll come with you."

And why would he want to do that? I pictured trying to conduct an interview in the presence of the Beast Lord. The journeyman would take one look at him and run for the hills screaming.

"No."

"You always say that word," he said. "Is it supposed to mean something?"

"It means I don't want you to come with me. The moment you muscle your way into the room, he'll clam up out of sheer self-preservation. Let me handle this."

We started up the stairway. Our quarters were at the very top and I really could've used an elevator right about now.

Curran kept his voice even. "Somehow I have managed to deal with the People just fine for almost fifteen years without your help."

"As I recall, you almost had yourself a war. And I won't be dealing with the People. I'll be dealing with one specific journeyman, facing sanctions and scared out of his mind."

"If you think you'll be able to get anywhere near Ghastek without me, you're crazy," Curran said.

I stopped and looked at him. "I will take my boudas and personal guard, dress them in black, put them on horses, and ride up to the Casino. Then I will pick the scariest-looking shapeshifter in the bunch and send him in to announce that the Consort seeks an audience. Do you really think the People will keep me waiting for long?"

It's good that we didn't have any kindling or paper around or the sparks flying from our butting heads would set the Keep on fire. We were both tired and pissed off.

Above us Jim rounded the corner on the landing and came to a dead stop, obviously wondering if he could get away with turning on his foot and going back the way he'd come without our noticing. Curran turned to face him.

That's right, you're busted.

Jim sighed and headed toward us at a brisk pace.

Tall, his skin the color of rich coffee, and dressed all in black, Jim looked like he was carved from a block of solid muscle. Logic said that at some point he must've been a baby and then a child, but looking at him one was almost convinced that some deity had touched the ground with its scepter and proclaimed, "There shall be a badass," and Jim had sprung into existence, fully formed, complete with clothes, and ready for action. He was the alpha of Clan Cat, the Pack's chief of security, and Curran's best friend.

He braked near us.

"Have you vetted the Wolves of the Isle yet?" Curran asked.

"No."

"Who are the Wolves of the Isle?" I asked.

"It's a small pack from the Florida Keys," Curran said. "Eight people. They're petitioning to join us and for some odd reason our security chief is dragging his feet on the background checks."

Jim waved the stack of paper in his hand. "The security chief has two thefts, four murders, and an abandonment of post to deal with."

"Murders?" I asked.

Jim nodded.

"I gave my word to the wolves," Curran said.

"I'm not opposed to admitting them." Jim spread his arms. "All I'm saying is let me make sure the people we have are safe before we add any more to them. By the way, Kate, did you review the Guild documents I sent you?"

Deflecting attention, are we? I gave him my tough stare. It bounced off Jim like hail from the pavement. "Somewhat. I was busy."

"See?" Jim pointed to me. "Your mate is doing the same thing I'm doing. Prioritizing."

I would get him for this. Oh yes.

Curran looked at Jim. "Do you need my help with the background checks?"

A muscle in Jim's face jerked. "No, I've got it."

Ha! He didn't want Curran in his hair either. "Don't worry, he's coming with me to investigate things."

"In the city?" Jim asked.

"Yes."

"That's a great idea. You both should go. To the city."

Curran and I looked at each other.

"He's trying to get rid of us," I said.

"You think he's planning a coup?" Curran wondered.

"I hope so." I turned to Jim. "Is there any chance you'd overthrow the tyrannical Beast Lord and his psychotic Consort?"

"Yeah, I want a vacation," Curran said.

Jim leaned toward us and said in a lowered voice, "You couldn't pay me enough. This is your mess, you deal with it. I have enough on my plate."

He walked away.

"Too bad," Curran said.

"I don't know, I think we could convince him to seize the reins of power."

Curran shook his head. "Nah. He's too smart for that."

We finally made it up the stairs, through the long hallway, up the second flight, and into our quarters. I dropped my bag down, shrugged out of my sword and scabbard and took a deep breath. *Aahh, home.*

Generally, tackling someone from behind is very effective, because the person doesn't know you're coming. However, after being tackled a dozen times, the victim becomes accustomed to it. Which is why when Curran made a grab for me, I danced aside and tripped him. He grabbed my arm, then we did some rolling on the floor, and I ended up on top of him, our noses about an inch apart.

He grinned. "You're jealous."

I considered it. "No. But when you stared at that woman like she was made of diamonds, it didn't feel very good."

"I stared at her because she smelled strange."

"Strange how?"

"She smelled like rock dust. Very strong dry smell." Curran put his arms around me. "I love it when you get all fussy and possessive."

"I never get fussy and possessive."

He grinned, showing his teeth. His face was practically glowing. "So you're cool if I go over and chat her up?"

"Sure. Are you cool if I go and chat up that sexy werewolf on the third floor?"

He went from casual and funny to deadly serious in half a blink. "What sexy werewolf?"

I laughed.

Curran's eyes focused. He was concentrating on something.

"You're taking a mental inventory of all the people working on the third floor, aren't you?"

His expression went blank. I'd hit the nail on the head.

I slid off him and put my head on his biceps. The shaggy carpet was nice and comfortable under my back.

"Is it Jordan?"

"I just picked a random floor," I told him. "You're nuts, you know that?"

He put his arm around me. "Look who's talking."

We lay together on the carpet.

"We can't let the necklace kill that boy," I said.

"We'll do everything we can." He sighed. "I'm sorry about dinner."

"Best date ever. Well, until people died and vampires showed up. But before that it was awesome."

We lay there some more.

"We should go to bed." Curran stretched next to me. "Except the carpet is nice and soft and I'm tired."

"You want me to carry you?"

He laughed. "Think you can?"

"I don't know. Do you want to find out?"

It turned out that carrying him to our bed wasn't necessary. He got there on his own power and he wasn't nearly as tired as he'd claimed to be.

Morning brought a call from Doolittle. When we arrived at the medward, Roderick was sitting on the cot, the same owlish expression on his face. The necklace had lost some of its yellow tint during the night. Now it looked slightly darker than orange rind.

I crouched by the boy. "Hi."

Roderick looked at me with his big eyes. "Good morning."

His voice was weak. In my mind the necklace constricted around his fragile neck. The bone crunched . . .

We had to get a move on. We had to get it off him.

Doolittle led us toward the door and spoke quietly. "There is a definite change in the color of the metal. He's beginning to experience discomfort."

"So that thing is getting hungry," Curran said.

"Probably." Doolittle held up a small printout. A pale blue stripe cut across the paper. The m-scan. The m-scanner recorded specific types of magic as different colors: purple for the undead, green for shapeshifter, and so on. Blue stood for plain human magic—mages, telepaths, and telekinetics all registered blue. It was the basic human default.

"Is that the necklace or Roderick?" Curran asked.

"It's the boy. He has power and it's obscuring whatever magic signature the necklace is giving out." Doolittle pointed to a point on the graph. I squinted. A series of paler sparks punctured the blue.

"This is probably the necklace," Doolittle said. "It's not enough to go on. We need a more precise measurement."

We needed Julie. She was a sensate—she saw the colors of magic with more precision than any m-scanner. I stuck my head out into the hallway and called, "Could someone find my kid, please, and ask her to come down here?"

Five minutes later, Julie entered the medward. When I'd first found her, she'd been half-starved, skinny, and had had anxiety attacks if the protective layer of grime was removed from her skin. Now at fourteen, she had progressed from skinny to lean. Her legs and arms showed definition if she flexed. She was meticulously clean, but recently had decided that the invention of brushes was unnecessary and a waste of time, so her blond hair looked like a cross between a rough haystack and a bird's nest.

I explained about the necklace. Julie approached the boy. "Hey. I'm going to look at the thing on your neck, okay?"

Roderick said nothing.

Julie peered at the metal. "Odd. It's pale."

"Pale yellow? Pale green?" Any tint was good.

"No. It looks colorless, like hot air rising from the pavement."

Transparent magic. Now I had seen everything.

"There are very faint runes on it," Julie said, "hard to make out. I'm not surprised you missed them," she added.

"Can you read them?" Curran asked.

She shook her head. "It's not any runic alphabet I was taught."

Doolittle handed her a piece of paper and a pencil and she wrote five symbols on it. Runes, the ancient letters of Old Norse and Germanic alphabets, had undergone several changes over the years, but the oldest runes owed their straight up-and-down appearance to the fact that historically they had to be carved on a hard surface: all straight lines, no curves, no tiny strokes. These symbols definitely fit that pattern, but they didn't look like any runes I'd seen. I could spend a day or two digging through books, but Roderick didn't have that long. We needed information fast.

Curran must've come to the same conclusion. "Do we know any rune experts?"

I tapped the paper. "I can make some calls. There is a guy—Dagfinn Heyerdahl. He used to be with the Norse Heritage Foundation."

The Norse Heritage Foundation wasn't so much about heritage as it was about Viking, in the most cliché sense of the word. They drank huge quantities of beer, they brawled, and they wore horned helmets despite all historical evidence to the contrary.

"Used to be?" Curran asked.

"They kicked him out for being drunk and violent."

Curran blinked. "The Norse Heritage?"

"Mhm."

"Don't you have to be drunk and violent just to get in?" he asked. "Just how disorderly did he get?"

"Dagfinn is a creative soul," I said. "His real name is Don Williams. He packs a lot of magic and if he could have gotten out of his own way, he would be running the Norse Heritage by now. He's got a rap sheet as long as the Bible, all of it petty stupid stuff, and he's the only merc I know who actually works for free, because he's been fined so many times, it will take him years to get out of the Guild's debt. About two years ago, he got piss-drunk, took off all of his clothes, and broke through the gates of a Buddhist meditation center on the South Side. A group of bhikkhunis, female monks, was deep in meditation on the grounds. He chased them around, roaring something about them hiding hot Asian ladies. I guess he mistook them for men, because of the robes and shaved heads."

"And why didn't anybody point out the error of his ways to this fool?" Doolittle asked.

"Perhaps because they are Buddhists," Curran said. "Violence is generally frowned upon in their community. How did it end?"

"Dagfinn pulled a robe off one of the nuns and an elderly monk came up to him and hit him in the chest with the heel of his hand. Dagfinn did some flying and went through the monastery wall. Bricks fell on his face and gave him a quickie plastic surgery. Since the old monk had raised his hand in anger, he went into a self-imposed seclusion. He still lives near Stone Mountain in the woods. He was greatly revered and the monks got pissed off and went to see the Norse Heritage Foundation. Words were exchanged and the next morning the Foundation gave Dagfinn the boot. The neo-Vikings will know where he is. They kicked him out, but he's still their boy."

Curran nodded. "Okay, we'll take the Jeep."

"They don't permit any technology past the fourteenth century AD in their territory. You'll have to ride a horse."

Curran's face snapped into a flat Beast Lord expression. "I don't think so."

"You can jog if you want, but I'm getting a horse."

A low rumble began in Curran's throat. "I said we'll take the Jeep."

"And I said they will put an axe into your carburetor."

"Do you even know what a carburetor is?" Curran asked.

I knew it was a car part. "That's irrelevant."

Doolittle cleared his throat. "My lord, my lady."

We looked at him.

"Take it outside my hospital before you break anything." It didn't sound like a request.

A careful knock echoed through the door. A young woman stuck her head in. "Consort?"

What now? "Yes?"

"There is a vampire downstairs waiting to see you."

CHAPTER 4

The vampire sat on his haunches in the waiting room, an emaciated monstrosity. Vampires were nocturnal predators. Daylight burned their skin like fire, but the People had recently gotten around this restriction by applying their own patented brand of sunblock to their undead. It dried thick and came in assorted colors. This particular vampire sported a coat of bright lime-green. The sunblock covered the undead completely, every wrinkle, every crevice, every inch. The effect was vomit-inducing.

The vampire turned its head as I walked in, its eyes focusing on me with the intelligence of its navigator, sitting in an armored room miles away. The nightmarish jaws opened.

"Kate," Ghastek's dry voice said. "Curran. Good morning."

"What are you doing here?" Curran asked.

The vampire folded itself, perching in the chair like some mummified cat. "I have a direct interest in determining the nature of that necklace. We have suffered great losses, we must account for them. Have you found a way to remove it?"

"No," I said.

"So the boy's life is still in jeopardy," Ghastek said.

Thank you, Captain Obvious.

"It's being handled," Curran said.

"I would like to be involved in that handling."

"I'm sure you would," Curran said. "It's hard to believe, but I go whole days without worrying about your likes and dislikes."

The vampire opened its mouth, imitating a sigh. It was an eerie sight: his jaws unhinged, his chest moved up and down, but no air came out.

"I believe in civil discourse, so please forgive me if I sound blunt: you took a child away from his parents against their will. In other words, you abducted him by force. Last time I checked, that constitutes kidnapping. I have a very capable staff, which, should I give the word, would present a very compelling case to the Paranormal Activity Division."

"The PAD can bite me," Curran said. "I also have a very capable staff. I'll drown you in paper. How would you like to be sued?"

"On what grounds?" The vamp looked outraged.

"Reckless endangerment." Curran leaned forward. "Your journeymen dropped two vampires in the middle of a crowded restaurant."

"There were extenuating circumstances and you were unharmed."

Curran's eyes acquired a dangerous glint. "I'm sure the public will take that into account, especially after my people plaster the sordid horror story of the Arirang Massacre over every newspaper they can find."

The vamp bared its fangs.

Curran's upper lip trembled in the beginning of a snarl.

I stabbed a throwing knife into the table between them.

The man and the monster fell silent.

"There is a child being slowly choked to death upstairs," I said. "If the two of you could stop baring your teeth for a second, you might even remember that."

Silence stretched out between us.

"I simply wish to help," Ghastek said.

Yeah, right.

Curran's face looked set in stone. "We don't need you."

"Yes, you do," Ghastek said. "You have the necklace, but I have Lawrence. He dated Amanda for over a year. I think you will be interested to know that Colin Sunny, Amanda's father, has a sister. She is married to Orencio Forney."

"Orencio Forney, the DA?"

"Precisely," Ghastek said. "After yesterday's affair, the Sunnys are staying in Forney's house. I trust you understand the implications."

I understood them, alright. The Sunnys had just become untouchable. If the Pack attempted to pick a fight with the DA, the tide of negative publicity would drown us, not to mention that every cop in the city would make it his personal mission to complicate shapeshifters' lives whenever possible.

Curran's face hardened into that blank, unreadable expression. He saw the writing on the wall as well, and he didn't like it. "Have you asked for an interview?"

"In the politest terms possible. We were extremely persuasive, but they are unavailable for comment."

"They aren't asking for Roderick?" What the hell?

"No, they are not," Ghastek said. "I found it extremely odd as well. The DA has circled the wagons. If you want any background on the boy and his mother, our Lawrence is your best bet. Give me access and I will share."

I looked at Curran. We needed that background.

His face was unreadable.

Come on, baby.

"Fine," he said.

A wise man once told me that a man's house said a lot about his soul. Over the years I had come to the conclusion that was complete bullshit. The Keep, with its foreboding, grim towers and massive fortifications, might have indicated something about Curran's need to protect his people, but it said nothing about how much responsibility he dragged around. It said nothing about the fact that he was fair and generous. And it sure as hell gave no hint that underneath all that Beast Lord's roaring, he was hilarious.

The Casino, on the other hand, looked like a beautiful mirage born of desert heat, sand, and magic. White and elegant, it nearly floated above the ground of the large lot decorated with fountains, statues, and colored lamps. All that beauty hid a stable of vampires. Undead, forever hungry, and gripped in the steel vise of navigators' minds, haunted its slim minarets. A casino milking money from human greed occupied its main floor, and deep inside it, the People brewed their schemes and machinations with the ruthless precision of a high-tech corporation, interested only in results and profits.

I parked the Jeep and peered at the Casino through the windshield. I didn't want to go in. Judging by the surly look on his face, Curran didn't want to go in either.

We opened our doors at the same time and headed toward the Casino.

"We're doing this for the child," Curran said.

"Yes." It was good to remember that. "We're just going to go in and talk to them."

"And not kill anybody," Curran added.

"Or anything."

"And not break things."

"Because we don't want a giant bill from the People."

"Yes." Curran's face was grim. "I'm not giving them any of the Pack's money."

I nodded. "We'll be good, we won't have to pay any damages, and then we'll come out and take a nice shower."

"Wash the stench off. I can smell the bloodsuckers from here."

"I can *feel* them from here."

I could—the sparks of vampiric magic tugged on me from the white parapets.

"Thanks for doing this," Curran said.

"Thank you for coming with me."

Get in, get out, don't cause a giant war between the Pack and the People. Piece of cake.

We passed through the tall arched entrance guarded by two men with curved yataghan swords. The guards wore black and looked suitably menacing. They very carefully didn't look at us.

Inside, a deluge of sound assaulted us: the noises of slot machines, refitted to work during magic, metal ringing, music, beeping, mixing with shouts from the crowd surrendering their hard-earned money for the promise of easy cash. Lemon-scented perfume drifted through the cold air—the People were keeping their customers awake, because the sleeping couldn't gamble.

Curran wrinkled his nose.

"Almost there, baby," I told him, zeroing in on the service entrance door at the far end of the vast room.

A large overweight man spun away from the machines and ran into Curran. "Hey! Watch it!"

Curran sidestepped him and we kept walking.

"Asshole!" the man barked at our backs.

"I love this place," Curran said.

"It's so serene and peaceful, and filled with considerate people. I thought you'd enjoy the ambiance."

"I adore it."

We passed through the service entrance. One of the journeymen, a man in black trousers, a black shirt, and a dark purple vest rose from behind the desk.

"How can I help you?"

"It's alright, Stuart." A woman descended the stairway on the side, walking into the room. She was five two and looked like an anatomical impossibility created from adolescent boys' dreams. Tiny waist, generous hips, and an award-winning chest, wrapped in dusky silk. Her hair fell down past her butt in red wavy locks, and when she smiled at you, you had a strong urge to do whatever she asked. Her name was Rowena and she ran the People's PR department and piloted the undead for a living.

She was also in debt to the witches, which in a roundabout way caused her to be in debt to me. If I asked a favor, she had to grant it, a fact we both carefully hid from everyone.

"Mr. Lennart. Ms. Daniels." Rowena fired off a beautiful smile. "Lawrence is waiting for you upstairs. Follow me, please."

We followed, Rowena's shiny perfect butt shifting as she walked up the stairs two feet in front of us. Curran heroically didn't look at it.

She led us to a small room with a two-way mirror. One would've expected a table, severe gray walls, and chairs bolted to the floor in an interrogation room, but no, the walls were cream with a delicate pale lattice carved at the top and the furniture consisted of a modern sofa and two soft chairs companionably arranged around a coffee table. Lawrence sat on the edge of the sofa. He looked pale and his eyes were bloodshot.

We sat in the chairs across from him.

"Do you know who we are?" Curran said quietly.

Lawrence nodded. "I've been briefed. I'm supposed to cooperate."

I pulled out a notepad from my pocket. "How long did you know Amanda?"

Lawrence swallowed. "Three years. She was admitted as an apprentice right after her high school graduation."

"How long had you dated?" I asked.

"Thirteen months next week," he said. His voice was hoarse. He cleared his throat.

"Tell us about her family," Curran said.

Lawrence sighed. "She didn't like them."

"Why not?" I prompted.

"She said her mother was very cold. Aurellia would go through the motions, make sure that Amanda and her brother were fed and appropriately dressed. She was very specific about their schedule. The Steel Calendar, Amanda called it. If they had a doctor's appointment or a school trip, it was put on the calendar and there was no deviation allowed from it. Amanda had perfect attendance her entire four years in high school. No matter how sick she was, her mother would send her to school. Never late. But there was no love or real warmth there."

"And her father?" Curran asked.

"Colin worships the ground Aurellia walks on." Lawrence gave a bitter laugh. "It's like he is blind when she's in the room. The only time Amanda could talk to him was when her mother was otherwise occupied. She couldn't wait to get out of that house. She told me that's why she enlisted with the People. The apprentices qualify for room and board in the Casino."

"Was her mother upset because Amanda did this?" I asked.

"Aurellia doesn't get upset. She's like a pretty robot," Lawrence said. "Never screams. Never loses her temper. I don't think she cared one way or another."

"Have you ever interacted with the parents personally?" Curran asked.

"Yes. We went to a dinner once. Colin seemed normal. Aurellia didn't speak, except when she ordered her food. I got a feeling she does only what is required of her, and talking to me or Amanda wasn't required."

"What about the necklace?" I asked.

Lawrence took several shallow rapid breaths.

We waited.

"It was a gift," he finally said. "It arrived at the house one Christmas, addressed to Colin. He took it out of the box—it was in a glass case—and tried to open it, and then Aurellia took it out of his hands. They put the necklace, still in its glass box, and displayed it on the wall in their foyer really high up. Amanda was about fifteen at the time. She loved it. She said she used to stand there and look at it all the time, because it was so beautiful. She was never allowed to touch it. They had a break-in six months ago. The burglars took some jewelry, money, and somehow got the necklace down and made off with it. She was really upset about it."

Lawrence looked at his hands. "I saw it at a pawnshop a week ago. I bought it for her. I . . . I killed her. She was so nice, so beautiful. She would sing little songs sometimes to herself when she was thinking about something or when she made coffee. And I killed her. She put it on and she just . . . she just died. I was right there and I couldn't do anything . . ."

We stayed with him for another ten minutes, but Lawrence was done.

Ghastek waited for us in the hallway.

"Please tell me he's on suicide watch," Curran said.

"Of course," the Master of the Dead said. "He is under the care of a therapist, he's given access to the priest, and he is watched even when he sleeps. However, if he truly wants to kill himself, there is nothing any of us can do. It is unfortunate. He is nearing the end of his five-year journeymanship. We've invested a lot of money and time into his education."

Of course. How silly of me to forget: the People didn't have employees, they had human assets, each of which came with a price tag attached.

"I've examined your drawing of the writing on the necklace," Ghastek said. "You said it appears to be a runic script of some sort but the characters are unfamiliar to me. How accurate is this drawing?"

"As accurate as humanly possible," I told him.

He raised his eyebrows. "Are you familiar with the term 'human error'?"

Are you familiar with the term "knuckle sandwich"? "The person who copied the runes from the necklace is an expert at what she does. Just because you don't recognize the script doesn't mean it's not runic in origin. The Elder Futhark alphabet has undergone many modifications over the years."

Ghastek took out the copy of Julie's drawing. "I've studied this subject extensively and I've never seen a rune like this." Ghastek pointed to a symbol that looked like an X with a double left diagonal arm.

Well, of course. He didn't know it, therefore it couldn't possibly be a rune. "Both Fehu and Ansuz runes have double arms. Why couldn't this rune have one? If you tossed it into a collection of runes and told a layman to pick out one that doesn't belong, he wouldn't grab that one."

Ghastek gave me a condescending look. "The term 'layman' refers to a nonexpert by definition. Of course a nonexpert wouldn't be able to single out this rune, Kate. We could throw stars and spirals into the mix and he would be unlikely to pick those out either."

You conceited ass.

Curran cleared his throat.

I realized I had taken a step toward Ghastek. No killing, no punching, no destruction of property. Right.

"We're taking this matter to an expert," Curran said.

"I think it's prudent, considering the circumstances."

Oh, well, so good of him to give us his permission.

"Where is this expert?" Ghastek asked.

"At the Norse Heritage Foundation," I told him.

Ghastek wrinkled his face into a semblance of a disgusted sneer, as if he'd just stuck his head into a bag of rotten potatoes.

"You're going to see the neo-Vikings?"

"Yes."

"They're ignorant, loud buffoons. All they do is sit in their mead hall, get drunk, and punch each other when their masculinity is threatened."

"You don't have to come," I told him.

Ghastek let out a long-suffering sigh. "Very well. I'll get my vampire."

CHAPTER 5

I was riding a horse called The Dude. The Dude, who also answered to Fred if he was feeling charitable, was what the Pack stables had called a "Tennessee Walker Blue Roan." The blue roan part was somewhat true—the horse under me was dark gray, with the colors nearing black toward the head and the ankles. The Tennessee Walker part . . . Well, some Tennessee Walker was probably in there, but most of it was definitely a coldblood horse. A massive coldblood horse, close to twenty-five hundred pounds. I was betting on a Percheron. Sitting atop The Dude was like riding a small elephant.

The presence of a vampire presented Curran with a dilemma. He refused to ride a horse, but he refused to let me travel in the company of an undead without backup either, so a compromise had to be reached. We stopped by the Cutting Edge office to get Andrea. Unfortunately, she was out. Apparently some shape-shifters had been murdered and Jim had pulled her in to head that investigation, a fact that he, of course, had neglected to mention. We kidnapped Derek and Ascanio instead.

Derek was our third employee. Once my sidekick, then Jim's spy, then a chief of Curran's personal guard, he was now working for Cutting Edge to acquire experience and figure out what it was he wanted to do. When I'd first met him, he'd been barely eighteen and pretty. Now he was close to twenty. Some bastards had poured molten silver on his face. The bastards were now dead, but he'd never healed quite right.

Ascanio was our intern. He was fifteen, as beautiful as an angel, and a bouda or werehyena. Bouda children rarely survived adolescence, as many of them lost the fight for their sanity and went loup—so Ascanio was treasured, babied, and spoiled beyond all reason. Unfortunately, he'd gotten in trouble one too many times and was turned over to me to train, because it was decided I was least likely to kill him.

Derek and Ascanio rode their horses behind me, bickering quietly about something. Ahead of me, the lime-green nightmare that was Ghastek's vampire trotted along the road in a jerky, looping gait. Most vampires eventually lost their ability to run upright, reverting to quadruped locomotion as the Immortuus pathogen reshaped its victim's body into a new nightmare predator. I had come across very old vamps before. They didn't even resemble their former human shapes. But the vamp Ghastek piloted was only a few months old. It loped forward, switching between scuttling along the ground one moment, and shambling two-thirds upright the next like some grotesque puppet on the strings of a drunken puppeteer.

Next to the vampire cantered a freakishly large black poodle. His name was Grendel, he was my dog, and while he wasn't the sharpest tool in the shed, he loved me and he was handy in a fight.

A few dozen yards behind us, an enormous lion trotted. When shapeshifters transformed, their animal forms were always larger than their natural counterparts, and Curran the Lion wasn't just large. He looked prehistoric. Colossal, gray, with faint darker stripes staining his fur like whip marks, he moved along the road at an easy pace, seemingly tireless. Which was why I'd ended up with The Dude. I had walked into the stables and told them I'd be traveling between a vampire and a lion the size of a rhino and I needed a horse that wouldn't freak out. True to the stable master's recommendation, The Dude seemed unflappable. Occasionally, when Curran flanked us, he would flare his nostrils a bit while the other two horses shied and made panicked noises, but mostly The Dude just pounded his way forward in a straight line, convinced that the lion was a figment of his imagination and that the vampire ahead of him was just Grendel's deformed mutant brother.

We were our own three-ring circus. Sadly, we had no audience: to the left of us the forest rose in a jagged line, and to the right a low hill climbed up, rocks and grass, before running into another line of trees at the apex.

"I've never met the neo-Vikings," Ascanio said.

"A good portion of them are mercs," I said over my shoulder. "They're a rowdy lot and not really what you would call true to tradition. Some are, but most are there because they saw a movie or two in childhood and think 'Viking' is a noun."

"It's not?" Derek asked.

"No. Originally it was a verb as in 'to go viking.' The Norse Heritage guys wear horned helmets, drink beer out of a giant vat, and start fights. As neo-Viking communities go, they are better off financially than most, so they can afford to have some fun."

"Where do they get their money?" Derek asked.

I nodded at the curving road. "Around that bend."

A couple of minutes later we cleared the curve. A vast lake spread on our left. Blue-green water stretched into the distance, tinted with bluish haze. Here and there green islands ringed with sand thrust through the water. To the right, an enormous mead hall built with huge timbers rose from the crest of a low hill like the armored back of some sea serpent. As we stood there, two *karves*, the longboats, slid from behind the nearest island, their carved dragon heads rising high above the lake's surface.

Ascanio raised his hand to shield his eyes.

"Lake Lanier," I told him. "The Norse Heritage Foundation built a river fleet of Dragon Ships here. They're not the only neo-Vikings in the region. There are several Norse groups along the Eastern seaboard and quite a few of them want to cruise up and down the coast in a proper boat. The Norse Heritage sells them boats and trains these wannabe raiders for shallow water sailing. They also give vacationers a ride for the right price. They're kind of touchy about it, so I wouldn't ask if they do children's parties."

Ascanio cracked a smile. "Or what, they'll try to drown us in their beer vat? 'Try' being the operative word."

We started toward the mead hall. Midway up the hill, the vampire paused when a man walked out in the middle of the road from behind a birch. Six and a half feet tall, he stood wrapped in chain mail. A cape of black fur billowed from his shoulders. His war helm, a near perfect replication of the Gjermundbu helmet, shielded the top of his head and half his face. The stainless steel had been polished until the sun's rays slid off of it, as if he wore a mirror on his head. The man carried an enormous single axe on a long wooden handle. I'd tried to pick up the axe once and it weighed ten pounds at least. He was slower than molasses in January with it, but it looked impressive.

Derek focused on the big man. "Who is that?"

"That's Gunnar. He's the Norse Heritage's idea of a security detail."

"What, all by himself?"

I nodded. "He's sufficient."

Ghastek's vampire stared at the giant Viking, motionless like a statue, while the Master of the Dead mulled the situation over. The bloodsucker turned, scuttled toward us, and fell back in line behind my horse. Apparently, Ghastek had decided that his vamp was too precious to risk.

We drew closer.

Gunnar took a deep breath and roared, *"Vestu heill!"*

Ow. My ears. "Hello, Gunnar."

He squinted at me through his face mask and dropped his voice down. "Hey, Kate." He sounded slightly out of breath.

"Good to see you."

He leaned on his axe, pulled the helmet off, and wiped sweat from his forehead, revealing reddish hair braided on his temples. "You heading up to see Ragnvald?"

"Yep."

"All of you?"

"Yep."

"Even the lion?"

The lion opened his mouth, showing his big teeth. *Yes, yes, you're bad. We know, Your Majesty.*

"Even the lion."

"What about?" Gunnar asked.

"Dagfinn. You've seen him around?"

Gunnar took a moment to spit into the dirt, making a big show of it. "Nope. And all the better for it."

Bullshit. "Too bad."

"Yeah." Gunnar waved me on with the helmet. "You're good to go."

"Thanks."

We rode on.

"He lied," Ascanio said.

"Yep." Gunnar knew exactly where Dagfinn was. He took his cues from Ragnvald, and since he wasn't talking, the jarl probably wouldn't be talking either. This would not go well.

We rode up through the wooden gates to the mead hall.

The rest of the settlement sat lower down the hill, past the mead hall: solid wooden houses scattered here and there. People walked to and fro, men in woolen tunics and cloaks, women in ankle-length gowns and *hangerocks*—woolen apron-dresses. They were an assorted crew: some were white, some were black, some were Hispanic. A couple to our right looked Chinese. Norse Heritage took everyone in. Viking wasn't a nationality—it was a way of life. As long as you thought you were a Viking, you had a place at their table.

People gaped at Curran as we passed. The vampire and the rest of us got significantly less attention.

As we dismounted before the hitching rail, I saw a familiar black Shire stallion in the pasture, segregated by himself. The huge horse stood almost eighteen and a half hands tall, the white feathers at his huge feet shaking every time he moved. A pale scar snaked its way up the horse's left shoulder. *Hello, Magnus. Where is your master?*

The stallion stared in my direction and bared his teeth. *Now horses were giving me crap.*

"Mind your manners," I murmured.

"Best behavior," Ascanio assured me.

Mentioning that I was talking to a horse who couldn't hear me would've totally cramped my boss style, so I nodded and walked up to the mead hall.

A large, rawboned woman barred my path. A large gun hung on her right hip and a small axe hung on her left.

"Hrefna," I acknowledged her. We had run into each other in the Guild before. She was good with both knife and sword and rarely lost her temper.

"Kate." Her voice was quiet. "The lion has to stay outside."

"He won't like it."

The lion shook his mane.

"I can't let him inside," Hrefna said. "You bring him in, someone's going to make trouble just to see if they can put his head on their wall. I've got to do my job. It's your call."

I looked at Curran. The lion melted. Skin stretched, bones twisted, and human Curran straightened. He was completely nude. Gloriously nude.

Hrefna raised her eyebrows.

Curran pulled jeans and a shirt from my saddlebag.

"Well," Hrefna said. "I always wondered why you went all shapeshifter. Explains things."

The vampire next to me rolled his blood-red eyes.

We walked inside the mead hall. The vampire, shapeshifters, the dog, and the lion man followed me.

A huge room greeted me. Twin rows of evenly spaced out tables ran parallel along the length of the chamber. Originally the Vikings had tried to have the tables joined in two lines, but they couldn't sweep under them, so they went to Plan B, which made their mead hall resemble a barbarian cafeteria. People mulled around the tables. Some ate, some talked, some oiled their weapons. The tables ran into a raised platform at the opposite end of the hall. On the platform a man sat in a large chair carved from driftwood and lined with furs. His shoulders stretched his blue woolen tunic. His face, framed by a glossy black mane of hair, was dark and carved with sharp precision. A narrow gold band rested on his head.

He glanced at us. Dark eyes took our measure. He noted Curran, frowned, and looked away pretending he hadn't seen us. Curran preferred to stay anonymous. Not many people besides the city heavyweights knew what he looked like. Ragnvald was trying to decide if the polite thing to do was to acknowledge Curran or pretend he wasn't there.

Before we left on this fun trip, we had discussed our strategy, and I volunteered to take point. If Curran came in his official capacity as the Beast Lord, there would be formal greetings and ceremony and the whole thing would take much longer than needed. Besides, I knew the neo-Vikings better than he did, so it made sense for me to take the lead. Curran decided to go as what he referred to as a "redshirt." Apparently it was the term for some sort of disposable attendant from some old TV show.

"Is that the jarl?" Ascanio whispered behind me.

"Yes."

"But he's Native American."

"Choctaw," I told him. "The Vikings don't care how you look. They care how well you swing your axe."

I headed down between the tables with my little entourage at my back. This would have been so much easier if I had come by myself.

About ten feet from the platform Ragnvald decided he couldn't ignore us any longer. "Kate! *Vestu heill!* Long time no see."

Not long enough. "Hello, Ragnvald. These are my associates." There. I didn't mention Curran by name. That should clue him in.

Ragnvald pushed himself off the chair. Upright, he was over six feet tall. He took a step off the platform and nodded to me. "I was just thinking of you."

"It's probably because you saw me walk through the door and then pretended I wasn't here for the last couple of minutes."

Ragnvald's face split into a grin. "I just couldn't believe my eyes. The alpha of the shapeshifters popping in unannounced. I'm shocked."

Oh, you sonovabitch. He was still trying to turn this into some sort of spectacle. "I'm not here in that capacity."

Ragnvald tapped his band. "This never comes off. Best to remember it now. But come on, we'll talk business." He raised his voice, shaking the nearby cups. "Someone bring drinks to our guests."

Why did everyone have to be so damn loud all the time?

Ragnvald nodded to a side table. "Please."

He took a seat and I sat across from him. Curran joined me. The vampire tried to follow but a large woman in chain mail barred his way.

A girl half my age swept by and slammed two giant tankards filled with beer on the table. Ragnvald held his up. I smashed my tankard against his. Beer splashed. We raised the tankard and pretended to take much bigger gulps than we actually did.

Curran drank his beer. Apparently, my taking the lead meant he went mute.

The young woman sashayed over to Ascanio and Derek and led them to a neighboring table. Judging by how hard her hips were working, she was open for business.

"So, what brings you to our mead hall?"

"I'm looking for Dagfinn."

Ragnvald grimaced. "What has he done now?"

"Just got some weird runes I need him to translate for me."

Ragnvald spread his arms. "We haven't seen the man. You should talk to Helga about the runes."

I had made some calls this morning. "We did talk to Helga. Talked to Dorte and old man Rasmus, too. They can't help us. Dagfinn is our best lead for now."

A huge older man staggered into the hall. Thick through the shoulders and slabbed with what my adoptive father had called hard fat, he moved in that peculiar careful way drunks do when they have trouble putting one foot in front of the other and don't want to pitch over. His leather vest sat askew on his large frame, his face was ruddy from cold or too much booze, and his long graying hair hung down in two braids, tangling with a mess of a gray beard.

It's all fun and games until the drunk Viking Santa shows up.

"I don't know what to tell you." Ragnvald drank a tiny swallow of his beer. "He isn't here. We expelled him months ago."

"Is that so?" Curran said.

"It is," Ragnvald insisted.

The soused Saint Nick zeroed in on the vampire sitting on the floor by the table where the shapeshifters were looking at their beer. The drunk blinked his bleary eyes and shambled toward the vamp.

"I hear the Guild is having a meeting soon," Ragnvald said.

"That's what I've been told," I said.

The older Viking pointed at the vampire. "What is this shit?"

Nobody answered.

Santa upped his voice a notch. "What is this shit?"

"Settle down, Dad," a younger man said from the corner.

Santa pivoted to the speaker. "Don't tell me to settle down, you stupid son of a whore."

"You don't talk about Mom that way."

"I'll talk about her . . . I'll . . . what is this shit?"

"I also hear that the Pack has been called in to mediate." Ragnvald looked at me for a long moment so I'd register that it was important.

"Aha."

"We have fifteen full-time members in the Guild," Ragnvald said.

I nodded. "I know. You put in what, eight years?"

"Seven and some change."

Santa rocked back, took a deep breath, and spat on the vamp. Awesome. "Are you going to do anything about that?"

Ragnvald glanced over his shoulder. "That's Johan. He's just having a bit of fun. About the mediation, Kate."

"What about it?"

The vamp unhinged his maw. "Only a fool fights with drunks and idiots," Ghastek's voice said.

"Are you calling me an idiot?" Johan squinted at the vamp.

People at the other tables stopped eating and trickled over to watch closer. They smelled a fight coming and didn't want to miss the show. This wasn't going well.

The vampire shrugged, mimicking Ghastek's gesture. "If a certain drunk spits on my vampire again, he will regret it."

Johan leaned back, a puzzled expression on his face. Apparently, Ghastek had managed to stump him.

"Which way are you leaning?" Ragnvald said.

Nice try. "Where is Dagfinn, Ragnvald?"

"I've told you twice now, he isn't here."

"You've got to be kidding me. His house is here, his mother still lives here, and his stallion is out in the pasture."

"He gave him to his mother," Ragnvald said.

"He gave Magnus to his mother?"

"Yes."

"That horse is a bloody beast. Nobody can ride him except Dagfinn. The only reason Magnus hasn't bitten Dagfinn's hand off by now is because every time he tries, Dagfinn bites him back. And you're telling me Dagfinn gave him to his mother? What is she going to do with him?"

Ragnvald spread his arms. "I don't know, use him for home protection or something. I'm not a psychic. I don't know what goes through that man's head."

"You mean me?" Johan roared. "You mean I'll regret it?"

Oh no. He finally got it.

"Do you see any other fat old drunks making a spectacle of themselves?" Ascanio asked.

Johan swung over to Derek. "You! Slap a muzzle on your girlfriend."

Derek smiled. It was a slow, controlled baring of teeth. I fought a shudder. The couple of guys to the left of us grabbed their chairs.

"Derek, we're guests," I called out.

Curran chuckled quietly to himself. Apparently he found me amusing.

"They need a lesson in hospitality," Ghastek said.

"I'll show you hospitality." Johan sucked in some air.

"Don't do it," Ghastek warned.

Johan hacked. The gob of spit landed on the vamp's forehead.

"Suck on that!" Johan pivoted to Derek. "You're next!"

Ascanio shot from his seat in a blur and punched Johan off his feet. Vikings swarmed. Someone screamed. A chair flew above us and crashed into the wall. Grendel bounced in place, barking his head off.

Ragnvald heaved an exasperated sigh. "Which way are you leaning, Kate? Veterans or Mark?"

"Are you going to tell me where Dagfinn is?"

"No."

Bastard. "Then I guess I don't know which way I'm leaning."

Ragnvald looked at Curran. "Seriously?"

Curran shrugged his broad shoulders. "It's her show."

A tankard hurtled through the room and crashed against Ragnvald's back. He surged to his feet roaring. "Alright, you fuckers, who threw that?"

The second tankard took him straight in the forehead. He staggered and lunged into the full-out brawl raging in the middle of the mead hall. Fists flew, people growled, and above it all, Ghastek's vamp crawled up the wall to the ceiling, its left paw gripping pissed-off Johan by his ankle.

I sighed, jumped on the table, and kicked some Viking in the face.

My butt hurt, because a Viking woman had kicked me from behind while I was busy, and the motion of my horse wasn't doing me any favors. The red spot on my shoulder promised to bloom into a baseball-sized bruise, but other than that I'd gotten away scot-free. Derek sported a cut across his chest and Ascanio, whose shirt had somehow gotten mysteriously ripped to shreds in the heat of the battle, was black-and-blue from the neck down. It wouldn't last more than a couple of hours and by the evening the lot of them would look like new, while I would still be nursing a sore shoulder. Shapeshifters.

The wind brought a whiff of hops from Ghastek's vamp loping next to me. The Vikings had tried to drown it in the barrel of beer and most of its green sunblock had come off, so Ghastek had ended up rolling him in some mud to keep the skin damage to a minimum. The mud had dried to a nasty crust and the vamp looked like something that would come out of Grendel's tail end.

Grendel had spent most of the fight barking and biting random people and was now smeared with someone's vomit.

Curran had escaped unscathed, mostly because when people tried to assault him, he punched them once and then they didn't get up. He walked now next to my horse in his human form, a big smile on his face.

"What?" I asked him.

"Good thing you took the lead on that one," he said. "It could've gone badly and degenerated into a huge brawl."

"Screw you."

"Oh, I hope you do, baby."

In your dreams.

"And that's why I don't like visiting the neo-Vikings," Ghastek said, his voice dry. "They're an uncivilized, idiotic lot and nothing good ever comes from it."

"They started it," Ascanio said.

"Of course they started it," I growled. "They're Vikings. That's what they do."

Ghastek cleared his throat. "I can't help but point out that now Dagfinn knows we're looking for him. He may go into hiding."

"Dagfinn doesn't do hiding. If he isn't involved in this mess, he'll show up on my doorstep demanding to know what's going on. If he is involved, he'll show up on my doorstep, waving his axe and trying to crush skulls. Works either way."

"So we wait?"

It made me grit my teeth. I'd hoped we'd get a hold of Dagfinn today. Roderick was running out of time, but there wasn't anything else we could do. "We go home and wait."

CHAPTER 6

※

We parted ways with Ghastek and the four of us—
Curran, Derek, Ascanio, and I—made our way back to the
Keep. Jim waited for us on the stone steps as we rode into the
courtyard.

"What happened to you?"

"We went to see the Vikings," I told him.

"This is nothing," Curran said. "You should've seen what
happened to the vampire."

Jim smiled.

I dismounted and gave The Dude's reigns to a shapeshifter
kid from the stables.

"Some people are here to see you," Jim told me.

"What people?"

"From the Guild."

Argh. "Fine. How's the boy?"

"Doolittle says he's the same. Your guests are in the
second-floor conference room, third door on the left."

I marched to the second floor. Grendel decided to accom-
pany me. Five people waited in the small reception hallway by
the third conference room, guarded by a female shapeshifter.
One of them was Mark, the late Solomon Red's self-appointed
successor, and the other four were Bob Carver, Ivera Nielsen,
Ken, and Juke, collectively known as the Four Horsemen. Most
mercs were loners. Sometimes, when the job demanded it,
they paired up the way Jim and I did, but groups of more than
two were rare. The Four Horsemen were the exception to the
rule. They made a cohesive, strong team. They took rough
jobs and finished them efficiently and mostly aboveboard, and
they were respected by the rest of the mercs.

The two parties stopped glowering at each other long enough to contemplate my dog.

"What the hell is that?" Bob asked.

"It's my attack poodle. Did you agree to come here at the same time?"

"Hell no," Juke said, shaking her head with spiked black hair. "We were here first. He just showed up."

"I made an appointment," Mark said. "Once again, you're bringing your bully tactics to the table."

"You're an asshole," Ken told him.

"And you're a thug."

Why me?

This was the first time I'd heard about an appointment. I made a mental note to ask Jim about that and pulled a quarter from my pocket. "Heads." I pointed to the Four Horsemen. "Mark, you're tails."

I flipped the coin into the air and slapped it onto the back of my wrist.

"Tails." I nodded at Mark. "Let's go."

We stepped into the conference room, I shut the door, and we sat at a large table of knotted wood.

"What can I do for you?"

Mark leaned forward. He wore a crisp business suit and a conservative burgundy tie. His dark brown hair was cut in that executive/politician style: not too long, not too short, conservative, neat. His nails were clean and manicured, his chin showed no stubble, and he smelled of masculine cologne. Not overpowering, but definitely detectable.

"I'd like to talk to you about the Guild arbitration," he said.

And here I thought he'd made the trip to chat about the weather. "I'm listening."

Mark looked at the dog. Grendel gave him an evil eye.

"I'll cut to the chase: I'd like to take over the Guild."

Ambitious, aren't we? "I kind of gathered that."

"I'm not popular. I don't wear leather and I don't carry guns." He braided the fingers of his hands into a single fist and rested it on the table. "But I make the Guild run. I make sure the customers are happy, the profits are made, and everyone gets paid on time. Without me the whole thing would collapse."

I had no doubt it would. "I'm waiting for my part in this."

"Your vote will be the tiebreaker," he said. "I'd like us to come to some sort of arrangement."

He'd just dug a lovely hole for himself. I waited to see if he would jump into it.

"Of course, I understand that sufficient compensation is in order and our arrangement would have to be equitable and mutually beneficial."

And he had. I sighed. "Mark, the problem isn't that you can't run the Guild. The problem is that you think 'white collar' is a noble title."

He blinked, obviously taken aback.

"In your world, everyone has a price," I said. "You don't know what mine is, but you think you can afford it. It doesn't work like that. You could've gone many ways with this. You could've argued that with the leadership of the Guild in limbo, nobody is getting paid. You could've pointed out that the longer this goes on, the more talent the Guild will lose, as experienced mercs move on to new jobs to feed their families. Offering to bribe me was the worst argument you could've made. My opinion isn't for sale."

"I meant no offense," he said.

"But you did offend, and you've demonstrated that you have no idea how to relate to me. A lot of guys are like me, Mark. Yes, you make the Guild run, but you lack the elemental understanding of what makes mercs tick, probably because you never were one. If I wanted to endorse you, which I don't, I'd have to defend my position before the Guild, which I find difficult under the circumstances."

He chewed on that for a long minute. "Fair enough. So you'll vote for the Horsemen then?"

"I don't know yet."

"Thank you for seeing me." Mark got up and left.

The door had barely had a chance to swing open before Bob shouldered his way in and dropped into one of the chairs around the table. Ivera followed, uneasy, watching me.

Bob was the leader of the Horsemen. If our world had spawned any veteran gladiators, he would be one of them. He was on the other side of forty and built with that mature strength and endurance that would make him a tough opponent even for people half his age. He might not be as fast as he used to be, but he had plenty of experience and he used it. Ivera was a tall, large Hispanic woman. She was nasty in a fight and a firebug—fire mage—on top of it.

The other two members of the Horsemen remained outside. Ken, a Hungarian mage, measured out words like they were gold and Juke, well, Juke was barely twenty and made up for her lack of experience in natural viciousness and a hot temper. She was fast and she liked to talk trash. I understood the urge. I liked to talk trash too, but twenty year-old me would've chewed Juke up and spat her out.

I looked at the two veterans. "What can I do for you?"

Bob leaned forward. The chair creaked and I almost winced. He was a big guy and the chair was none too sturdy.

"I'll come right to the point," he said. "Solomon was one of us. A merc. A working stiff."

"Actually, Solomon only worked as a merc for the first three years after forming the Guild, and given that he's been underground for a few months, we can drop 'working' from his description."

Bob plowed ahead. "All the same, he knew what it's like to be out in the field. He knew how to take care of the guys. The man had a heart, unlike that prick. He'll bleed us dry if we let him."

"By 'that prick' you mean Mark?"

"Who else?"

I nodded. "Just checking."

Bob knocked on my desk with his scarred knuckles, making a point. "That pencil neck wants to run the Guild. Between the four of us, we'll do better. Someone's got to look out for the guys."

I spread my arms. "More power to you. What do you want from me?"

Bob scooted forward. The chair groaned. "Solomon, you, and Mark are the only people with any sort of official designation other than Guild member, except for the clerk and the payroll ladies. You were the first of us to make it into the Order and you did good work as a liaison. People remember that. And now you're the Beast Lord's . . ." He groped for a word.

"Mate," Ivera told him.

"Yes, that. You have street cred. The mercs will never follow Mark. You know it, I know it, Ivera knows it."

I glanced at Ivera. "What do you think?"

"What he said," she said grimly.

I leaned back. They wouldn't like it, but it had to be said. "Three mercs go on a gig. One bails midway through the fight, the second dies, the third loses a hand. Are they eligible for Guild disability pay?"

Bob thought about it. "The guy that ran off gets nothing, that's abandonment in progress. The dead guy's next of kin gets thirty percent. The guy without a hand gets disability."

I sighed. "The first question to ask is how long any of them have been in the Guild. You have to hit the five-year mark to qualify for disability and do seven years to qualify for the death benefit. Until then, you die, your family gets a flat ten grand from your standard life insurance. The next question is, when did the first guy take off? If he did it once the fight started and the danger was evident, the Guild is entitled to garnish his wages, because his abandonment in progress becomes abandonment in imminent danger. How much do we garnish, Bob?"

Muscles played on his jaw. "I don't know."

"Then we move on to disability. How much do we pay? What's a hand worth? Does it matter if he was right- or left-handed?"

"I don't know," Bob said again. His eyes told me he didn't like where I was headed.

"Neither do I. But you know who does? Mark. I can call Mark right now and he'll rattle it off the top of his head. Let's talk contracts. Who provides the ammo for the Guild supply room? How much of a discount do we get from them? The Guild has a deal with Avalon Construction to clear the magic hazmat at their prospective construction sites. It's a sweet contract, so you know there were perks. Bribes. Gifts. How much and to whom?"

Bob growled a bit. "All this stuff can be learned."

I nodded. "Sure. But how long will it take you? The Guild has been without a leader for what, six months now, and you still haven't learned any of it. Would it even matter by the time you finished learning?"

Bob crossed his arms. "You could do it."

"No, I can't. First, it's not my job. I've got my hands full with the shapeshifters and my own business. Second, what little I know I've learned only because it came up during my tenure as a liaison. It would take me ages to find it in the Guild's Manual. For better or worse, Solomon made Mark the sole brain behind this operation and Mark has years of experience. You don't have the knack for wheeling and dealing, Bob. You're a good solid tactician. You know what the gig needs and you're good at picking the right people and getting it done. The mercs look up to you. But bargaining isn't your thing."

Bob's eyebrows crept closer together. "You'll be backing Mark then?"

"I will tell you what I told him. I don't know yet."

Bob nodded and handed me a piece of paper. I scanned it. A formal summons with my name on it. The top left corner boasted "code X" in bold. Priority ten. Either I made this meeting, or the Guild would suspend me.

"Not that it would matter," Bob said. "But we did all manage to agree that you need to pick somebody by Monday."

Ivera got up and put her hand on Bob's shoulder. "We should go."

He started to say something and changed his mind. I watched him get to his feet. He nodded to me. "Later."

I dragged myself upstairs to the infirmary. Roderick was playing checkers with a shapeshifter boy. The collar on his neck had gone from orange to canary yellow.

I climbed the million stairs to our quarters, asked the guards to order some food from the kitchen, and took a shower. When I came out, Curran was sprawled on our giant couch, his eyes closed.

I flopped next to him. "Help."

The blond eyebrows rose a quarter inch. "Mhm?"

"The mercs aren't going to reach a consensus." I lay next to him on my side, propping my head up with my hand. "No matter who I pick tomorrow, they won't like it. Mark can run the Guild, but the mercs despise him. The mercs can do the jobs, but the admin stuff leaves them clueless."

"Make them work together," Curran said.

"Not going to happen. They hate each other."

"If fourteen alphas can meet in the same room every week without killing each other, so can Mark and the mercs. The Guild has been without leadership for months. The people are tired and they want a strong leader. Not a tyrant, but a leader who inspires confidence. You need to walk in there and roar until they cringe. Demonstrate that you are strong enough to take away their freedom to choose, make sure it sinks in, and then give some of the choice back to them on your terms."

Hmm.

"Tie it back to Solomon Red, too," Curran said. "It's basic psychology: under Solomon things ran, when he died, they broke. The more time passes, the more rosy the times of Solomon look to the average merc. So if you attack them from the 'Let's go back to the good old days' angle, they will fold. Make them think that following you is what they want to do."

"You scare me sometimes," I told him.

He yawned. "I'm totally harmless."

Someone knocked on the door. A bit soon for the food.

"Yes?" Curran called.

Mercedes, one of the guards, entered. "There is a man outside, my lord. He is big, he's wearing a cape, and he's got a giant axe. We're also pretty sure he's drunk."

Dagfinn.

"What does he want?" Curran asked.

"He says he wants to fight the Beast Lord."

CHAPTER 7

✦

Curran and I stood in the arched entrance to the Keep's courtyard. Dagfinn waited in the clearing outside. He was six feet eight inches tall, and he weighed a shade above three hundred pounds. None of it was fat. Dagfinn looked hard. His broad shoulders strained his tunic, his biceps had trouble fitting into the sleeves, and his legs in worn-out jeans carried enough muscle to make you wince at the thought of him kicking you. His curly hair fell over his shoulders in a dense reddish wave. He'd trimmed his beard, but his red eyebrows overshadowed his eyes.

He stood brandishing a battle axe etched with runes that matched the tattoos on his arms. The blade of the axe flared at the toe and heel, its razor-sharp edge spanning a full twelve inches. Combined with the four-foot haft for extra power, the axe sheared flesh and bone like an oversized meat cleaver.

"Look, I fought this guy before. Maybe you should talk him away from the cliff. He's drunk and isn't in his right mind."

"He challenged me," Curran said. "There will be no talking."

"Suit yourself," I told him. Mr. Make Fun of My Leadership wanted to have it his way. Well, he'd get it.

Around us the shapeshifters were piling out onto the battlements. Every balcony and parapet facing in Dagfinn's direction was occupied. Great. An audience was just what we needed.

"Anything I should know?" Curran asked me.

"The axe is magic. Don't touch it. Dagfinn is pretty magic, too. If you kill him, I'll be really mad at you. We need him to read the damn runes."

Curran stretched his shoulders and walked out into the clearing.

"I heard you were looking for me," Dagfinn growled. His voice matched him, deep and torn about the edges.

"She has some runes she wants you to look at."

Dagfinn leaned to the side to look at me. "Kate? What the hell are you doing here?"

"I live here."

"Why?"

"Because I'm with him now."

Dagfinn looked at Curran. "You and her are . . . ?"

"She's my mate," Curran said.

Dagfinn swung his axe onto his shoulder. The runes sparked with pale green. "Well, how about that? You know what, I don't care, I'll still beat your ass, but I like her so I won't kill you."

Curran's eyes turned gold. "Thanks."

Dagfinn waved his arm at him. "Well, go on. Do your transforming thing."

"No need."

"Oh, there is a need," Dagfinn assured him.

"Are you going to talk all day? I'm a busy man," Curran told him.

"Fine. Let's get to it." Frost condensed on Dagfinn's hair. His skin turned dark. He grew, gaining half a foot of height, his shoulders spreading wider.

"Have fun, baby," I called.

Pale tendrils of cold spilled from Dagfinn's body. The icy mist danced along his skin, clutched at the runes tattooed on his arms, and drained down in a brilliant cascade onto his axe. The weapon burst with bright green.

I braced myself against the stone wall. Dagfinn swung his axe.

Curran jumped aside. A flash exploded to the left of him, blinding white and searing. Thunder slapped my ears. An air fist slammed into me. Curran flew a bit and rolled up to his feet.

A three-foot hole smoked in the grass where Curran had stood. Dagfinn roared like an enraged tornado. A blast of frigid air whipped from him, striking at Curran. The Beast Lord dodged again.

Dagfinn remained firmly planted. The last two times we'd fought, he'd moved at me and I'd taken him down. There were dozens of ways to use an opponent's movement against him: trip him, knock him off balance, gain control of a shoulder or a leg, and so on. Dagfinn must've decided not to give Curran that chance.

Dagfinn spun the axe. A barrage of frost missiles shot out. Curran leaped back and forth, circling Dagfinn. On the battlements the shapeshifters roared and howled.

"How are we doing, baby?" I called out. *Serves you right, Your Furriness. Next time, listen to me.*

"Trying not to show off," Curran yelled.

Dagfinn brought the axe down. A sonic boom smashed into me. Curran flew backward.

"Bring it!" Dagfinn roared.

The shapeshifters booed.

Curran bounced back up and dashed forward.

Dagfinn spun, but the Beast Lord was too fast. He dodged left, right, and collided with Dagfinn. The huge Viking staggered back from the impact, whipped around, picking up momentum, and charged, roaring, gripping the axe with both hands, and bringing it up for an overhead blow.

Move, honey. Move.

Curran lunged forward.

What the hell was he doing?

Dagfinn chopped down with all his strength.

Curran caught the axe with his right hand.

Dagfinn *stopped*.

Holy shit.

The Viking strained, right leg forward, left leg back. Muscles rippled on his arms. Frost ate at Curran's hand, but the axe didn't move.

"Done?" Curran asked.

Dagfinn snarled.

Curran raised his left hand. His fingers curled into a fist.

"Not in the head!" I yelled. "We need his brain intact."

Curran yanked the axe forward. Dagfinn jerked back, trying to regain his balance, and Curran swept his left leg from under him. Dagfinn crashed down like an oak chopped at the root.

Curran tore the axe out of his hands and tossed it aside. Dagfinn swung at him with his right fist. Curran leaned out of the way and sank a vicious punch straight down into Dagfinn's gut.

Ow. I hurt just from looking. The shapeshifters watching on the wall made sucking noises.

Dagfinn curled into a ball, trying to gulp in a lungful of air, which was suddenly missing.

Curran pulled Dagfinn up, swung him over his shoulder, and carried the Viking toward me.

Oh, you crazy sonovabitch.

Curran dumped purple-faced Dagfinn by my feet. "Here is your expert, baby."

The shapeshifters on the wall whistled and howled. *Why me?*

"Thanks, show-off," I told him. "Let me see the hand."

"It's fine."

"The hand, Curran."

He held it out. Blisters covered his right palm. Frostbite, probably second-degree. It had to hurt like hell. Lyc-V would fix it in a day or so, but meanwhile he'd have to grit his teeth.

"I said don't touch the axe."

He leaned over and kissed me. The shapeshifters on the walls cheered.

Dagfinn finally managed to remember how to breathe and swore.

I leaned over him. "He won. You're going to read my runes now."

"Fine," Dagfinn growled. "Give me a minute. I think something's broken."

According to Doolittle, nothing was actually broken. Dagfinn treated the diagnosis with open suspicion, but given the circumstances, he decided to deal with it. Curran, on the other hand, got a plastic bag with some sort of healing solution tied around his hand. He liked it about as much as I expected.

"This is ridiculous."

"With the bag, the hand will be usable in two hours," Doolittle informed him. "Without the bag, it may be usable by tomorrow. It's your choice, my lord."

Curran growled a little, but kept the bag on.

I put Julie's drawing in front of Dagfinn.

He squinted at it. "Whoa. Was this on a weapon?"

"No, it's on a gold necklace that's killing a child. Looks like Elder Futhark, but not exactly. Is this a spell?" I asked.

"This isn't Elder Futhark."

"What is it?"

"It's dvergr."

I sat down into the nearest chair. "Are you sure?"

Dagfinn pulled back the sleeve of his tunic, displaying his tattoos. "Look here."

The last two characters on his shoulder matched the last two characters on Julie's paper. Dagfinn drew his fingers along the tattoo. "This says, 'Wielder of Axe Aslaug, born from the blood of Earth shaped by the hands of Ivar.'" He tapped the paper. "This says, 'Apprentice of Ivar.' Yeah, I'm sure."

"What is dvergr?" Curran asked me.

"Dwarf," I told him. "Old Norse dwarf: magic, powerful, skilled with metalwork. Makers of weapons for the gods. They're often portrayed as embodiments of greed—they lust after power, women, and most of all gold."

"Hey now!" Dagfinn raised his hand. "Most experts believe this to be a later development. The dwarf myths probably take their root in nature spirits . . ."

"Dwarves like in Tolkien?" Curran asked.

I wish. I dragged my hand over my face. "One time, four dwarf brothers, the sons of Ivaldi, created some magical gifts for the gods. Two other dwarf brothers, Brokk and Eiti, became jealous of all the praise and bet Loki, the trickster, that they could make better gifts. He wagered his head. The dwarves won and then wanted to murder Loki. The gods wouldn't let them do it, so Brokk sewed Loki's lips shut with wire. These are not the jolly, drink-beer-and-go-on-an-adventure type of dwarves."

"The one I met was a good guy," Dagfinn said.

"You think the Ivar whose apprentice wore this necklace is the same Ivar who made your axe?" Curran asked.

Dagfinn nodded. "I was about fourteen or fifteen. I was wild back then, not like now."

Curran and I looked at each other.

"So my uncle Didrik, he was a Viking, took me to the mountains to this valley. We met a smith there and my uncle talked to him and then left me there for the summer. It didn't go well at first, but Ivar and me got along finally. I liked it there. When Didrik came to get me, Ivar made me this axe and put the runes on me. Right arm"—he slapped his right biceps— "controls the axe. Left arm is my oath. I can't ever kill a defenseless person or force myself on anyone, or the axe will turn on me."

"I heard you broke into the monastery looking for Asian ladies," Curran said.

"Asian ale," Dagfinn said. "I wasn't looking to rape anybody. I was looking for the beer. None of them would talk to me, so I kept trying to grab them to make them hold still so I could ask where the beer was. I had a bit to drink that evening."

The light dawned on me. "Dagfinn, they are Buddhists. They don't brew beer. You needed the Augustine Brothers two miles to the south. You went to the wrong monastery, you dimwit."

"Tell me something I don't know," Dagfinn growled. "Anyway, can I see this collar?"

We took him in to see the boy. Roderick shrank a little. "Don't be scared," Dagfinn said. He examined the collar for a little while and we returned to the other room. Dagfinn sat down in his chair, while Curran leaned against the wall, watching him and emanating menace.

"Could be Ivar's work," Dagfinn said. "I just don't understand why. The dwarf I knew wouldn't hurt a child."

"What about his apprentice," I asked. "What do you know about him?"

"Never met him, but it looks like this collar must have belonged to him or at least his apprentice. Maybe Ivar will know more, if we can locate him."

"Can you find the valley again?" I asked.

He shook his head. "There is a trick to it somehow. I'd meant to ask Didrik about it, but he died. I've tried to find him on my own. I've been all over the Smoky Mountains and nothing."

He was holding something back, I could feel it. "What are you not telling me, Dagfinn?"

He hesitated.

"It's going to kill the kid," Curran said.

"He might know," Dagfinn said.

"He who?"

"You know. *He.*"

My heart took a dive. This was getting better and better.

"He who?" Curran demanded.

I stepped closer to him and lowered my voice. "The Vikings know of a creature. He's been trapped on their land for a very long time. They don't like to say his name, because he might hear and kill them at night."

"Don't tell me you're thinking about it," Dagfinn said.

I spread my arms. "I'm out of ideas."

"Kate, please tell me you haven't been to see him before, right? Right?" Dagfinn asked.

"No. This will be my first time."

"Why?" Curran asked.

"He catches your scent when you go to see him," Dagfinn said. "It takes him a while, but once he learns the scent, he never forgets it. People who go to see him twice don't come back. Their bones stay on that hill."

"We're going to need backup," I said, thinking aloud.

"Don't look at me," Dagfinn said. "I like you and all, but I've been once. I ran like a little girl and barely got out. I can't go again."

"Backup won't be an issue," Curran said.

I shook my head. "We can't bring anyone we can't afford to lose."

"She's right," Dagfinn said. "I hired a crew. Six people. I was the only one who got out and only because *he* ate them first. My advice, hire someone you don't know and tell them up front it's a fight to the death. They're just flesh speed bumps for him." He looked at me. "You need to talk to the Cherokees."

"Yes, I know." Thinking of going to see Håkon sent ice down my spine.

"Well, I'm out." Dagfinn rose. "Thank you for the fight,

I had fun, we should do it again sometime. It was nice knowing you."

Curran pushed from the wall. "I'll walk you out."

"I can find my way," Dagfinn said.

"I'm sure you can. I'll save you the trouble." Gold rolled over Curran's eyes.

Dagfinn sighed and they left.

I went up onto the roof. We had set up a small dining area there, two chairs and a table. Lately, every time we sat down to eat in our kitchen, someone would knock on the door with some bullshit emergency, so when we didn't feel like being interrupted, Curran and I would go up to the roof and eat in peace. His Furry Majesty was threatening to drag a grill up there and "cook meat" for me. Knowing him, "grill" meant a giant pit and "meat" stood for half a deer.

I sat on the low stone wall bordering the top of the roof. It was late afternoon, and the sun was slowly rolling to the west. The stone wall was nice and hot under my butt. Summer was coming.

I sat, enveloped in warm air. It felt nice, but not hot enough to chase away the ice built up on my spine. I didn't want to visit Håkon. Several people I knew had gone to see him. Only two had come back, and Dagfinn was one of them.

The world blinked. The magic vanished, snuffed out like a candle by a draft. A mixed blessing: as long as the magic was down, the necklace wouldn't constrict Roderick's neck any further, but we couldn't see Håkon without it.

Voron, my adoptive father, had always warned me that friends would make me soft. When you cared about people, you forged a bond, and that bond made you predictable. Friends weren't for me. Greg, my now-dead guardian, took that a step further and added lovers to that ban. When you loved someone, your enemies would use it against you.

Neither of them had predicted that being in love and being loved in return made you value your life much higher. I liked my life. I had a lot to lose now.

Curran emerged from the door, pulled the bag off his hand,

and tossed it into the garbage can we kept up here for the times we ate outside. He walked in complete silence, like a tiger stalking through the forest, quiet and confident. I liked to watch him, provided he didn't know about it. His ego was threatening the ozone layer as it was.

Curran sat next to me and put his left arm around my shoulders and kissed me. There was a slightly possessive edge to the kiss.

"Through the Guild and no."

"Hmm?" he asked.

"You were about to ask how I know Dagfinn and if we were ever more than friends. We never were friends, actually. I got suckered by the Guild into bringing him in twice. He was wanted for unpaid fines and destruction of property."

Curran grimaced. "No, it never crossed my mind that you'd be with Dagfinn. He's an undisciplined idiot. Give me some credit. I know you better than that."

I shrugged and leaned closer against him. "This is fucked up."

"Yes, it is. Can you think of any other way to find Ivar?"

"No. Maybe Doolittle can try removing the collar during tech?"

Curran shook his head. "I asked. He says it will kill the boy. He says we have thirty-six to forty-eight hours, depending on how long the magic lasts. There is a good chance the next magic wave will be the boy's last."

Two days before Roderick with his owlish eyes died, choked to death.

"Do you remember a few years ago a detachment of PAD disappeared? Eleven cops, armed to the teeth? It was in the papers?"

"Yes."

"That was Håkon."

"Is that his name?"

I nodded. "I didn't say it in front of Dagfinn so he wouldn't freak out. Whoever we take will die. If we don't take anybody, the boy will die."

"We explain it and ask for volunteers." Curran drew me closer. "Those are the choices we make."

"I'm tired of those lousy choices." If you put all the people I'd killed together, their blood would make a lake. I was wading through it and I had no desire to make it any deeper.

We sat next to each other, touching.

If Curran asked for volunteers, the Pack would cough some up. I would have to look at their faces, I would witness their deaths, and then I would have to tell their families about it, assuming I survived. Assuming Curran survived.

The thought pissed me off. We'd do it. There was a child on the other end of that equation, so yes, we would grit our teeth and do it. But it made me so mad. I could've strangled Aurellia if I got my hands on her. She knew what the collar did, and she had deliberately chosen between her husband and her son.

"Can Håkon be killed?" Curran asked.

"No. The Cherokees have tried for years. All they can do is contain him on that hill. If he's destroyed, he just reassembles himself." I growled. "I don't want to do this."

"I know," he said.

"Do you think less of me?"

"No." Curran stroked my back. "Like I said, these are the choices we make, and sometimes every choice is bad, and then you sit by yourself and remember all the horrible shit you had to do and have done, and you deal with it. It will eat you alive if you let it."

I straightened and touched his cheek. "Well, you don't have to sit by yourself anymore. We'll sit together."

He caught my hand and kissed it. His eyes turned dark. His fingers curved into a fist. He looked predatory. "I wish I could rewind back to that second and crush her skull before she put the necklace on the kid."

"I know. I wish there was a way to get to her."

He looked at me. "I thought about it. If we approached Forney's house at night . . ."

"Curran, we can't break into the house of the DA. The fallout for the Pack would be enormous."

"I know, I know." Muscles played along his jaw. He hated to have his hands tied and so did I. "But if we use someone outside of Atlanta for the DA job . . ."

"It's a bad idea. Even I know it's a bad idea."

He looked at me. He was still thinking about it.

"No," I told him.

Curran swore.

Screwing with the DA would get us a witch hunt in a hurry. He knew it and I knew it. No, there had to be another way. Some way where the boy survived and our people didn't die.

I sighed. "I envy navigators sometimes. All they do is sit in the Casino and drink coffee, while the bloodsuckers run into dang—"

I stopped in midword.

Curran's eyes lit up.

"You think he'll go for it?"

"Oh yes. Yes, he will go for it." He jumped off the wall. "Come with me."

"Shouldn't we have some sort of a plan? Ghastek isn't an idiot. We can't just call down to the Casino and tell him, 'Hi, we're going on a suicide mission, wanna bring some vampires to be our bullet meat?'" Bloodsuckers were expensive. The very idea of taking four or five of them into danger with minuscule chances of survival would give Ghastek an aneurysm.

"I have a plan." Curran grinned at me.

"Please enlighten me, Your Majesty."

"I'm going to make Jim figure it out," Curran said.

"That's it? That's your plan?"

"Yes. I'm brilliant. Come on."

I hopped off the wall and we went down the stairs.

If anybody could figure out how to rope Ghastek into this scheme, Jim would be the man. Served him right for all those times he'd pushed me into the line of fire.

Payback is a bitch.

We trapped Jim in one of the conference rooms and explained our brilliant plan.

"This is payback, isn't it?" Jim glared at me.

"Don't be ridiculous," I told him. "As the Consort of the Pack, I'm far above petty revenge."

Jim tapped the clipboard with several pieces of paper on it against his forearm. "I'll do it if you go to the Guild tomorrow."

"You'll do it, because I asked you to," Curran said.

Jim turned to me. "Will you do the Guild thing?"

I had a dying kid on my hands and all he cared about was Guild idiocy. "Maybe. I don't know yet. I'm kind of busy at the moment."

Green flashed in Jim's eyes. He yanked a piece of paper from the clipboard and thrust it at me. It looked like a long list.

"What is this?"

"This is the list of all the phone calls I've gotten about this shit in the last week and a half. The mercs have gotten every damn member to call me here." He shook the list in Curran's direction. "You want to know why your background checks aren't done? This is why! I could get it done if your mate would stop dicking around and just deal with it."

Oh, it's like this, then. "Then I have a great idea. Since they're all calling you, why don't *you* stop dicking around and deal with the Guild. You have the same time in as I do."

"I have a job!"

"So do I! Why is your time more important than mine?"

The clipboard snapped in Jim's fingers. He dropped it on the ground and raised his hands. "You know what, I'm done. I quit."

"Oh my God, seriously?"

Jim wiped his hands against each other and showed them to me.

"Is that you washing your hands off?"

"Yes."

"Really? So what, you're going to retire and open that flower shop you always wanted?"

Jim's eyes went completely green.

"Enough," Curran said. An unmistakable command saturated his voice. Jim clicked his mouth shut.

I crossed my arms. "I'm sorry, is this the part where I fall to my knees and shiver in fear, Your Furriness? Silly me, I didn't get the memo."

Curran ignored the barb. "What's your problem with the Guild?"

"The only way to resolve it involves me being entangled in running it and I don't want to do it." I waved my arms. "I have the Consort crap and I have the Cutting Edge crap and whatever other bullshit the two of you throw my way. I don't want to go to the Guild every month and deal with their crap on top of everything else."

Curran leaned toward me. "I have to dress up and meet with those corpse fuckers once every three months and be civil while we're eating at the same table. You can deal with the Guild."

"You, dress up? Wow, I had no idea that putting on your formal sweatpants was such a huge burden."

"Kate," Curran snarled. "They're not sweatpants, they are slacks and they have a belt. I have to wear shoes with fucking laces in them."

"I don't want to do it! I hate the ceremony crap." I so didn't need the Guild politics in my life. It was complicated enough, damn it. "I don't have time for it."

"Everybody hates the political stuff," Curran growled. "You'll do it."

"Give me one reason why."

"Because you know those people and some of them are your friends. The Guild is sinking and they're losing their jobs."

I opened my mouth and clamped it shut.

"Also, because I'm asking you to do it," Curran said. "Will you please resolve this, baby?"

I would punch him. I would punch him straight in the face, hard. "Fine. I'll need a lot of backup for the Guild."

Curran looked at Jim. "Make sure she has everything she needs."

"Okay," Jim said. He picked up the pieces of his clipboard, pulled a piece of paper out, and handed it to me with the pen. "Write it down."

I did and gave it back to him.

Jim read it. "I'll take care of it, Consort."

"Thank you, Alpha."

If it had been raining, our voices would've frozen it into hail.

"Is there anything else?" Jim asked Curran.

"No."

Jim nodded and left.

"I hate you," I told Curran.

He chuckled. "You'd hate me more if Jim quit. We'd have

to find a replacement. I don't trust that many people. Just think how much more shit you'd have to put up with."

"Don't," I warned him.

"Mhm, Kate, the chief of security. Sexy. Who better to guard my body than the woman who owns it?"

"Curran, I will punch you."

"Rough play." Curran pretended to shiver in excitement.

I raised my fist and tapped his biceps lightly.

"You knew it was inevitable," he said.

I knew. The moment Jim sent me the file I had known exactly how it would end. But I'd put up a valiant fight. "Yes, but I don't have to like it. Can we eat now? I'm starving."

"Oh so am I forgiven?" he asked.

"Sure. The next time you decide to flex your claws and come up with a plan to invade the home of a high-ranking civil servant, I'll bark, 'Enough!' and expect to be obeyed, how about that?"

"You told me no," he said.

"And?"

"And I didn't like it."

"You can't assault the DA's house, you crazy bastard!"

"And you can't check out of the Guild's mess. We both have to do things we don't want to do. I consider us even."

I rolled my eyes and we went upstairs to our cold food.

"I know what that ass is getting from me next Christmas," I said.

"What?"

"Clipboards. Lots and lots of clipboards."

CHAPTER 8

Before the Shift and the return of magic, a person's power could be readily judged by the kind of car they drove, by the clothes they wore, and the company they kept. In post-Shift Atlanta, visual clues still proved true in some cases, but not nearly often enough. A bum in tattered jeans and ragged cloak could walk out into a crowded street, raise his arms, and the sky would tear open and weep a rain of lightning and hail the size of coconuts, leveling everything in a three-mile radius.

That's why post-Shift Atlanta's movers and shakers preferred both a show of power and dressing to impress. Still, if you did dress like a badass, you had better be able to back it up.

When I woke up in the morning, a pair of gray jeans, a gray T-shirt, and a gray leather jacket waited for me, folded on top of a gray cloak edged with fur. Just as I requested. Gray was the Pack color. I was going to put on a show for the Guild and this was my costume for it. I put the clothes on, added my boots, my saber in the back leather sheath, my throwing knives, and my wrist guards filled with silver needles. I braided my hair away from my face and examined myself in the mirror. I was broadcasting dangerous loud and clear.

Normally I stayed away from clothes like that. The less attention I drew when I worked, the better. Most mercs knew I was good at my job, but I wasn't very impressive. I didn't put on a show. Some of them had problems with me, most didn't. Today was different. Today I needed to be less Kate Daniels and more Pack Consort. I needed to knock them off balance, so they wouldn't question why I showed up there and told them what to do.

I marched into the bathroom, where Curran was brushing his teeth. His blond eyebrows crept up. "That's your Council meeting outfit from now on."

I laughed. "Cloak or no cloak?"

"Definitely cloak," he said.

I tried the cloak on in front of the mirror.

Curran came up behind me and nuzzled my neck.

"Is that your gun or are you just happy to see me?"

"Mhm, a challenge." He nipped the skin on the back of my neck, sending electric aftershocks down through me. Some men got excited by white lace and a translucent negligee. My love muffin got excited by a woman dressed to murder. There was probably something deeply twisted about that. Lucky for me, negligees were never my thing.

He kissed me again. "You're finally getting the hang of this whole badass thing."

"I was always badass."

"No, you thought you were badass and talked a lot of crap." He wrapped his arms around me.

Aha. "Let me go."

"You have time." He kissed my neck again. Every nerve in my body came to attention.

"No, I don't. I have people waiting." I pulled free from him and kissed him back. He pulled me close, locking me within his arms. *Mhm, Curran.* I really didn't want to leave.

"Come on."

"No. Have to go."

"It won't take long."

"Who would that be fun for, exactly? Your seducing techniques need work." I untangled myself and escaped, before he thought of something else to say to change my mind.

It took me ten minutes to stop by the medical ward.

Roderick's collar has faded to lemon yellow. The skin around it had turned bright red, inflamed. It hurt just to look at it. I crouched by him. "How are you doing?"

"I'm okay, thank you."

"Does it hurt to eat?"

"A little," he said.

"I'm going to see someone today to figure out how to take that thing off."

He just looked at me with his big eyes. Deep down, he must've been scared. His sister had died. His parents were gone. But he held it all inside and he wasn't about to let me in.

Before I left, Doolittle drew me aside. His face was bleak. "You must hurry."

"I'll do my best," I told him.

When I walked into the morning light, ten Pack vehicles waited for me. The crews of the vehicles stood in front of them wearing identical gray. Jim stood to the side, surveying the troops. I approached him.

"Satisfied, Consort?"

"How long are you going to be pissed off?" I asked him. We both kept our voices low.

He stared straight ahead.

"Jim, we had a verbal disagreement. I was an ass, but you withheld information. The way you're acting, you'd think I got some guys to jump you and work you over until you woke up with bites on your legs and bruises all over your body."

"It's different now, because we're both Pack. I've told you I was sorry about that. Are you going to keep dragging it out every time?"

"It was a shitty thing to do."

He locked his teeth, making his jaw muscles bulge.

I sighed and started toward the cars. "Suit yourself."

"I always do," he called out.

I turned around and flipped him off.

He glared at me.

I kept walking.

"Kate!" he called out.

I turned.

"Eduardo is your second. You need to talk to him. He wants you to practice something."

I nodded.

"Kate!"

I turned around.

Jim approached me. "Do you need me to watch your back for this Guild thing?"

"I got it. Thanks," I said.

"Anytime."

I went in search of Eduardo. Jim was an ornery bastard, but

he did have my back. At least he wasn't mad anymore. I would probably have to make a peace offering all the same. The werejaguars were difficult creatures.

I'd have to get Dali to help me pick a gift. That way there would be no misunderstandings.

The Mercenary Guild made its headquarters in a converted Sheraton Hotel on the edge of Buckhead. In another life the hotel, built as a hollow tower, had a solid glass front, complete with a rotating glass door. Now massive steel gates marked the entrance. As our procession rolled up to the hotel, I could see a few mercs milling about and smoking. Most of the Guild personnel were probably inside already. Perfect.

Next to me, Eduardo leaned forward in the Jeep's driver seat. A werebuffalo from Clan Heavy, he was over six feet tall and layered with thick muscle. His hair fell down his back in a black mane. His square chin and deep-set eyes said that he would rather die than back down. That impression was one hundred percent correct. I had a problem with a part of his plan and argued with him about it until I turned blue in the face, but he wouldn't budge, which was probably why Jim had assigned him to be my second for this venture.

"Wait until we line up before you go in, Consort," he murmured.

"Kate." We'd been on a first-name basis for a while now.

"Not today, Consort."

The ten Jeeps turned in unison, parking next to each other in front of the building. The mercs at the entrance forgot to suck at their cigarettes and stared.

The car doors opened. The shapeshifters stepped out, forming two lines with a military precision, their faces solemn. I glanced at Eduardo.

"Not yet," he said.

The shapeshifters marched into the Sheraton, looking like they would chew through anybody dumb enough to stand in their way.

"I'm going to get out and go ahead. Derek will open your door. When you exit, keep walking, like you own the place," Eduardo said. "We've got your back."

"Watch it, bison," Jezebel growled from the backseat. She was one of the two bouda advisors Aunt B, the alpha of the werehyenas, had attached to me. "You talk to her like she's a child."

I held up my hand. "It's okay. I got it."

"No worries," Eduardo said. "You'll do fine."

There were few things I hated more than being the center of attention. Especially if the crowd was large.

Eduardo stepped outside. The passenger door behind me opened and Jezebel and Derek got out. Jezebel was six feet tall, moved like a predator, and had enough hard muscle on her to make me think twice about trying to take her on. Derek was leaner and younger, but his face and bearing made an instant impression.

Derek opened the door. "My lady."

The arrogant, self-assured face of my aunt flashed before me. I would be Erra for today.

Eduardo stomped toward the Sheraton like a mountain with a "make my day" face.

I stepped out and marched on the Guild, imagining there was an army at my back.

Eduardo cleared the iron gates, sucked in a lungful of air, and roared. "Make way for the Consort!"

Oh boy.

Eduardo stood to the side. I strode through the gates and the lobby. Eduardo fell in behind me.

Before the Shift, the hotel was a many-star establishment, complete with an on-the-premises restaurant, a coffee shop, and a happy hour area raised on a three-foot platform. Mercs filled the main floor now. The twin lines of shapeshifters had sliced through the crowd, forming an empty corridor leading toward the platform. They stood like statues, hands behind their backs, feet together. A lone table waited for me. Mark sat on the left, his face pale. On the right Bob Carver and Ivera gawked at me with owl eyes.

I walked to the platform with my head held high, my cloak flaring. The entirety of the Guild focused on me. *Super.*

At the platform Eduardo sped up, drawing even with me. He took a knee, locked his left fist on his right wrist, and offered me the makeshift step.

Do not fall, do not fall, do not fall . . .

Without breaking my stride, I stepped onto his arms and then onto the platform.

We'd practiced it at least two dozen times before we had left for the Guild.

The three shapeshifters—Derek, Eduardo, and Jezebel—turned, their backs to the platform, and glowered at the crowd. Derek carried a large wooden box. The two lines of shapeshifters stepped to the left as one, snapping into a wider stance.

Someone gasped.

Showtime.

"I speak for the Pack," I said, putting all my power into my voice. "We hold twenty percent of the Guild. The admin group holds forty. The veterans hold another forty."

You could hear a pin drop.

"You've had months to choose a leader. You have failed and asked the Pack to break this deadlock. This is my proposal to the Guild. Listen well, because there won't be another."

They were listening. *Thank you, Universe, for small favors.*

"Solomon Red envisioned this Guild as a place for independent men and women to earn their living in the way they see fit. We must continue the course he plotted for us."

It was bullshit. Solomon Red didn't have that grand of a vision, but Curran had suggested it, so I plowed on ahead.

"Point One. The Guild will appoint a chief administrative officer to oversee day-to-day operations and the financial security of the Guild. I nominate Mark for this post. Point Two. The Guild will appoint a chief personnel officer to protect the interests of its members, oversee the zoning of scores, and the assignment of gigs. I nominate Bob Carver for this post. Point Three, the Guild will create the post of Pack liaison officer, who will represent the Pack's interests in the Guild as its third largest shareholder. I will be taking over this post. Together the chief administrative officer, chief personnel officer, and Pack liaison officer will form the Guild Committee, which will meet on the fifteenth of every month. All matters of policy concerning the Guild will be resolved by vote of the committee members."

I looked down. The shapeshifter at the end of the left line stepped forward and unfolded a small table. The shapeshifter from the end of the right line placed a tall stack of index cards and three pens on the table. Derek stepped forward and put his wooden box in the center of the table.

"The Guild will now vote," I announced. "Each of you will write your merc ID on the card, add one word: YES or NO, and drop it into this box. I give you this last chance to save the Guild and your jobs. Don't blow it."

Two hours later, two hundred and forty-six mercs voted yes, thirty-two voted no, and sixty-one dropped blank cards with their IDs into the box, abstaining. I made a show of congratulating Bob and Mark and got the hell out of there.

CHAPTER 9

✦

I went to see Immokalee, a Cherokee medicine woman, after leaving the Guild. She spent half an hour making supplies for me and another half an hour trying to convince me that going to see the draugr was a Bad Idea. I knew it was a Bad Idea. I just didn't see any way around it.

I got to the Cutting Edge office just after noon. The Dude and a cart containing one very sedated deer waited for me in the parking lot. A female shapeshifter I didn't know sat on the cart with a sour expression on her face. It took me only a moment to figure out why. Next to the cart, hiding in the shade, crouched a vampire. It was thin, wiry, and covered in purple sunblock from head to toe, as if some giant bubble of grape bubblegum had exploded over it.

Jim had done it. I felt like jumping up and down. Instead I gave the vamp my flat stare.

"There are more inside," the female shapeshifter informed me.

I stepped into the office. Curran sat at my desk, drinking a Corona from my fridge. In front of him, four vampires sat in a neat row in the middle of the floor. Two matched the purple delight outside, one was Grinch green, and the last one blazed with orange.

"I get the sunblock," I said. "But why do you have to paint them like Skittles?"

The orange vamp unhinged its jaws. "The bright color helps to make sure they're completely covered," an unfamiliar female voice explained. "It's easy to miss a spot. When they're young, they have a lot of wrinkles."

Ugh. "What is the meaning of this?"

"Kate," the green vamp spoke with Ghastek's voice, "it has come to my attention that you are planning to see a creature in the

Viking territory with the purpose of finding a means to remove
the necklace from the child. An undead creature. That explicitly
violates the terms of our agreement to resolve this matter jointly."

I looked at Curran. He shrugged.

"And how did you know this?" I asked.

"I have my methods."

How in the world had Jim pulled this off? I'd have to buy
him all the clipboards in the world.

"Ghastek, this is not a pleasure trip," Curran said.

"You can't go," I added.

"Why ever not?"

"Because this undead will murder your vampire hit squad
and I have no desire to get that bill," Curran said. "Do yourself
a favor. Sit this one out."

Wow. He went there.

The vamp's red eyes bulged, struggling to mirror Ghastek's
expression.

"Kate, perhaps you need to explain to your significant
other that he is in no position to give me orders. Last time I
checked, his title was Beast Lord, which is a gentle euphe-
mism for a man who strips naked at night and runs around
through the woods hunting small woodland creatures. I'm a
premier Master of the Dead. I will go where I please."

Once again I rode The Dude. Curran chose to drive the cart.
We traveled side by side. Ghastek took point, while three of
his journeymen flanked us. The fourth, the orange vampire,
trotted next to me. It was piloted by Ghastek's top journeywoman. Her name was Tracy and as navigators went, she
wasn't too bad.

Ghastek's vampire reached Gunnar's fork, marked by an
old birch. Predictably, Gunnar lumbered out. "Come to see
Ragnvald again?"

"Going to the glade." I nodded at the cart. The deer's moist
dark eyes stared at the Viking.

Gunnar's spine went rigid. "To see *him*?"

I nodded.

"Don't go," he said.

"I have to."

He shook his head and stepped aside. "It's been nice knowing you."

I touched the reins and our small procession rolled on.

Ghastek dropped back, drawing even with The Dude.
"Why the secrecy?"

"The Vikings don't like to say Håkon's name. The glade
isn't that far from here and he might hear."

"What is he?"

He and Curran had that in common. Wave a secret in front
of them and they would foam at the mouth trying to learn it.
"He's a draugr."

The vamp hopped on the cart and peered at me, its eyes only
a couple of inches from my face. "A draugr? A mythical Norse
undead that's supposed to guard the treasure of its grave?"

"Get off my cart," Curran growled.

The undead hopped down. The vampire's grotesque face
twisted into an odd expression: the corners of its cavernous
mouth pinched up, while its lips gaped open, displaying its
fangs. It stared at me with blood-red eyes and bopped its head
forward and back a few times.

"What are you doing?"

"I'm laughing at you."

Kicking the vampire in the face with my foot would be
counterproductive at this point.

"When I was a journeyman, I spent eighteen months in
Norway, looking for draugar. I've camped in cemeteries in sub-
zero temperatures, I've scoured fjords, I've dived into sea caves
in freezing water. It was the worst year and a half of my life. In
those eighteen months I didn't find any credible evidence of the
existence of draugar. Trust me when I say this: they don't exist.
Hence, my use of the word 'mythical.' As in, 'not real.'"

I briefly contemplated punching the vampire in the nose. It
wouldn't hurt Ghastek any, but it would be immensely satisfying. "This draugr exists. Plenty of people have met him."

"Oh, I have no doubt that they have met something, but it
wasn't a draugr. Don't you see the signs? The mysterious glade,
the path to which is guarded by a giant. The legendary undead
with magical powers, who you can only meet once, and those
who disobey that rule die a gruesome death." The vampire
waved his front limbs, fingers spread. "Woo-ooo. Frightening."

"Do you have a point?"

"Those bearded, horn-helmeted bandits are conning you, Kate."

"You've got to be kidding me."

"There's no need to feel bad about this. You're a capable fighter, proficient with a blade, and you have intelligence and tenacity, but you don't work with the undead. You have very little familiarity with the basic principles of necromancy, beyond its most practical applications. You lack the tools to recognize the hoax."

The urge to grab the mind of the nearest vampire and use it to beat Ghastek's vamp to a bloody pulp was overwhelming. Perhaps that was why Voron had insisted on steering me away from necromancy. He'd known there would be times that the temptation to show off would be too much.

"No worries. It's a forgivable mistake," Ghastek said. "However, it'll cost us a day and the use of five vampires."

"Humor me."

"Oh, I intend to. I've had a stressful day and breaking this farce open will prove a wonderful way to vent the pressure."

The vampire sauntered off.

"He doesn't like to be wrong," Tracy's vamp said. I caught a hint of humor in her voice.

I couldn't care less if he liked it. As long as his vampires stood between me and the draugr, it would buy me a couple of extra seconds to get away.

The old road led deeper and deeper into the forest. The trees grew taller and thicker, their long limbs thrusting at each other, as if trying to push their neighbors out of the way. Mist swirled between the trunks, first an ethereal haze shimmering along the ground, then a thicker blue fog that hugged the road, lying in wait. It swallowed the sounds: the hoofbeats of the horses, the creaking of the cart, and the occasional sigh from the deer in the back. All seemed muted.

Ahead a stone arch rose above the path, gray slabs of rocks tinted with moss. I halted The Dude. The cart rocked to a stop.

"There's a path leading north just past the arch. We go on foot from here." I hopped off the cart. "I need one of you to carry the deer."

A purple bloodsucker crawled up on the cart. Sickle claws sliced at the rope securing the animal, and the vampire pulled the deer off and slung it over its shoulder.

"Which way will you be coming on the way back?" Curran asked.

"The glade is northeast from here." I pointed to a tall oak to the left.

Curran pulled me close.

Ghastek's vampire rolled his eyes.

"Remember the plan?" Curran said in my ear.

"Get in, get the information, and run like hell out of there."

"See you in a few hours."

I brushed his lips with mine. "See you."

I grabbed my backpack and headed up the path.

The mist grew thicker. Moisture hung in the air, tinted with the odor of rotting vegetation and fresh soil. Somewhere in the distance a bird screamed. No movement troubled the still woods. No squirrels chattered in the canopy, no small game scurried away at our approach. Nothing stirred except for the vampires gliding alongside the path, their emaciated shapes flashing between the trees.

The path veered right and opened into a small glade. Tall pines framed it, the enormous dark trunks scratching at the sky. A carpet of dark pines needles sheathed the ground. Here and there rocks thrust from the forest floor.

"Put the deer right there." I pointed to the center of the glade. The vampire unloaded the deer and hopped aside.

"I suppose we wait until the magic returns?" Ghastek inquired.

"You got it." I sat on a fallen pine.

The vampire's shoulders rose up and down. Ghastek must've sighed. "I suppose we might as well treat this seriously." The vampire raised his left forelimb. A long yellow claw pointed at a tall birch on the left. "Observation Post there." A claw moved to the right to a pine on the other side of the glade. "Another OP there. Give me a perimeter assessment."

Two purple vampires scattered, took a running start, and scrambled up the indicated trees. The third dashed into the bushes. Only Ghastek and Tracy remained. His vampire sat on my right, her vampire sat on my left. Peachy.

A minute passed. Another.

Ghastek's vamp lay down. "If half of the things said about draugar were true, it would revolutionize necromantic science. According to legend, they're the spirits of warriors who rise from the grave to guard their buried possessions. They see the future, they control the elements, they shapeshift into animals. They turn into smoke and become giants."

"Not at the same time," I told him.

"What?"

"You said they turn into smoke and become giants. Not at the same time. They're solid in giant form."

"You're still clinging to this fallacy?"

I leaned forward. "What would you have done if you had found a draugr in Norway, Ghastek?"

"I'd have tried to apprehend it, of course."

"Suppose you live in a small village in Norway and you know a draugr is nearby. You bring him live game once in a while and you hope to God he leaves you the hell alone. Now some geeky hotshot foreigner shows up on your doorstep and explains to you how he's going to go annoy this terrible creature for the sake of 'necromantic science.' You try to explain to him that it's not a good idea, but he treats you as if you're an idiot child."

"I never treat people like infantile idiots," Ghastek said.

I looked at him.

Tracy cleared her throat carefully.

"Go on," he said.

"Would you take this foreigner to this undead monster and risk pissing it off, or would you steer him as far away from the draugr as possible and hope he'll go away eventually?"

"That's a sound theory, with one exception. I'm not that gullible."

Fine. "Bet me."

The vampire stared at me. "I'm sorry?"

"Bet me. If the draugr is a hoax, I'll owe you a favor."

"And if he's real?"

"Then you will bring me a quart of vampire blood."

"And why would you need vampire blood, Kate?"

Because I needed it to experiment with making armor out of it, that's why. "I want to calibrate the lot of new m-scanners the Pack bought." He didn't need to know I was practicing to see how much of Roland's talent had passed to me.

A hint of suspicion slid into Ghastek's voice. "And you need a quart of blood for that?"

"Yep."

The bloodsucker became utterly still as Ghastek mulled it over.

"If I win this silly game, you will tell me why Rowena came to see you after the Keepers affair."

Sucker. "Deal."

"Excellent." He put emphasis on the "x" and the word came out slightly sibilant.

"You need a fluffy white cat. That way you can stroke it when you say things like that."

Tracy's vamp made a small noise that might have been a clearing of a throat or a choked-up laugh.

A purple vampire popped out of the bushes, dragging something behind it. The bloodsucker strained, tight muscle flexing across its back, and heaved what looked like a large collapsed leather tent into the open.

"We found human bones," the vampire reported.

"In the ravine?" I asked.

"Yes, ma'am."

I knew about the spot. Immokalee had described it to me this morning, trying to scare me into not going. A few dozen yards to the north, the ground dropped sharply into a narrow fissure lined with human skeletons. Some still held their weapons. When a draugr sucked the flesh off your bones, he did it quick, like jerking a shirt off a body.

"We also found this." The vampire indicated the tent.

Ghastek's vampire raised the top edge, exposing a dark opening, and vanished into it. The leather shifted, mirroring the vampire's movement inside it. The bloodsucker emerged into the clear air. "The design is ill-conceived. It is clearly too large for one person, but it has no structure or method of remaining upright as a tent, and besides, this side is completely open to the elements. Perhaps it's some sort of communal sleeping bag?"

"It's not a sleeping bag," I told him.

"Would you care to enlighten me?" Ghastek said.

"Look at it from above."

The purple vampire leaped onto the nearest tree and scurried up into the branches. A long moment passed and then it dropped on the ground next to me without a word.

"What is it?" Tracy asked.

The vampire's face was unreadable, like a blank wall. "It's a glove."

The wind stirred the tree branches. The world blinked, as the tech vanished, crushed under the onslaught of a magic wave. Cold froze the glade. The other vampire burst from the bushes and came to rest by Tracy.

In the distance something wailed in an inhuman voice, its forlorn cry rising high above the treetops.

Gloom claimed the clearing. It came slowly, like molasses, from the dark spaces deep between the roots, washing over trees, leaching color from the greenery, drenching it in shadows, until the shrubs and foliage turned dark, almost gray. Behind the gloom, mist rose in thin wisps, tinted with an eerie bluish glow.

A crow cried overhead, its shrill caw impossibly distant.

"They are putting on quite a show," Ghastek said.

"Yep." I nodded. "Going all out. Viking special effects are out of this world."

I pulled a canvas bundle out of my backpack and untied the cord securing it. Four sharpened sticks lay inside, each three feet long. I picked up a rock and hammered the first of the sticks into the ground at the mouth of the path. That was the way I'd run when it came time to get the hell out of there.

I moved along the edge of the clearing, sinking the sticks in at regular intervals.

"What is the purpose of this?" Ghastek asked.

"Protection."

"Have I given you a reason to doubt my competence, Kate?"

"No." I pulled a black box out of my backpack, took a black cloth out of it, and unfolded the cloth to extract an old pipe. The medicine woman had already packed it with tobacco.

"What is this?"

"A pipe." I struck a match, puffed to get the pipe going, and got a mouthful of smoke for my trouble. The pungent tobacco scraped the inside of my throat. I coughed and started to circle the clearing, blowing smoke as I went.

"What sort of magic is this?" one of the journeymen asked.

"Cherokee. Very old." If life was perfect, I'd have Immokalee herself do the ritual. It took years of training for the medicine woman to reach her power, but none of the Cherokees would go near the draugr. Unlike me, they had common sense. All the chants over the sticks and the pipe had been said already. All I had to do was follow the ritual and hope Immokalee's magic was potent enough to work when an incompetent like me activated it.

I finished the circle, put the pipe away, and sat back on the log.

A pair of tiny eyes ignited by the roots of an oak to the left. No iris was visible—the entire eye was an almond-shaped slit of pale yellow glow.

"Left," Tracy said. Her voice was perfectly calm.

"I see it," Ghastek said.

Another pair sparked to the right, about a foot off the ground. Then another, and another. All around us the eyes fluoresced, clustered around tree trunks, staring from the underbrush, peering from behind rocks.

"What are they?" Tracy asked.

"*Uldra*," Ghastek said. "They're nature spirits from Lapland. They live mostly underground. I wouldn't provoke them. Stay in the clearing."

The eyes stared at us, unblinking.

A blast of icy cold ripped through the clearing. The *uldra* vanished as one. On the ground, the deer moaned, coming up out of its drugged state.

Here we go.

I reached into my backpack and pulled out a small leather satchel, a small plastic bear full of honey, and a canteen. No turning back now. I got up off the log and walked over to the center of the glade where a large stone waited. Ghastek's and Tracy's vampires trailed me.

I brushed the leaves from the stone. The inside of the rock had been hollowed out into a stone basin, large enough to hold about three gallons of liquid.

"When the draugr appears, don't talk to him," I said. "The longer we talk, the more time he has to lock onto our scent. We'll have to fight to get clear anyway. No need to make things harder."

No response.

"Ghastek? Do you understand me?"

"Of course," he said.

"The Cherokee have set protective wards on the mountain. If we make it to the pillars by the road, we're safe."

"You said this before," Ghastek informed me.

"I'm just reminding you." This wouldn't go well.

I set the canteen on the ground and loosened the drawstring cord securing the pouch. It opened into a square of leather in the palm of my hand. Inside lay six rune stones chiseled from bone, and a handful of beat-up silver coins: two etched with a sword and hammer and four with the Viking raven.

I cast the runes into the basin. They clicked, rolling from the stone sides. It took me a second to unscrew the canteen. Ale splashed on the runes, drenching the bone in liquid amber. The scent of malted barley and juniper wafted up. The bluish mist snapped at it like a striking snake.

"Patience, Håkon. Patience."

I poured in the rest of the ale, emptied the honey into the basin, and stirred it with a branch. Magic spread from the runes into the honey and ale. I reached in and pulled the runes out, all except two: the rune of enemy binding and *Þjófastafur*, the rune that prevented theft.

The mist hovered by me.

I took a deep breath, grabbed the deer by the head, and heaved it onto the basin. Moist brown eyes looked at me.

"I'm so sorry."

I pulled a throwing knife out and slit the animal's throat in a single quick swipe. Blood gushed into the basin, hot and red. The deer thrashed, but I held its head until the blood flow stopped. The basin was a third of the way full. I stepped back and hefted the coins in my hand. They jingled together, sparking with magic.

"I call you out, Håkon. Come from your grave. Come taste the blood ale."

Magic pulsed through the glade, ice cold and shockingly powerful. It pierced my skin, ripping its way all the way into my bones. I recoiled. Panic crested inside me like a huge black wave. Every instinct I had screamed, "Run! Run as fast as you can."

I clenched my teeth.

The air reeked of fetid, decaying flesh. It left a sickeningly sweet patina on my tongue.

The mist congealed with an eerie moan and a creature stepped forth to the basin. A thick cloak of half-rotten fur hung off his shoulders, shielding the chain mail that covered him from elbow to the knee. The fur had thinned to long feathery strands, smeared with dirt. Long colorless hair spilled from his head in a tangled mess. His skin was blue, as if he had an intense case of argyria.

The draugr dropped by the basin, dipped his head, and lapped the blood like a dog. Death had sucked all softness from his flesh. His face was a leathery mask of wrinkles, his nose was a misshapen nub, and his lips had dried to nothing, baring a mouth full of long vampiric teeth. His eyes were awful: pale green, and completely solid, as if made of frosted glass. No iris, no pupil, nothing. Just two dead eyes behind an opaque green membrane.

I gave him a couple of seconds with the blood and squeezed the runes. They warmed my skin, forging a link to the two left in the blood ale. "That's plenty."

The undead raised his head. Blood dripped from his chin. A voice came, hoarse, like the creaking of trees in the wood. "Who are you, meat?"

Not good. "I've come to trade. Fair trade: fresh meat for an answer."

The draugr dipped its head toward the blood. Magic pulsed from the runes. The creature let out a long sound halfway between a sigh and a growl.

Ghastek's vampire moved to stand next to me.

The undead swiveled to the bloodsucker. "You bring me dead meat?"

"No. Dead meat guards me. Dead meat has no power over the ale. If you want to talk to dead meat, that's between you and it."

The draugr rose above the basin, shoulders hunched over. "Dead meat speaks?"

Ghastek shifted the vampire another step.

"I wouldn't," I told him.

The vamp halted. "Who are you?"

Would it kill him not to screw with my thing?

The draugr leaned on the stone. "I'm Håkon, son of Eivind. My father was a jarl and his father before him was one. The blood ale calls to me. Who are you, meat, that you interrupt my feeding?"

"I'm Ghastek Sedlak, Master of the Dead."

The draugr's mouth gaped wider. The creature rocked back and forth. "Dróttinn of the dead. I am dead. Do you style yourself my master too, little dead meat?"

Full stop. "Don't answer that. Your ale is getting cold, Håkon. Have a taste."

The runes in my hand cooled. The undead took a step toward me, then turned, as if drawn by a magnet, dropped on his knees and drank deeply, sucking up the blood in long greedy swallows.

"How did you come to be here?" Ghastek asked.

Damn it all to hell.

The draugr turned its unblinking eyes to the vampire and raised his head from the blood for a moment. "We came for gold."

"All the way from Norseland?"

The draugr shook its head and drank.

"Kate," Ghastek said. "Make him talk. Please."

How do I get myself into these things? I gripped the runes. The draugr ducked down, trying to lick the blood, got within two inches of the red surface and stopped.

"From Vinland. The north *skrælingar* brought us gold to trade for weapons. They told us they bartered with the southern tribes for it. They said the southern *skrælingar* were soft. They were farmers, they said. Our seers had scryed the source of the gold, in the hills, not far from the coast. We took two ships and went looking for it."

"Did you find the gold?" Ghastek asked.

The draugr reared back, his teeth on display. "We found woods, and giant birds, and *skrælingar* magic. We were retreating when a *skræling* arrow found me."

"Is that why you rose? To punish the native tribe?" Ghastek asked.

He just wouldn't stop talking.

The draugr's clawed hands scratched the stone of the basin. Magic snapped from him, flaring like a foul banner. The hair on the back of my neck rose.

"To punish them? No. I rose to punish the ingrate dogs who threw me into a hole in the ground like a common thrall. Not one of them bothered to even place a stone to mark my grave. I killed some of them and ate their flesh, but a few still lived. I've searched for them, but I can't find them."

"You can't find them, because they've been dead for a thousand years," I told him. Damn it. Now Ghastek had me doing it.

The wrinkled mask of the draugr's face twisted in derision. "So you say."

Ghastek's vamp leaned forward. "If you're so powerful, why don't you just leave?"

"He can't. The Cherokee wards are locking him in. No more questions."

"In that case—"

I brought my fist down on the vamp's bald head. *God, that felt good.*

The vamp whipped around, glaring at me in outrage.

"Shut up," I told him and turned to the draugr. "Blood ale, undead. If you want any more, you will grant me my boon."

The draugr rose, slowly. His fur mantle closed about him. Cold spread from him. My breath turned into a wisp of vapor.

"Ask."

"How do I find Ivar the Dwarf?"

"He lives in a hidden valley," the draugr said. "Travel to Highlands and find Cliffside Lake. At the north edge of the lake, you will see a trail leading you to the mountain scarred by lightning. Make the offering of gold, silver, and iron, and the dwarf will permit you to enter."

I released the runes and backed away. "The blood ale is yours."

"It's grown cold."

I kept backing up.

Magic accreted around the draugr like a second cloak. "I do not want it. I want my blood hot."

Mayday, mayday. "That's not the deal we made."

I passed the stick guarding the road.

"I make deals and I break them."

The wooden stick between us shivered in the ground.

"There is no escape, meat."

The cocoon of the draugr's magic burst with icy fury, snapping at me with dark fingers. The stick shot from the ground and pierced the draugr's head.

I ran.

Behind me a wail of pure fury tore through the forest and Ghastek's voice barked, "Secure the creature!"

Magic exploded with mind-numbing intensity. My eyes watered. The breath in my lungs turned into a clump of ice. The path veered right. As I took the turn at a breakneck speed, I saw the draugr, towering over the trees, a mantle of dark magic streaming from his shoulders as he ripped a vampire in half with his colossal hands.

"I have your scent," the giant roared. "You won't escape!"

The translucent flood of magic crested the edge of the glade and rolled down, chasing me.

The forest turned into a blurry smudge of green. I flew, jumping over the roots. Weeds slapped me.

The harsh stench of rot filled my mouth. Around me the trees groaned, as if pulled upright by an invisible hand. My throat burned.

I could almost see the road through the shrubs.

The path turned left and I leaped straight down, praying the old injury to my left knee wouldn't flare up. The brush snapped under my weight and I tore down the slope, squeezing every last drop of speed out of my body.

A deep roar shook the ground.

No way to dodge, no direction to take but down.

A shadow fell over me. I threw myself forward. I rolled once, twice, catching a glimpse of a colossal clawed hand raking the forest behind me, flipped to my feet, and burst onto the road.

The pillar loomed to my right. I sprinted to it.

The air whistled. Something large crashed on the road ahead of me, bounced, and sprung to its feet. Ghastek's vampire. Deep gashes scoured its flanks, oozing thick undead blood onto the sunblock. It looked like it had gone through a shredder.

The trees creaked behind me. The draugr had made it onto the road.

I ran like I'd never run before in my life.

The vampire froze for a fraction of an instant and galloped to the pillars.

My feet barely touched the ground. In my head my bad leg snapped like a toothpick.

The draugr's magic whipped at me, slashing at my back. I went airborne, rolled, and hit the ground hard. My head swam. I rolled to my feet.

Taller than the trees, the enormous undead towered above me, his eyes spilling icy green mist. Ragged chain mail hung from his torso. Colossal iron pauldrons guarded his shoulders. Huge chunks of his flesh were missing, and bone glared through the holes.

Holy shit.

The draugr raised a foot the size of a car. His magic swirled about him in a stormy cloud.

Curran in his warrior form shot out of the treetop, flying through the air like a gray blur.

I stood still, presenting a clear target for Håkon.

The draugr stomped forward.

Curran smashed into the back of the undead's neck. Bone crunched. The draugr spun, and I saw Curran ripping into the space between the neck vertebrae with his claws. Undead gristle flew.

The draugr roared, trying to swat at the Beast Lord. His head began to droop.

Two ribbons of green magic snapped backward from the draugr, aiming for Curran.

Oh no, you don't. I opened my mouth and barked a power word.

"Ossanda." Kneel, you undead sonovabitch.

The magic burst from me. It felt like someone had sunk claws into my stomach and tore out the muscle and my innards. The world went black for a tiny moment. I'd sunk a lot of magic into it.

The horrible creak of bone snapping rolled through the air. The draugr's bony knees hit the road. The forest quaked.

I took a running start and sprinted at him.

The dazed undead raised its huge hands, trying to grab me. I veered left, avoiding the gnarled bone fingers, and scrambled up the giant's body, climbing the chain mail.

Above me, Curran snarled.

The draugr slapped his chest, missing me by a couple of inches.

I pulled myself onto his shoulder and ran down the iron plate to his neck. Curran was ripping into the gristle. The undead flesh tore under his claws, and snapped back, regenerating.

I pulled Slayer and chopped at the gap he'd made. My saber smoked from the contact with undead flesh. The gap widened.

Curran grasped the edge of the two vertebrae and forced them apart. I cut into the cleft, slicing through the connective tissue.

Cut. Cut. Cut.

Cartilage crunched.

Magic stung me, weaving about me in green strands.

"Wait!" Curran growled.

I stopped my sword in midstrike. Curran jumped into the gap, his clawed feet on the edge of one vertebra, his hands on the other. He strained, pushing them apart. Steel-hard muscle bulged on his frame, shaking with effort.

The draugr howled.

Curran snarled, a vicious, short sound born of strain.

With a sickening screech, the draugr's head fell and rolled off his body. The colossal torso toppled. I jumped and landed on the road, my sword in my hand. Curran dropped down next to me.

We ran. We sprinted to the pillars.

Behind us an eerie, unnatural noise announced the draugr reassembling himself.

The green vampire that had fallen on the road picked itself up and chased after us.

We were almost to the pillars.

A shadow fell over us.

Curran spun. His head melted, reshaping into a lion's head. The Beast Lord roared.

The sound was like thunder. Deep, primeval, arresting, it froze the marrow in my bones. My instincts screamed and tried to drop me to the ground in a small quivering ball.

The draugr screeched to a halt.

We dashed forward.

The pillars flashed by our sides. I ran to a stop and turned around, my ribs hurting.

The undead giant strode toward us.

The pillars flashed with deep amber.

The draugr smashed into an invisible wall. Streaks of

orange lightning clutched at his flesh. A deafening wail slapped my ears.

"I will kill you! I will gnaw the flesh off your bones! I will pick my teeth with your femurs!"

I vomited onto the ground.

Next to me Curran patted my back, his breath coming in ragged gasps.

The vampire next to me collapsed. The gashes on its body knitted together. A new pale skin slid over the cuts and began to smoke.

"You owe me vampire blood," I told him.

"Yes, yes." Ghastek sounded sour. "Do hand me that canvas before he burns to death."

I jerked the canvas off the cart and held it up. "I just want to hear you say it."

The vamp squirmed.

I shook the canvas a bit.

"Fine. The draugar do exist."

"And I was right."

"You were right. The canvas, Kate."

I draped it over the vampire and looked at Curran. "Did you hear that?"

"I heard that." Together we picked up the vampire and heaved the bloodsucker into the cart. "I still don't believe it, but I heard it."

Two vampires dashed past the raging draugr, one purple, one orange. The remains of Ghastek's super-squad.

"Over here," I waved. "Run to safety!"

"Could the two of you gloat a little more?" Ghastek said.

"Oh I could," I said. "I definitely could."

The vampire pulled the canvas back and peeked out, staring in the direction of the glade. "Double or nothing."

"What?"

"Double or nothing, Kate. I can take him."

Ghastek was a gambler. *Knock me over with a feather.* I sat on the cart. The draugr would rip them to pieces in ten minutes, tops.

"Knock yourself out," Curran told him. "We'll wait right here."

"Don't take too long," I told him. "We have a child to save."

CHAPTER 10

❖

I knew that something was wrong by the look on the face of the werewolf who opened the door to the Pack's safe house. The Pack owned several properties in the city, and after we were done clapping and cheering at the sight of Ghastek's complete and utter failure, Curran and I had made a beeline for the nearest one to wash the undead nastiness off. The magic had fallen and with technology once again reasserting its grip on the world, Curran was eager to trade the cart for a Pack Jeep.

When the male werewolf opened the door, his eyes had that particular look to them that meant some catastrophe had happened.

"What is it?" Curran growled.

The werewolf licked his lips.

"Out with it," Curran said.

"Andrea Nash has been seen in the city, interviewing business owners."

"She is frequently in the city," I said. "And interviewing is her job. She's investigating some murders for the Pack." Which I would look into as soon as we got Roderick out of that damned necklace.

The werewolf took a small step back. "She's doing it in her beastkin shape."

"Come again?"

"She's walking around in her beastkin shape. And some clothes."

All unaffiliated shapeshifters within the Pack's borders were required to present themselves to the Pack within three days. Until now, the Pack had been able to deny all knowledge that Andrea was a shapeshifter, mostly because Curran made a very public point of ignoring it and nobody cared to bring it up.

Well, he couldn't ignore it any longer. Andrea had pretty much made sure of that.

It made no sense. Andrea almost never used her beastkin shape. In fact, she pretended to be human most of the time. Going out in her fur and claws for her would be equivalent to me taking off my clothes and parading through the city naked.

Something had happened. Something really bad.

I looked at Curran. "I guess we'd better go back to the office."

I walked through the office doors carrying a vampire's head smeared in green sunblock. I had picked it up after the draugr had punted it out of the ward zone. It was beginning to smell and needed to be buried in ice ASAP.

Andrea sat at her desk. She was wearing her beastkin shape, a perfect meld of human and hyena. It was a shape that could get her killed. Andrea's father was a hyenawere, an animal who turned into a human. That made her beastkin, and many older shapeshifters would want to murder her on sight.

"Want" being the operative word. Andrea could take care of herself. On top of that, I would help her, and Curran had made it plain that this was a prejudice he would not tolerate. He was waiting outside now in a parking lot a block away. I had asked him to give us a few minutes.

Andrea's feet were on the table. Her T-shirt was torn, her pants were in tatters, and a mess of blood and tissue stained both. She wiggled her clawed toes at me.

"Hey."

"Hey." Andrea raised her hand. There was a bottle in it. She was drinking.

I went into the kitchen, got a ceramic dish from under the sink, and deposited my vampire head inside the fridge. Then I came back, shrugged out of my sword sheath, and sat in the chair.

"What are you drinking?"

"Georgia Peach Iced Tea. Want some?" Andrea shook the bottle at me.

"Sure." I sipped it. FIRE. "What the hell is in this?"

"Vodka, gin, rum, sweet and sour, and peach schnapps. Lots of peach schnapps."

I'd never seen her drink before. "Do you actually get a buzz from this?"

"Sort of. It lasts for about thirty seconds or so and then I need another gulp."

I tried to think. Derek was back at the Keep, but I was pretty sure Ascanio should have reported to the office this morning. "Where is the bane of my existence?"

"In the shower, freshening up."

Damn it all to hell. "Oh God, who did Ascanio screw now?"

"No, no, he's covered in blood."

"Oh good." Wait a minute. "The kid is covered in blood and we're relieved. There is something wrong with us."

"Tell me about it." Andrea eyed me. "Not going to mention my beastkin appearance?"

"I like it. The torn pants and gore-stained T-shirt is a nice touch."

She pointed her foot at me. "I was thinking of painting my claws a nice shade of pink."

Those claws were three inches long. "That would take a lot of nail polish. What about some golden hoops in your ears instead?"

Andrea grinned, baring a row of sharp fangs. "It's a definite possibility."

Okay, you know what, screw this. "What happened?"

"I saw Raphael this morning. I'd called him last night, because Jim put me on some shapeshifter murders and I needed to interview him. I wanted a chance to apologize."

Raphael, you spoiled moron, what the hell did you do?

I took her bottle and drank from it. I needed some alcohol for the next part. It tasted vile. I swallowed it down anyway. "How did it go?"

"He replaced me."

"He what?"

"He found another girl. She is seven feet tall, with breasts the size of honeydew melons, legs that start at her neck, bleached blond hair down to her ass, and her waist is this big around." She touched her claws together. "They are engaged to be engaged."

Of all the stupid, idiotic things . . . "He brought her *here*?"

"She sat in that chair right there." She pointed at a chair. "I'm thinking of burning it."

Andrea loved Raphael the way birds loved the sky, and until a minute ago I would've sworn that he would have run into fire for her. "Did you punch him?"

"Nope." Andrea shook her head. "After he told me that his new sweetheart's best quality is that she isn't me, it didn't seem like it would make any difference."

"Is she a shapeshifter?"

"A human. Not a fighter. Not that bright either." The false cheer evaporated from her voice. "I know what you'll say—it's my own fault."

I wish I knew the right words to say. "Well, you did check out of his life. You checked out of my life for a while."

"Yeah, yeah." Andrea looked away.

Raphael was spoiled. He was handsome, and treasured by both his mother and Clan Bouda in general, but he was never known for being mean or cruel. He was also the male alpha of Clan Bouda. He had to have known exactly what sort of risks he faced by bringing another woman and shoving her at Andrea. He had to have done it to provoke a reaction. The next time we met I'd pound his face into ground beef.

Still . . . I couldn't believe that there was no method to his madness. He'd chased Andrea for months and he'd won her, then lost her. Perhaps this was some sort of stupid attempt to make her chase him.

"Are you going to fight for him?"

Andrea stared at me like I was crazy. "What?"

"Are you going to fight for him, or are you going to roll over on your back and take it?"

"Look who's talking. How long did it take you and Curran to have a conversation after that whole dinner mess? Was it three weeks or more like a month?"

I arched my eyebrow at her. "That's different. That was a misunderstanding."

"Aha."

"He brought his new main squeeze here after you called him with a peace offering. That's a slap in the face."

"You don't have to tell me that. I know." Andrea growled.

"So what are you going to do about it?"

"I haven't decided yet."

I wasn't sure she felt Raphael was worth fighting for. But once, when I was in a really bad place, Andrea had told me that she felt like being with Raphael had healed her. She'd said he was picking up broken pieces of her and putting them back together. Well, all the pieces had fallen again, and Andrea was trying to reassemble herself on her own.

I'd seen Andrea fight. I'd seen her in unguarded moments, taken over by bloodlust and rage. Raphael would have to tread very carefully, because whether she decided that she wanted him or revenge, nothing would stop her.

I tried to pick my words carefully. "Nothing is free. If you want it, you have to fight for it."

"I'm thinking about it," she said. "How did your day go?"

"I got some head. It was vamp, but still."

"That good, huh."

"Yup."

"I have a glass monster corpse for you. It's in the freezer."

I gave her a nice smile. "You shouldn't have."

"It's a bribe for putting up with my psychotic break."

The car motor started up. Curran had gotten tired of waiting.

"That's my ride," I said.

The door swung open, and Curran walked in. I held my breath. Having Andrea and him at each other's throats would be more than I could take.

Andrea rose to her feet.

A show of respect for the Beast Lord. I decided that breathing was a good thing.

Curran nodded to Andrea. I got up too, walked over to him, and kissed him, just in case he was entertaining any violent thoughts. He winked at me.

"Hold on, let me grab the vamp head." I went to the back and got my head.

When I came out, carrying the head in a plastic bag, Andrea and Curran were still in one piece and had been joined by a freshly washed Ascanio.

I waved at Andrea, and Curran and I went to the car. Ascanio tried to linger behind, but Curran looked at him, and the kid decided he'd better follow us.

We got into the car and pulled away.

"And how did your day go?" I asked Ascanio.

He turned to me, a dreamy look on his pretty face. "We killed things. There was blood. Fountains of blood. And then we had barbecue."

Why me?

When we walked through the doors of the Keep, Doolittle was waiting for us. Roderick's necklace had turned the color of white gold. He was having trouble breathing. The next magic wave could be his last.

Ten minutes later we rode out of the Keep in a Pack vehicle. Curran drove. I sat in the passenger seat, holding a bowl of jewelry and bullets for our offering. Doolittle and the boy sat in the back. Roderick whistled with every breath, and Curran drove like a maniac to the north leyline, his hands locked on the wheel, his face a grim mask. We reached the leypoint in record time and he didn't slow down as he drove the Jeep off the ramp into the invisible magic current. The magic clutched the car and dragged it north to the mountains. Whether magic or technology was in ascendance, the leylines always flowed and I was damn grateful for their existence.

The current carried us to Franklin, spitting us out at a remote leypoint, and from there we drove up a winding road to the Highlands. It used to be a ritzy destination, beautiful lakes and waterfalls wrapped in emerald-green forests that spilled from the sheer cliffs. Million-dollar homes, leisure boats, play ranches with pampered horses . . . But the magic had wrecked the infrastructure and the residents quickly learned that the mountains in winter are much less fun without electricity and takeout. Now the homes lay abandoned or taken over by die-hard locals. Little villages sprang up here and there, small remote communities whose residents peered suspiciously at us as we drove by.

Cliffside Lake was beautiful, but we had no time for sight-seeing. Eight hours after we had left the Keep, we stood by a mountain scoured with white lightning whip marks.

I had expected an altar, or some sort of mark to show the right spot, but there was nothing. Just a cliff.

I dumped a bowl full of jewelry and bullets onto the rocks. They scattered, clinking. "Ivar?"

Nothing happened.

Doolittle's face fell.

"Ivar, let us in!"

The mountains were silent. Only Roderick's hoarse breathing broke the quiet.

We should've gotten here sooner. Maybe the offering worked only during a magic wave, but as soon as magic hit, the necklace would snap Roderick's neck.

"Let us in!" I yelled.

No answer.

"Let us in, you fucking sonovabitch." I hit the mountain with the bowl. "Let us in!"

"Kate," Curran said softly. "We're out of time, baby."

Doolittle sat down on a rock and smiled at Roderick, that patient calming smile. "Come sit with me."

The boy walked over and scooted onto the rock.

I sagged against the mountain wall. *It didn't work. All this and it didn't work.*

"It's pretty up here," Roderick said.

It wasn't fair. He was only a boy . . . I buried my face in Curran's shoulder. He wrapped his arms around me.

"Can you hear the birds?" Doolittle asked.

"Yes," Roderick said.

"Very peaceful," Doolittle said.

I felt Curran tense and looked up.

A man walked up the path. Broad and muscular, built like he wrestled bears for a living, he had a wide face, lined with wrinkles and framed with a short dark beard and long brown hair. He wore a pair of soot-stained jeans and a tunic.

His gaze fell on Roderick and the necklace. Thick hairy eyebrows crept up above his pale blue eyes.

"What are you guys doing up here?" he asked.

"We're looking for Ivar," Curran said.

"I'll take you." The man looked at Roderick and held out his hand. "Come, little one."

Roderick hopped off the rock and walked over. The dark-haired man took his hand. Together they walked up the steep mountain path. We followed.

The path turned behind the cliff, and I saw a narrow gap in the mountain, its walls completely sheer, as if someone had sliced through the rock with a colossal sword. We walked into it, stepping over gravel and rocks.

"Where are you folks from?" the man asked.

"Atlanta," I said.

"Big city," he said.

"Yes." None of us mentioned the necklace choking the boy's throat.

Ahead the sun shone through the gap. A moment and we passed through and stepped into the light. A valley lay in front of us, the ground gently sloping to the waters of a narrow lake. A watermill turned and creaked on the far shore. To the right a two-story house sat on the lawn of green grass. A few dozen yards to the side a smithy rose and behind it a garden stretched up the slope, enclosed by a chain-link fence. Further still, pale horses ran in a pasture.

The necklace clicked and fell off Roderick's neck. The dark-haired man caught it and snapped it in half. "I'll take that, then."

Roderick drew a breath. Tiny red dots swelled on his neck, where the necklace had punctured skin.

"No worries," the man said. "It will heal in the next magic wave."

A shaggy gray dog trotted up to us, spat a tennis ball out of his mouth, and pondered Roderick with big eyes.

"That's Ruckus," the man said. "He'd like it if you threw the ball for him."

Roderick picked up the tennis ball, looked at it for a moment, and then tossed it down the slope. The dog took off after it. The boy turned to us.

"Go ahead," Doolittle told him.

Roderick dashed down the slope.

"So you're Ivar," I said.

"I am."

It finally sank in. The necklace was gone. Roderick was safe. My legs gave a little bit and I leaned against the nearest tree.

Ivar studied me. "Oh now, that's not good. Why don't y'all come down to the house? Trisha was making iced tea before I left. It should be about done."

As if in a dream I followed him down to the house. We sat on a covered porch, and Ivar brought a pitcher of tea and some glasses.

"Why make a necklace that would strangle a child?" Curran asked.

"It's a long story." Ivar sighed. "I take it you know what I am?"

"A dvergr," I said.

"That's right." Ivar looked at his hands. They were large, out of proportion to his body. "I work with metal. As long as I can remember, the metal spoke to me. Some things I make are harmless. Plows, horseshoes, nails. Some are not. I have made a blade or two in my time. The thing is, once the blade is out of your hands, you can't control what it's used for. I try."

"Like with Dagfinn?" I guessed.

Ivar nodded. "How is that boy doing?"

"Well," Curran said.

"Good to hear. He had a bit of a temper, that one." Ivar looked out at the river's shore where Roderick and Ruckus chased each other. "Trisha is my second wife. My first one, Lisa, well, she was . . . The best I can figure, she was elfin. No way to know for sure, of course. She showed up on my doorstep one day and stayed. She was beautiful. We had a daughter, but the valley life wasn't for Lisa, so one morning I woke up and she was gone. Left the baby with me. I did my best to raise her. She had hair like gold, my Aurellia. But I must have done a lousy job raising her. There was never any warmth in her, no empathy. I don't know why. She was fully grown when a young man came down to the valley. He said he wanted to apprentice himself to me. To learn about smithing. I don't take apprentices, but the boy had talent, so he and I made a bargain. He would stay with me for a decade."

"Ten years is a long time," I said.

"It's enough to learn how not to do harm," Doolittle said.

Ivar threw him a grateful look. "You understand. You can't teach the craft in ten years. I'm past eighty and I still learn new things every day. But I thought a decade would be long enough to teach him what you should make and what you shouldn't and when. Can't just hand that kind of power to a man and let him loose in the world without guidance. So Colin and I made a bargain. He would wear the collar and stay here in the valley to learn all I could teach him. If he left the boundary of the valley before the time was up, the collar would kill him. He understood that there was no turning back. Once he put on the collar, he had to stay here for ten years."

"Aurellia decided to leave?" Curran asked.

Ivar nodded. "She had no skills. There's a school down in Cashiers, and I tried to take her there, but she quit. Didn't care for it. Didn't care for the metalwork either. Thought it coarse and common. It's my own fault: I had explained money to her and that in the outside world you can't just live off the land and barter the way we do here. So she decided Colin would take care of her. One day I went up in the mountains to the old Cooper mine, and when I came down, they were gone. I had warned Colin that even if he managed to take the collar off, it would try to find him again and he wouldn't be able to resist. The way I figure, Aurellia got it off him somehow and they must've sold it. There was a lot of gold in that collar."

Now things made sense. Colin made the money. She needed him alive to take care of her. Roderick was just incidental.

"Colin doesn't do metal smithing anymore," I told him. "He's an accountant. I don't think he even remembers his time here. They way he acted when he saw the collar, I don't think he knew what it was. He and Aurellia had a daughter. The necklace killed her. That's their son." I pointed down toward the valley where the boy and dog played. "Aurellia put the necklace on him to keep it off Colin."

Ivar's face jerked. "The necklace was never meant to follow the blood. It was only meant to keep Colin here."

Roderick came up the stairs. His face was flushed. "We don't have to go yet, do we?"

I would not take him back to that bitch.

Ivar looked at his grandson. There was a sadness there and

regret. A lot of regret. I could see the resemblance between them now: same dark hair, same serious, somber look in the eyes.

"Do you like it here?" Doolittle asked.

Roderick nodded.

The medmage looked at the dwarf. "Second chances don't come about often."

Ivar's face went slack.

"He's right," Curran said.

Ivar took a deep breath and smiled at Roderick. "Roderick, I'm your grandfather. Would you like to stay here for a while? With me?"

Roderick looked at Doolittle.

"It's your choice," the medmage said. "You can come back with me, if you would like."

Roderick mulled it over.

"I never had a grandfather before," the boy said.

"I never had a grandson before," Ivar answered.

"Can I go swimming?"

"Yes," Ivar said. "Your grandmother will be back from the market soon. We'll have us some lunch and you can go swimming. The water's cold but you might enjoy it. Our kind does."

Roderick smiled. It was a tiny hesitant smile. "I would like that."

Ivar got up and offered the boy his hand. "Would you like to see my smithy?"

Roderick nodded. The two of them walked off the porch together, hand in hand.

The three of us sat on the porch, watched the river, and drank the iced tea.

"What about Aurellia?" I asked.

"She's still married to the DA's brother-in-law," Curran said. "A woman told me it would be a bad idea to do anything about that."

"I wouldn't worry about Aurellia," Doolittle said, watching Ivar and Roderick by the smithy. "I have a feeling she'll get what's coming to her."

EPILOGUE

Atlanta Avery hospital reported an extremely troubling case: a local woman, Aurellia Sunny, has aged forty years overnight. The medmage professionals theorize that accelerated aging occurred due to a gold ring that arrived in the mail and was left on Mrs. Sunny's front porch. The ring has since dissolved into her skin and is impossible to remove. The aging process is continuing and the family has been advised to make the proper arrangements. PAD Detective Tsoi, the lead investigator on the case, had the following advice for residents: "Don't accept gifts from anonymous parties. If you don't know who the package is from, don't open it."

The Atlanta Journal-Constitution

ABOUT THE AUTHORS

Ilona Andrews is the pseudonym for a husband-and-wife writing team. Ilona is a native-born Russian, and Andrew is a former communications sergeant in the U.S. Army. Contrary to popular belief, Andrew was never an intelligence officer with a license to kill, and Ilona was never the mysterious Russian spy who seduced him. They met in college, in English Composition 101, where Ilona got a better grade. (Andrew is still sore about that.) Together, Andrew and Ilona are the coauthors of the *New York Times* bestselling Kate Daniels urban fantasy series and the romantic urban fantasy novels of the Edge. They currently reside in Austin, Texas, with their two children and numerous pets. For sample chapters, news, and more, visit www.ilona-andrews.com.

*A romantic urban fantasy novella set
in the world of Kate Daniels!*

From *New York Times* Bestselling Author
ILONA ANDREWS

MAGIC DREAMS
A companion novella to *Gunmetal Magic*

Shapeshifting tigress Dali Harimau finds herself
in deep waters when she must challenge a dark
being to a battle of wits—or risk losing the man
for whom she secretly longs.

Magic Dreams previously appeared
in the anthology *Hexed*
and is now available as an eSpecial.

❋

facebook.com/Ilona.Andrews
facebook.com/ProjectParanormalBooks
penguin.com